# Acknowledgments

Jagged Little Edges, edition two.

On May 30, 1997, the life I lived in addiction came to an end. I stopped running and got help at the Edgewood Treatment Center on Vancouver Island. When I walked through the front doors, I thought my life was over. But in fact, it was only beginning.

To my children,
You are my heart. I love you forever. We have come a long way since those dark days. I look forward to new adventures!

144 people die each day from an overdose. Millions of families are grieving the unnecessary loss of their loved one. Addiction is a highly treatable illness, but due to stigma, only one in ten persons will seek help. If you or someone you love suffers from this disease, I hope reading Jagged Little Edges will encourage you to reach out. Admitting you need help is not an act of weakness, but one of great courage.

Dedication

This book is dedicated to all those who lost their life to addiction:

There for the grace of God, go I.

**Jagged Little Edges** that's how it had felt for her as long as she could remember. Like cuts, coming first in words, as they tore little pieces of her innocence, trust, and self-worth. Evolving into the physical form, with a smack to the head, a cuff to the ear and at times, welts and bruises on her backside. But by far, the greatest damage of all was what you couldn't see. A soul, torn asunder, left with an open wound, a vast emptiness and a hunger that screamed to be fed.

# PART ONE

# CHAPTER ONE

Lyndsey bolted upright in bed. The rapid beat of her heart an old and familiar friend. A gust of sour breath escaped between her dry lips. Her mind raced. *Shit.* It happened again. Darkened figures dissolved, as the last traces of the nightmare vanished. It wasn't unusual for her to experience bad dreams, but lately, she was haunted by a sense of impending dread. Something was very wrong.

Cool moisture gathered between her breasts. She absently rubbed them, noticing once again how sore they were. Exhausted, she stretched, not wanting to get up. The bed beneath her was soft and warm and far too inviting. Lyndsey fought the urge to lie back down. Morning, she hated mornings. It was her worst time of day. Tired and irritable she tossed the covers off and quickly dressed.

As she climbed the stairs, her family was already up. The toilet flushed down the hallway. A plate rattled in the kitchen. A hair dryer turned on in her sister's room. They were everyday sounds. Noises you heard in every family, except for one thing missing.

Voices.

You rarely heard voices in this home, and if you did, they were loud and angry. Lyndsey hardly knew them, her family, and couldn't remember if she ever did. Just like any prisoner, she was counting down the days until she was out on her own.

At the top of the staircase, she glanced around. All clear. On tiptoes, she crept down the corridor and entered her parent's room. Thank God. Their bedroom was empty, the bed not yet made. As a little girl, she experienced horrible nightmares. Lyndsey would enter their room trying to be quiet. Looking for solace, terrified and filled with panic she lay on the floor next to her mother's side of the bed, hoping she wasn't discovered and sent back to her room. Swallowing the scream inside, she lay on the floor. It was cold and hard, and yet a thousand times more comforting than what had awoken her.

Lyndsey blinked, pushing the memory aside. In the corner of the room up against a wall, was their dresser. On top of the dresser was a pack of Players cigarettes. Her last butt smoked yesterday seemed a long way off. Lyndsey opened the pack, shook out three then took one more.

A crumpled handful of bills and some change rested next to the cigarettes. Lyndsey paused, then scooped up a five dollar bill and a handful of coins. Amidst the clutter were five little white pills. Lyndsey took two, pocketed them and walked to the kitchen.

Her mom, wearing a purple housecoat was busy at the sink. "Don't forget your lunch Lyndsey." She reminded.

Lips pursed, she never bothered answering. It was a strange

relationship she, and her mom had. They didn't have anything in common. At times she wanted to shake her Mom so hard her head would fall off. At other times she wished she could put her arms around her, talk to her and protect her. Save her maybe. She never would though. She couldn't remember the last time she'd put her arms around any of them.

As she left for school that morning, a burning heat rose up in her throat. It was an all too familiar sensation of indescribable loneliness. She felt *bad,* not as in doing something wrong bad. Stealing from her parents didn't bother her conscious at all. She felt justified, a kinda secret revenge for the hell she called her childhood. This bad was different, stemming from not having said goodbye or even thank you, to her mother. For a moment she let it bother her. Then she did what she always did. Lyndsey pushed it from her mind.

On her way to school, she stopped meeting her girlfriend in their usual spot. She felt closer to Kelly than anyone else. Lyndsey had a burning need to make sure Kelly and all her friends were happy. She would do anything for them. They were her family. To them, she'd never say no. She'd spend hours on the phone with them, saying what they wanted to hear, and fixing their problems. She wished she could be with them all the time. Lyndsey wanted to know everything about them. She was obsessed with them, and wanted them need her just as badly.

As she and Kelly arrived at school, they hugged one another before heading through the front doors. Her first class was English. Lyndsey liked this class, but she would have died before admitting it. The teacher was engaging, and secretly, she thought he was pretty cool. Two cute boys sat next to her. She was tongue tied and interested, she also felt weird around them. The boys teased her, trying to engage her in conversation, making jokes and playing around. She was awkward with the attention, yet she wanted it so badly. Their game was one she didn't know. It was confusing too, for she knew how to flirt and fight, but she'd never learned how to play. In the end, all they got back from her was an aloof mask of disinterest and scorn. It wasn't the message she wanted to send.

Lyndsey reached into her pocket, the school desk making a great privacy screen, and removed the pills. No easy task. Her jeans were so tight she'd used her father's pliers to pull the zipper up that morning. She studied the pills. They were white with a rooster on them. Not sure what they were she put one back, forcing it deep into her pocket. The other she eyed warily, before placing it between her lips. It felt strange and foreign, sticking to the roof of her mouth. With barely enough spit to swallow it down, she gagged, wishing for a drink to chase away the chalky, bitter aftertaste.

Not sure what to expect, she opened her textbook, lowered her head and closed her eyes. Her body relaxed, and she started to drift, listening to the teacher's voice as he read her into her morning nap. Lyndsey dozed, almost asleep and yet still aware. When the bell ended her English class, she walked to her locker and put her books away. Her next class was math. She hated math. Besides, she was so behind there was no point in going. Lyndsey checked her pockets again. She had enough money for a coffee and maybe even a pack of smokes, too.

The coffee shop was right across the street from the school. All her friends hung out there. Lyndsey plunked herself down sitting at their usual table. It was big enough for six but many more had crammed around it. The waitress came by and took her order. Lyndsey asked for coffee only. She wasn't hungry although she'd eaten no breakfast. The constant smoldering anger bubbling in her stomach kept her full.

The restaurant smelled of bacon grease and smoke. It didn't go well with the anger and coffee mixing in her stomach. She felt queasy and wondered if she might be coming down with the flu.

As Lyndsey rubbed her stomach, the door opened. A tall, good-looking young man entered. Lyndsey waved at him and said, "Jason, over here."

A lopsided grin shaped his lips as he sat down beside her. Jason was older than she by five years. He'd already graduated and was working. She knew he was interested in her, but she didn't feel the same way. She liked him, but not like that. Still, it was pretty cool, he could buy her beer and she enjoyed talking to him. His chin sprouted a decent enough beard. His voice was deep and gravelly as he called for the waitress. Jason ordered a plate of French fries and a beer. It was early, but that didn't bother either of them.

A strange tingling sensation began in her scalp. She felt weird, off balance and light-headed. Her pulse soared. Her cheeks were warm like someone turned the heat up inside her. Lyndsey babbled, talking and couldn't stop. Words came out fast and faster. Her eyes opened wide, her pupils dilated. The burning edge in her stomach smoothed out leaving behind a soft, warm and sensuous flow. Jason even looked more attractive, and she liked him more than when he first sat down.

She felt *powerful*. She felt *awake*. She felt *alive*.

Jason offered a fry. She turned him down with a grin. There was no way she could eat. Lyndsey felt like she'd never have to eat again. Not bothered in the least by her lack of appetite, Jason offered her a sip of his beer. She drank down half and lit up another smoke. He ordered another beer and rubbed her leg. Laughing gently, she swatted his arm. He didn't belong to her. He had a girlfriend. It didn't seem to bother him though. Jason didn't play by the rules either.

God, she felt great. She loved this feeling! She could sit here and do this all day long. For her everything else ceased to exit. Lyndsey smiled, feeling relaxed as they joked back and forth, flirting, touching at times and teasing. She let Jason think maybe, sometime in the future, there *might* be a possibility of him getting what he wanted from her.

Lyndsey liked the power she had over him. It was intoxicating. She sensed if she gave him what he wanted, he'd find her less appealing. Her power, if you could call it that, would be diminished and there was no way she would let that happen.

Most of her day was spent hanging out, drinking coffee and visiting with various friends. She couldn't remember ever being so talkative and didn't notice when breakfast turned into lunch. Other customers came and went as she sat drinking, smoking and gossiping.

The day passed in a happy blur. Eventually, she returned to

school. It was late and the school day was almost over. It seemed as if minutes, not hours, had passed since she'd first sat down at the table. The warm fuzziness began to fade, and she gathered her belongings with a sense of dread. She felt bitchy, and a headache was brewing. The smooth flow running through her lessened and edginess crept back in.

Lyndsey started home. People were everywhere, all trying to exit the building at once. The schoolyard was loud. Lyndsey was agitated. She avoided the mass of bodies, walking fast, with her head down.

Weird, a short time before she'd felt love for everyone. Now she couldn't wait to be on her own. Although she yearned to feel a sense of belonging and connection, she rarely ever did. Today was the first time she felt equal to others and comfortable in her skin.

Lyndsey wondered if her connection came from the little white pill. She still wasn't sure what ailment the pill relieved.

But she was sure she'd be taking another one soon.

# CHAPTER TWO

Suzy, her little dog, was waiting by the back door when she got home. Her tail wagged back and forth, and she yipped with excitement. Lyndsey stooped down to give her a quick pat and cuddle. Suzy was special. Lyndsey never felt irritated with her as she often did around people. Her stomach rumbled, and suddenly Lyndsey was starving. The fridge held nothing she wanted, so she put together a peanut butter and jelly sandwich. With a glass of milk in her hand, Lyndsey headed for the stairs.

In the quiet of her bedroom, Lyndsey thought about him. She'd met him six months ago on a grey, rainy morning. She hadn't been into walking to school, so instead, she'd hitched a ride. It didn't bother her to hitch rides. She knew it was dangerous and that alone appealed to her. She'd not been standing there long when he passed. To her surprise, he veered right and pulled off the road. He backed the car up to where she was standing. His window came down. A pungent smell wafted towards her announcing he'd just finished smoking a joint.

"Where are you going?" he asked.

Lyndsey felt herself getting all flushed. She didn't want to tell him she was going to school. He looked older than her. Mean, even. So she made up a lie. She was quick with the bullshit. It was a skill she'd accumulated over the years. She found it often protected her and saved her from getting caught in the web of lies she called her life.

"Just going to do a little shopping," she replied.

He gave her a strange look, half knowing and half sneer.

As they headed toward the town's only mall, she looked over and studied him. His eyes were slits, shot through with red. His hair was long and stringy and could use a good wash. He wore a denim jacket, jeans and a wrinkled, dirty T-shirt with a logo she couldn't quite make out. On his feet, he wore scuffed black boots.

He watched her studying him. Again that sneer. "I've got a few beers back at my place," he stated.

"Oh?" she asked.

"You wanna come over," he questioned.

She did, and she didn't. He looked dangerous, and she'd never seen him before. Not giving herself a chance to change her mind, Lyndsey blurted out. "Sure."

He cranked on the steering wheel narrowly missing a passing car. He did a U-turn in the middle of the street. Cars on both sides of the road honked at them. He laughed loudly and gave them the middle finger in return. He turned the music up to a level that made further conversation impossible. By the looks of him, talking wasn't going to be his strong suit anyhow.

He drove fast. Lyndsey held on tight, her fingers biting deeply into the sides of the seat and tried to breathe. He passed anything that dared to be on the road. On sharp corners, she closed her eyes. When he noticed her reaction, he laughed again and drove even faster. When they arrived at his place, his car shuddered to a stop. He cranked the e brake and turned to her. She got a closer look at him then. He looked crazy and if possible, even scarier than before.

"Get out," he demanded.

She got out and followed him into the house, strangely terrified and turned on at the same time. Her heart was racing. Adrenaline rushed through her body making her feel cold and clammy at the same time. His house was dark. The curtains pulled shut. He flicked on a light. Lyndsey looked around and noticed in one corner there were big black garbage backs stacked to the ceiling.

"You smoke?" He questioned.

"Of course," she replied. She waited for him to offer her a cigarette but instead he got out some rolling papers and what she thought might be pot. She'd never seen it before and didn't want to try it.

He lit up. The joint was pencil thin and rolled expertly. He took a long toke, exhaling smoke through his nose. "Take it," he demanded, handing her the joint.

Lyndsey took the joint hesitantly. It didn't burn like a cigarette. It burned sideways. The smell was revolting and made her want to throw up. She took a small toke. Her eyes started to water.

"Take another," he insisted.

She took another small toke. As she inhaled, her lungs felt like they were on fire. For a moment she couldn't breathe. Gasping, she started to cough. Deep, rasping coughs that sent tears streaming down her cheeks.

"One more," he said. "This time hold it in."

Lyndsey took another toke. She held the smoke in as long as she could. Lyndsey exhaled, and passed him the joint.

He took a few more hits, pinched off the end and stuffed it back into his cigarette pack. Then he walked over to his stereo and punched a few buttons. The room filled with sound. The music seemed to have a life of its own. The beat synchronized with her heart and she could feel it moving in her. It pulsed in her veins, going straight up her spinal cord and into her brain. Her head buzzed. Her tongue felt strange. Thicker, pastier, and leathery. Her eyes felt different too, drier and swollen. She was glad it was dark. She wished she could turn off the one light still on.

"Supper," her Mom called from above.

Lyndsey shrugged off thoughts of *him* and returned to the present moment. She debated going upstairs. Spending time with her family was the last thing she wanted to do. But if she didn't, one of her parents would come down to see why she wasn't coming to the table. It would be nothing but nasty if her father came down and she'd feel guilty if it were her mother. If she didn't eat dinner with them not only would she pay, but so would her mother and the rest of her family. With no good options, she rose and stomped up the stairs.

Her family was sitting around the table in their usual spots when she got there. No one talked. They never did. She wasn't hungry when she sat with them. Just being in their presence provoked hurt, bringing a golf ball sized lump to her throat. She picked up her fork and started forcing the food down. It was difficult. Every time she took a bite her throat would close, choking her.

But she had a trick up her sleeve. She'd take a bite of food and then a sip of milk to help push it down. She tossed the occasional morsel to her little dog waiting eagerly under the table. The tension at their table was unbearable; their silence was deafening. The meal was fast and quickly over. They all scattered, going their separate ways, strangely relieved not to be in each other's company any longer.

Lyndsey returned to her room. She checked the stash of stolen cigarettes she kept hidden in her drawer. She found one. It was smashed and partially smoked. She headed out the basement door to light up, her little dog at her side. The butt tasted nasty. Old and dried out, but she needed it. Her body craved that hit of nicotine. She'd been smoking since she was twelve. To most people, it would seem very young to be smoking. However, Lyndsey had never felt young, and to her, there was nothing strange about it.

The phone rang as she entered the house. Running as fast as she could, she answered it. She didn't want anyone else to hear his voice, and somehow she just knew it would be *him* on the other end. Her family didn't know him, they'd never met, but they did know *of* him. Just some fairy tale bull shit she'd made up to appease them. Besides, they weren't interested in much she was doing anyway.

Breathless from her short run, she answered the phone. Just as she'd thought, it was him. He was loaded and slurring his words. She hated when he got like this. She could barely understand what he said but recognized the anger in his voice. For a moment she was glad she was at home. He was away working out of town, doing what she wasn't quite sure. She'd learned not to ask many questions.

The phone hung limply in her hand. She didn't know what she felt for him. It was confusing. Love at times, contempt always, fear for sure. His words cut deep. He raged at her accusing her of cheating on him, saying she was nothing but a bitch, a slut, a whore. Eventually exhausted, he ran out of names to call her. Then he started to cry, claiming he couldn't live without her and he loved her.

She was numb. His insults did not affect her. She'd heard them all before. The irony was she'd been a virgin when they met. She'd given him her most prized possession, and now she was paying for it. It wasn't strange to her he called her these names. In her limited experience, it's what you did when you loved someone. She'd watched her parents argue all her life. Her mom saying little and her father bullying them all. She'd grown up with name calling.

Images from the past raced through her mind. She'd never gone to war, but she'd been in one. Her childhood had been a battleground, her father the enemy. Lyndsey never knew why her family was at war, or why they'd all gotten so good at hurling explosives at one another. It wasn't something they never discussed. They never really talked at all. She couldn't remember one real conversation. Just orders, always orders and God forbid you disobey, for the punishment was severe.

Lyndsey sat on her bed deep in thought, her fingers twirling in her hair. Sometimes she pulled little strands out, other times she just twirled. Around and around her finger, the ritual soothed her somehow. She lay down on her bed with her little dog Suzy at her side. The hard mattress squished her breasts, and she noticed once again how tender they were. She thought back to her last period. When was it? She'd never been very good at keeping track of them. There was never any reason too. The few times she'd had sex with *him*, well, you couldn't get pregnant that fast!

There was no way she was pregnant.

Nope.

No way.

# CHAPTER THREE

The next day was Friday, her favorite day of the week. Lyndsey fell asleep early the night before and woke up feeling rested. With her mascara brush in hand, Lyndsey peered in the mirror. She looked pale and applied more blush to her cheek, then washed it off. Still not satisfied, Lyndsey put it on again.

Lyndsey looked in her closet for something to wear. Nothing appealed to her. She tried on one outfit after another. Her frustration grew as the pile of clothing on her bed mounted.

She knew something must look good on her and yet when she looked in the mirror she couldn't see it. To her eyes, she looked fat, ugly, and her nose was too big. Lyndsey yanked the jeans from her body and tossed her clothes around the room. Then she screamed, trying to get rid of the ugly image she'd seen in the mirror.

Lyndsey swept the clothes on her bed onto the floor. She eyed the mess and pulled at her hair. Her dirty jeans from yesterday lay on top of the heap. The loose change had spilled from the pockets and on top of one quarter was one white pill. Lyndsey scooped it up and pooped it in her mouth. Her experience yesterday told her she would feel better soon. Lyndsey bit into the pill and grimaced. She disliked its bitter taste and the way it burned the back of her throat. But she swallowed it anyway. It tasted as if she'd bitten into a dandelion.

Her room looked like a bomb had gone off in it. She eyed the mess as she sat on her bed and waited. Impatiently willing the pill to hurry, she felt all the nastiness of her life creep back in. Pain engulfed her. Hurt consumed her. At times like these, she could do nothing for herself other than to hold on and breathe, rocking back and forth, back and forth and trying not to go insane.

Eventually, the pill did its job. The ugliness loosened its grip, like a big fist unclenching, letting go. Lyndsey got off her bed and began picking up her clothes. She stuffed them into drawers and hung some on hangers. The rest she shoved under the bed.

When she was ready, she glanced into the mirror a final time. This time she saw nothing hideous at all. Her cheeks were pink, and she looked, well, pretty. Lyndsey's confidence return and she headed out the door.

By the time she got to school, she was *flying*. Lyndsey talked to people she would normally avoid. She was in a big bubble of happiness as she moved through the crowd.

Lyndsey caught up with her girlfriend just as she was about to enter the school. "What are you doing tonight?" She asked.

"I'm not sure yet. We can figure it out later." Kelly replied. "Gotta go, Lyndsey, I'm late for class."

Lyndsey watched her walk away. No way was she going to wait for later. She wanted to get the party started right now! She continued down the hallway looking for someone to hang out.

John stood in front of his locker at the end of the hallway. His eyes widened as he watched Lyndsey approach. John had a locker full of goodies and he'd been trying to share them with her all year. Today was his lucky! Lyndsey liked this feeling and wanted more.

"Hey, John." She greeted.

John stared at her, not sure how to reply. "What do you want?" He asked.

"What you've been offering," Lyndsey replied.

"Like what?" He prompted.

"Like what's in your locker." She grinned. John was known around school as Mr. Party. He had a reputation of giving freely, drugs, booze, and himself. They walked toward his locker. He took out his key and opened the lock. The locker door swung open, and he reached inside for something she couldn't see.

"What have you got?"

"You'll find out."

They walked out of the school together and got into his car. John's family had a lot of money and had just bought him a brand new Camaro. It was a beauty. Black with gunmetal flake mixed in. Shiny chrome, the tires were fat, the rims spotless. It smelled nice too. They drove out of the school parking lot. As John turned onto the main road, he cranked up the stereo.

"Where are we going?" She asked.

"Sit back and enjoy the ride," John said with a grin and a wink.

Lyndsey did something quite unusual then. She sat back and did as told.

A few minutes later they pulled into the liquor store. John got out of the car and held up a finger. "Stay put." He turned on his heel heading to the entrance of the store then veered left. Lyndsey wondered what he had in mind. Neither of them was old enough to go into the store.

John stood beside the door watching people enter and exit the store. It was a busy place. She wondered if John was trying to work up the nerve to go in. She spotted one guy who didn't look much older than them. John approached him, and they headed around the back of the building. For a minute she lost sight of them.

She recognized the guy John had spoken to as he re-entered the store. Lyndsey couldn't see John anywhere, and she was starting to worry the stranger had done something terrible to him. With growing concern, she saw the man exist the store again before he turned to head around back.

Lyndsey opened the door. "Hey!" She called out.

He ignored her and turned the corner. Lyndsey didn't know what to do. The keys were still in the ignition, and she thought about driving the car around back to see if she could find John. Just as she was about to turn the key, someone yelled. Lyndsey looked up and saw John running towards her. He wore a huge grin, and it lit up his face.

"Whoop, whoop!" He yelled. "Move over!"

As she slid into the passenger seat, John climbed in and threw a heavy paper bag onto the back seat. "What the hell is that? Where did you go?" She asked.

"That's pure pleasure." John winked at her. "I asked that guy to bootleg for us. The bastard charged me an extra twenty bucks, so you better be nice!"

She wouldn't even bother replying to that. John drove them to a nearby beach. The beach was usually busy, bustling with families, children playing and the elderly walking their dogs. It was early though, and they had it to themselves. They moved further down the beach. The day was cool, and Lyndsey shivered. The high she'd felt earlier was fading.

John offered her his coat. She wrapped herself in it as he opened the bag revealing the contents inside. He pulled out a bottle of Southern Comfort and six long-neck Budweiser beers.

John crumpled the bag and tossed it to the side. He unscrewed the cap from the Southern Comfort, put the bottle to his lips and took a long pull. "Smooth." He murmured, smiling with the word.

John passed the bottle to Lyndsey. She grabbed it like she would a lifesaver in stormy seas. She'd never tasted this liquor before, but John was right. It was smooth. It poured easily down her throat. After a long drink, she handed the bottle back. John screwed the lid on and grabbed two bottles of beer. He twisted the top off one and handed it to her. Then he opened one for himself. John got busy gathering wood to make a fire, giving Lyndsey a moment alone.

A few people had entered the park since they first arrived. A father and daughter were playing on the beach. The man chased his little daughter in the sand. The little girl squealed with laughter when her father caught her. The man tossed his little girl up in the air, catching her safely in his arms, then tossed her back up again. Their squeals of delight traveled down the beach to her ears.

For a moment she listened, smiling. Their laughter rang out with joy. She could feel their love. A sense of longing came over, her and she wondered what it would be like to trust someone to catch you.

There was a time, long ago, when she had that. She was shopping with her father. They were in a mall and she was holding his hand. She was excited and chattered incessantly, her happiness barely contained, her legs breaking into little joy skips and hops as she walked beside him. She'd felt so special that day, just like a fairy princess.

Three older boys walked in front of them, pushing and shoving each other and goofing around. The grip on her hand tightened as her father reacted to the sight. The boys said something that made her father mad. He clenched his fist and told the boys never to say that word again.

Not knowing what the word meant she asked. "Daddy, what's a prick?"

He'd been her hero. She looked up at him with such adoration, pure innocence, and love. Thinking of princesses and dolls, she never saw it coming. It blindsided her, his hand smacked her to the ground. Her tiny body hit with such force; she couldn't breathe. The physical pain was great, but it was nothing compared to a broken heart.

Lyndsey gave her head a shake, pulling back from her thoughts. They were such a waste of time. At sixteen she had life all figured out. If she were tossed into the air, no one would be there to catch her. She would crash to the ground. And she'd already experienced enough crash landings to last a lifetime.

The only one she would *ever* trust again was her.

Lyndsey staked her life on it.

# CHAPTER FOUR

John returned with an armload of wood. He set it down, retrieved the crumpled bag and set to work starting a fire. "You want another drink?" He asked, offering her the bottle.

This time Lyndsey took two long pulls, guzzling as much as she could without choking herself.

"Hey, hey, slow down!" John said. "There are two of us here you know!"

Lyndsey didn't care how many were here at the moment. She just wanted the ache to stop. The alcohol warmed her. Lyndsey didn't know if the heat coursing through her was from the fire or the bottle, but it didn't matter. She finished off her beer.

John fished in his coat pockets pulling out a pack of cigarettes and a clear plastic baggy. Inside of the baggy was a cream-colored powder. John dug into his jeans pocket and pulled out a wad of Kleenex. She wasn't the only one wearing tight jeans.

"What's that?" Lyndsey pointed at the powder.

"MDA." John shrugged. "They call it the love drug." He poured a little powder onto a sheet of Kleenex, rolled it up in a ball and popped it into his mouth. "Cheers." He mouthed through the Kleenex. With a long pull from his beer, he swallowed and grimaced. A moment later he tore off another sheet of Kleenex and repeated the process, handing the bundle to Lyndsey.

"Why is it called love drug?" She held the little package up to her face for closer inspection. It was a sizable mound, and she didn't think she could swallow it.

"What are you, chicken?" John goaded.

That pissed her off. To show John just how wrong he was about her she put it in her mouth. The Kleenex came apart as it settled on her tongue. Lyndsey gagged. It tasted horrible. Vile. The unexpected burn brought tears to her eyes. Lyndsey grabbed his beer and guzzled it down. There was a strange aftertaste like licorice. She helped herself to another beer, trying to wash away the taste.

John laughed. "Pretty gross isn't it. Here, have a smoke. It'll help."

Lyndsey lit up, filling her lungs with smoke. He was right. It did help. She snuggled deeper into his coat. It was nice here. She loved the smell of the sea. It was mysterious and eternal. The sound of the waves lapping nearby relaxed her.

She felt hypnotized as she watched the tide pull the surf in and out, in and out, in and out. The ocean sounds soothed her frazzled soul and a sense of calm, came over her. Lyndsey glanced over at the fire. Why had she never noticed how beautiful flames were? They seemed to dance just for her.

Her body tingled, warmed from the nearby heat. The sting of smoke in her nostrils was pungent with a thick woodsy smell. The colors in the fire were incredible! The flames danced seductively, changing hues like a kaleidoscope, orange, red, yellow, blue and white. The flames shimmied and shook as she watched, fully absorbed. She couldn't take her eyes off the spectacle. Lyndsey sat in wonderment and awe.

Lyndsey got lost in her watching and time passed. She

looked over at John and noticed he was also watching the flames. She could see the flames through John's eyes. The two had become a part of each other and no longer needed words. She moved closer to the fire, its beauty drawing her near. The flames were soft, warm and comforting.

"Careful it's hot!" John laughed.

His voice sounded funny like it was coming from far away. Lyndsey laughed too. For a few minutes, they watched the flames together in silence. Then John moved closer to her. They sat side by side, in complete harmony.

Lyndsey became *more* than herself. She joined with the fire, with the ocean, with the sand, with the trees, and with John. The fire burnt down as she watched. Lyndsey was fascinated by the coals now revealed. Chilled, she rose to put on more wood. She wobbled as she got up. Lyndsey howled with laughter. Somehow it was hilarious she could barely stand.

Her fingers were rubbery. Still, she managed to throw more wood on the fire, bending to sit back down and falling as she landed. Another outburst of laughter. Lyndsey stretched her legs one sneakered foot landing close to the flames. She held it there, watching as the heat melted and reshaped the end of her shoe. She'd never seen anything funnier in her life. They both laughed, hysterical now. Her tears mixed with the wood smoke and she laughed until her face ached. Lyndsey pulled her sneaker from the fire and leaned against John.

It was getting dark when Lyndsey found herself waking up. Not that she'd been asleep exactly, she hadn't. It was more like coming too. Her world had been perfect and then the buzz wore off. Now she felt anxious.

Lyndsey looked over at John. He was still staring into the flames with a dazed expression on his face. Dread took her breath away. Worry filled her thoughts, and it came back to her with a rush. She was late. Lyndsey was in supreme shit and needed to get home ASAP!

"John. John." Lyndsey shook him.

"Hmm."

"John!" Lyndsey shouted.

Slowly the dazed look on John's face disappeared to be replaced by irritation. "What!" He demanded.

"I have to get home." Lyndsey blinked back tears. Her muscles tensed with dread. Anxiety crawled up her throat as she stomped her feet in the sand.

"Relax." He whispered, trying to pull her closer.

She pushed him away. "Come on!" Lyndsey urged, gathering up handfuls of sand and throwing them on the fire.

"Hey, what are you doing?"

"John, I need to go home!"

John blinked, fully coherent now and took a closer look at Lyndsey. Her face was tight with worry, her fists clenched at her side. "Okay, okay, we're on our way."

They picked up the empty bottles, Lyndsey moving quickly, John more slowly. Finally, they turned to walk back to the car. The ride to Lyndsey's house was quiet, uncomfortable and awkward. Neither of them had much to say after such a strange shared intimacy.

Lyndsey recalled another time when she was late. Her family

was seated around the table eating dinner when she walked in. Her father was enraged by her late arrival. He grabbed her by the ear, smacking her in the head as he pulled her down the hallway. She worried her ear might come off; he pulled so hard. She cried and begged. "No Daddy, no, no, *please!* I'll be a good girl from now on." She was going to get walloped and hoped it wouldn't be with the belt. The pain from that was like being cut in two. It was more than her child-sized body could handle.

Lyndsey chewed on a thumbnail, determination hardening her jaw. She'd never cower again. As they neared her house, Lyndsey saw most of the lights were out. John gave her a questioning look and she instructed him to pull around the back. Quietly, she closed the passenger door and said goodnight.

On tiptoes she crept up the back steps avoiding the third one, it's creaking sure to give her away. She twisted the doorknob, holding her breath. Noiselessly, she entered the kitchen. It was empty. She tiptoed down the hallway and passed the living room. The outline of her father either asleep or more likely passed out on the couch, caused her pulse to skyrocket.

She prayed the roaring of her heart wouldn't wake him. She made it to the stairs undetected. The staircase disappeared behind her as she hurried to her room. Suzy looked up from her bed as she entered. Without bothering to undress, she climbed in and joined her furry little friend. The bed was soft, and the blankets were heavy. Lyndsey pulled them to her chin, hugged her pup and curled up next to her.

She twirled a strand of hair she thought about her day. It was surprising how fast it had gone. She thought about John. He was nice, accommodating, never pushy or demanding. Yes, he was nice. But maybe *too* nice. He was sweet and well, boring. She felt drawn to him like a brother or a friend. He wasn't in the least bit edgy, and she could never be attracted to anything less.

As Lyndsey drifted off to sleep, her last thoughts were of *him*.

# CHAPTER FIVE

When Lyndsey woke up, she had no idea of the time. With no windows, her room was like a cave. The house was quiet, and she felt as if she'd slept for a long time.

Lyndsey was in a dark mood. It was a heavy, sucking misery. She was a hostage, held against her will, by feelings of hopelessness and despair. Her toes curled with impatience, and she seethed. Her thoughts were dark, her mood foul.

Time passed, she drifted off to sleep. When she woke, her black mood shifted to gray.

Lyndsey climbed out of bed. Hunger drove her to the kitchen. She was pouring herself a bowl of cereal when her sister entered. They were close in age but nothing else. They fought viciously, hitting each other, biting at one another, grabbing fistfuls of hair. She'd learned a long time ago not to trust her. Anything she told her sister in confidence would be used as blackmail against her. Lyndsey didn't like her sister, but she would protect her. If anyone tried to hurt her, they'd have to go through her first

In the kitchen, neither of them spoke. Both aware it would take very little to have the fists flying again. For the moment they called a truce. Her sister poured a glass of water and left the kitchen. Alone once more, Lyndsey's thoughts returned to him.

She wondered where he was and who was with him. Wherever he was, he was trouble. Lyndsey thought about the last Saturday they'd spent together. He'd picked her up from her house, leaving the car parked down the street. She'd been out in the backyard weeding a patch of the garden when she heard his whistle, looking up she'd spotted him over the fence.

He was in his usual state, stoned, looking half-crazed only he'd washed his hair. She never knew when he would show up. Sometimes she'd go weeks without hearing from him. Lyndsey rose from her knees, knowing as she did there would be hell to pay for leaving. She calculated the cost was worth the price of seeing him. Lyndsey met him beyond the fence, and together they walked to his car.

He wasn't alone. Two of his closest buddies were with him. She wasn't very comfortable around these two. He was even meaner when they were there. His friend Larry was the quiet type; only a lot went on behind his eyes. Lyndsey got the impression he didn't like her much. He seldom spoke to her, and if she asked him anything, he answered her with contempt.

Mark was the complete opposite. Where Larry was tall and lean, Mark was short and stocky. Mark would spend hours talking *at* her, often making no sense at all. At first, she'd tried to follow his conversations, but learned quickly not to bother. She'd never seen Mark sober. Most of the time Mark was intoxicated and could barely stand up, let alone speak clearly. He was always trying to hug her or plant a wet kiss on her cheek. Lyndsey climbed into the back seat, pushing Mark's hand out of the way before sitting down. The fumes coming from his breath made her eyes water.

"Ssshhhllynds," he acknowledged before drifting off, his chin resting on his chest. A small dribble of drool escaped his lips and ran down his chin where it hung before falling on his already filthy shirt.

The car took off in its usual manner, gears grinding, tires squealing. The old familiar lurch in her stomach fluttered as they sped off. Larry looked at her with a scowl, advising her they were going to pick up a car.

"Oh? Whose car?"

Larry didn't have to say it. His face said it for him. S*hut the fuck up*. They drove out of town along a stretch of bumpy highway to a beach on the outskirts of their small city. When they arrived the parking lot was almost empty.

Lyndsey shivered as he turned to her. She rarely called *him* by his real name and only if he insisted. His real name did not do him justice. It should have been asshole, jerk, or bully. So Lyndsey just called *him*, him.

"I want you to follow Larry and me in my car."

"Where are you going?" She said it out loud and then wished she could take it back. This time she got the look from both of them.

Rather than ask again, she replied. "Okay." Lyndsey didn't have much practice with driving other than the odd foray in her mom's car. Late at night, she would sometimes sneak a joy ride around her neighborhood. It was exhilarating, and she loved breaking the rules.

She watched him with Larry as they approached an SUV. It was shiny and new. Lyndsey wished she had a car like that. The two men tried the doors with little success. Larry pulled a strange looking tool out from under his shirt and went to work on the driver's side window. Before long they were inside the car doing something to the steering wheel.

*Oh my God, oh my god.* Now she knew what was happening. To her horror, she saw they'd started the car. It moved fast, pulling out of the parking lot and leaving her to follow. She glanced in the back seat wondering if Mark could drive while she made a run for it. But Mark lay sprawled on his back not moving. Lyndsey shook her head and started after them, lurching wildly in the car.

They drove farther out of town, turning down an old gravel road. The road was in rough shape with many potholes. Lyndsey slowed to a crawl. One particularly deep hole had Mark bouncing off the ceiling.

"Cchhheezus," he slurred. The word sounded wet as if formed of its own from the drops of spittle collected on his shirt. It was hard to see. The dust thickened on the road ahead, stirred up from the car in front. The road became less and less until she was driving on nothing more than a barely etched track, just wide enough for the tires to pass over.

They came into a clearing, an open gravel patch surrounded by trees. Using hand signals, they instructed Lyndsey to pull the car as far to the edge as possible. The stolen car sat parked in the middle of the patch. Lyndsey, glued to her seat, watched the two of them getting ready for the task ahead. Larry pulled everything out of the trunk. He removed a blanket, a small odd shaped tire, a weed eater and a small tank of gas. When Larry bent again, he came out with tools, a car emergency road kit, and a tire iron. He put everything on the ground except the tire iron. This he held in his hand. Larry must have liked the way it felt because his lips turned up in one of his rare, strange looking grins.

Him was under the dashboard cutting the stereo free. Yellow, white and red wires poked through his fingers. Watching him turned her on. She liked a man who knew what he wanted. Him was a practiced thief. He knew what he was doing, and it wasn't long before he had the stereo out. He plunked it beside the car and turned to the speakers where he repeated the process. As he was finishing up he grabbed the CD case and added it to the pile growing next to the car. With their newly acquired possessions transferred from the stolen car into the trunk of the car Lyndsey was driving, all but one item remained. The tire iron in Larry's hand.

Larry eyes locked on hers. Goosebumps kissed her skin. Larry was a crazy badass. He shook the tire iron at her and bared his teeth. Her eyes widened and her breath caught in her throat. Lyndsey imagined him beating her over the head, her skull breaking open like an over-ripe melon.

But it never happened. Instead, Larry turned away from Lyndsey and headed for the stolen car, running, tire iron held high in the air. Larry hurled himself at the car's windshield and attacked. His iron came down again and again. His screams accompanied the cracking of the glass. Larry hammered in rage, his face turning red. He pounded with a vengeance, hitting the windshield and hood from every angle. He kept smashing the car until there was nothing left but bent, twisted metal and jagged shards of glass. Larry stopped suddenly and crumpled to the ground as if all the air had escaped his body.

In all this excitement Lyndsey was having trouble catching her breath. She peered through her fingers, watching him calmly walk over to Larry. He ruffled his hair, patted his cheek and took the tire iron from his hand. He turned to the car and started his demolition. Quietly and with precise blows, he circled the vehicle. Whack, whack, whack, whack, the metal shrieked like a beaten child crying out all around them. It was too close to home. She ached for the car. She didn't want to watch it anymore. She felt sickened as if the car had once been a living thing, full of life and now it lay in a mangled ruin, broken and slaughtered. As if to agree with her, the car gave a dying shriek. Lyndsey closed her eyes.

Forcing them open, she made herself watch. Him was a cool customer. Just like an ice sculpture, his movements were precise. He turned the container of gasoline upside down in the car. When there was nothing left, and it was empty, he tossed it inside and pulled out a pack of matches. With a flick of his wrist, he struck the match, waiting a moment until the flame was just right. He used the single flame to light the rest of the pack on fire. Carefully, he placed the flaming mass inside the car.

The boys moved away from the vehicle, heading in her direction. Smoke poured out of the bent window frames. The smell of burning upholstery filled the air with a horrible stench. Quickly before they could reach her, she jumped into the back seat feeling more comfortable sitting with Mark.

The car lurched off the path turning back the way they'd come. They'd only traveled a short distance before he pulled to the side of the road. Not wanting to ask questions she just watched as he got out of the car, going to the trunk and lifting out a garbage bag. It looked the same as the ones she'd seen stacked up in his living room. He reached into the bag and pulled out a green brick. Him removed a wedge from the brick, then returned the brick and bag to the trunk.

A weird mask with a hose attached to it came out next. Arms full, he carried his possessions to the front of the car and handed Larry the mask. The rubbery mask fit snugly on Larry's head. He reached across the front seat taking a pinch of pot from the wedge and sprinkled the weed into a little tin attached to the hose. Then he lit it. Clouds of dark gray smoke filled the inside of the mask. Larry's face disappeared behind the smoke screen. Lyndsey hoped he would choke on it, but he didn't. Worse yet, he took off the mask and handed it to her.

"Your turn." They both said in unison.

Not bothering to argue, she put on the mask. It was heavy and suffocating and smelled like burnt rubber. It was cold and repulsive. Another pinch of weed went into the tin, and she sucked in lungfuls of bitter smoke. It swirled around her, blinding her with its oily cloud. For a moment she panicked and tried to yank the mask from her head. Vaguely, she could make out Larry holding it firmly in place. Another plume of smoke, another lung full, again and again. By the time the mask came off she barely felt it her head.

Her face was slimy and coated with smoke. The back seat didn't appear to hold anything she could clean herself with, so she settled for her sleeve. Her scalp tingled, feeling weirdly thick as she scrubbed her face. Her eyes felt swollen, red and ugly. Her tongue grew twice its size in her mouth. She hated this feeling and tried to push it away. If she weren't careful paranoia would set in.

The only one who never used the gas mask was Mark. He remained sprawled on the back seat beside her, tossing out the odd mangled word. Lyndsey willed herself to calm down and relax as she listened to the music. The upbeat tempo turned out a catchy tune, and before long she was singing to it. The words flowed from her. Her fingers tapped in rhythm. Her head rested on the backrest too heavy to hold up. Her eyelids thickened, and she closed them.

Music had always been her savior. It flowed smooth and easy, chasing away the dark places and soothing her *jagged little edges.*

# Chapter Six

Her arm felt heavy like it belonged to someone else. Lyndsey pushed the cereal around her bowl. It was a soggy mush in her mouth. She put the bowl on the floor for Suzy to clean up. She felt slightly nauseous and hoped it meant her period was on the way. She could hear her parents down the hall, their voices raised in another argument. Lyndsey wasn't bothered by their loud voices. It was their silence that frightened her.

The clock above her head read one pm. She had never slept that late. She wondered what her friends were doing. Just as she was thinking about giving them a call, her dad walked into the kitchen. Her body automatically tensed as she waited for whatever cutting comment he'd direct at her today. Silence echoed off the kitchen walls, and she took a closer look at him.

Her dad didn't look so hot. His mean look was missing. In its place was a more subdued mask. His hair stuck straight up. Black and gray beard stubble dotted his face. He wore the same clothes as the day before minus the suit jacket. Only his clothes were crumpled now with a new addition of a red smear (ketchup?) on his once white shirt. Her father headed straight for the refrigerator and pulled out a beer. He popped the top off and took a long pull. When he put the bottle down it was half empty. Still thirsty, he opened the cupboard and took out a bottle of rye. He filled his glass half way. Not quite steady he sat down, bringing the bottle with him.

"You want a drink?" Her father asked her.

"What?" Was this a trap he was setting for her?

He repeated his question. His voice was different, softer, less harsh and threatening. Lyndsey took another long look at him then. Her dad's face hung slack, and his eyes were bloodshot. It dawned on her that he had probably been up all night. His hand shook as he lifted the glass to his lips. Understanding he was sick, Lyndsey relaxed in his presence.

It wasn't a normal relationship they had by any means. Not that Lyndsey knew what normal was. She didn't even know him when he wasn't drinking. Sober, he was mean, cruel, and always looking for a fight. Like somehow being him was such a miserable experience he couldn't bear it without inflicting his pain on somebody else. That somebody else was her and the rest of her family and they'd all grown weary. He walked to the fridge, slanting slightly to his right as he retrieved another beer.

"Do you want a glass?" He asked.

"No thanks."

He sat down with her, handing her the bottle. He'd never offered her a drink before, and she wasn't sure what to make of it. She'd seen him like this many times. It was the only time she ever felt even slightly close to him. He seemed more at peace this way, happier and friendlier. He liked to talk to her when he had the booze in him. She was all ears as he spoke, telling her about his troubles. Telling her more than a daughter should ever know. She felt loved at times like this when he showed her attention. She felt important too like she mattered to him. These were rare moments, and she wanted every crumb she could get.

The alcohol hit him, and his head started to droop. His hands, which had been holding up his head, were no longer strong enough to support it. It wouldn't be long now before he couldn't hold up his head at all. He reached out to pour more rye and knocked the glass off the table. It shattered on the tile floor below. Lyndsey rose to get the broom and cleaned up his mess. When the glass was picked up and the table wiped off, she sat down to finish her beer.

Her father was asleep. Passed out cold. At least it *looked* like he was sleeping. His head lay flat on the table, his mouth open and he snored lightly. She'd never seen him look more at peace. Once again she felt a sense of affection mixed in with a longing for what could have been. Lyndsey shrugged it off. Time to get him to bed. Lyndsey reached for her dad, and they stumbled down the hallway. She from the weight of him and he from the weight of the bottle. Lyndsey put him to bed, tucking him in as she would a small child and quietly tiptoed out of the room.

A wave of emotion left her restless. A tear trickled down her cheek, and she rubbed it away. What she needed was something to take her mind off her troubles. Lyndsey knew just the right person to call. After a few rings, Dee answered, sounding out of breath. "Did I catch you at a bad time?" Lyndsey asked.

"Nope," Dee replied. "Just vacuuming the house so I can get some money for tonight. There's a big party at Sheila's house. Are you going?"

Lyndsey pondered the question for a moment before replying, "Yeah, I'll be there."

They agreed to meet up in a few hours and walk the half mile to Sheila's place together. She hung up wondering if she'd made the right decision. She could wait for him. It was Saturday. It wasn't unusual for him to call or show up. She didn't want to hang around the house waiting though and frankly some of his charm, if you could call it that, was wearing a little thin.

Lyndsey entered her bedroom already starting to feel anxious about what she would wear. Her clothes had to be just right, not only in the way they looked on her but how she felt in them. Lyndsey searched her closet pulling out T-shirts, hoodies, sweaters, brown cargo pants and her favorite pair of jeans. She chose the jeans and lay on her bed to pull the zipper up, but even with the pliers to help she couldn't close the top button. Lyndsey pulled so hard the skin peeled off her finger. But no luck. Maybe they'd shrunk in the dryer? Lyndsey thought about wearing them anyway, with the button open. But in the end, she decided to go with the cargo pants.

More pockets to put her confiscated loot in, she reassured herself. As she pulled the cargo pants on, she noticed they too were more snug than usual. She finished dressing in a hurry. As she put on her makeup, she refused to meet her eyes in the mirror.

Back in the kitchen, she opened drawers searching for a container of sorts. The small space was crammed full with her mom's Tupperware. In the far back corner, she spotted just what she was looking for a plastic drinking bottle that would do nicely. On tiptoes, she opened the liquor cupboard and began taking out the bottles. There was a vast assortment lined up on the kitchen counter, and she eyed the contents. Lyndsey poured six ounces of Vodka into the water bottle and topped it off with Kahlua. Then she took the vodka bottle to the sink and poured six ounces of water back into the bottle. Lyndsey knew her father wouldn't miss a few ounces. More than likely he'd just think he'd drunk more than usual, but just in case she added a few more drops.

Lyndsey scooped the pack of cigarettes her father had left behind. She thought about taking the car. She didn't have her driver's license yet, but it didn't matter. Her dad wouldn't wake until morning, and if her mom found out, she wouldn't say anything. Lyndsey thought her mom knew more than she said. Although she would never admit it, her mom did her best to protect her from her dad by not ratting on her. Deciding against the car, Lyndsey left the house. Once outside she pulled out the bottle, gave it a shake and took a drink.

The first time she'd ever stolen liquor from her parents was a few years back. Her parents were out attending a Rotary function, and her friends were over hanging out. They were raiding the fridge when Lyndsey had a better idea. She opened the liquor cabinet displaying all the pretty bottles crammed inside. Alcohol was taboo, and that made it so much more fun than forbidden left-overs. She pulled out the bottles and set them on the counter. They sampled every bottle, taking small sips from each one. Lyndsey filled a water bottle with a mixture of alcohol taken from each bottle before returning them all to the cupboard. Bored with staying in the house, they walked to a nearby school. A motley crew of neighborhood kids hung out there, and Lyndsey was more than happy to share her pilfered alcohol with them.

They took turns, passing the bottle among them. One of her girlfriends spun in circles. "Try it!" Sheila urged. Lyndsey watched Sheila take a pull on the bottle, pass it off to the person next to her and then spin. Her arms open wide she twirled around and around, with each spin she went faster. They all laughed and took turns drinking and spinning. What a blast! She'd never laughed so hard or had this much fun. Before the bottle was empty and her friends had to go home. Cindy wasn't feeling well and thought she might throw up. Lyndsey thought her friends weren't very good drinkers. They acted silly and felt sick. She wished they could drink like her. Finally, she found something she did better than her friends!

Not ready to go home she met up with Dee. They had just started hanging out. Dee was razor thin with a beak-like nose and brown mousy hair. What she lacked in looks she made up for in personality. Dee was sweet. She never had a bad thing to say about anyone. She wasn't like her other girlfriends who liked to gossip and trash people. Lyndsey was totally at ease around her and wow could the girl party! Dee was lucky. She could come and go as she pleased. They stopped outside the house they dubbed Party Central.

Lyndsey stalled as Dee entered through the front door. At times she felt awkward among her friends. She didn't trust them, yet she loved them and yearned to feel at one with them. She envied their confidence and innocence.

It was hard to explain. Lyndsey didn't feel good enough. Like she wasn't worthy of them. They had something she didn't.

Lyndsey wasn't sure what the missing ingredient was, but she felt it deeply. So she adorned her imaginary barbed coat, the one that kept her safe in situations like this and walked through the door.

The house was crowded, standing room only. She looked around and spotted Sheila. Sheila stood in a small circle with five of her closest girlfriends. Lyndsey walked in their direction and said. "Hey!"

The girls all talked at once, their faces animated with excitement as they pointed fingers around the room. They critiqued each person, criticizing their clothes, hair, and makeup. Their small group made up a panel of judges in a contest known only to them. They did this quite often but tonight they had to shout over the loud music just to be heard.

It was bittersweet. Lyndsey's friends who were considered some of the hottest in their school. She tried to join in. She tried to belong. But it had never felt right for her, trashing other girls. She didn't get quite the same high from it that she saw in them. She noticed their eyes lit up when they became the center of attention. Their words came out fast. It was like a feeding frenzy. They took shots at the people in the room, outdoing one another, lying, exaggerating and shredding reputations.

Lyndsey moved on looking for Dee. She found her in the living room. Dee was curled up on the couch sitting with a couple of the guys from their school. Lyndsey joined her, pulling out her pilfered bottle. Mindful there wasn't much left she drank slowly. She noted Dee was getting pretty drunk. Dee blew her a kiss then toppled onto the couch. She landed on one of the guys.

Not at all embarrassed Dee sat up and jumped into his lap. While on his lap she kissed the boy beside her. Lyndsey grinned. Dee didn't seem bothered by all the hang-ups that plagued her. Dee was a free spirit. Oh, some would call her far harsher names, but those weren't Lyndsey's names for her.

Manny dropped down beside her. A few years back she'd had a HUGE crush on him. At the time she felt sick with love just looking at him. But he hadn't been interested in her, and it was pathetic the way she had trailed after him, trying to get his attention and settling for crumbs.

It was like that with her. At one time or another, she had believed herself to be in love with half the guys in the room. Not that she'd ever told them that. It didn't take much from them either, a nod in her direction, a compliment, eye contact or a few words. It was like she was starving and they were food. She fell in and out of love the way she changed her clothes – every day. One moment her new crush was her entire world, she was high just being around them and the next moment they ceased to exist. Poof. Gone. And she couldn't for the life of her understand what she'd seen in them. Strangely it was after they didn't matter she found they noticed her. She wasn't sure why it was like that. She wanted them close and then pushed them away.

Manny tried to engage her in conversation, but his slurring words were anything but sexy. By the looks of him, he'd had way too many. He was cute though, like a puppy dog cute. His sweet cheeks were just right for pinching. Instead, Lyndsey ruffled his hair. She was feeling generous. A few drinks had loosened her up. She and Manny were wrestling on the floor having fun when he opened his mouth and ruined it.

"I looove you, Lyndsey." He slurred into her ear. "Lesss go to my place."

Lyndsey pushed him aside. It was as if he'd thrown ice water over her. She was pissed! She wasn't an easy lay! Unlike Dee, Lyndsey had only been with one guy, and honestly, she didn't like it. She didn't see what all the fuss was about. Sex was gross. It made her feel dirty and ashamed. Rather than tell Manny this, she painted an imaginary target on his face and started firing.

Lyndsey was small, not a physical threat, but her words could cut you to pieces. She insulted Manny, attacking his character until he was in tears. Then she shamed him for crying.

Not able to sit with him a moment longer she rose and went looking for Dee. Lyndsey looked in the kitchen, seeing an older crowd. They gathered around a table with powered white lines spread across it. A guy with a goatee held a short straw to his nose snorting a line. She moved away from the kitchen. For a moment she forgot about finding Dee needing instead to find the bathroom. She passed by a long line of guys waiting at a door in the hallway.

"Where's the bathroom?" She asked.

"Down there." A skinny blonde guy answered, pointing further down the hallway.

Lyndsey wondered why they were lined up by the door. She pushed open the door to the bathroom. Her hand searched the wall for the light switch.

"Hey!" A female voice yelled as her hand hit the switch flooding the room with light.

A couple lay entwined on the floor. Lyndsey caught a glance of bare ass before hurrying out of the room. She continued her search for Dee. Lyndsey went downstairs pushing through a crowd of people. No Dee. She checked the laundry room, the family room, no Dee. She wondered where the hell Dee had gotten too. She guessed she must have left. Had she been ditched? Disappointment rolled over her.

Not sure if she should stay she decided to give the house one more go around looking for Dee. She didn't want to be here tonight. It was like she was on the outside looking in. She watched her girlfriends dancing in the living room, their circle of six swaying to the music. She thought about joining them but decided against it. There hadn't been near enough liquid in the bottle she sipped. Sober she felt stiff, awkward and self-conscious when dancing. Lyndsey wasn't eager to experience those feelings again.

She went over to say goodbye, and their cheery protests rang in her ears as she left the house. God, she hated the way she thought. She wanted to trust them. She wished she wasn't so sarcastic and well, bitter.

Lyndsey held a piece of herself back from others. Truthfully, there wasn't a living soul who knew her thoughts. She didn't feel lonely though, for she was most comfortable when she was alone. Alone, she could relax and not be on guard at all times. Lyndsey walked off into the black night heading for home.

The darkness was soothing. Lyndsey loved being outside. It didn't matter that it was the night. She was unafraid. There was nothing out here that would hurt her. Lyndsey had always enjoyed a special understanding of the outdoors. She thought nature was beautiful no matter what the weather or time of day. All you had to do was *look* to understand how magnificent it truly was.

When she was a little girl she would watch the clouds for hours, looking for animals, angels and objects she could identify. The soft billowy shapes entertained her. Trees gave her comfort. Blades of grass, hope. Rocks were like old friends in different shapes and sizes. She loved the wind nipping at her ears and pulling the hair from her face. As a little girl, she'd played in a field nearby. The grass was twice her height making it perfect. She'd run and play for hours there. In the tall leafy field, she had an ideal home and family where she made up fun new games every day. This safe place was her haven. It sheltered her as she napped in it, wrapped in the long leafy blades.

There little Lyndsey slept peacefully as her leafy sentinels towered above her, protecting her from all that was evil.

# CHAPTER SEVEN

Lyndsey heard the phone ring as she stepped out of the shower the next morning. Her mother called down to her.

"Lyndsey, it's for you."

Lyndsey towel dried her hair as she wandered into the family room wondering who was on the phone. "Hello?" Silence. "Hello?" Lyndsey tried again. "Hello?" A sniffle then silence. "Who is this?" She asked growing tired of the mystery.

"Lyndsey?" The person on the other end spoke so quietly she could barely hear her.

"Yes?" Then it came to her. "Dee?"

"Lyndsey, I need help." Dee sounded like she was crying. Her voice was almost unrecognizable. "Can you come over?"

"I'll be right there," Lyndsey assured her.

She left by the basement door wanting to avoid her family and the questions they were sure to ask. It wasn't long before she arrived at Dee's. Her house was small, the yard a mess. Dee didn't know where her dad lived. She had no brothers or sisters. It was just her and her mom. Well, it was more like just Dee. Her mom was never home.

Lyndsey opened the front door not bothering to knock. The living area was filthy. Cobwebs hung from the curtains and the place was thick with dust. The end tables held overflowing ashtrays and a large mound of clothes took up one end of the couch. Next to the couch was a very full kitty litter box giving off a horrible smell. Lyndsey sidestepped the mess and walked to Dee's room.

"Dee?" Lyndsey called, opening the door. "Oh, Dee!" Lyndsey cried, spotting her on the bed.

Dee was lying in a pile of dirty bedclothes curled into a tight ball.

Lyndsey sat on the bed beside her and touched Dee's shoulder. "Dee, are you awake?" She gave her a small shake.

Dee lay motionless curled tight on the bed. Lyndsey looked around the room wondering how she could help. She noticed a glass of water sitting on the night table with a cigarette butt floating in it. Next to the glass of water was a bottle of pills. Lyndsey picked the bottle up to get a closer look. The prescription was made out to Dee's mom. The name of the pills was Halcion and the bottle said to take one before bed if you were experiencing difficulties sleeping.

"Oh, Shit!" Alarmed now, Lyndsey gave Dee a much rougher shake.

"Whhaaa." Dee murmured.

"Dee, wake up!" Lyndsey shouted.

One eye opened a crack. Dee sprawled like a rag doll. Her body all limp and floppy. Her head hung loosely. Lyndsey didn't know what to do, but she'd read somewhere that it was important to keep them awake. She was pretty sure Dee had taken her mom's sleeping pills and she hoped to God it wasn't too late.

Lyndsey pulled on Dee trying to get her to stand up. Dee was too rubbery and all she succeeded in doing was rolling Dee out of bed and onto the floor. Dee hit with a plop. It must have hurt.

Lyndsey heard Dee grunt. She got on her knees beside her, pulling Dee's body onto hers. She used the bed to help pull them both up. Straining under the weight, she just barely managed to hold onto her friend.

Standing, she walked slowly around the room with Dee hanging limply from her. She knew she should call 911. But she wanted to wait a little longer to see if Dee might wake up on her own. They walked for a while, Lyndsey slapping Dee's cheeks.

"Come on, Dee! Wake up! Wake up! Wake up!" She chanted the words over and over again.

She felt like her arms were going to fall off. Dee was heavier than she looked. Dee's head hung loosely, her hair was a tangled mess and mascara smeared her cheeks.

Panicked she screamed into her ear. "Dee wake the fuck up!"

Dee groaned, it was weak, but it filled her with hope and she renewed her efforts. Walking and chanting into her friend's ear, Lyndsey circled the small house trying to keep Dee alive.

Her efforts paid off. Dee started moving her legs walking with her instead of just dragging. Dee's body grew less limp as it regained muscle tone. Feeling relieved, Lyndsey seated Dee at the kitchen table and sat down next to her.

"Oh my God, Dee! What in the hell did you do?"

Slowly, laboriously, Dee tried to tell her. She faltered as her words slurred and had to start again. Lyndsey listened as Dee told her about the party last night. How she'd gotten drunk and was having such a great time. Dee remembered sitting on many laps and flirting with different guys. "Lyndsey, I felt so loved." She confessed. "I went into the bedroom with George. It was getting pretty hot in there. We were laying on the bed making out when I must have fallen asleep. The next thing I remember I'm waking up and someone is on top of me, and Linds, it wasn't George!" Tears ran down Dee's cheeks, and she turned her head away.

Lyndsey was feeling overwhelmed. All she said was "Oh, Dee."

"Anyway," Dee sobbed. "I kept falling asleep and waking up. It was like I was dreaming and each time I woke up there was a different guy on top of me."

Lyndsey leaned in closer straining to hear. Dee's words hitched, coming between gulps of air. Mucus ran from Dee's nostrils as told the story, her voice low. "And that's not the worst part. I really thought it was a dream. I mean, I really wanted it to be, but it wasn't. Linds it's a nightmare and it's real!" Dee cried, stuffing a fist in her mouth.

Lyndsey's chest was tight with anxiety. She wanted to help her friend but didn't know what to do.

"It gets worse. " Dee locked eyes with Lyndsey. "The last time I woke up I was outside. It was so cold and I didn't have my coat. I felt sick, and my pants were unzipped. I looked around and I…" Dee stopped and blinked away fresh tears. After a few breaths, she was able to go on. "I...was...a...I was um...laying on a bag of...ah...trash. You won't believe this Lyndsey, but they put me out with the trash! I was just...*garbage* to them!"

"Oh, Dee." Sorrow filled her voice.

Dee was overcome with sobs and started to hyperventilate. Lyndsey put her arms around her and rocked her like a babe.

They stayed that way, rocking back and forth for a long time. When she could Dee continued. She told Lyndsey she'd walked home. Cold, alone and in such pain she wanted to kill herself. She thought about throwing herself in front of a car. But it was late and there weren't many on the road. Besides, she didn't want to do that to anyone.

When Dee got home her mom wasn't there and she felt sick. She vomited a few times then climbed into bed. Dee looked up from her thoughts and admitted. "I couldn't sleep, my mind kept replaying it. Over and over I saw myself waking up with the trash. I couldn't make it stop."

Lyndsey was so pissed! "Those assholes." She blurted.

Dee rubbed her head. "I thought I was going crazy. I laid awake for hours and I just couldn't bear it anymore. I remembered my mom's sleeping pills and decided to take them. I took four and then regretted it. I didn't know if I'd taken enough to kill myself, so I just sat on my bed waiting to die."

Lyndsey's heart was breaking. It hurt so badly listening to Dee tell her story.

"I started to feel really strange." Dee went on. "I could barely move. I remember calling you and then nothing else."

Lyndsey thought about the line-up of guys she'd seen waiting by the door last night. Now she knew what they'd been waiting for. Her blood boiled. How stupid of her! She didn't tell Dee she'd unknowingly stood right outside the door as they took their turns with her. Feeling helpless with the knowledge and somehow at fault, Lyndsey experienced a strong urge to leave the house. But she didn't run. At least not right away. They talked for a little longer. Dee promised she wouldn't hurt herself again and thanked Lyndsey for her support.

Eventually, they ran out of words. It got awkward then, neither knew what to say or do to make things better. Lyndsey stayed a little longer fussing over her friend trying to reassure herself that Dee would be okay.

Finally, it was Dee who encouraged her to go. As Lyndsey got up to leave she looked at Dee again. Dee sat in the chair, holding onto herself and rocked back and forth. With no one to comfort Dee, she hugged herself. Last night's mascara looked like tattooed tracks running down her cheeks.

Outside Dee's house, her mind spun. *Fuck, fuck, fuck, fuck.* Lyndsey walked home on overload. She felt small and insignificant. She was helpless and useless. She gnashed her teeth biting her tongue accidentally.

At times like this, she wanted to hit herself. *If only* she'd looked harder. *If only* she'd opened the door. *If only* she and Dee hadn't gone. *If only* she'd said something to Dee when she was sitting on the couch.

*If only.*

White hot anger uncoiled in her gut causing her stomach to grumble as she walked. Her jaw was rigid and clamped tightly closed. She wanted to scream in frustration. Fuck you unfair Gods of the world! Her body was stiff with rage. She walked as fast as she could and swallowed her screams. Silencing the pain inside, she willed it gone. Hardening her heart, she didn't whimper. Instead, she did something far more dangerous. She grew another barb.

Over the next few weeks, Lyndsey spent a lot of time alone. She read tons of books and hung out with her sweet little dog, Suzy. She took long walks hoping nature could heal the hole growing in her soul. She didn't call Dee and she felt badly about that. She didn't know how to make what happened to her friend better and she couldn't face that awkward feeling again.

Sometimes Lyndsey was so disgusted by humanity. They looked so harmless and yet they had an evil coiled inside them just waiting to pounce on their next innocent victim.

In her experience, people were wolves in sheep's clothing who claimed to care about you and preyed on your love.

# CHAPTER EIGHT

The school year was coming to an end. Students and teachers alike were looking forward to the holidays. It was a frenzied week and excitement was in the air. Lyndsey had chosen this week to harvest the "tomato plants" she'd planted in her socials class. Her teacher, Mr. Fraser, loved plants and brought his to the classroom. He lined them up along the thick windowsill fitted with a small greenhouse.

Lyndsey stayed late after class one day, planting the tiny germinated seeds into the available pots. Throughout the year Mr. Fraser had lovingly watered, fed and pruned these strange looking "tomato plants." He told his students he never had children and thought of his plants as his family.

Lyndsey had gotten the seeds from him. He'd taught her how to germinate them and then prune the leaf to produce a more potent bud. Lyndsey didn't have a green thumb and the ones she'd planted in the garden at home didn't look anywhere near as green or leafy as Mr. Fraser's. That morning Lyndsey had stolen a small pair of shears from her father's garden shed. After class that day, she cut all the leaves from the plants leaving just stalk behind. Lyndsey looked at the bare stumps and was reminded of early winter when the trees looked naked and vulnerable from having shed their leaves. It was the worst time of year for her. She shrugged off the image, stuffed her cuttings into a large backpack and hurried out of the room.

Her first class the next day was social studies. She'd felt nervous about attending the class and thought about skipping it. She decided it might look more suspicious if she wasn't there. So instead, she arrived a few minutes early warily watching the door. The bell rang and the room filled with the rest of her schoolmates, Mr. Fraser in their midst. He took attendance and then stood to write on the board. Mr. Fraser was elderly and seemed old to be teaching. He dressed in suits and wore starched white shirts and matching ties. His shoes were always polished to a high gloss. He taught as if reading from a textbook, his speech crisp and precise. His tone never varied and it often lulled Lyndsey into one of her comforting naps.

With a dry marker in hand, Mr. Fraser stood by the board. His hand stilled as he glanced out the window, his eyes stopping on the greenhouse. His forehead wrinkled as he peered at the strange looking plants before marching over for a closer inspection. Time slowed as Lyndsey waited for his reaction. At first, there was only silence as he looked at the plants and then back at his class with a bewildered look on his face. His look changed to one of understanding as reality dawned on him. A heart-wrenching groan escaped his lips and his face crumpled. Lyndsey heard him cry, "Oh no, oh no."

Lyndsey could barely watch. She didn't like seeing Mr. Fraser in distress and fervently wished she could glue the leaves back on. Mr. Fraser shook with grief. Lyndsey felt sickened with disgust like she'd beaten a small child. Her classmates found his behavior entertaining and laughed at his distress.

Shakily, Mr. Fraser made his way out of the classroom. The

students were left unattended and the classroom filled with loud laughter, flying books, and paper airplanes. Lyndsey sat at the center, again observing, again apart. She hoped it had been worth it. The devastation she'd seen on Mr. Fraser's face today told her the price had been far too high.

She hoped Mr. Fraser would be okay. Maybe she could plant more seeds back in there for him. Tuning her classmates out, she thought about him again. This summer they were going to be spending a lot of time together. He was going to teach her how to turn the leaves in her backpack into something much more potent. He said they'd sell the final product and make enough money to take off. They'd go somewhere else and start over.

Lyndsey knew he had a strange grip over her. She felt repulsed in his presence and yet unable to break free. He had power and control over her, and Lyndsey didn't like it. She was afraid of him and yet at the same time, she wanted to please him. It made no sense and she'd stopped trying to figure it out. The best she could come up with was she was hooked on him. Like an addict who craved the drugs that were killing them, she'd do what he wanted. She'd seen him smile once. That was all it took. His smile went straight through her landing somewhere between her heart and her head, overriding caution and sense of self-preservation. She'd experienced such an overwhelming and heady rush seeing it. Just once and she was hooked.

Her father was away much of the summer. Her house was very different when he wasn't around, Lyndsey's mother was more relaxed. She could come and go as she pleased. Lyndsey settled into a routine. She lived for the nights and slept away the days.

Lyndsey woke late one afternoon, not even sure what day it was. Waking out of a deep sleep she felt a sharp pain stabbing deep inside her pelvis. Cramps, she thought. The elastic of her panties cut into her flesh adding to the discomfort. Not able to stand them one minute longer she pulled them off. Her pelvis was on fire, sharp pains ripping through her. There was wetness between her legs. It was warm and sticky. The pain intensified and her dark room shrank around her as the pressure built. Lyndsey felt an achy burning that she'd never experienced before. It hurt! She was about to get up when another pain hit. This one was deeper. It felt like something had ruptured or torn. She writhed in agony, the pain all but muting her voice.

Animal instinct took over as she twisted on her bed. Heaviness spread through her pelvis and pain shot up her back. Somewhere in the back of her mind, she was sure she was dying. She hoped it would be quick then she thought no more, her body taking over as it writhed and twisted on the bed.

Pain rode her building to a torturous crescendo before finally easing off. The pressure lessened leaving behind a dull throb. Between her legs was a large mass. It was warm and felt like the liver she'd once cooked for her dad. It smelt like that too; a coppery blood smell scented the air.

Lyndsey lay there for a while, wiping her hands on the dirtied sheets, exhausted. She must have made a hell of a mess. She'd never had a period like that before, but she guessed it must be making up for the few she'd missed. Blood seeped out of her. Dazed, she thought she better get up and clean up the mess. But first, she just needed to lie here a little longer. Drifting, Lyndsey was asleep once more.

She dreamed she was a butterfly cocooned in cotton. She floated. A gush of warm fluid escaped between her legs and awakened her. Lyndsey shivered, the warmth she'd been laying in was now cold. A deep ache throbbed in her pelvic region.

Little bits of a foreign substance adhered to her legs and the sheet covering her. Another sharp pain ripped through her as she climbed out of bed. On shaky legs she made her way over to the light, fumbling with the switch. Bright light flooded the room. Lyndsey turned to view the mess she'd made passing the mirror as she did so.

She stopped dead in her tracks. The sight in the mirror was so startling that for a moment she wasn't sure what she was seeing. From the waist down she was covered in blood. Little black dots made their way up her body. Her legs were stained crimson, and blood trickled down them. She retraced her steps walking back to the bed and looked down. It took her a moment to understand. She stared not really seeing. Then recognition hit with a chill.

Lyndsey's heart cracked wide open as she stared at the remains. It was the most precious gift a woman could ever receive.

There on the bed was a little piece of her and a little piece of him.

# CHAPTER NINE

Lyndsey spent the next night with him. She never mentioned she'd just miscarried and lost their baby. She didn't tell him she'd wrapped the tiny little mass in a face cloth and buried it under the cherry tree. She would never get that vulnerable with him. They didn't have that kind of relationship. Lyndsey never thought to ask for support because she'd never received it before. It wasn't a loss. She was a lone wolf. Besides, if she told him, he might be angry with her and blame her for losing their child. So instead, she said nothing and avoided the confrontation by acting as if there wasn't a huge missing part of her.

When she arrived at his place, he grabbed her by the hand and showed her his prize possession. It was downstairs in the basement, in a room sealed off with thick plastic. A weird ventilating system blew cool air across rows of baby plants that grew in red rocks. Water lined the ground cloth. He showed her how the system operated. Using words like cultivation and a good hydro grow room. With an intense expression, he explained how metal halide grow lights functioned and talked about nutrient reservoirs system.

Lyndsey grew bored and stopped listening. She wasn't in the least interested in hearing any of this. The room was hot and humid, the air rich with the skunk-smell of his growing plants.

They left his grow room and entered a smaller one. Cute! This cubicle looked like a miniature kitchen. There was a table, two chairs, a kitchen counter with a four burner cook top, and a small freezer. On the cooktop, she saw a big funny looking pot, like the one her mom had at home. A tube trailed down from the pot ending in a container on the ground. From the freezer, he removed their harvested marijuana and a jug that held blue liquid inside it. He rinsed the pot with the liquid, telling her to pay attention.

Lyndsey drifted off again. She wondered what her girlfriends were doing. Maybe she'd give them a call later. She never noticed the tense silence when she was shoved up against the wall. Stunned, she looked up at him. His eyes were bulging, and the edges of his mouth held little white specks of foam. His hand moved to her neck, holding her there pinned against the wall. She froze like a deer caught in a hunter's scope, intuitively knowing not to say a word.

He raged at her spraying spittle on her face as he went. He berated her for not paying attention, slapping her face to make his point. She held her breath, trying to remain calm so she wouldn't do anything further to enrage him. He squeezed her throat, holding it so tight little white spots danced before her eyes. He shook her till she thought her neck would snap. Lyndsey's head banged painfully on the wall. When he was sure he'd made his point, he let her go and turned back to the task at hand. As if nothing out of the ordinary had just happened, he continued instructing her on how to make the oil.

This time Lyndsey paid closer attention.

When the oil was ready, he poured most of it in little glass vials. Leaving a small amount, he reached into a drawer and pulled out a knife. He inserted the knife under the stove element and turned on the burner. Lyndsey didn't have a clue what he was doing but knew better than to ask. When the knife was cherry red, he placed a drop of oil on the tip. A thin trail of smoke plumed upward. He inhaled the smoke through a small straw. His permanent scowled disappeared and his brow relaxed, the anger finally dissolving from his face. He blew out a smoky breath, his eyes twinkling. His *happy place* was being a red-eyed, stoned-out mess.

He grinned and pointed a finger at her. "Your turn."

Lyndsey didn't have the courage to argue. He moved the chair closer to her telling her she would need to sit down. Then he handed her the straw. He put a small drop of oil on the hot knife. Lyndsey lifted the straw and inhaled. Surprisingly, it was smooth. It was less harsh than the product it came from. She felt herself falling, now she knew why she needed the chair. Without it, she would have landed on the floor.

Her mind floated free from her body, drifting far above and she looked down seeing them both. He was peaceful and gentle as he took her by her arm. Guiding her back up the stairs, he eased her onto the couch. This time she *felt* the music come on, entering her system with an electric charge. Pink Floyd, she thought vaguely. *Hello, hello, hello, is there anybody in there?* The words of the song suited her life perfectly.

Time ceased to exist. Her body felt weightless. Her legs moved on their own accord. Lyndsey wandered outside and sat under a large tree. The night sky above her was black and lit with thousands of tiny, bright lights. Pinpoints of sheer dazzling brilliance and depth. She reached out to pluck one from the sky, her fingers grasping only air. She felt the earth shift as it moved on its axis. The magnificent night sky swaddled her, folding her in its arms as it danced, bright lights twirling all around her. Mesmerized Lyndsey became aware of him. He looked so handsome, as he took her by the arm and lead her back to the house. They lay down on his bed together. Wrapped in his arms, she was content. It was the most precious moment she would ever share with him. His arms cradled her, lulling her into a false sense of security.

Feeling safe for the first time ever, she wasn't in the least prepared for the horror to come.

# CHAPTER TEN

Summer passed quickly, and she got an unwanted education in horticulture and chemistry. The knowledge helped her sell the marijuana-based products to her schoolmates, with instructions to give every cent of the sales to him. Sometimes, he gave her a few dollars back for her efforts.

Lyndsey had seen Dee around from time to time. She didn't look good. Dee was even thinner than she'd been before. When Lyndsey asked if she wanted to hang out, Dee was hesitant. Dee said she was too busy so maybe another time. Dee seemed to be avoiding her, but that wasn't what bothered her most. Lyndsey was worried because Dee couldn't look her in the eye.

With summer ending and her last school year soon to begin, Lyndsey thought about her girlfriends. She hadn't seen them much this past summer which was unusual, because before this they'd been joined at the hip. She knew they were probably pissed at her. They didn't like him and told her so. He didn't like them either, and she'd felt awkward in the presence of both. He couldn't stand her girlfriends, and it was obvious.

Lyndsey had meant to spend time with them. They'd called her so many times in the early summer, but she was always busy with him. They hadn't called for a while now, and Lyndsey knew the next call would have to come from her. At one time she'd been closer to them than anyone else in the world. She wouldn't have gone a day without hearing from them, let alone the whole summer.

But she had changed a lot that summer and didn't feel like the same girl anymore. She was a woman now. And the thought of hanging out, talking about clothes, makeup, boys, and girl bashing didn't appeal to her at all. She'd outgrown her friends, like the way you outgrow your favorite pair of jeans. You know they don't fit, but you keep wearing them anyway.

That year Lyndsey loaded up her locker with the specially wrapped packages from him. Mr. Party would have some serious competition! He'd shown her how to suck all the air out of the bags, leaving the dope fresher and with no smell to give it away. He'd also given her some glass vials to keep in her locker. She'd even pilfered a bottle of the small white pills from her dad. One night she'd overheard him telling her mother he got the pills from the truckers. The truckers used them to stay awake on long hauls. Her dad called them speeders only this time there was no picture of a rooster. Other than that, they looked the same.

She got lucky. Her dad never noticed the missing bottle. He took the white pills in the morning and the new blue ones at night. He drank mostly on the weekends now. For a time her family came to a cease-fire. Arguments happened occasionally, not daily. But when they did happen, it was an ugly mess. They all went their separate ways. Although her family lived under the same rood, they were strangers to one another.

Lyndsey hadn't heard from him in the last month. She settled into her life, hanging out with her girls and having fun at Party Central. She flirted with the boys and sold illegal goodies from her locker. All the small bags of weed were gone, and only a few vials of oil remained. Lyndsey kept the cash from the sales rolled up in a sock in her drawer. She was tempted to spend some of it but refrained, remembering the look in his eyes when he held her by her throat against the wall. Still, with the passing of time, it didn't seem quite as scary.

The little white pills became a way of life. She loved the way she felt, energetic, happy, and took them most days. On the days she didn't, she felt irritated, jumpy and lethargic. That summer Lyndsey lost ten pounds. Her body slimmed out, the last look of her childhood fading as a more mature beauty replaced it. She'd never really liked the way she looked before. But it dawned on her now she'd become if not beautiful, then certainly pretty. She spent more time on herself and got good at applying makeup and getting her hair just right. She even dressed in tighter clothing, if that was possible, making sure to emphasize her small waist and large breasts.

She wondered if the little white pills had something to do with the changes in her. She wasn't hungry when she took them, and they gave her confidence and courage. Wow, Lyndsey thought, who knew one little pill could be so powerful. Lyndsey got more attention those first few months of her final school year than any of the previous years combined. Boys who never talked to her before were suddenly hanging around. She turned heads. She'd only just realized this wandering through the mall after school one day.

A small circle of men stood to one side of the crowded mall. Walking fast, she sped past them, and as she did, they turned their heads to follow her. Lyndsey didn't have a clue what they were looking at. She thought maybe she'd spilled some food on herself, or worse yet, her periods had soaked through the back of her pants. Her cheeks grew bright pink at the thought, and she glanced down to be sure. Finding nothing amiss, she looked around wondering why they were staring. She turned to them briefly when one of the older men smiled and whistled at her. She was mortified and wanted to crawl under a rock. Lyndsey moved away from them as fast as she could, hearing their catcalls as she walked. It didn't take long for her feelings of embarrassment to wear off. She thought over the brief encounter and experienced a heady rush.

The rush had worn off the next day as she walked to school. It was raining again. The sky was grey with nasty black swollen clouds hanging above her. She was in an ugly state of mind. It was the end of October. This time of year all you had to look forward to was grey skies and cold, wet rain. Lyndsey longed for a hot shower even though she'd one earlier that morning. She felt infectious with misery, feeling it in every pore of her body. On days like today, it was so hard to be her.

Lyndsey had forgotten her umbrella and the rain was ruining her hair. Maybe she should turn around? Instead of going to school today she would climb back under the warm bed covers and stay there. Roused from her thoughts, she heard him before she saw the car. Its familiar screech and rattle drew closer. Lyndsey looked up from the puddle and noticed he was approaching *fast!* His car veered left then right and then aimed right for her. Instead of hitting her at the last minute he pulled to the side stopping next to her and splashed water all over the bottom of her pants. The water was cold and she was soaked from the thigh down.

"Fuck you! You're an asshole!" She screamed.

Lyndsey grabbed the door handle giving it a hard pull. Getting in, she turned ready to blast him some more, but the words died right there on her lips. He looked mean. His lips pulled down, his eyes dark and cold. His forehead was wrinkled, and a large vein stood out on his left temple. His jaw was thrust forward set in an angry stance. He looked at her and fear stole her breath.

At times like these, she had to be so careful, as if she was handling glass. One wrong move and it could shatter all around her. She willed the defiance right out of her body. It wasn't that difficult, and she found herself naturally adapting to a more meek behavior, one that appeased him and wouldn't set him spiraling into another rage.

Lyndsey bit her tongue and lowered her head as the car sped off. She waited for him to speak first. After a moment he did. Nothing romantic like *I'm sorry* or *God, I've missed you.* Unless he was high, he never spoke like that.

Instead what came out was, "Where's my money?"

"In my drawer at home."

He changed directions and pulled into the alleyway behind her house. "Go get it."

She entered her yard through the back gate. Careful to hug the fence line she remained hidden. Noiselessly, she opened the basement door creeping through the hallway and into her room. She opened the drawer slowly, every squeak sounding like a gunshot in her small room. Her hand searched in the drawer for the money sock. It would help if she could turn the light on but she didn't want to chance it. Her fingers picked up a bra, panties, and socks. But no money. When she was starting to panic, she felt the hard lump wedged up against the corner of her drawer. Lyndsey ran her fingers over the sock material feeling the bills inside. She pulled the socks holding her money out and stuffed them into her bra. Something brushed against her leg, and she nearly screamed. A wet nose pressed up against her jean-clad leg. Lyndsey reached down and gave Suzy a pet. Her puppy jumped up on her legs. Lyndsey picked her up and gave her a quick cuddle. With a final kiss to Suzie's head, she put her down. She better hurry. She didn't want to make him angry. Well, any angrier than he already was.

Lyndsey retraced her steps and hurried back to the car. As she slid into the passenger seat, he grabbed the money from her and began counting it. Sitting quietly, she watched. He counted it twice before putting it away. He placed the bills in the glove compartment and then reached over and patted her knee as if to say *good work*. Then he rolled down his window, threw out her socks and pressed hard on the gas pedal. As she clutched her seat, she noted his face had relaxed, and he seemed in a better mood.

When he finally spoke, it was to tell her he was picking up Larry and Mark. They had business plans and were leaving town for the day. She asked if she could come too and after a moment's hesitation, he nodded. Happy now, she settled back into her seat. She wasn't sure where out of town they were going, but she was glad to be tagging along.

It wasn't long before Mark and Larry were in the car with them. This time she remained in the front seat. The car was ripe with the alcohol fumes coming from Mark. Lyndsey cracked her window and tried ignoring the smell. They drove for forty minutes, heading south of town into farming country. The car was warm and to add to the stink was the smell of fertilizer from the freshly plowed fields. The rain came down sideways, entering through her cracked window and washed her face. The wipers flew across the windshield. The scenery in front of her twisted from the rain and the trees blurred.

Mark was quiet today. Lyndsey turned to look at him. He met her eyes and looked away. He looked sick. His eyes were red. His skin shiny with oil and tinged with yellow. She'd seen something in his eyes before he'd looked away. She knew what it was and her heart went out to him. What she'd noted in Mark's eyes was the shame. It was that - I'm a loser - look. As if he were a wounded puppy Lyndsey opened her heart up to him. She wished there was something she could do to help him ease the pain she spied there.

But before she could think of anything to help Mark the car slowed pulling off the road and parking on the edge of a large pasture. Larry took plastic bags out of his coat pocket and handed one to Lyndsey. As they got out of the car, Larry said they were going to pick mushrooms on the farmer's field. And Larry had come dressed for it. He had on a long rain jacket and tall rubber boots. On his head, he wore a baseball cap, the brim stretching far over his forehead to keep the water out of his eyes.

When Mark climbed out of the backseat, he hunched over, gripped his stomach and threw up. He groaned, a trail of yellow dripping on his chin. On trembling legs, he grabbed a beer from the trunk. His hands shook so badly he missed his lips. He tried again, this time getting it right, and guzzled the entire can.

Mark hurried after them as they walked. The field was large and muddy with tall blades of grass sticking up. Mud sucked at her shoes making it hard to walk. Black and white dairy cows grazed all around them. Lyndsey loved animals and wanted to pat one. On her way to the nearest cow, her arm was yanked roughly from behind her. She stopped, turning to face him. He looked down his nose at her, his face twisted with fury. He was angry again. It didn't take much to piss him off, and she wasn't sure what she'd done this time.

"Stay with me," was all he said.

Lyndsey followed behind him as they walked deeper into the pasture. Off in the distance was a tiny dilapidated shack. They moved in the opposite direction, and he warned her not to go near the shack. She stepped over numerous cow patties and was surprised when he knelt down and began sifting through a big pile in front of her. His hands were filthy with cow shit which he wiped on his jeans. He checked a few more piles before finding what he was after. Tiny brown mushrooms peeked through the cow shit. He picked them, placing them inside his bag. Then he walked to the next pile and repeated the process.

Mark stooped over a patch, swaying. He managed not to fall as he pulled mushrooms from the ground. Mark stopped pulling and poured beer over the pile of mushrooms in his hand. Then he popped them into his mouth and chewed. Mark saw she was watching and gave her a big grin before bending over another pile. Lyndsey saw Larry further down the field filling his bag as well.

Lyndsey poked at a cow pile with the edge of her shoe. It smelled like rotting hay. She bent over for a closer look and noticed a tiny brown nipple sticking out of the pile. She used her foot to kick the cow shit aside. Underneath was a good size patch. Lyndsey bent and yanked the rubber caps from the ground. It rained hard. Water dripped from her nose and mixed with the mushrooms below. Her hair was soaked and hung in long, loopy tangles. Her hands were wrinkled, and her feet were a soggy mess, but at least they were still warm. Lyndsey picked as fast as she could, trying to stay warm and lessen the time they had to spend in this field.

They'd been picking for some time when a loud *boom* thundered overhead. "Oh, Shit!" He muttered, standing next to her. She looked at him in astonishment.

"Run!" he shouted.

They all took off at once. Mark dropped his bag and returned for it. Boom! A second shot rumbled through the air. This one was even louder than the last. As Lyndsey was running her shoe came off in the mud. She pulled it free with a loud plop. Her heart pounded wildly; sure she'd be shot in the back. As she ran, she looked over her shoulder and saw an old man. He was dressed in jean overalls and holding a rifle in his hands. His beard was long and grey and trailed in the wind as he ran after them. Pausing, he stopped to take another shot.

She ran as fast as she could, not stopping to put her shoe back on. Boom. Boom. Twice more the rifle fired. This time when Lyndsey looked over her shoulder, the farmer was farther away. Their youth and speed had outdistanced him.

The four of them made it to the car, covered in mud, out of breath, and huffing hard as they piled in. "Oh my god, he was shooting at us!" Lyndsey said, grasping her mud-encrusted sneaker and shivering with delayed shock.

Larry looked at her. "It was just bird pellet. It won't kill you. But it stings like hell."

Mark, Larry and him laughed at Lyndsey, who was shivering and covered in mud. She looked back at them and joined in. The four of them laughed long and hard until tears rolled down their face. Lyndsey felt wildly alive and hysterical at the same time.

There was something quite heady about being shot at and living to tell the tale.

# CHAPTER ELEVEN

The heat inside the car dried the mud on her face to an itchy mask. Lyndsey scratched at it longing for a hot shower. As they pulled into his driveway, she gathered her belongings and followed them into the house. Once inside her sense of humor started to fade. She noticed another large hole in the wall. It was directly above the phone. *Must have been some call. I wonder who he was talking too.* Of course, she never asked. Instead, she walked past as if she hadn't noticed.

Lyndsey went straight to the bathroom and rinsed the mud from her clothing, as best she could. Then she pulled his brush through her tangled snarls. With a smelly facecloth, she swiped at her face. Her eyes locked on a large jagged hole above the mirror. It wasn't the only one, either. Many dents peppered the wall. The largest of them being the one over the toilet. Uneasy now, she cleaned the sink. The water mixed with the mud making a frothy brown brew. Old toothpaste stained the sink bowl. Determined to clean every nook and cranny she polished between the faucets with the smelly facecloth. Now that the sink was clean she looked around for something else to tackle, not yet ready to leave and face him. Lyndsey thought about cleaning the toilet but looking down she couldn't bring herself to do so. The bowl was disgusting, stained a rusty-brown-red and looking like something had died in there. With nothing else to clean she left the bathroom.

Water was running in the kitchen, and Lyndsey followed the sound. Mark sat at the kitchen table still covered in mud. In his hand, he gripped his familiar trademark. His forever can of Lucky.

Larry and him stood next to the kitchen sink. With a paper towel, they carefully cleaned the mushrooms, removing all the mud and fecal matter from them. Once the mushrooms were clean, they left them on a fresh piece of paper towel to dry. Him spoke in his science teacher voice explaining to Lyndsey the art of cleaning and drying mushrooms.

"We'll take them downstairs and leave them under the heat lamp to dry." He gave her a hard stare and then continued. "Once they're dry, we'll package them to be sold."

Lyndsey paid rapt attention. She was a quick study and had learned to pretend interest. Even as her thoughts wandered, she kept her eyes glued to him.

With the lesson over they returned to the living room. Larry lit up a joint. Lyndsey helped herself to a beer as they passed it around. She shook her head when it came her way. She didn't know why they liked weed so much. It made her feel horrible. When she got stoned, she couldn't wait for it to be over. Smoking weed made her hungry and paranoid. She felt ugly when she smoked it and she thought the guys looked ugly, too.

Mark passed around a handful of mushrooms, first taking a few for himself. Lyndsey took four. They looked clean, and they smelled musty, like dirt. Out of manure, they weren't repulsive at all. Biting into them, they were firm and rubbery. They didn't taste awful, but just in case Lyndsey took a mouthful of beer and chased them down.

Then she lit up, helping herself to Mark's pack. Leaning back against the couch, she relaxed, knowing that for the moment at least, it was safe to do so. Closing her eyes, she let her head rest on the back of the couch cushion.

One of her favorite bands was playing on the stereo. The music was mellow, and she hummed along with it. When she knew the words, she sang them quietly. The music moved in her, swelling her heart. Music always had that effect on her. Her mood lifted as it played and she smiled, drifting away.

Sometime later Lyndsey felt cramping in her stomach. It wasn't intense, just a minor twinge. Something weird was happening to her saliva. Her mouth pooled with water and she swallowed more than usual. Her fingers tingled as she let herself drift. She wasn't worried at all. Her flesh was prickly as if there were an electric charge running through it, every cell and skin particle open and conscious. Her mind was like a giant eye looking around the room. She wondered if this feeling was love. In her mind, she left the room for space beyond it.

The four of them sat together, each absorbed in their hallucinations and enthralled by the magical mystery of it all. The music enhanced their experience. The living room changed into a cave, its deep depths filled with beauty. They spoke from time to time each blown away by their experience. The furniture looked more vivid, becoming works of art. Lyndsey was warm like she was sitting on a sunny beach. Shapes shifted and the sofa she sat on morphed into a magic carpet. Lyndsey was euphoric and snuggled closer to him.

The beautiful bubble burst to the sound of retching. Larry was asleep on the couch across from her. She must have moved around a lot during the night and finally curled up into a tight ball. At the opposite end of the couch, was him. He was still asleep, with his mouth hanging open. He snored lightly and with his eyes closed, he almost looked almost peaceful. But it was just a mirage. She was well aware of the anger hiding underneath those closed lids.

Deep retching noises from another room interrupted her thoughts. Lyndsey got off the couch and hurried down the hallway. Mark was in the bathroom hunched over the toilet. His whole body heaved wracked by nausea. She looked around for something that would help him and spied the smelly facecloth. Lyndsey rinsed it out under the faucet and placed the cold cloth on Marks' forehead. She hoped it would ease his discomfort, and held it firmly in place as his body convulsed. Looking down, Lyndsey saw what was coming out of him and almost threw up, herself. Bright yellow bile mixed with nasty black chunks floated in the toilet bowl.

Should she call an ambulance? Mark looked like he was dying! His skin was cold and clammy and had that weird yellow color again. The whites of his eyes even looked yellow.

Mark's body continued to heave, even when it was empty, producing nothing more than a thin stream of yellow spittle.

Lyndsey feared he might rupture something vital; he heaved so hard. Not sure if she should call for help and not knowing what else to do, she just stood there with him. Horrified and feeling useless, she held the cloth to his head and wiped the messy chunks from his lips.

Exhausted, Mark slipped to the floor and hugged the toilet bowl. He started to shake. "Please get me a beer."

It was the clearest she'd ever heard him speak. The slur in his voice was missing, at least for the moment.

"Quick!" Mark urged, his tone laced with panic.

Lyndsey ran to the fridge, flung open the door and flinched when it crashed against the counter. The loud noise made her hands shake. She reached in grabbing the first beer she could find. It wasn't one of Mark's. He must have drunk all his the night before. She knew the beer belonged to him and she hesitated for a moment. She felt torn. A noise from the bathroom ended her indecision, risking his rage she took the beer and ran back to Mark.

Mark was lying on the floor beside the toilet. The cloth had slipped from his head, and his body shook all over. She handed the can to him, but he was unable to hold it. His hands resembled a flock of birds flapping their wings.

Lyndsey opened the can for him, wondering if she should get a straw to help him drink.

"Can you pour it in my mouth?" Despite his shaking body, his words rang clear.

Lyndsey held the can upright and poured the liquid down his throat. Mark swallowed greedily. His shaking eased, and then he started to gag. Bolting upright, he threw up all the liquid she'd just fed him.

"That's better," Mark sighed.

Stunned, she couldn't believe it when he asked her for

another drink. "Come on Mark!" She blurted. "I can't give you more it's making you sick!"

Mark shook his head and groaned. "No, it's not. It's making me well. If I don't drink the entire can right now, I'll get really sick. I'll have another seizure, and I'd rather die than have to go through that again."

Not knowing what else to do, she did as Mark asked. She carefully fed him the beer in small sips, praying it would stay down and not spew all over her. She was in luck. He managed to keep it down, and his hands were not shaking nearly as hard now. Mark told her he could drink the next can on his own.

Lyndsey was disgusted. She'd never seen anything like this before. Sickened by what she'd seen, she vowed to herself she wouldn't end up like Mark. Mark was killing himself. There was no way in hell she'd ever let herself get like that.

Lyndsey wondered if she should go home. Wherever the hell home was. The house where she slept had never felt like home. When she was younger, it was her prison, and it filled her with anxiety and dread. Her father had been her prison guard. One wrong word to him and she would end up bent over her bed, begging for mercy, from a man that had none.

Lyndsey remembered the day her pleading stopped. She was in her room, waiting for him to come in and beat her with his belt. Lyndsey was shivering, and her stomach heaved with anxiety. She'd felt weak and helpless and in utter despair. A strong, calm voice came to her. *He can't hurt you*, it said.

She knew there was no one in the room with her and yet she heard the voice and felt its comforting presence. Alone in her room waiting, she came to understand that although she could do nothing about the beatings, she could take away her dad's pleasure. By not pleading, begging or cowering, she didn't think he would derive the same satisfaction from beating her.

Her dad entered her room and pulled off his belt. He folded it in two and held it high above her. His arm swung back to increase the impact it had on her flesh. The belt sliced through the air descending with a whistle. It cut through the air as it would soon cut through her flesh. Then it landed with a loud crack. Lyndsey bit her tongue and never said a word. The belt came down over and over and over again. With each new whack, her hatred grew.

The comforting presence she felt earlier stayed in the room with her. It gave her strength and took away her fear. Lyndsey felt it growing in her, blocking out panic and giving her calm. When his arm grew weary he finished whipping her and she rolled over.

Lyndsey raised her head, her eyes dry and looked directly at him. She never blinked. Instead, she smiled. The smile spoke of bitterness and hate, pity and loathing. And somewhere, deep, deep, down, love. Still smiling, she stared at him. The man who stood above her had always been her very own, private monster.

This man, her father.

# CHAPTER TWELVE

When him fell asleep, Lyndsey walked home. It was early, a bit after nine she thought. She needed a shower, a toothbrush, and a meal in the worst way. As she neared her house, she noticed her father's car wasn't in the driveway. No surprise there. But her mom's car wasn't there either, which was odd. She was usually home at this time of day. Curious she walked around the back of the house. Her mother's car was there but parked in a different spot. Lyndsey didn't know if this was a good sign or a bad one.

Not sure what she'd find, she entered the house heading straight for the kitchen. She opened the fridge door and saw last night's dinner. Chicken casserole was her favorite. She scooped some out on a plate and popped it in the microwave. At the smell of food, Suzy trotted into the kitchen. Lyndsey shared from her plate, setting it on the floor when she was finished. With her hunger satisfied, Lyndsey headed for the shower. The food didn't agree with her, and as she sat on the toilet, it occurred to her this was probably the payback for the mushrooms she'd eaten last night.

Fed and showered Lyndsey felt pretty good. She decided to walk to school and attend her afternoon classes. She'd just arrived at her locker when she spotted Dee.

"Dee!" Lyndsey shouted and waved.

Dee had her arms full of books, and her backpack bulged.

She walked as if in a trance.

"Dee!" Lyndsey called again.

This time Dee heard and she looked up. She turned as if to walk away and then stopped. Lyndsey walked over to her noting Dee looked awful. Her emaciated body curled around the books she carried. Lyndsey thought they might weigh more than Dee did.

Her eyebrows shot up. "Lots of homework?" Lyndsey teased, joking because she'd never known Dee to do homework before.

"No. I'm dropping out."

"What? You mean as in quitting school?"

"Yeah, as in," Dee nodded. "I hardly ever go anyway, and I can't even look at anyone since…well, you know. I can't stand it here. It's such a waste of time. Anyway, I've met this guy, and he kinda hooked me up."

"Hooked you up? What do you mean?"

"Well, I figure if the guys are going to take it for free, I might as well get paid for it." Dee shrugged. "Jack helps with that. He finds the guys then he waits outside my room to protect me. That way no one can ever take advantage of me like *that* again. He gives me something that helps me feel better. I think I'm in love with him, Lyndsey." Dee shifted her backpack and continued. "And I'm moving in with him this weekend. Jack made me realize school is just a waste of time. Linds, I'm making money now. I have to give him some, to help with expenses and all. But I don't mind."

Lyndsey was stunned. "Isn't Jack that biker guy? What do

you mean he gives you something that makes you feel better?"

"Don't freak out, Lyndsey. It's just a little powder. It mellows me out, so I don't think about that night. Sometimes I snort a little bit," Dee grabbed Lyndsey's arm, her eyes bright with excitement "and Jack just showed me how to smoke it. I *love* smoking it!"

"Is it coke?"

"No, it's heroin. It's nice. Kinda like taking a warm, relaxing bath. I've been using it for a few months now, and I love the stuff. All the bad things you hear about heroin is bullshit, and anyway, it's not like I'm shooting needles into my vein. You gotta meet him, Linds. He's really sweet, and you'll like him. He bought me a cell phone. He wants to know where I am every minute. Isn't that adorable? I'll ask him if you can come over this weekend. We can hang out and listen to tunes. Hey, maybe we can smoke a little H together. You have to be careful with it though. The first few times I used it, I puked my guts out. But I'm passed that now and it has been *so* worth it. Nothing in my life has ever felt this good. Jack is even buying my clothes. He says he wants to pick them out for me. He asked about my friends, and I told him I don't have many, except you. Jack says that's okay because I'm going to be busy with him. I wouldn't have time for a lot of friends, anyway. He wants to introduce me to the rest of the guys in the club. Jack wants to know who I talk to and every little move I make. He is so interested in me. Jack says I'm a bit rough around the edges, so he's teaching me to speak differently. He even gives me hand signals when he wants me to talk. Isn't that cute? It will be official this weekend, but

I'm already staying there. Mom knows, but she doesn't care. One less mouth to feed and all."

Not knowing what to say, Lyndsey just stared at Dee and closed her mouth.

Dee prattled on. "I better keep Jack away from Mom though. She'd be all over him. Jack's place needs a little help. It's definitely a bachelor pad. He doesn't want me touching anything. But, I don't know, maybe some flowers would help. I'll have to ask him. I'll give you my number so we can make plans for the weekend. If I say you have the wrong number, hang up and I'll try and call you later. Jack is overly protective. He doesn't want me talking to anyone. He must really love me, don't you think?" Not giving Lyndsey a chance to respond, Dee said, "I gotta go. I'm meeting Jack, and I don't want to be late." Dee waggled her fingers at Lyndsey and tottered off, staggering under the weight of the books.

Lyndsey didn't have a good feeling about Jack and hoped things would work out for Dee. Oh my God though, selling her body, that was brutal! Maybe she should go to Jack's place this weekend and try and talk some sense into her.

Walking home from school, Lyndsey found her thoughts returning to Dee. One of the things Lyndsey liked about Dee was that she felt safe. Dee was comfortable to be around. She had no rough edges. Lyndsey had never heard her say a bad thing about anyone and she feared Jack was manipulating Dee's naivety.

At home in the kitchen, Lyndsey found the note. As she picked it up, the fridge clicked on with a loud hum. She jumped, and her imagination ran wild, picturing her family slaughtered in another room. Goosebumps rose on her skin at the thought.

Her heart rate slowed as she read her mother's words, *Lyndsey, your father and I will be away for the next week. Your sister is staying at her friend's house while we're gone. Look after yourself. There's plenty of food in the fridge. No parties and go to school! See you when we get back.*

That was it. Nothing about where they'd gone. No words of love, just a few sentences. It was as if they'd been in a hurry and she was a last minute afterthought. The story of her life. She held the note reading it for the second time. The words sunk in as it dawned on her she had the house to herself. A rush of excitement swept over her, and she turned to the stereo. Changing the station from country to rock, Lyndsey cranked the tunes. The loud music shook the walls and the pictures hanging from them.

Lyndsey lit up a smoke and sucked greedily. She loved the nicotine rush. Christ, it felt good. She couldn't wait to be living on her own with nobody to tell her when to get up or go to bed. She'd do whatever she felt like, whenever she felt like doing it. But what she most looked forward too was knowing she could finally relax and breathe. Not living in constant tension and always walking on eggshells. It was a liberating thought and Lyndsey couldn't wait to experience it.

Sure it must be her lucky day she opened the fridge door. *Come on, come on, be there.* She was in luck! A bottle of beer called her name from the bottom shelf. Lyndsey pulled it out and popped the top. For a moment she just enjoyed the yeasty smell and then she put the bottle to her lips and took a huge swallow. It was delicious, ice-cold and bubbly. She liked the taste of beer, especially when it was this cold. The first one was always the best. The second one never tasted nearly as good.

Lyndsey lit up another smoke and sat in her father's favorite lazy boy. There were rules around his chair. Rule 1 – he was the only one allowed to sit in it. Had he seen her there she would have earned another cuff or some overly exaggerated response. Sitting in his chair was a massive fuck you, and she was enjoying every minute of it.

For a moment all was well. Lyndsey rocked back and forth, listening to the music, sometimes singing along, and enjoying the peace. Thinking of Dee again, Lyndsey pulled out the piece of paper Dee had given her. On it was Dee's new cell phone number. Lyndsey picked up the phone and dialed. Dee answered on the third ring.

"Hi, Dee, it's Lyndsey, my parents have taken off. I have the house all to myself and thought you might like to hang out. We could watch a movie or listen to tunes. And there are chilly-ones in the icebox."

"Oh, I'm sorry Linds, I can't. Jack's having a huge party tonight, and he wants to introduce me to some of the guys. Why don't you come to his place? I'm sure he won't mind, and I would feel better if you were there, too. Say yes. Please, Lyndsey?"

Lyndsey thought about it and then asked. "You're not going to be, um, working, are you?"

"Oh Linds," Dee giggled. "Of course I'm not. I only do that when Jack schedules me. He's kinda like my manager in that way. He says a hot babe like me can make a lot of lonely men very happy. I'm kinda like public service in that way, don't you think, Lyndsey? Anyway, tonight is purely party time. No business involved and I'm sure he wouldn't want me to do that with his friends now, would he?" Dee gushed.

Lyndsey ran through various scenarios. She could stay home and wait for him. She was pretty sure he wouldn't be calling though and the idea of staying home all night doing nothing didn't appeal to her.

By now the beer was giving her a small buzz. She hadn't eaten much today, and she could feel it. Lyndsey wrapped a piece of hair around her finger and paced, weighing the pros and cons. She didn't know anyone there, and Jack sounded like a real winner. But she didn't like the idea of Dee being alone with these strange men, without someone to watch her back.

"Lyndsey? Are you still there?"

"Yeah, I'm here," Lyndsey replied. "What time should I come over?"

Lyndsey thought it was her choosing to go to Dee's that night. What she didn't understand was it wasn't her choice. The two beers Lyndsey consumed, chose for her. But it wasn't until much, much later that she would know this.

And by then, the damage was unbelievable.

# CHAPTER THIRTEEN

Lyndsey drove her mother's old car to Jack's house. It was a standard, and she had trouble getting it into reverse. Trial and error prevailed, and after grinding a few gears, she got lucky and hit the right spot. She jerked out of the alley and stalled the car. It came to a rocky stop, and Lyndsey started it again. With the gear shift in the right slot, she pulled out of the alleyway. It wasn't long before she began to feel confident, quickly getting the hang of the gears. Lyndsey thought she probably drove better after she had a couple of beers in her. She felt more confident with beer. She was looser, relaxed, and it was easier to drive that way.

On the way to Jack's house, she passed a cop. Lyndsey looked down at the speedometer and noticed she was doing a few clicks over the speed limit. It occurred to her that she'd be in big shit if she were pulled over, but it was just a thought. She felt indestructible, like the rules no longer applied to her. Lyndsey laughed, it was a heady thought.

Jack's driveway was nothing but a dirt road. Lyndsey slowed to a crawl as she navigated the potholes and rocks. The driveway was twisty and in the darkness, she could barely make it out. Lyndsey drove off the road and had to fight the gear shift to get it in reverse. After a few tries, she managed to get the car back on the road.

The night was black, and she could barely see. Lyndsey turned on the high beams and continued her crawl. After a few more bumps and lurches she came out into a large field. Jack's house stood in the center of the field. His house resembled an old barn. The roof sloped at an odd angle as if it might cave in. Motorcycles and an old pickup truck parked in front. Hers was the only car there. The front door was wide open, and there were people on the deck. Lyndsey parked between two bikes. She could barely make out the Harley Davidson crest as she pulled in. The bike looked mean. Its insignia should read I'm boss!

Lyndsey thought only a really badass guy would ride a bike like that and for a moment she reconsidered going in. Maybe she should turn around and leave right now? After a moment's pause, she got out of the car and headed towards the house.

As she entered the front door, she saw Jack. He stood in the midst of a small crowd. There were people everywhere. She didn't know any of them, and some appeared to be her grandparents' age. They didn't look like her grandparents though. These men and women dressed in black leather pants and vests. On the back of their vests was a patch with the name of their club and city.

Some of the men wore long hair tied back with a bandana or braided in a long tail that trailed down their back. There were big bellies and lots of tattoos. The women had tattoos also, and a few looked like they'd bought into the slogan *burn the bra*. There were younger members, too. One of them turned and walked in her direction.

This dude walked using his whole body. His hips jutted out towards her. His lips pulled back in a snarl, exposing cracked and rotting teeth. His eyes looked like little black bullet holes.

He stepped close and asked, "Who do you belong to, sweet thing?"

Nasty! He smelled like he hadn't bathed in a long time. His hands were black with grease, and his arms covered in colorful ink. She stared at his ink. Not sure how to respond she didn't say anything.

"Who do you belong to?" He asked again and spat a foul stream of black liquid on the floor next to her.

Lyndsey jumped and moved her foot. "What?" She had no idea what he meant.

He gripped her arm in a painful hold. "I'm going to ask you one more time, and you better have the right answer. Who are you here with?" He questioned and twisted her arm behind her.

Lyndsey looked into his eyes and wished she hadn't. Madness stared back at her. His eyes reminded her of a rattlesnake she'd once seen on a trip to the zoo with her seventh-grade class. This guy was deadly, cold, coiled, and ready to strike.

Lyndsey stammered, "Dddeee. Dee asked me to come."

The tension on her arm eased off immediately.

He was all smiles now. "Oh, why didn't you say so? Any friend of Jack's girl is a friend of ours. Are you working for Jack?"

"Aaah, no, just...hanging out with Dee tonight," she said, trying to think of some way she could get this vile creature away from her and find Dee.

"They call me Weasel, come with me. I'll take you to see Jack."

Obediently, Lyndsey followed Weasel through the crowd. Good name for him. He looked like a weasel. As they walked through the people, Weasel smacked the odd back and punched a few arms on his way. The skinny little guy sure knew how to throw a punch. It wasn't just the guys he tortured, either. He stopped by some of the women and whispered in their ear. Weasel pinched their rear, and grabbed their tits, making them squeal. As he spotted Jack, Weasel grabbed her by the arm and steered her over to him. Lyndsey was sure she'd have a few bruises to show for tonight.

"Hey, Jack, I found this pretty little thing looking for Dee," Weasel said. He shoved her at Jack, pushing her so hard she stumbled.

Jack reached out to steady her. "Thanks, Weasel, I'll take it from here."

Weasel, sensing dismissal, looked at Lyndsey and said. "If you get lonely, come and find me."

Yeah right, she thought. I'd rather take my chances with that rattlesnake. At least there was an antivenin for that. Lyndsey ignored Weasel and turned to Jack. She'd seen him before, but never this close. She'd heard about him though. Jack had a nasty reputation as a very bad dude.

He was probably ten years older than her. He was quite good-looking in a macho sort of way. Jack was dressed in black leather, too. The back of his vest also sported a colorful patch. Jack had no shirt on under his vest, allowing her full view of his upper torso. He wasn't one of the big-bellied members. Jack looked like he worked out at the gym and frequently. His upper arms bulged with muscles, and his forearms were thicker than her legs. His stomach was lean and hard, his six-pack of abs peeking out through the opening in his vest. Jack's chest was hairless and smooth and looked as if he had recently oiled it. He flexed his pecs causing his chest muscles to dance up and down.

"Like what you see?" He grinned down at her.

Actually, she did. Lyndsey continued studying him. His hair was black and thick. His eyes were green, and there was a cleft in the middle of his chin. Black stubble covered his cheeks leaving him with a five o'clock shadow. His skin was tanned golden brown making his white teeth pop. His lips were full and made for kissing. Just looking at him she felt her pulse skyrocket. Now she understood how Dee had fallen prey to his charm.

"Where's Dee?" Lyndsey blurted, cutting to the chase.

"You must be Lyndsey?" Jack's gorgeous green eyes drilled into hers. "Dee told me all about you. She is in the back. She's, ah, busy right now, if you know what I mean. I'll get her for you in a minute. Why don't you grab a beer and hang out for a while? You look kind of uptight. Just chill."

Jack's back disappeared into the crowd. It seemed like history was repeating itself with Dee missing at another house party. Lyndsey felt uneasy and thought she would go looking for Dee, rather than waiting for Jack to get her.

Lyndsey wandered through the living room and kitchen. The house was small, and the floorboards were loose and sticking up. If you weren't careful, you'd find yourself tripping over them. There were a few buckets placed around the room to catch water from the leaky roof. Paint peeled off the walls in large flakes, and someone had drawn a lewd picture on the exposed drywall. A large penis drawn in felt pen covered the entire wall. The hallway leading off the kitchen sloped to the right. Lyndsey side-stepped a hole in the floor and turned around. No one was at this end. The hallway was vacant.

"Dee," Lyndsey called. "Dee, where are you?"

Lyndsey came to a door. It was slightly open and she put her eye to the crack. Lyndsey spied Dee's back. She was sitting on the bed tying something around her arm.

"Dee?" Lyndsey questioned. "Didn't you hear me calling you?"

"Lyndsey, don't come in!"

Completely ignoring her, Lyndsey burst into the room. "Jesus Christ, Dee! You invite me to this fucking party, and then I can't even find you. I got mauled by this little creep and…" Her words trailed off as she saw what Dee was doing.

Dee sat on the bed with a rubber hose tied around her arm. On the bedside table was a spoon with a piece of cotton and liquid in it. Beside the spoon was a needle. A candle burned next to it, scenting the room with its waxy smell.

"You shouldn't be in here, Linds," Dee shook her head and picked up the needle. She took off the orange cap and inserted the pointy tip into the cotton. Lyndsey watched spellbound as Dee drew the liquid from the spoon. As if Lyndsey weren't even in the room, Dee held the needle up for closer inspection. Dee pushed down on the plunger, and a small droplet of liquid escaped the sharp point.

Lyndsey watched in disbelief.

"If you don't want to see this you'd better leave right now," Dee advised. Her voice sounded funny, flat, dead.

Lyndsey couldn't move. She watched Dee put the end of the hose in her teeth. She bit down and used her teeth to yank the hose tight. A vein bulged, and Dee picked up the needle and started poking her veins. She seemed to have forgotten Lyndsey was there. Lyndsey watched, horrified, as Dee butchered herself. She poked one vein after another in her attempt to get high.

Dee must have tried six or seven times before she got it right. Each time Dee pushed the needle deep into her arm she'd mumble, "Shit, I missed. Shit, I missed." Then she'd repeat the process, desperately searching for another vein. Her previous pokes still oozed, dripping little blood trails down her arm. White bumps and welts rose with each missed hit. Finally, Dee found a vein that worked, and she emptied the bloodied syringe.

Lyndsey thought she might throw up. She hated needles. She remembered getting a vaccination when she was five. She'd watched the nurse drawing a bunny rabbit being stung by a bee on her arm. The needles sharp sting was so unexpected Lyndsey panicked just seeing one.

Her mouth watered and she worked hard to push nausea back. Whatever was in that needle worked fast! Lyndsey was pretty sure it was the heroin that Dee was "just smoking." Dee spat out the rubber hose, and her head drooped. Lyndsey looked at her arm, noticing the track marks running down them. There was old bruising too, and a big boil covered the inside crook of her elbow. It must hurt like hell. Lyndsey couldn't believe anyone would willingly do something so devastating to themselves.

Dee's head slanted to the left, resting on her shoulder. Her eyes closed and she murmured sounds of contentment. Lyndsey thought she looked pathetic. Dee was a junked out mess. If this was her idea of a good time, she didn't want any part of it. The needle still hung from Dee's vein, and Lyndsey gave her a shake. "Dee, for Christ's sake's' wake up!"

Dee opened her eyes and gave Lyndsey a glassy stare. "Sooo good," she slurred. "I'm in heaven."

"No, Dee, you're not! You're in hell, and you're sick. You can't ever do this again!" Panicked, Lyndsey's mind raced, looking for something she could say or do to fix Dee. As if finding the right words, might magically make her well. But before she could say anything, Dee's eyes closed again, and her head fell forward.

In this strange position, Dee got up from the bed. Standing, she swayed in a rocking motion. Her head bowed as if praying to the heroin gods. Dee appeared to be sleepwalking. She moved around, but she wasn't awake.

Lyndsey felt sick to her stomach, watching her friend. Dee stood in a bent over crouch. She swayed back and forth catching herself every time she was about to topple over. The stuff in Dee's needle must make her head heavy because Dee couldn't hold it up for long. For a minute Dee got her head up before it fell back down. Her mouth hung open, and her face was slack. Dee's eyes rolled back exposing the white undersides.

This time Lyndsey didn't touch her. She never took Dee in

her arms. Lyndsey wasn't sure how to make Dee better. She stared at her friend for what seemed like an eternity. She watched her until she couldn't watch any more. The stuff in the needle was poison.

Heroin was evil, corrupt and it was destroying Dee.

Her friend was broken.

Dee had clearly entered hell.

# CHAPTER FOURTEEN

Goosebumps rode her body like an unwanted guest she'd picked up in a horror show. Lyndsey left the room needing to escape the nightmare scene she'd just witnessed there. Running down the hallway, she forced herself to slow down and stay calm.

Going to Jack's place was a bad idea.

A large group of the big bellies blocked her way as she entered the living room. The noisy room grew quiet. Lyndsey could feel eyes staring at her. She lowered her head and quickened her steps.

"Hey, darlin', an old man in a sleeveless t-shirt spoke, "why don't you come on over here and rub the Buddha?"

The big bellies surrounded her. "Nice tits." A mean grey-haired man with a tear-drop tattoo under his eye reached over and pinched her nipple. Lyndsey moved out of his reach and side-stepped their groping hands.

A thin man with a long red beard pinched her ass with such brutality it brought tears to her eyes. His pinches would leave a mark. She was going to be black and blue tomorrow. Lyndsey blinked back tears. She must not show any weakness.

She took a deep breath and squared her jaw. Lyndsey stared hard at the mean ring-leader and said. "Stop it!"

She must have said something funny because they all started to laugh.

The thin man said. "Hey, Rooster, you gonna listen to the little lady?"

Rooster didn't look impressed. One eye narrowed making the tear tattoo under it more pronounced. Before she could run, he grabbed her, holding her firmly against his body as his hands wandered up and down pinching as they went. Lyndsey could feel his meanness with every pinch. His old fingers were like steel. Rooster cupped her ass, gave it a few light strokes and then dug in and twisted hard.

The pain was bad. But she held herself together.

Finally, he grew bored of toying with her. Rooster put his hands on her shoulder and gave her a hard push. Lyndsey hit one of the big bellies and landed on the ground.

She landed on her backside trying to catch her breath and get up. Only she wasn't quick enough. One of the big bellies reached down and grabbed her by her hair and yanked her up.

The thin red-bearded one undid his fly and grinned at her.

Caught in a game of cat and mouse, Lyndsey tried to crawl away.

The thin red-bearded man took a step towards her when Rooster knocked him out of the way.

Rooster grabbed her and pulled her close. He wrapped one meaty arm around her waist and with his free hand began to unbutton her blouse.

Lyndsey froze as Rooster's buddies egged him on with hoots and hollers. Numerous hands groped her exposed flesh. Rooster held her in place as his friends touched every part of her. He took his arm from her waist and wrapped it around her neck holding her body firmly against his flabby midsection. His fingers squeezed her throat, and she panicked.

Lyndsey bit down on his arm as hard as she could. With a mouthful of his hairy arm between her lips, she tasted blood.

Rooster's arm loosened on her neck, and she pulled herself free. "Fuck off and leave me alone!" Lyndsey wiped the blood from her mouth trying not to shake.

"You gonna take that, Rooster?" A big belly asked.

He wasn't.

Rooster grabbed her and shoved with all his might. Having no time to put her hands out, Lyndsey hit the ground with a bone-jarring crunch. She saw stars when her head hit the uneven floorboards.

Rooster planted one foot on her chest and pinned her down. He took his belt off, looked into her eyes, and said, "I'm gonna hurt you bad, *real bad.*"

A comforting calm came over her. It was like there was two of her. She was on the floor and she was above it. Lyndsey detached from what was happening to her physical body below and watched, safe, from above.

Rooster puffed hard on his cigar making the ash cherry red. Then he blew smoke rings at her face. Rooster took the cigar out of his mouth and placed the burning end between her breasts. Lyndsey heard her flesh sizzle. She could smell her burnt skin but felt no pain. Lying there on the cold floor, she looked beyond Rooster into another place.

Rooster re-lit his cigar. Lyndsey's flesh must have put it out, she thought, without emotion. Rooster's cheeks huffed in as he puffed his cigar. When the ash was bright red, it began to descend.

Only this time it never connected. The cigar was tossed high into the air, with Rooster following it.

Jack stood above her. Lyndsey came back to her body with a jolt.

The old boys backed away from them, giving Jack the space his body seemed to demand. Jack pulled her up and carried her in his arms. As is she weighed no more than a sack of potatoes he informed his friends. "She's off limits, boys." With that, he walked away leaving the big bellies with their mouths open.

Jack carried her out of the house. She squirmed and tried to get free, but he just threw her over his shoulders and kept walking.

Blood rushed to her head as she hung upside down. Lyndsey kicked his shins, but he only held her tighter. She pounded his back with her fists. "Put me down!"

Jack kept walking, ignoring her demands and flailing body. When they reached her car, he released her. Lyndsey slid off him and landed on her feet. She was *furious*! How dare he treat her like a child? Standing as tall as she could, her shoulders back and her anger making her feel stronger than she was, she lit into him.

"How dare you treat me like a child! Who the fuck do you think you are? What the hell -" She broke off as he placed a hand over her mouth.

Her nostrils flared at the intimate connection. Black long lashes connected to Jack's beautiful green eyes. He smelled of citrus and spice. Her pulse skyrocketed. Jack held her close, the hand covering her mouth kept just enough pressure to still her words but not to hurt her.

Jack's beautiful green eyes looked at her with sorrow.

Lyndsey tried to back up a step.

What she couldn't handle, what she'd never experienced before, was someone showing her kindness. Jack cared, and it made her breathe hard. She didn't understand why he would give a shit, but he did. She could see it in his eyes.

As if she were a puppy, Jack patted her on the head and opened her car door. He helped her inside and took the keys from her shaky hands. Jack started the car for her and waited in silence as the engine warmed. Lyndsey blew on her stiff fingers trying to defrost them.

Satisfied that she was good to go, Jack softly closed the door. He looked at Lyndsey through the driver's side window and motioned her to roll it down.

Her hands shook, and her insides quivered, but she managed to lower the window.

Jack leaned through it and placed his lips on her ear. His breath warm against the cold, "go home," he whispered. "And don't ever come back." To make his point he raised his voice, but just a little. "Please. If you know what's good for you, don't ever come back here."

His words weren't mean or dismissive. They were soft, warm and genuine. Lyndsey noted how carefully he delivered them.

Jack kissed her hair. Pulled his head from the window and gave a little tap to the top of her car. She knew what he meant, *get going.*

Lyndsey rolled up the window and backed away from him. Looking in the rearview mirror, she watched him as long as she could. Jack grew smaller and smaller. Turning the corner, Lyndsey caught one last glimpse of him.

Then she drove off into the cold night.

# CHAPTER FIFTEEN

Lyndsey took her time going home, driving slowly and paying close attention to her speed. Her body was cold, and her teeth chattered. The shock she'd been feeling wore off. In response, she was shaky as she held tightly to the gear shift. Her breath came in little hitches and her newly branded chest hurt. Tears crawled up her throat and burst from her lips in great racking sobs. Her face was hot, and her throat was sore and swollen.

The windshield fogged from her warm breath. Lyndsey couldn't see much and wiped away the moisture. Water pooled in her mouth as she tried to pass the lump lodged in her throat. Little bubbles of pain she'd kept hidden for years began to burst.

*Scared little girl, POP.*

*Hurt little girl, POP.*

*Lonely little girl, POP.*

*Please, somebody, see me, POP.*

*I want to be loved, POP.*

Buried pain rose in her chest like a large ocean swell, coming in waves that rolled through her body.

Lyndsey parked the car in the alley, wondering how she'd managed to drive home. The ride was a blurry as if it hadn't been her driving but someone else. Her body had merely gone through the motions of shifting gears, accelerating, braking, and steering.

Jack's image haunted her. Kindness killed her, she didn't

know what to do with it, and she felt overwhelmed by the raw emotion it evoked in her heart.

Wrung out and exhausted, Lyndsey lay down on her bed. Suzy jumped up and joined her. Lyndsey pulled her close, cuddling her sweet little pup in her arms. As she drifted to sleep, Suzy licked her face and washed the tears from her cheeks.

She slept until noon the next day. She would probably have slept longer, but hunger pains woke her up. Lyndsey was stiff and sore. She touched her burned chest. It was tender and gooey. Lyndsey got up and walked to the bathroom mirror for a better look. The led-lights above the mirror were bright. As her eyes adjusted to the brightness, she got a good look at her wound.

The red circle of flesh was puckered and oozing with ash embedded at the center. Oh, and it hurt like hell! Lyndsey reached under the sink and pulled out the first aid kit. She dabbed antibiotic ointment on her burn hoping it wouldn't get infected.

With her burn taken care of Lyndsey walked to the kitchen and topped up Suzy's water bowl. After she refilled her pup's kibble, she poured herself a bowl of cereal. Lyndsey wasn't much on cooking, but today she had a craving for bacon and eggs with pancakes smothered in butter and syrup on the side. Instead, she made do with the cereal.

Lyndsey thought about last night and wondered how Dee felt this morning. Lyndsey worried about her. It was a lifelong habit, really. It was weird, but she felt the strongest affection for things that were, well, broken.

She always rooted for the underdog.

There was a time years ago when she'd been coming home from a friend's house. It was dark, and she was late. As she was crossing the street, a cat stepped out in front of her, nearly tripping her when it brushed up against her leg. She could barely make it out but saw something in its mouth. As she bent down to take a closer look, she thought it might be a bird. Lyndsey reached out and gently pulled on the little creature in the cat's mouth. She didn't want to injure the bird further, so she was careful. Lyndsey could feel the tiny skeleton thrashing in its attempts to get away. A long thin wing protruded from the cat's mouth, and she pulled on it.

Lyndsey freed the bird and held it up to the street light to see if it was injured. Before she could get a good look, the strange-looking bird sank its beak into the flesh of her finger. It was a heavy little thing and pulled her finger down. The birds bite hurt like crazy. Lyndsey held the bird carefully and walked to the streetlight where she got her first look. Lyndsey almost fainted when she what was there. *Dangling from her finger* was *not a cute little bird but a hideous looking rat!*

A shrill scream tore from her lips and she shook her hand back and forth, trying to dislodge the gross little creature. The rat released its grip on her finger and fell to the ground. It bounced off the concrete, righted itself, and tried to crawl away. Only it didn't walk so well. The rat scrabbled at the ground, dragging its legs.

Lyndsey didn't step on bugs or hurt any living creature. Well, except for mosquitoes and wasps. And she didn't think they should count. Her heart broke seeing the injured rat. She forgot about her earlier aversion and bent to pick it up. She would take it home and see if she could splint its legs. Maybe she could fix them? She couldn't leave it here to die.

Lyndsey scooped up the rat to cuddle it, but before she could bring it close, it bit her again. Jesus Christ that hurt! She shook the rat from her hand, and it fell to the ground. Only this time it didn't try to crawl away. Maybe now it understood she was only trying to help, she hoped so anyway and bent down to pick it up again. As she held the rat it went limp in her arms. It squeaked a message only another rat would understand, but at least it didn't bite her. Lyndsey walked home as fast as she could knowing the poor little thing didn't have much time left.

Out of breath, she reached the back door. The rat trembled as she flung the door open. Her mom was there in the mudroom, pressing her father's shirt. She looked up from the ironing board and noticed the rat. Her face went white as she snatched up the broom beside her and knocked the rat out of Lyndsey's hands. Then she screamed, and the poor broken little rat dragged itself into a corner. Mom took hold of Lyndsey's arm, pulled her into the kitchen and called for her father.

Lyndsey held her finger high in the air while her Mom turned on the tap. As cold water splashed over her swelling digit, Lyndsey looked at her finger and couldn't believe what she saw. The end of her finger was swollen twice its size!

As her dad entered the kitchen, her mom wrapped a clean tea towel around her injured finger and her father whisked her out the door. The shot she got at the hospital stung worse than the bite from the rat. By the time she was finished at the hospital her finger was throbbing.

Her father was angry with her for picking up the rat. The ride home was silent. Lyndsey made sure not to complain or say her finger hurt. One wrong word could set him off, and she didn't want to chance it.

Lyndsey opened the front door and ran off looking for the rat. It wasn't in the laundry room where she'd last seen it. Lyndsey looked behind the door and in the kitchen, but she didn't see it anywhere. Worried now, she found her mother and asked if she'd seen it.

Her mom nodded. "It's outside in the garbage can."

"In the garbage can?" Lyndsey worried the poor thing would be cold. "What's it doing in there?"

"I didn't want it to bite anyone else. " Her mom said and touched Lyndsey's finger. "So I killed it with the broom and swept it into the garbage can."

"What! No!" Lyndsey screamed and ran from the room. *Please don't let it be dead.* She went straight for the garbage cans on the back porch. Lyndsey lifted the lid and peered in. Nothing there but bags of garbage stacked one upon another. *Good*, replacing the lid she prayed her mother was playing a joke on her. Maybe the little rat was sleeping behind the washing machine, its legs healing as it slept. Fingers crossed, she lifted the lid on the second can and looked inside. No bags of garbage piled up in this one. It was almost empty except for one tiny broken body, lying curled on its side at the bottom of the can.

For some morbid reason, the memory of the rat made her think of Dee. Lyndsey hoped her friend didn't end up like that rat. All alone, broken and curled into a little ball as she breathed her last breath.

As she stepped into the shower, Lyndsey pushed away images of last night. The hot water beat a comforting melody on her back. She breathed in steam and relaxed. Lyndsey stood under the shower turning front to back until the hot water, grew cool. Lyndsey scrubbed away Rooster's filthy touch. She avoided her burned breast and tried not to think about Dee. As the lather circled the drain, dark thoughts crept back in.

The best way not to think was to keep busy. So that's what she did. Lyndsey took extra care with hair and makeup. Sometimes if she could get her makeup just right, she would feel better.

But her makeup trick wasn't working today. Disturbing images flashed vividly through her mind. She wondered if other people went through this. Did everyone feel crazy at times? Lyndsey never told anyone about the stuff that went on in her head. They weren't happy thoughts. They made her feel anxious.

Lyndsey thought something very important was missing in her. But she had no idea what it was. She knew the missing piece was on the inside, it felt empty, like a big void. Lyndsey was feeling it now. It was an intense yearning for something. She just wished she knew what it was.

Feeling the need to move Lyndsey grabbed the leash and hooked it to Suzy. For once it wasn't raining. Sunshine spilled through the trees, making her laugh. Lyndsey walked the familiar streets waving to the neighbors she saw on the way.

It was weird how you could live in one place for so long and not really know anyone. Oh, Lyndsey knew their names and they talked about the weather, but they didn't *know* her. No one did. Lyndsey picked up her pace. She didn't want to talk to her neighbors, only wave at them. She didn't like idle chit-chat. It felt phony to her. And it was work. Head down and walking fast, a frail voice called her name.

"Lyndsey," Mr. McDonald motioned, come here.

Shit, she hadn't been fast enough. Forcing herself to look cheerful and interested, Lyndsey crossed the street to listen to the old guy talk about the weather again.

Mr. McDonald wore a green and white vest and a yellow cap on his head. His eyebrows resembled two shaggy grey caterpillars. He looked through the rim of his glasses at her and said, "all this rain is making my arthritis act up."

"Oh." It was lame, but it was all she could think of.

"They have me on so many medications I don't know if I'm coming or going," he complained.

She could relate to that one.

Mr. McDonald switched topics and began telling her about his roses. "They don't like all this grey…" he trailed off, waiting for her response.

Looking at him, she had one of her strange thoughts. She imagined herself taking off the pleasant mask she wore, and showing him her real self. She wondered if he would turn from her and run off screaming, hoping to save his precious roses from what he glimpsed.

Lyndsey was sure if he looked hard, he'd see the darkness hiding just below her smiling surface.

# CHAPTER SIXTEEN

Lyndsey heard the rumble of his car before it arrived. She climbed the stairs knowing he'd be there soon. She didn't know why he liked loud cars. His car sounded more like a motorcycle than a car. He'd purposely bought a beefed up muffler system that sounded broken to her ears. His muffler was loud and annoying, kind of like he was.

She grabbed her purse from the kitchen chair where she'd left it and gave Suzy a little pat. Lyndsey locked the back door and ran to meet him.

Lyndsey strapped the seat belt around her waist and said. "Hey."

His nodded at her and replied. "We're going on a trip."

"Oh?" Lyndsey imagined lush hotels with swimming pools and spas. She hoped they had room service and a mini bar. "Where are we going?"

"Not far. About six hours from here. We'll spend the night and be back tomorrow. No more questions, now," his brow crinkled and he shot her *the look.*

Feeling excited she grinned. "Okay, give me a sec. I've got to grab a few things." Lyndsey ran back to the house and loaded her suitcase with makeup, toothbrush, special shampoo and conditioner, and enough clothes for any event.

Then she put out an extra bowl of kibble for Suzy and topped up her water bowl. She wished she could bring her little pup with them, but caution said no. She could imagine him in one of his rages tossing her small dog out the window. Nope. Not a good idea to bring her at all. Suzy was safer at home. With a final glance at Suzy, Lyndsey picked up her suitcase. It was heavy and awkward and banged against her legs. The extra weight slowed her steps. As she neared the car, she saw he had the trunk open for her. Lyndsey handed him the suitcase.

"Christ," he complained. "What have you got in there?"

"I wanted to make sure I had enough clothes."

"Didn't you listen? We're only going for one night." His voice rose.

Lyndsey acted quickly. She'd gotten good at saying the right thing to him. And the right thing to say was *always* what he wanted to hear.

"I want to look pretty for you. I brought extra clothes so you can choose an outfit for me." Lyndsey gave him a kiss on his cheek. It seemed to soothe him, a little.

She didn't know why but it seemed important to him that she understood he was boss. Lyndsey thought he liked her company, but only if she kept her mouth closed and paid close attention to him.

There was a certain sexiness to his mean. He looked good today. His hair was washed and curled around his neck. His cheeks were smooth, he had shaved and spicy-sweet cologne scented the air. His nose was too big for his face. It was beak-like and more suited to an eagle or hawk. Or some other large bird of prey.

She looked away before he noticed her staring at him. He

removed a pencil thin joint from behind his ear and lit up. Marijuana was his medicine. It soothed the anger from his face. He took two long tokes and then offered her one. Lyndsey refused, praying it wouldn't set him off. Luckily, it didn't. He relaxed into his seat as the weed took effect.

Lyndsey was glad he smoked a lot of pot. She didn't like him when he was straight which, thankfully, wasn't very often. He turned the music up, and they took off. As they drove out of town, she sat back in her seat and looked out the window, prepared to enjoy the ride.

They'd been on the road a few hours when he said they should stop. Him was in a good mood today. He wasn't angry. Instead, he was talkative, which rarely ever happened. Lyndsey drank it all in. He told her Mark and Larry had wanted to come with them on this trip, too. But he wanted to spend time alone with his special pretty girl, so he told them no.

Lyndsey felt warm all over. She loved when he called her special and pretty. She could almost believe it, and for a moment, all was right in her world.

They pulled into a restaurant parking lot. The billboard overhead advertised the daily specials. As he opened the front door for her, the waiter greeted them. Lyndsey wanted to sit at a table by the window. They had to wait a few minutes for the busboy to clear away the dirty dishes and wipe down the table. Lyndsey looked around the restaurant. The delicious food smells made her stomach grumble with anticipation. The menu on the blackboard announced lasagna and garlic bread as the daily special. She thought it looked good.

The waiter came back and showed them to their newly cleaned table. He held the chair out for her. Lyndsey sat down feeling flustered. With a thick Italian accent, the waiter rattled off the specials. Only he spoke to her, barely glancing at him. After taking their drink orders, he withdrew giving them time to choose their meal.

Dear God, it was back. Tension, so thick, she felt like she would choke on it. She didn't want to look at him, already knowing what she would see. Bracing herself, she glanced in his direction. His face wore its familiar sneer. When he was angry, his nose looked even bigger. His lips thinned out into pencil lines, and his eyes drilled little bullet holes in her.

What had she done wrong now?

The waiter not noticing the tension at the table whipped out his order book, and studied her face. Lyndsey looked at the ground and placed her order. Her appetite was gone. Him ordered, his tone condescending. She almost hated him for sounding like this. She stole another glance at him. Her anger grew as she looked at him. God, he was ugly, sitting there, his face all twisted up and matching his cold heart.

It was a silent meal like the many she'd eaten with her family, all of them sitting at the kitchen table and jamming food into their mouths. As they chewed, their insides swelled with frustration, betrayal, hurt, and anger. It wasn't an appetizing combination. One more time Lyndsey couldn't wait for a meal to be over.

They walked back to the car in silence. As she slid into her seat, he sped off. They hurtled down the highway as she fought to latch her seat-belt. Lyndsey never said a word. Afraid her voice might set him off. He drove with reckless abandon as if defying death. The scenery through the windshield was a blur. They whizzed past telephone poles and other vehicles. Lyndsey held her breath, praying he wouldn't lose control of the car.

They drove for a long time like that, the pedal to the metal while death hovered near. It wouldn't take much at this speed. One wrong move on the steering wheel and they'd both be gone. Her life was in his hands now, and she was terrified.

After what seemed like hours but was probably thirty minutes, he slowed down. The tension in the car eased off as he let up on the gas pedal. Traveling at a safer speed, he settled back in his seat, turned the music up loud, and drove.

Finally, they reached their destination. As far as cities went this was the biggest one she'd ever been visited. Approximately three million people lived here, Lyndsey had never seen so many cars or tall buildings. Caught in a traffic jam, they crawled through the streets of the downtown area. Lyndsey was sure she could have walked faster than the speed they were driving. There was an ocean of people marching down the sidewalks. Lyndsey wondered where they were all going. The city people walked with purpose and hurry.

His earlier rage forgotten him pointed out the various cultures, points of interest, and the panhandlers. He pulled the car into a tight spot, parking between a Beemer and a Mercedes. He put some change into the meter, took her by the arm, and steered them down the street. They walked like that for some distance. This part of the city wasn't very nice. The buildings were older and not as well cared for. There were fewer people on this street, and a many of them appeared dazed and lost. Some were dressed in layers and of grubby old clothing, and they walked, sat, or lay on the sidewalk, mumbling to no one, or yelling at each other. A few of the grubby-dressed people yelled at nothing at all.

"Oh my God," Lyndsey pointed. "What's wrong with them?"

He pushed her hand down. "They're homeless and mentally ill, and most are drug addicted or alcoholics." He shrugged. "Don't feel bad for them. They're weak-willed, they let the bottle or needle beat them. They live mostly on the streets and beg for money to buy more dope or booze."

"We have to help them." Lyndsey took the spare change from her pocket and dropped it in the can belonging to a disheveled man sitting on the sidewalk. He sat on a filthy blanket, and there was a shopping cart filled with garbage and empty cans and bottles, next to him.

Him gave her a nasty look. He gripped her arm painfully and marched her down the street. Wagging a finger under her nose, he said, "Don't talk to them, don't give them money, and don't look at them!" To emphasize his point, he pinched the soft flesh underneath her arm.

Blinking back tears she walked beside him wishing she'd never come on this trip. They walked another two blocks and then came to a stop in front of a shop with graffiti art drawn on the windows. Inside the shop were a six small tables with chase loungers beside them. Heavy metal music played in the background. The people working in the shop wore ink with graffiti tattoos.

One of them approached, "what can I do for you?" He had piercings in his nose, chin, eyebrows, ears, and one painful looking one through his lower lip.

Lyndsey had seen tattoos before, but his body was much more than that. He was like a picture, filled with beauty and vivid color, his skin was the frame. Lyndsey was surprised when him asked for a tattoo. He reached into his pocket and pulled out a folded piece of paper. Opening it, he smoothed away the wrinkles and held it out. As she looked over his shoulder, she saw the crude drawing. It was a shield with a crown of thorns at the top and two crossed swords at the bottom. The shield read *Born to Rule*.

Intrigued she sat in the waiting room and watched him pull off his shirt, leaving his chest and arms bare. Him would benefit from lifting weights. He was lean, bordering on skinny. He pointed to his upper arm where he wanted the tattoo placed. He watched closely as the area was swabbed, shaved, and disinfected.

Lyndsey thought his tattoo would look better on his chest. His arm wasn't big enough to receive a drawing of that size, but she knew better than to suggest it.

It was quite fascinating watching as his picture came to life. The tattoo needles dipped into his flesh over and over again. It must hurt like hell, but he looked like he was enjoying it. Him never flinched as the needles drew their painful picture on his arm..

He wasn't a baby that was for sure. He never whined or pulled his arm away. The man tattooing him asked if he wanted a break, but he didn't. He just sat that there, watching, smoking, and looking at her.

She felt kind of weird watching him. That strange, twisty, compulsive, lovesick feeling she got every once in a while when she looked at him. Him continued to stare at her as the needles pierced his flesh, and she looked back.

They stayed like that, watching each other, while her stomach did flip-flops.

Lyndsey didn't know it then, but she would never feel that kind of attraction again.

At least, not for him.

# CHAPTER SEVENTEEN

They walked back to the car, their arms touching as they walked, together, yet a million miles apart. He rolled his sleeve up, exposing his new artwork. The area around his tattoo looked swollen and red. The petroleum jelly made it all shiny, and she thought he looked funny as he stopped to peer in the windows they passed, flexing his arm and checking out his new tattoo.

They passed more homeless people and shopping carts. Some held signs reading *I'm hungry please help me.* This time she resisted giving them money. But to do so, she couldn't look at them or meet their eyes. Lyndsey didn't understand why, but she when she made eye contact with people she felt responsible for them. Like some weird bond passed from her to the other person, binding them in a way she couldn't explain.

Back in the car they drove a short distance and pulled into a parking lot. The parking lot sat next to an ugly old brown brick building. The building was four stories high. Moss grew between the cracks in the brick. The building was what she would consider, a tear-down. Around the front door was a group of shabbily dressed people. The shopping carts parked next to them held blankets and clothing.

Him slammed the door as he got out and she followed behind. A man bumped into her never noticing he had. He stumbled off, slapping his face and muttering to himself.

"We're staying here." He nodded to the decrepit building.

What? Here? Lyndsey couldn't believe it. She'd imagined something far nicer than this seedy, run-down building.

Him wasn't interested in Lyndsey's opinion. He opened the trunk, took their luggage from it and walked off. Lyndsey hurried to catch up with him. She didn't want to be left alone out here.

He stopped just steps away from the front door and turned to her. "It's a hostel, but we can have a private room. We have to share the bathroom though. It's cheap, and we're only here for one night. It's either here or the car."

Lyndsey closed her mouth afraid of what would slip out. When they got closer, she saw *GENTLEMENS CLUB* written on the front door. "What does that mean?" she asked, jerking a thumb at the door.

"Don't worry about it. Ladies aren't supposed to stay here, but they can visit the rooms. We will pretend you're a visitor."

One of the visiting *ladies* across the street called out to them. "Hey honey, you look like you could do with some *real* company." She gave Lyndsey a dismissive look.

Lyndsey's spine stiffened.

The *lady* cackled her twisted Siren's call, "I'll do things to you she ain't never heard of! Let her watch if you like, might even teach her a thing or two. Gonna cost you extra though."

Lyndsey's cheeks grew hot. The *lady* was a real prize. She had cracked lips with a big cold sore on one corner. Her teeth were dark with decay and her hair hung in greasy coils. She had dark pouches under her eyes. Lyndsey figured she was somewhere between twenty and fifty. Her face wore the look of a hard life. Lyndsey couldn't imagine anyone wanting to spend time with her much less kissing those cracked lips.

Him just kept walking, not even glancing in the woman's direction. He told Lyndsey to wait outside while he went in to register. The human wreckage was unbelievable, and for a minute she felt sad. It was terrible that people lived like this.

He wasn't gone long. As he opened the door, Lyndsey got her first glimpse of the hostel. It was dark and musty. They climbed the stairs carrying their suitcases. He took her larger one, and she held his small bag. The stairway was dirty, and Lyndsey reminded herself not to touch the handrail afraid she might contract some infectious disease.

They climbed all the way to the fourth floor. The hallway smelled of cat piss and she covered her nose. Some rooms had open doors and she glanced inside seeing men lying prone on their beds. Correction, old men. Many were partially unclothed, wearing only underwear and socks.

Him stopped at the door and inserted his key. The door opened with a creak and then stuck. He shoved it open with his foot and stepped inside. When she saw the room, her heart sank even farther. Paint hung in strips from the walls. The bed was a single cot with a green army blanket folded at one end. At least the sheets looked clean. A pedestal sink stood in one corner of the room, its leaky faucet dripping a rusty trail.

Him put their cases on the floor. Neither one of them said a word as he laid Lyndsey on the bed. She wouldn't call it making love. There was nothing *loving* about it. It was a chore. Something Lyndsey needed to do, and get out of the way. He never noticed her burned chest. Most of her clothes were still on, and she was grateful for that small barrier. She closed her eyes as he lay above her, grunting. Her fists clenched at her sides and she prayed for it to be over quickly.

It was.

He rolled off her and walked to the sink.

They hadn't spoken words of love. They never cuddled or touched. They didn't share their hopes, dreams, or their heart's desires. They never even looked at each other.

Lyndsey felt used, ugly, dirty, and broken. She looked down at the carpet, ashamed, not wanting to see him at all. She wished she were invisible.

At that exact moment, she started to hate him.

She already hated herself.

That happened years ago.

# CHAPTER EIGHTEEN

Lyndsey needed to wash. She looked at the sink she decided against it. No privacy. Him didn't seem bothered by washing in front of her. But she wouldn't do that. Instead, she gathered her toiletries and left their room in search of the bathroom. In an open doorway, one resident sat upright on his bed. Seeing Lyndsey pass a look of astonishment crossed his face.

"Hey!" He called to her. "Hey girlie, come here."

Lyndsey picked up her pace leaving the old man behind. His calls echoed down the hallway.

"Hey girlie, come back here! Come give Papa a kiss!" The old goat's laughter turned to a full-blown coughing fit.

*Good, she hoped the sick old pervert choked on his words.* His shouts woke the other residents, and they came to their doorways to see what was happening. Lyndsey paused, wondering if she should go back.

An old man reached his wrinkled arm out to her. "Hey dolly, come here and keep me company."

Lyndsey acted as if she hadn't seen or heard him and stopped in front of a door marked *GENTS.* Where was the *LADIES* room?

*Oh well, Gents it is.* Lyndsey pushed opened the door praying it was empty and had a lock. She was in luck! As locked the door her body trembled. What kind of place was this? She imagined all the old geezers lining up outside her door waiting to for her to come out.

The water was cold. Lyndsey splashed some on herself washing the necessary parts and finished quickly. Then she braced herself for the trip down the hallway. Lyndsey opened the door just enough to peer out. The hall was vacant. No long line awaited her. They had either gone back to sleep or left the building, but just in case she ran past every open doorway.

Later that night they went to a nearby club. Instead of asking for her ID the doorman seated them at a nearby table where the waiter took their drink order. Him had a Rye and Coke, and she ordered a Singapore Sling. Her drink came in a tall glass with a slice of orange and cherry on top. A tiny umbrella held it all together. The umbrella was adorable!

The sling was tasty and easy to drink. With just a few sips it was gone. Lyndsey ate the fruit and slipped the umbrella into her purse. The waitress came by, and she ordered another one.

The music was loud. The vibrations of the bass made their drink glasses rattle. The dance floor crowded with bodies. Some of those bodies were barely clothed. Lyndsey looked on in wonder as they danced with complete abandon. She'd never done anything with complete abandon. She was way too conscious of others and never fully relaxed in their presence.

Lyndsey was in love with the club. In this dark, smoky atmosphere she felt right at home. Chewing the ice from her second drink, she was surprised to see it was empty.

"Slow down. Those drinks are expensive! You can have beer from now on." He gave her his ugly look as if that were all it took for her to obey.

A pretty waitress stopped at their table. Around her hips, she wore a gun belt. "It's happy hour," she smiled. She held her tray with one hand using her other to pour two shots of amber liquid into two tiny glasses.

Lyndsey smiled up at her. The woman obviously enjoyed her job.

"It's on the house," the waitress grinned and moved on to the next table.

Lyndsey picked up the tiny tumbler and smelled it. It was nasty! She set it back down and watched the people at the next table, pick theirs up. They clinked the glasses together, laughed and shouted "cheers!" Then they poured the drinks down their throats.

As if she'd done it a thousand times Lyndsey copied the table beside them. Holding her small tumbler against his, she smiled and said "cheers." Then she swallowed the entire contents.

Holy Shit! It burned! Her eyes watered. She coughed and gasped as the potent liquid robbed her of breath. "Whew! What was that?"

"It's Tequila or a better way to say it is *to kill ya.*"

"*To kill ya* is right!" Lyndsey could already feel the effects. The alcohol tasted like gasoline. Her face was hot and warmth coursed through her entire body. It energized her with its heat and made her feel bold and free.

Lyndsey jumped up needing to move. She reached for him and dragged him to the dance floor. They squeezed into a small spot. Their bodies pressed tightly together. For a moment she was repulsed, but the music quickly soothed her discomfort. The beat was intoxicating, and she pushed him from her thoughts as she moved with the rhythm and the bodies around them.

They hadn't danced for long when he jerked her from the dance floor. She was pissed as she trailed after him. It was so unfair! Why did he have to ruin everything? They sat, saying very little to each other. Lyndsey picked up the beer the waitress delivered while they were dancing. She didn't like the taste, but she loved what it did for her. She drained her entire glass and reached for his. Right this minute, he didn't scare her. To hell with him! Ignoring his scowl, she emptied his glass.

The music was hypnotic. She rose from the table moving her hips and needing the bathroom. Lyndsey found the woman's washroom just beyond the bar. The brightly lit interior had sinks and mirrors lining one side. Lyndsey pushed open a stall door.

"Hey! How about knocking!"

Embarrassed, Lyndsey started to back out.

"Now that you're here…" The woman trailed off.

Uncertain, Lyndsey eyed the pretty woman bent over the back of the toilet. On the toilet tank were long white lines of powder. The woman bowed her dark head put a rolled up bill to her nostril and inhaled the line. Thick, glossy black hair hung down her back. Her nails were long, painted red with jewels embedded in the tips.

"Want a line?" She asked.

It seemed like a good idea. Lyndsey copied the woman, holding the rolled up bill to her nostril. She bent over the largest line, took a deep breath and inhaled. It hit with an explosion almost taking the top of her head with it. Her nose burned and the taste in her throat was like battery acid. Her nose began to drip, and her mouth felt numb.

The pretty woman never introduced herself. She just finished off her coke and left.

Lyndsey sat down to pee. She couldn't believe how much her nostril hurt. Lyndsey stared into the mirror as she washed her hands, checking her nose for blood. She couldn't see any but just in case and to minimize the damage, she placed a few drops of water below her nostril and breathed in.

As she exited the women's room Lyndsey headed for the dance floor. She pushed into the swarm of bodies, at one with the massive crowd. Flesh touched flesh as they moved together like waves in an ocean rolling to the beat of the music, they danced.

Lyndsey danced for a long time. She was free of inhibitions among the sea of bodies. Sweat beaded on her upper lip and the back of her neck. She had a ton of energy! It was like she'd been plugged into the wall and recharged. Electricity sizzled through her bloodstream.

The dancers dwindled until Lyndsey was the lone dancer. The music slowed then ceased altogether. Taking a few final carefree bumps and grinds, Lyndsey turned to head back to him.

He sat alone at the table staring at her. His face was all ugly again. The sneer was back, and for just a moment Lyndsey wished she had a camera so she could take a picture of him. She wanted to show him how ugly his sneer looked but didn't think he would be agreeable to a snapshot at the moment.

By the time she reached the table, she could feel his anger. It came off him in cold waves like a big old nasty storm cloud.

Lyndsey shivered, little prickles of apprehension coursing through her.

He didn't say one word to her.

He didn't have to. His face said it all.

Meekly she gathered her belongings and followed his disappearing back into the night.

# CHAPTER NINETEEN

The magical effects of the white powder wore off. Lyndsey felt awful. Her stomach twisted with dread and anxiety crept back in. Her mind raced with doubts and *what-ifs* as she followed him to the car. The drive back to the dingy hotel was tense. She thought he would speed off into the night, but instead, he drove slowly, other cars passed them as if they were standing still.

Lyndsey wished she could think of something to say to ease the tension. But nothing came to mind, and the silence screamed. She was on dangerous ground. But it wasn't the first time she'd walked on eggshells. She'd spent a good portion of her life on them.

Climbing the stairs to their room, she felt as if she were walking the plank. She dreaded arriving at their door. Her heart beat harder with each step. It was dark, and the hotel looked much better in the gloom. It never occurred to her she could run, or change directions, or make a million other choices which didn't involve giving her will over to him. She never had choices before. In her experience, it was better to get the punishment over with as quickly as possible.

As Lyndsey walked through the doorway, she braced herself. He didn't turn the lights on. She felt along the walls finding the bed and sat down waiting for what would come.

She didn't have to wait long.

His words flew like bullets. He called her every filthy name she'd ever heard and some she hadn't. His insults fueled his rage to a frenzied pitch, and he grabbed her from the bed and shook her violently. Her jaw snapped shut, and her teeth rattled. Him hit her in the mouth and split her bottom lip. She licked the blood from her lips as he took her by the throat and squeezed. He dragged her by the hair, up and off the bed and threw her across the room. She hit the floor hard, her arm breaking the fall. It made a popping noise on impact and pain exploded in her shoulder.

Him shook her again and then released her.

Quiet as a church mouse, she lay there, testing her arm by moving it in small circles. It hurt like a son of a bitch, but she didn't think it was broken. Hatred and rage for him seethed in her. All men were bastards. She wished the rotten sons of bitches in her life would get the job right. Why only beat her *half* to death? Why not go all the way? She was sick of being someone else's punching bag and vowed never to let it happen again. The next time someone tried to hurt her, she'd fight back. She didn't care if it killed her. She already felt dead anyhow.

The floor was cold, and she blinked back tears. *Why did bad things always happen to her?* A lump formed in Lyndsey's throat and she pushed it down. She wouldn't cry. She lay curled up until he came to her again.

Then it got weird.

Him held her close and stroked her hair, saying he hated to hut her. But it was her fault. He must teach her a lesson.

For a while, she knew he'd be okay. Nice even. He might even feel bad for the pain he'd inflicted and try to make it up to her. She wished he could be like this all the time. It was easy to forgive him when his fingers soothed her brow, and he kissed her cheeks and told her he loved her.

Easy to forgive maybe, but she wouldn't forget.

Lyndsey didn't get much sleep that night. Him curled around her, and she laid still. Lyndsey wondered why. Why did people tell you they loved you and then hurt you? Lyndsey traced a finger on her lips. They were swollen and tender. Her head ached where he grabbed her by the hair. Her throat was raw. But it was her arm that hurt the worst. It throbbed in sync with her heartbeat. All in all, it wasn't the worst beating she'd ever had. On a scale of one to ten, it was probably only a five. She knew physically she would heal.

Her mind drifted back to a time when she was little. Lyndsey was overflowing with love and joy, innocence and trust.

No, she couldn't be hurt worse than she already was. The physical beating she'd just received paled in comparison. The real damage happened years ago. It was done in the name of love by a man she called her Daddy.

The next day was a long one. Her arm was swollen and hurt terribly. Him offered her a pain pill insisting it would help. With no drinking glass in their room, Lyndsey swallowed it dry. Her sore arm was useless. One-handed she tossed her clothes into her suitcase, then brushed her teeth.

Him sat on the bed running his hands through his hair. The sheet covered his lower half, leaving his chest bare. Him looked better with his clothes on. Naked, he was scrawny with a sunken chest. His arms and legs were spindly little twigs. His tattoo stood out in bold contrast to his pale skin. It looked funny on his arm.

*BORN TO RULE* raised in black ink. Lyndsey wondered who he thought he was ruling. Hitting women didn't count for much in her books. She would like to see him go up against another guy. She didn't think he'd be *BORN TO RULE* then. It was more likely he'd be *BORN TO GET HIS ASS KICKED*. The image brought a small smile to her lips. Him was a coward and Lyndsey couldn't for the life of her understand what she was doing here with this man. It made no sense to her whatsoever. She couldn't understand this attraction. The more she knew him, the more she loathed him and yet, here she was. She must be screwed up. Lyndsey hoped she would get her shit together, soon.

They stopped for breakfast at a fast food place. Even their meal choices were opposite. Lyndsey had fruit and yogurt, and him had a breakfast burger.

Him swallowed half his burger in one bite and then said, "I have a stop to make before we head home."

Lyndsey didn't reply. His recent beating gave her permission to be less attentive to him. Besides, she was starting to feel all floaty and had to concentrate to get the spoon in her mouth. Her eyes were heavy and her shoulder had stopped throbbing. Warmth spread through her and chased away her aches and pains. Her body felt boneless and droopy. She was vaguely aware of being walked back to the car. Him buckled her into the seatbelt as she floated, light as the clouds above them.

Lyndsey had never felt so content. Her physical body

disappeared, she was weightless. She was bubble-wrapped in love. No jagged little edges disturbed her bliss. Maybe this is what it was like to be in the womb. A nurturing environment where you were protected, and loved. Fed and housed by your host, connected by blood and umbilical cord, where the beat of their heart sustained your life. Sheltered, growing, and *always* safe.

They parked in an alleyway. Him locked the car doors and said he would be right back. The buildings were high, and people swarmed the street. They looked like ants, marching this way and that. A tabby cat foraged in a garbage can nearby. Lyndsey thought the cat was hungry, and she wanted to find it food. Her fingers were clumsy and didn't work right. It took a few tries to undo her seat belt and open the car door.

Lyndsey staggered in the direction of the cat. It hissed at her as she approached. The cat was skinny. It's orange and brown fur matted in filth. Lyndsey kneeled down. "Here kitty, kitty."

The cat didn't budge. Its bright green eyes sized her up. Lyndsey stayed low, hand out and spoke softly. "I won't hurt you. I want to help."

As if the cat understood, it moved towards her.  The little cat rubbed against her leg as she ran a hand over its back. The poor thing was all fur and bones. As she stroked the underside of the cat, she was surprised to feel engorged nipples. This cat was pregnant! Now she really must help. Lyndsey remembered the half-eaten sandwich and water bottle in the car.

Lyndsey returned to the car with the little cat following behind her. She grabbed the sandwich and tore a piece from it.

She offered the morsel to the cat. It took it from her hand and turned, running back in the direction of the garbage cans. Lyndsey chased after the cat and came to a stop in front of a green bin. Little mewling sounds alerted her to another reality. The cat wasn't pregnant. It had kittens!

Lyndsey walked around the garbage bins and saw six furry little kittens peeking from a pile of rags. The tabby nestled down among her kittens, eating her snack as the kittens stepped over each other in their attempt to nurse.

The tiny babies were adorable! One little fellow was smaller than the rest. The kitten's fur was orange and it had big blue eyes. The baby tried to feed but had trouble crawling over the other kittens. Lyndsey pulled one of the bigger kittens off the cat's teat and placed the tiny orange one there. It began to suckle. The bigger kitten was not happy. It pushed the runt aside, stepped on its head and latched on to its mother.

Lyndsey picked the tiny kitten up. It was floppy, kind of like she felt at the moment. Lyndsey placed the kitten inside her shirt next to her heart. The baby was cold, and she wondered what she should do. The kitten mewed a weak cry from between her breasts.

That cinched it. It needed milk, and Lyndsey would find it. Lyndsey walked down the alley until she came to a busy street. On the corner was a grocery store. Lyndsey crossed the street and walked in that direction. The problem was she didn't have enough money. Her fingers dug deep into her pockets and pulled out two nickels, one dime, and six pennies. Shit, that wasn't going to buy much. Lyndsey looked at the people passing by on the street. She thought about pan-handling for her starving kitten, but couldn't do it.

Lyndsey pushed opened the store door hoping to think of something. A small Asian man stood behind the counter. He looked frail and old. But he had eagle eyes and watched her every move. If the store sold hot cups of coffee, she could take some cream. After checking out the aisles and not finding coffee, Lyndsey walked to the icebox at the back of the store. On the shelves were different sized containers of milk. Lyndsey picked up the smallest one and looked at the price. A buck twenty-nine. Cream would probably be best, but she didn't see any, so she picked up the small carton of milk and walked to the front counter. On her way, she passed a bin of bubble gum and pulled out two pieces.

The eagle-eyed man never lost sight of her. He wore a serious expression on his face as she placed her items on the counter. He spoke with a heavy Asian accent announcing the total.

Lyndsey placed her coins on the counter.

He frowned pointing at her coins. "Mo' money."

Acting as if she didn't understand him, Lyndsey picked up her items and walked quickly to the door.

The little man blew a gasket. "Sief! Sief!" He shrieked, as she pushed open the door. Then he grabbed her by the back of her shirt, trying to detain her.

Lyndsey wasn't strong, but she got through the door.

The back of her shirt tore leaving him with a handful of cloth.

Lyndsey fled down the street hoping the man would find some compensation in that small victory.

She wasn't a thief. The few times she'd stolen from her family she was justified in doing so. Normally, she would never walk into a store and take a container of milk. But this time the end justified the means.

And she hadn't stolen the bubble gum.

She'd left more than enough money to cover that.

# CHAPTER TWENTY

The small carton of milk wasn't easy to open. Even though it read *open here,* it still stuck and when Lyndsey applied pressure, it popped open and spilled milk on her. At least she had it open, now what could she use for a nipple? Lyndsey dipped her finger in the cold milk thinking it might be a satisfactory substitute. She opened her shirt and pulled the kitten free. It gave a pitiful meow. Lyndsey placed her milk soaked finger in the kitten's open mouth and prayed. She nearly shouted with joy when a small, sand-paper tongue began to suckle.

Over and over again she dipped her finger into the container of milk. The kitten lapped hungrily. Worried she would overfeed it, she withdrew her finger and closed the carton of milk. Lyndsey opened her suitcase and took out her oldest sweater. She wrapped the kitten in it and placed the furry bundle in her purse. Should she return the kitten to its mother? Would it starve if she did? The thought of the little creature dying broke her heart. Lyndsey decided to keep the kitten, at least for a little while.

Mother Nature was a mean bitch. Why something this helpless and adorable would be left to starve was beyond her. There was a time, long ago, when she used to read books with happily-ever-after endings called fairy tales. She didn't know they weren't real. Lyndsey would pray and pray for their family to have a happy ending, only it never played out that way. No matter how many fairy tales she read, her family still struggled.

When Lyndsey turned ten, she threw away all her make-believe books. Life wasn't fair. Bullies ruled the day. And if you didn't wear armor you'd get mowed over. So she'd hardened herself. She stopped caring, but she still had a weak spot for the vulnerable, the innocent, and the ones who couldn't defend themselves and needed rescuing. Luckily she learned life didn't sting nearly as bad with the help of pharmaceutical aids. Under the influence, Lyndsey found her happy place. Still feeling a little floaty, she leaned back in her seat. Warm content and at peace, she fell asleep.

*Something was crying.* Lyndsey's eyes blinked open. The sky was darker than when she'd drifted off. Little mewling sounds came from her bag in the back seat. She reached for the kitten before noticing him had returned. He sat motionless in the car beside her, watching as she unwrapped the little bundle of fur. When she opened her sweater she saw it had gone to the bathroom. Feces clung to its fur. It was hungry and latched on to her finger.

Worried him would make her get rid of the kitten she cleaned up the mess. But he just watched, never saying a word. His face was blank, his usual nasty sneer gone. For the moment all was well. As she fed the kitten, Lyndsey held it close loving the way it felt. With each tug on her finger, she fell more in love. When the kitten was full, she put it back in her sweater, and they drove home.

The trip back was quiet. Each lost in thought. He parked at Lyndsey's house and handed her six more pills. He told her to take them if she were in pain the next day. They never spoke of what happened or the ugliness between them. With the pills in her, it seemed like more dream-like than real. The brutality Lyndsey experienced at his hands was minimized by her morphine haze.

Lyndsey's parents got home two days later, her sister, too. Lyndsey wanted to show off her new kitten who she now called Sammy, but she fought the impulse. Her sister would love him, but she wouldn't be able to keep him a secret. At some point, Lyndsey would piss her off and then it would be game over for Sammy.

Where does one keep a kitten when they don't want anyone to find it? Lyndsey figured her school locker was as good a place as any. She hoped it wouldn't suffocate. Lyndsey was nervous about leaving it there and checked on it many times that morning. The kitten slept a lot, but maybe that's what babies did.

At lunch, she brought it into the cafeteria with her. Lyndsey sat down with Sheila and the girls. Things were cooler between them now, so much left unsaid. At least to her face, but she knew they talked about her when she wasn't there. Lyndsey told them almost nothing of what went on between her and him. They would be horrified. If she were honest with herself, which was a skill she hadn't yet developed yet, she would be horrified too.

Her friends gave Sammy a few cuddles and passed the kitten back to Lyndsey. They were much more interested in fashion and boys than a kitten. Lyndsey felt sad at the growing distance between herself and her friends.

Why couldn't she be more like her girlfriends? They were so

carefree and at ease with each other. They were like herd animals and liked to hang out in a pack. They seemed to find comfort in numbers. But Lyndsey had always felt more comfortable alone. She gained her strength from the trees and ocean, the animals and the little creatures she saw. The only animal she didn't trust was in the human form. Instead of feeling safe around them, she felt like prey.

Over the next few weeks, the kitten grew bigger. Now that it was moving around more, it wasn't safe to leave in her locker. So she made a home for it in the garage at the back of their house. Lyndsey fed Sammy dog food mixed with milk. He seemed to love it and purred whenever she was near.

A month went by, and she hadn't heard from him. Which was fine by her. Lyndsey slept more than she normally did. Not from depression or anything, she was just unusually tired. As soon as the school bell rang ending her day, she'd walk home and fall asleep. And she'd sleep until dinner.

At meal times she seemed to be starving, eating more than she ever had before. She developed new cravings and seemed to think about potatoes and vegetables and popcorn all the time. The one thing she couldn't stomach was meat. Lyndsey gagged at the smell of it cooking.

Her grades improved that semester. She attended all her classes, forgoing her usual coffee hangouts. She surprised herself with the good grades she received. She never thought herself smart and would make fun of her peers when they studied for upcoming exams. She wasn't making fun of them exactly. She just had a real problem with teachers telling her what to do. She never really saw the point in studying an ancient civilization or the various other pointless topics that seemed to be such a waste of time.

With her first A in social studies, she felt pride swelling within her. She wanted to show it off and yet she felt sort of embarrassed about it. She'd never really tried in school before, and it was good to know she wasn't stupid. She decided to shrug it off and threw it in the garbage. For some reason she couldn't figure out, doing good felt *wrong*. Like she'd let herself down and become one of the herds.

Lyndsey's thoughts warred with her heart. Sometimes the noise in her head was unbearable. She felt confused, as her thoughts overrode the pride she felt in seeing the A. The noise in her head didn't come in words. It was more like a dark cloud consuming anything positive that might be lingering. Like a mass of angry wasps, it buzzed about looking to sting any hope of achievement or well-being.

Anxiety crawled up her throat causing it to burn. Her chest felt tight, and she knew she needed to be careful now. Her thoughts could destroy her and if she weren't careful, they would. Before she'd found narcotic relief, she endured hours of emotional torture. Many times waking up in terror so great her body shook with it. She remembered those nightmares and prayed to God they were gone for good.

The discomfort increased. Lyndsey selected a strand of hair and twirled it around her finger. She touched the silky smoothness, twirling, twirling. Pulling gently, she teased the strands increasing the pressure as she went. It was starting to hurt now, the pulled strands causing her head to tilt to one side, her ear almost resting on her shoulder. Harder and harder she pulled. Maybe if she pulled hard enough she could pull the thoughts right out. The pressure on her scalp had her gritting her teeth. Her eyes watered, her jaw clenched. Groans came through her open mouth escaping her mind. Sounds of pain and despair popped out. Such private sounds. Ugliness voiced, forming from her vocal cords. The noise in her head slowly ceased as it found an exit. Lyndsey continued to pluck herself, pulling out roots of hair, as if the very act of plucking itself could pull out all the hurt and anger. Slowly she let her fingers relax. The strands of hair escaped falling once again down her back.

She felt emptied and spent.

Relaxed, and for the moment, at peace.

# CHAPTER TWENTY-ONE

She wasn't sure when she knew. It was gradual, almost like waking up. She'd been in class when she first felt it. A feeling, like butterfly wings, moving through her lower abdomen. When Lyndsey felt sick in the morning, she wrote it off as the flu. The sickness passed and other than sleeping more, she felt better than she had in a long time.

Lyndsey quit smoking too, almost. She still had the odd puff, but it made her feel nauseous. Her body filled out, and for the first time, she had color on her cheeks.

Her mother was giving her strange looks, or maybe it was just her imagination, but either way, Lyndsey tried to avoid her. Actually, it was pretty easy. Her mother was obsessed with her father – what he was doing, who he was with and if he was drinking, so she didn't notice Lyndsey anyway.

For a moment Lyndsey wished things could be different between them. A few of her girlfriends had close relationships with their mothers. They were able to talk with them about women things like changing bodies, periods, and boys. Lyndsey had so many questions and no one to ask. She could not imagine having *those* types of talks with her mom.

Lyndsey remembered the day she got her period. She experienced painful cramps and bloating. Feeling terrible, Lyndsey considered going home when she went to the bathroom and discovered blood. She was horrified, absolutely certain she was dying, and something had ruptured in her. Lyndsey panicked, not sure who to tell and found she was unable to confide in anyone. Had the blood been coming from anywhere else, she would have sought help. But the fact it was coming from *there* kept her mute.

All throughout the day she'd checked, hoping the flow of blood had stopped. It didn't so Lyndsey decided to cut her last class. If she was going to die, she wanted to do it in her bed at home.

Of course, that never happened. But on that particular day she really thought it might.

Going forward, Lyndsey learned to figure things out on her own. She never asked a direct question. It was more in what others didn't say and the way their faces looked when they didn't say it, that gave her the answers she sought. She'd gotten so good at not asking questions the most important one remained unspoken. She tried not to think about it. If she didn't think about it, then it wasn't real, and if it wasn't real then she didn't have to worry. Her recent problem simply ceased to exist and yet strangely, what she wanted most in this world was for it to be real. The very thing that was going to cause her untold misery and shame was something she wanted more than anything else in the world.

It wasn't real yet, and then it was.

She *knew*.

She just hadn't told anyone yet.

Lyndsey held tight to her precious little secret, counting down the days, then the weeks, and eventually, the months. Her body didn't change much, at first. Which allowed her to wear the same clothing she'd been wearing all along. For the very first time, she felt she had a purpose and began to understand why she was here.

A strange phenomenon occurred. Lyndsey was happy! She hummed with contentment. At night she would lay in her bed, wrap her arms around her stomach and imagine holding the tiny creation growing inside. One night as she stroked her belly she felt a strange flicker beneath her fingers. It felt like butterfly's wings, under her fingertips. Kind of like a zipper being opening just under her skin.

Lyndsey was amazed to think her body housed a tiny human. She couldn't wait to meet him/her. Stroking her stomach, over and over, she assured the tiny babe that everything would be okay.

Lyndsey lived in a magical realm of wishful thinking. She made promises in her heart and sent them to her womb.

*I promise I'll never let anyone hurt you.*

*I promise to always be there for you.*

*I promise I'll never hit you.*

*I promise I'll never let anyone else hit you.*

*I promise you'll always know you're important.*

*I promise you'll always be loved.*

*I promise to keep you safe.*

*I promise…* It became her mantra.

Lyndsey never realized her promises were sad truths mirroring her own life. She didn't know that most mothers didn't pray for their children not to be hit, but instead prayed they were healthy and had ten fingers and toes. She had no way to compare her experience with other Mothers. For this experience was to her as everything else in her life was top secret.

As time marched on Lyndsey grew bigger. Now she wore her father's shirt to school. She could still get her jeans on, but the rest of her spilled over the top making her look like a muffin. Lyndsey discovered that by wearing her dad's sweater, she could hide all the extra parts of her hanging over her waistline. She wasn't fat. There as just more of her. Her stomach was a hard bump, like a basketball, although not that big. Nothing else on her body had changed much. Her breasts might be just a tad fuller, her cheeks a wee bit rounder, but looking at her no one could tell.

No one knew her big secret. At least not yet.

Him hadn't been around in a long time. He didn't know her secret either. And she wanted to keep it that way. As long as she didn't tell anyone, she could dream about a bright future where everything would magically work out. Once the secret was out, not only would her family be furious with her, they would also try and ruin everything.

Lyndsey tried not to think about anything upsetting. She went to school, avoided her friends and for the most part, laid low. The baby continued to grow. Sometimes Lyndsey thought she could feel tiny hands and feet under her fingers. She was amazed and terrified at the miracle taking place within her.

Not long ago she dreaded going to bed early. Now she loved it and couldn't wait for dinner to be over. Lyndsey would crawl into bed, pull the blankets tight and spend hours alone with her little bump. She would make up fairy tales and silly stories. She spoke of love and hope and possibilities. In the far reaches of her mind, she knew her time was running out. But for now, she wouldn't allow herself to worry. Each time reality tried to push its way in, Lyndsey pushed it back out.

"It will work out."

"It has too."

Lyndsey whispered to the walls in her dark room, patting her stomach.

The dark walls were silent. Fear crept up Lyndsey's spine. At times like this, she needed parents desperately.

Lyndsey stopped talking to the walls and called to an entity she'd never seen before.

"Please," she begged.

If something was in the room with her it wasn't talking.

"Please," she tried again. "I need your help."

Lyndsey wasn't sure if this entity was God. Humans were fallible, and you couldn't trust them, she wasn't sure if she could trust God, either. But she found comfort in the idea that someone cared about her, even if she couldn't see or touch them.

Out of time and options, Lyndsey got down on her knees, folded her hands and hoped God would answer her prayers.

# CHAPTER TWENTY-TWO

Lyndsey was worried. Sometimes a day or two would go by without any movement. What if something terrible had happened? Was she eating enough? Was she eating too much? Was she getting enough sleep? Was she doing something wrong? How did one grow a healthy baby?

Time slowed as she waited for a kick or movement tell her all was right. Waiting was awful. Her mind spun dark outcomes and just when she couldn't take another minute of not knowing, butterfly wings rippled through her belly.

As hard as she tried to push it away, the truth of her situation set in. She was in serious shit. Worry and fear overwhelmed her. It was getting harder to hide her changing appearance. If anyone ever put their arms around her, they would have discovered her secret.

At least she didn't have to worry about being hugged at home. They weren't a touchy-feely family. Her girlfriends liked to hug, but they knew better than to try it with her. The one time she'd tried to hug them back, she felt stiff and awkward, and she'd hated it.

Lyndsey figured she was five months pregnant. She'd missed five periods anyhow. She finally worked up the courage to tell him. The conversation went horribly wrong. He was so drunk she wasn't even sure he'd remember, but she would.

It was a few weeks back. After not hearing from him for

months he phoned one evening and invited her over. Lyndsey didn't want to be with him anymore. Just hearing his voice made her skin to crawl. The attraction she had once felt for him was over. His nasty temperament repulsed her.

Not sure if she should go see him or stay home she sat on her bed and ran through scenarios. Should she go to his house or stay home? She didn't want to see him, but she did need his help. How could she raise a baby on her own? She was still in school, and she didn't have a job. He did though, and although she didn't know what it was, she knew he made good money doing it. And if she was going to pay for the upcoming baby expenses, she needed money and a lot of it.

Money was the deciding factor. Although she didn't want him anymore, she did need him.

When she got there, the small house was crammed with people. Him, Larry and Mark stood together in a small circle. The three stooges as she'd begun to think of them.

Most of the crowd were older guys she didn't recognize. Almost everyone had a joint in their hand, and the air was thick with smoke. Lyndsey worried breathing the air would hurt the baby and decided to make this a quick visit.

Him spotted her and walked in her direction. His vise-grip fingers grasped her by the arm and drew her close. Her skin crawled. She stiffened and got *the look*. God, he was grotesque. She'd like to reach over and smack that sneer right off his face. Of course, if she did that she might as well say goodbye to the money she hoped to get from him to help her raise the baby.

She had to play this just right. For the sake of the baby, she willed her body to relax and squeezed his hand.

"That's better," him lifted her chin so he could see her eyes. "Let's get you a drink."

Lyndsey knew it wasn't an offer. It was a demand. Would sipping a drink hurt the baby? She wished she knew more about pregnancy and babies. The little she knew about kids was from the few times she babysat at the neighbor's place. Their kids were six and eight, little brats who tore through the house throwing toys at each other. About pregnancy, she knew nothing at all.

Him gave her a beer, making a big deal out of it as if it were a precious stone. He even opened it for her as if saying *see what a great guy I am?* Yep, he was a great guy all right. A real winner. She sure could pick em.

Lyndsey took the beer from him. She wouldn't drink much of it but for the time being it was easier to take it than to explain why not. With the house full of people this wasn't the right time to tell him. She would wait until later when she hoped they would be alone.

She lost count of the times she said *no* that night. No to mushrooms and pot. No to hot knives in the kitchen. No to cigarettes and another beer.

Mark bumped into her with a smile.

Lyndsey smiled back. She really liked Mark even though he was the most physically messed up person she'd ever met.

"Hey Shhhlllyynnddsss," Mark slurred. "Where you been?"

"Around, here and there," she replied. This vague answer seemed to satisfy him. "How about you, what have you been doing?"

Redirection. It was a skill she'd learned long ago. Lyndsey didn't like talking about herself and found if she switched the question around and got the person talking about themselves, she could avoid it. Redirection worked great. In her experience, most people liked talking about themselves, and she liked, that they liked it.

Mark's chest puffed out. "I've been working on my car," he bragged.

Mark had an older model Chevy he was restoring and Lyndsey thought if he could ever stay sober long enough the finished product would be one sweet looking car.

"That's nice," she murmured.

They stood together in silence for a moment. Mark whistled along with the music. He had a fine whistle. Then he began to sing. Mark had a good voice. Behind his slurred words his tone was beautiful. His voice was deep and sent chills through her. Mark sang one song after another stopping only to take long drinks from his forever can of LUCKY. Mark competed with the loud music playing on the stereo system. It was ACDC, Guns N Roses, Metallica, and Mark. For a little while, her vote went to Mark.

It was weird watching people get wasted when you were sober. Mark got all droopy. His face got slack, and his eyes were slits. Mark was having trouble forming words, and his singing sounded like gibberish. Although his vocals weren't recognizable, she could still make out the tune.

Mark took a final swig from his can and slumped next to her.

He was soft and warm and completely harmless. For a minute Lyndsey snuggled him back, her large, pissed, teddy bear.

She could feel the stare and searched the room for him. Lyndsey assumed it was him staring, but he was busy talking to one of the stoners. His face was animated the way it got when he was selling one of his 'products' or when he was teaching someone how to grow them.

Lyndsey's eyes slid away from him and wandered the room. One of the stoners led his girlfriend down the hallway. The girlfriend didn't look so hot, she was pale and walked on wobbly legs, probably from too much booze and pot. Lyndsey was reminded of Dee and made a mental note to call her soon.

To the far right was the kitchen and Larry stood in its center. He stared at her, hostility written all over his face. Why did he hate her so much? She'd never understood it but she felt his dislike every time they were together.

The strange thing was he wasn't like that with everyone else. With other people, his face was soft, almost shy. When he wasn't looking at her like he wanted to kill her, he was actually quite attractive. Larry had big lips, dark curly hair, and an athlete's body. Lyndsey didn't know if he was into sports or not. She really didn't know much about him at all other than he didn't like her. A new song played on the stereo. Perfect timing! Lyndsey sang to the lyrics, *if looks could kill, I'd be lying on the floor, please, please, baby, don't hurt me no more.*

Lyndsey looked away from Larry, ignoring him. Maybe he was jealous? Hell, maybe Larry was gay and wanted him to himself. Christ, he could have him! She wished she could tell

Larry that.

The night finally wound down. It took a long time for everyone to clear out. Well, almost everyone. Mark was passed out on the couch, and Larry sat next to him. Lyndsey was getting anxious. She really needed to talk to him and had been working up her courage all night.

She tapped him on the arm "Um, can you come outside? I have something I want to talk to you about and its ppprivate," she stammered.

Him was in a good mood. His party was a success, and he had been the star. Him was the God of all stoners, and he loved it.

Him shook his head. "It's too cold out there, let's go to my bedroom."

*Shit*, that was the last thing she'd wanted to do. But she couldn't think of anything to say to stop it. If she hesitated, she would just make him made. Lyndsey needed him to be calm and not in a rage. So she did what she least wanted to do and followed his back down the hallway.

Alone in his bedroom, he was on her. She pushed him away. At first, he played along. Him wrestled with her, trying to pin her down and she kept pushing him off. He laughed and continued to grab at her, more forcefully now.

Lyndsey found her voice. "Please! I need to talk to you. It's important, and I need you to listen."

That got his attention. "What the hell is it?" he asked, not smiling anymore.

Lyndsey blurted, "I'm, ahh, I'm pregnant." Then she burst

into tears, saying she wanted the baby more than anything in the world and she would need his help with expenses. Lyndsey assured him he wouldn't have to worry about looking after the child because she would do it all.

Him was more focused on getting his immediate needs met. Communication had never been their strong suit. He didn't acknowledge Lyndsey's pregnancy. Instead, he groped her breasts and held her down.

Lyndsey panicked when his hands touched her stomach. She fought him off with everything she had. She wasn't fighting for her but the life of her unborn child. No way was she going to have sex with him. She had no idea if that would hurt the baby and she wasn't going to risk it. Lyndsey used her teeth and her nails, but in the end, she was no match for him.

Doing her best to protect her baby she curled into a little ball. Him punched her back and her arms, but he didn't get her stomach. They weren't hard blows. He wasn't very coordinated and only then did she realize he was very drunk. Seemingly frustrated at his inability to hurt her with his fists, him pulled the antenna off his black radio. It snapped with a thwack, and he whipped its long steel shaft in the air.

Him looked at her with crazy eyes.

Lyndsey shivered and looked away.

He flung himself at her. Lyndsey curled tighter, her knees shielding her stomach. Him pushed her onto her back and sat on her chest.

The skinny freak was incredibly heavy.

Lyndsey tried to push him off but couldn't.

Him wrapped the antenna around her neck and squeezed.

Lyndsey saw white flashes with orange starbursts.

Him grunting with effort squeezed harder and harder.

She couldn't breathe! Great white lights exploded beneath her eye-lids. Lyndsey hooked her fingers under the antenna and pushed back. She gained just enough room to take a breath.

It rattled in her lungs.

Him came to his senses. The madness simmering just under his surface slunk off into another room and he sniveled. He released his grip on the antenna, and Lyndsey removed it from her neck. He stroked her hair and said he was sorry. She shouldn't push his buttons, it wasn't his fault she made him so angry. Then he cried. Great big blubbery tears. Him said he loved her. He was sorry. Oh so sorry.

Lyndsey remained quiet, not wanting to chance another go around.

She would keep the antenna. She held it as she left his room closing the door softly behind her.

Lyndsey held onto the antenna for courage. She'd use it on him in a second if he tried to stop her from leaving.

She held onto the antenna as a reminder that never again, *ever*, would she be with him.

Lyndsey held onto the antenna because if she ever forgot her vow to stay away from him, she'd use it on herself.

But mostly she hung onto it because something told her to. Call it intuition. Or call it weird, but something told her the piece of broken antenna she held in her hand was a powerful lesson.

One she was still waiting to learn.

# CHAPTER TWENTY-THREE

It was time. Lyndsey had to tell. There was no way she could hide it any longer. The thought of telling had her breaking out in a cold, clammy sweat. Her heart pounded with fear, and her stomach did flip-flops. Facing a death sentence would have been easier. Her chest tightened as did her windpipe making it hard to suck air and bringing on a fresh wave of panic.

Lyndsey sat at the kitchen table trying to calm down. She took deep breaths in through her nose, and blew them out through her mouth. She'd seen a woman do this on TV and she hoped it would help. She felt silly as she took in large breathes of air through her nose, expanding her chest like a balloon. She blew the expelled carbon out. Air in. Air out. She felt silly, but it was working.

Lyndsey's throat relaxed. She wondered how she could tell her mom about the baby. Not coming up with any ideas, she wondered if she could just move away. Where would she go? She couldn't think of one person who she could turn to. Her girlfriends might be able to help for a little while, hiding her at their place. But eventually, she'd be found out and then what? What would happen after the baby was born? How would she pay for diapers, clothes, and food?

Feeling overwhelmed, she left for school. She couldn't think of any good ways to let her parents know about her pregnancy, so she did what she'd always done when life became too difficult. For the time being, she put it out of her mind.

Deep in thought, her fast-paced steps soon had her at school. Avoiding her friends, Lyndsey entered through the back door. Her girlfriends knew something was up, and they were giving her weird looks. They didn't know what that something was. It wasn't that obvious *yet*. They just looked at her a little longer like when you know something has changed, but you don't know what it is.

She was worrying about her problems when she bumped into Sheila.

"Hey, Lyndsey. Where you been?"

Sheila stood close. Lyndsey smelled the Juicy Fruit she was chewing.

Sheila arched one overly plucked eyebrow and said, "Did you get your sweater from the Goodwill bin?"

Lyndsey nodded, "I'm opting for comfort these days," she lied. "Don't you ever get tired of it? I mean the plucking, the waxing, and the makeup. And what about the clothes and hair that seems to take forever to get just right." Lyndsey rolled her eyes at Sheila.

Sheila chewed her gum faster, seeming at a loss for words. Then she sputtered, "No, I don't get tired of it! It's important we look our best." Sheila's eyes narrowed, and she pointed to Lyndsey's stomach. "Have you gained weight?"

"A little," Lyndsey admitted.

"I knew it! We just *knew* it! It's because of *him,* isn't it? You've been smoking a ton of weed, and we all know that munchies come with it and *look* what it's done to you!" Sheila waved a well-manicured finger at Lyndsey as if she were the Goodyear blimp.

Lyndsey was embarrassed and wanted to smack the smug look right off Sheila's face. Instead, she agreed with her. "You're right. I have been smoking way too much lately. But I'm cutting back now." Lyndsey figured agreeing with Sheila would stop any more questions and prevent the rest of her friends from intervening.

Sheila stared at Lyndsey like she was one of those slugs you see in the morning, the kind that leaves a slimy trail behind them. Then she shrugged and put her arm around Lyndsey. "We knew he was bad news but you wouldn't listen. Linds we don't like him. You could do so much better."

Truer words were never spoken, Lyndsey thought. *Man, if you only knew*. She wouldn't though. Lyndsey would never tell her, subjecting herself to countless hours of girlfriend gossip.

Lyndsey said goodbye and thanks and then she left for her last class.

Sheila smiled and waved, and walked off in the opposite direction.

Lyndsey knew it wouldn't be long before the rest of the girls approached her. She wondered how many times she might have to hear *we told you so*!

Sitting at her desk, Lyndsey noticed it had grown smaller. A big round basketball protruded from her abdomen. Lyndsey pulled the sweater away from her stomach and knew the gig was almost up. She vowed silently to herself that she would tell her mother as soon as she got home from school today.

She *would* tell her.

For sure.

Today.

The day passed in a blur of avoidance. Sometimes she felt like she was sleepwalking in a bad dream. One that never ended, and she couldn't wake up. Sitting on her bed that night, she searched for the magical words that would make everything okay. If only she could find them, Lyndsey thought she could persuade her Mom to help her with the baby. The right words were like a fairytale, one that came with a happy ending.

Lyndsey rehearsed her speech. *I'm old enough. I can get a job. I'll be the best mom. You won't have to help out at all. We don't have to tell Dad.*

No, that didn't seem right. Lyndsey grew more frustrated and desperate. Her head was pounding. Not even Suzy's snuggles helped.

Panic set in as her reality became clear.

There were no magic words. There was no fairytale ending. No Prince Charming was coming to save her (hers was an ugly troll, and she hoped he perished). Once again she was completely alone. Only this time, she wasn't. Inside her belly, a tiny bundle slept, as yet unaware of life's pressures and torturous decisions and nasty bogeymen.

In the end, it was simple.

Just like her grade school days, she left a note. When her father went to work that morning, she snuck into her parent's forbidden chamber. Note in hand, Lyndsey lifted her mother's pillow. For a split second, she stood on the verge, pillow in hand

and thought, *if I leave this note there is no going back. I can't lie my way out of it or run away from the outcome.* Lyndsey was good at running and the thought of facing up to such a life-changing reality sent terror and anguish coursing through her body. With a deep breath, she forced her hand open and placed the note on the bed covering it with her mom's pillow.

It seemed a simple enough thing to do. But one little note, with so few words, would have an enormous impact. It wasn't only her life after all, but all of theirs. She hoped she'd said enough and that her mother would understand. Suddenly feeling uncertain, Lyndsey snatched the note out from under the pillow.

*Mom, I've been dreading this. I don't know any easy way to tell you so here it is; I'm pregnant. At least five months and Mom, I want to keep the baby. I don't want Dad to know about this, or he will make me get rid of it. Please don't tell him!*

Lyndsey held the note and stared at it hard. Before she could change her mind, she shoved it under the pillow and left the bedroom. The door clicked softly behind her as she hurried down the hallway, grabbed her lunch from the counter said goodbye.

A deep sadness filled her. She needed her mother more than she ever had in her life. And the fact that she needed her left her feeling vulnerable.

Lyndsey had a rough day. As if waiting for a catastrophic event she white-knuckled every passing minute.

The stress was too much for her, bolting from the class she ran to the bathroom and made it just in the nick of time. With her head over the porcelain bowl, she ejected this morning's breakfast.

*Oh my God!*

Her hands shook as she cleaned herself up at the sink.

*Oh my God!*

What if someone had been in the washroom when she came rushing in?

*Thank God no one saw!*

Lyndsey rinsed her mouth with clean water and stared into the mirror at her reflection. She saw a pale version of herself who looked a lot older than she did just a few months ago.

The day passed slowly. She had a hard time catching her breath. Lyndsey side-stepped her joking classmates. Their hilarity seemed grossly immature to her now. As they hooted and hollered at their lockers, Lyndsey wondered if she was in hell. She was sick with dread, and her body shook so much she worried it might hurt the baby.

Time rushed forward and then slowed down.

At 3 o'clock the buzzer went, and she felt like dying. Her steps dragged as she walked home. Brain noise screamed in her head. She felt thick, jittery and swollen. Her fingers tingled, and her feet were freezing, heavy and encased in cement. Fear had wormed its way into every single aspect of her life.

Lyndsey's hands trembled. She could barely twist the knob. Lyndsey opened the back door as if there were a firing squad behind it.

There was a definitive line. Once Lyndsey crossed it, there would be *no* going back.

Just one more step and it would begin.

One little step.

Lyndsey took a deep breath, closed her eyes and crossed the threshold.

She was in.

# CHAPTER TWENTY-FOUR

All was quiet as she entered the house. It was an eerie silence, loud in its unexpectedness. Nothing rattled in the kitchen, there was no cooking smells in the house, and even the TV was off.

Lyndsey walked quickly to her room wondering if her mom was home and the really big question, did she read the note?

Her oversized purse slid off her shoulder, and she sat on the bed, pondering. What should she do? Lyndsey was tempted to hide in her room but staying here made her feel sick and anxious.

There was only one way to fix that. Lyndsey got up from her bed to look for her Mom and end the silence. Feeling light-headed and reminding herself to breathe, she called out, "Mom!"

No one answered back.

Lyndsey searched every room in the house eventually finding her mom in the garage sweeping the floor.

She stood at the door, her mouth half open, waiting for the bomb to go off. When it didn't, she said simply. "Hi, I'm home."

Her mom didn't acknowledge her. She swept dirt into the dustpan and emptied it into the garbage bin.

Lyndsey cut to the chase. "Did you get my note?"

Her mom turned to her. Her face was blank. "I got it." She admitted. "We can talk about it later, I need some time to think."

"Well...ummm...okay?" Confused and feeling more overwhelmed than ever she walked back to her room. What the hell? She hadn't been expecting that reaction. Lying on her bed, stroking Suzy she calmed. The feeling of fur beneath her fingertips was soothing. Lyndsey stroked Suzy over and over again.

Before long she found sweet oblivion.

Not in drugs or alcohol. Lyndsey wouldn't use anything harmful while pregnant. No, the oblivion she found was in sleep. Sweet, sweet, sleep. It was her new drug of choice.

As it turned out, *later* was more than a month away. They didn't discuss Lyndsey's note for that long. She was starting to show, and it was getting more and more difficult to hide her situation. Her sister made fun of her, calling her fatty, fatty, just assuming her widening middle was due to over-eating.

Her changing body looked hideous. Lyndsey felt worried and anxious all the time. Trying to hide her pregnancy was becoming a greater task than she could manage. If she wasn't worried about someone finding out, then she was worried about not feeling the baby move. If it wasn't the baby, then she worried about her changing body. How big would she get? Would her stomach shrink back to its normal size after the baby was born? Lyndsey had many questions, all bottled up inside her growing body. Every waking moment her head buzzed with more questions. She had a million questions and *no* answers. If there were anyone lonelier than her on the planet right now, she sure wouldn't want to be in their shoes.

Lyndsey was *big*. She imagined herself being poked with a pin, expelling all her worries and flying across the room landing an emptied hollowed out version of herself. She thought her life couldn't get any worse.

But it did, much worse.

Her parents called her to the kitchen table, their faces frosty and sitting rigidly in their chairs.

Lyndsey shriveled. She was getting smaller and didn't have a voice.

Her father started. There was no way in hell she was going to keep this child. What kind of a slut was she to get herself pregnant? His face red, he banged his fist on the table to emphasize his points. How dare she shame their family like that? He didn't want people thinking his daughter was a whore. She was a failure and had been a disappointment to him her whole life. Why couldn't she be like everyone else's kid, doing well and making plans for university?

On and on it went.

All his yelling must have made him thirsty. He poured himself a drink, half whiskey, half water. Experience told Lyndsey once he took that first sip the tension would ease off. One sip at a time, they would all breathe just a little bit easier.

Her mother sat frozen in her chair, not saying much. She didn't defend her daughter, or her head would have been on the chopping block.

Lyndsey sat at the table with them feeling nothing at all. It was strange because she'd made herself sick with anxiety in anticipation of this confrontation. She felt nothing. Maybe her body had gone into shock at some of the names her father called her. But more likely, she was just numb. Numb and empty and void. It wasn't a terrible place to be. She far preferred it to her previous feelings.

Her father downed his drink and poured another. Lyndsey sat mute. Her mother got up to cook dinner. Her dad continued to belittle her. He attacked her morals, her integrity, and intelligence. In the end, he gave himself away.

Yes, her dad was ashamed of her, but as she listened to him rant, she began to understand his shaming her character wasn't about her. Her father was more worried about himself and what other people would think of him. It really had nothing to do with her. His narcissism dictated his needs. He wasn't able to empathize with her feelings or have compassion for the devastation she faced as she tried to do what was best for her baby.

No her dad's verbal assault wasn't about her at all. It was about him. But then it always had been.

The next morning she got up and went to school as if nothing ever happened. In her pregnancy, she never cut classes. It was the best attendance record she had in years. Lyndsey knew she would have to tell her friends soon. It wasn't as if they were moral prigs. They weren't. Most of them had been with more than the one man, Lyndsey had. Two of her friends had even had an abortion. But none of them had gotten pregnant and told the world about it, in the way she was doing. They kept their pregnancy secret, hidden away and dealt with behind closed doors. She couldn't remember anyone going through school with a huge protruding stomach. The thought of waddling down the school hallways was more than she could handle right now.

Lyndsey ran into Sheila and the girls on the way home. She

was leaving for the day, side-stepping the large group of teens hanging outside the front of the building. Lyndsey shielded her stomach through the crowd, protecting her tummy from an unexpected elbow or being jostled by the kids goofing off around her. The schoolyard was loud with laughter and name-calling. Lyndsey felt a thousand years old as she hurried past them. Her classmates seemed so juvenile to her now.

Sheila and friends stayed on the outskirts of the crowd. Lyndsey looked in the other direction hoping they wouldn't spot her. Wishing she were invisible, she kept her head down. Just when she thought she'd gotten away with it, her name was called.

"Hey! Lyndsey! Over here!" Sheila called out to her.

*Damn it*. They had spotted her. Lyndsey turned and walked in Sheila's direction. All five of her once close girlfriends faced her. The looks on their faces said more than their words ever would.

Lyndsey wished that more people's faces would match their words. It was awkward when they didn't. Trying to unwind the thousand years she'd aged recently, she faced her friends. For a moment they reverted to what they knew, cute guys, gossip, drama, the next house party and their upcoming graduation. It was all so meaningless, and the effort to appear normal was exhausting. With a promise to call Sheila later, she walked away from her friends only to stop three steps later.

Horrified at what she was about to do, but not able to stop herself from doing it, she blurted, "I'm pregnant."

She didn't know who was more shocked, herself, for saying

it out loud, or her friends at her sudden delivery. As if the world had stopped there was a moment of silence, and then bedlam broke out.

Her girlfriends had questions. *Does him know? What does he think? Did her parents know? How could she be a mother when she was just a kid? Who would look after the baby? How would she buy clothes and feed it?*

They asked the same questions she'd asked herself. The five were fast and furious, talking over one another, their eyes sparkled, their words honeyed. Teen girls loved drama, and this was big!

Finally, Lyndsey asked them to stop. She didn't have the answers they sought. And she was tired, and she didn't feel well. Lyndsey left them there in the schoolyard, promising to call later where they could discuss her *situation* more openly.

Her cheeks burned as she walked away. She felt hugely relieved to be on her own and leaving them behind.

She braved a final look back. Her girlfriends looked stunned.

Lyndsey had just reminded them, all too vividly, of reality.

Only now did they glimpse what she'd know all along.

For the truth was, life sucks.

# CHAPTER TWENTY-FIVE

Lyndsey stood in front of the mirror staring at her bulging body. She was huge! Even her hair was fat. The beautiful glowing look she'd heard pregnant women get must have missed her because she looked hideous. But at least she'd seen the doctor. Had she'd known the physical would be so gross and invasive, she probably wouldn't have gone. And as if that weren't bad enough, she almost fainted when the nurse took her blood. Lyndsey found out she was low on iron and left the doctor's office with prenatal vitamin supplements and iron pills. After a week of taking them, she felt sick to her stomach and was constipated.

Looking at her twin in the mirror, Lyndsey was surprised to see her stomach move. It was amazing, and she felt the ripple effect deep inside her belly. She was in awe. Pregnancy was a miracle she couldn't comprehend.

The baby growing inside her was beautiful, but she was ugly. She looked like an anomaly, her stomach was covered in thin little crisscross marks. And something very strange had happened to her belly button. It looked pregnant too and popped out like a meat thermometer on a Butterball turkey. There was a weird brown line running up her stomach, and her breasts looked like they belonged to someone else. They were too big for her with ugly blue veins. Strangest of all was the clear fluid that had recently started to leak from them. She had no idea if this was normal or not. There was no one she felt comfortable asking questions, she didn't know a single pregnant person her age, and even if she did, the stuff that was happening to her body was way too embarrassing to discuss.

With so many changes she felt incredibly overwhelmed and scared. She seriously worried her stomach would burst open at any moment. Surely stomachs weren't meant to get this big? She didn't think she could stretch much further. She must be at maximum capacity. Hers was the first naked pregnant body she'd ever seen. She looked distorted, grotesque and ugly. Lyndsey couldn't bear another second of looking in the glass. So she turned her back to her reflection and got dressed.

Him called again. Another lovely phone call of nasty words and putdowns. Him said she was ruining his life. He was drunk. He called her a slut, a whore, a bitch, a fat bitch, and worse. Then he got really mean and said the baby growing in her wasn't his kid and she better not try and say it was. It went on and on. Him bullied her, hoping for what, she didn't know.

Lyndsey was sick of it all. Listening to him was like being at their funeral. And it was sort of. It was a funeral for their relationship. Each insult he slung at her was like a nail driven into their coffin. Him ranted on, sealing it permanently never to open again. By now she knew what was coming. Bullies were so predictable. Once they lost their power over you and you weren't afraid of them anymore, they switched tactics. Him started to snivel, saying how he loved her. Him couldn't live without her. Lyndsey knew if she didn't respond to his pleas it would be back to the threats.

Yawn. She didn't care.

Him used everything he had to manipulate her. At the end he tried a different approach, saying he didn't want her anymore. Him told her she'd never been good enough and he had already found her replacement. Then he abruptly handed the phone to his newer model. The woman laughed in Lyndsey's ear. She was drunk, too. They were a match made in heaven. Good riddance and good luck.

Lyndsey wished them both to hell and hung up the phone.

As she replaced the receiver back in its cradle, she saw the coffin being lowered slowly into the ground. There were no mourners there to grieve the passing of the casket. No one stood by shedding tears for the relationship that had just ended. Her most precious assets were never acknowledged. The casket hit bottom with a final thud. In it was something she could never get back. Lyndsey was the only mourner, and she paid her last respects. She shed a lone tear as she stared at the silken lined interior of the casket and waved goodbye to its two dead occupants, her youth, and her virginity.

Yes, she'd given him something she could *never* get back. She hadn't understood how precious her virginity was at the time. She'd trusted her judgment thinking she was, oh so grown up. He'd taken advantage of her. He had no respect for being her first, and he wasn't mature enough or man enough to care about her that way.

And to be fair, she had given it, so naively.

She'd known though, a small part of her. A little voice she ignored, telling her things she didn't want to hear.

Yes, she had made bad choices too. He hadn't been solely to

blame.

Lyndsey looked back one last time.

The large mound of dirt stood alone in a barren landscape hiding what had once been the story of a desperate little girl seeking love.

# CHAPTER TWENTY-SIX

Her back hurt. The ache was low and deep and painful as hell. Lyndsey experienced cramping, on and off, over the last few weeks. Every time a cramp hit she would break out in a fresh wave of panic, sure she was going into labor. She wasn't sleeping much either. She woke up every few hours needing to use the bathroom. It was getting difficult to move around.

Lyndsey was relieved she had broken her silence and found the courage to speak with her doctor. The doctor told her not to worry so much, everything was normal. What she was experiencing was just nature's way of getting her body ready to have the baby. The doctor said her cramps were Braxton Hicks contractions that tightened her uterus getting it ready for delivery. She saw her once a week now and brought in a new list of questions for each visit.

Her cheeks still grew hot as she asked questions. Many times she had to stop taking when her voice warbled, the telltale sign she was dangerously close to tears.

But she would take a few deep breaths and carry on. When she made eye contact with her doctor, Lyndsey had expected to see disgust written all over her face. After all, she was a disgraceful unwed teen who was pregnant, but that's not what she saw.

In fact, it was just the opposite.

Her doctor looked at her with concern. There was no judgment in her eyes. Concern yes, and maybe even a little caring, but nothing damming that said she had to put her mask back on to protect herself.

Lyndsey breathed a deep sigh of relief. She learned a lot from her doctor and looked forward to their visits.

Another twinge of pain shot through her back. She wished for a pain reliever but then worried it might harm the baby. With awkward movements, she did her best to get dressed. It wasn't an easy task. Just putting socks on could be quite an event. She struggled with balance as she bent over her beach ball middle, and put one sock on and then the other. Even this simple task left her breathing hard.

She and her mom scoured the thrift stores hoping to purchase clothing that reflected Lyndsey's style. She couldn't find anything that looked right on her in maternity wear, so she settled for a pair of fat lady jeans that someone had donated. Even with the extra-large size, it wasn't big enough. Her mom sewed in some stretchy material where the zipper should be to make up the difference.

Although they never really talked about the baby her mom helped where she could. Her father, on the other hand, had stopped talking to her period. Not one single word. It was a relief knowing she wouldn't have to engage with him any time soon. Her mom became the middleman. If she had to get a message to her dad, her mom passed it. The same went for her dad. If he had something to say to Lyndsey, her mom said it for him. It wasn't perfect, but for now, it worked.

Her friends tried to be supportive, kind even. But her big round belly was just too much for them. Teen pregnancy is like cold water in the face. It's a real downer among the flirty games they were used to playing.

Graduation was approaching fast. Lyndsey wondered if she would make it because the baby was so close to being born! Lyndsey, Sheila, Kelly, and the rest of her crowd had made plans years ago for this big event. They were all going to sit together and party the night away.

Lyndsey doubted she would be doing much partying. She wasn't even sure what the plans were anymore. When she asked Sheila or Kelly, she got only vague answers in return.

One afternoon at school she was sitting on the toilet when Kelly and Sheila entered. They spoke in their usual loud and dramatic voices. Before she could call out *hello,* Lyndsey realized they were talking about her.

Sheila huffed, "I'm *not* going to sit with her! It's embarrassing just knowing her. What the hell is she thinking?"

"Years ago we made a pact to sit together," Kelly added. "We pinky swore and promised. I feel so bad about breaking that promise. But I know what you mean. She is so embarrassing to be around. It's awkward, I mean what do you say, wow is your stomach ever huge?"

Lyndsey didn't move. She sat glued to the toilet seat.

Sheila and Kelly talked about her completely unaware she was sitting right next to them. Her friends felt sorry for her. They wished they could do something to help her, but they were embarrassed to be seen with her. They were doing their best to avoid her. When the school year was over, they would move on, without her of course.

Lyndsey had gone to school for thirteen years, but it was on this day she learned her most important lesson of all. One her family had taught her years ago, but it was even worse coming from her friends.

At first, she was numb and shocked. She'd known something wasn't right and things weren't as they seemed. So many times she'd imagined this, her friends talking behind her back, only to feel guilty and saddened that she had allowed herself to feel that way.

Lyndsey wanted desperately, urgently, to believe in *someone*. Someone who wouldn't hurt you or betray you. Someone who would stand beside you, *no matter what*. Someone who would be there for you *always*, even when you weren't there for yourself. Especially, then. She had hung onto the tiniest thread of hope that there was someone special. Lyndsey placed the thread of hope around her friends. She spent years sewing with that thread, but she guessed she should have used something stronger. For threads were so fragile and it was all unraveling.

*Someone* didn't exist. It was just a silly idea Lyndsey thought up in an attempt to make herself feel better.

Waves of grief hit with hurricane force. Lyndsey tossed about in a vicious sea of hurt and pain, anger, and outrage. Painful emotions washed over her, at times pushing her under as she fought to stay afloat.

Lyndsey sat on the toilet for a long time.

Long after Kelly and Sheila had gone, long after the final

bell rang, long after the noisy hallways became quiet and long after the stormy seas passed.

# CHAPTER TWENTY-SEVEN

A brutal knifelike pain awakened her, jolting her out of a dead sleep. The pain came again tearing through her uterus and down her back. It stopped for a minute and then started up again, ripping through her stomach and racing up her spine. Her back felt like it was on fire. Oh, my God, she was dying.

Lyndsey crawled out of bed and trudged up the stairs. Her pelvis throbbed with a giant muscle spasm. She moaned in pain and sweat ran down her brow. Lyndsey took two steps and stopped. The pain was so intense she couldn't walk. Instead, Lyndsey held onto the wall and waited. Just when she was sure she would die, the pain let up and passed.

Was this labor? She looked down at herself afraid of what she would see. Was she bleeding to death? Something had broken inside her that much she knew. Lyndsey looked for blood, but her immense stomach blocked her from closer inspection.

As the pressure began again, Lyndsey walked to the kitchen and called for her mom. Wave after wave of powerful muscle spasms hit her. Each new one brought more pain than the last. Lyndsey gritted her teeth and clenched at the arms of the chair.

"Mom!"

"Just a sec," her mother answered making her way into the kitchen.

Not comfortable sitting, Lyndsey stood up. Something

popped inside her and she wet herself. Rivers of warm water flowed down her legs and pooled at her feet. Lyndsey stared down in disbelief.

"Mom, I peed myself!" Lyndsey cried out in alarm.

With a hand full of towels from the linen drawer, her mother bent to clean up her mess. "Your water just broke, you didn't pee yourself. It means you're going to have the baby soon." Her Mom stood up with a wet towel in her hand, "I need to get you to the hospital."

Lyndsey held onto the kitchen counter as the pressure returned. The pain was beyond anything she'd ever experienced before. Wave after wave of intense contractions radiated through her pelvis and up her back. She stood swaying and moaning. In between the waves she'd managed to gasp, "Something's wrong, I'm dying!"

"You'll be fine," her mother assured her, causing her to panic even worse because she knew she wasn't fine. "Go and have your shower and get for the hospital. You still have time before this baby will be born."

Lyndsey couldn't imagine how she was going to have a shower when she was in the middle of dying, but she did want to be clean for her new baby. Maybe a hot shower would make her feel better. Lyndsey had to stop halfway down the stairs as another wave of pain hit. Calling them cramps would be like comparing the size of a baseball to a basketball. These were cramps on steroids. If she got out of this alive, she would never complain about ache or pain again. Ever.

It was bizarre how you could be writhing on the floor for one minute and the next you were almost normal.

*Almost.*

In those almost minutes, Lyndsey was able to get showered and remembered to pick up the bag she had packed. Inside it was an adorable little outfit she bought last month. Lyndsey still had some money left over from the vials she'd sold for him. In a way, he was contributing to the baby. Of course, he didn't know that, and she certainly wasn't going to tell him, and risk yet another assassination on her character.

Another wave of pain hit. Lyndsey groaned, and held onto the bedpost until it passed. Lyndsey opened her overnight bag and picked up the tiny blue outfit. It was a baby blue with a yellow and white teddy bear on it. She also placed a snugly plush teddy bear inside the bag with a comfy soft blue blanket. She didn't know what she would do if the baby were a girl, but oddly enough she knew it was a boy.

As Lyndsey took a final look around the room, she wouldn't let herself notice the missing crib or baby toys. She wouldn't think about the missing nursey decorations or the fact that she'd be returning here with empty arms.

Instead, she imagined herself lying in bed, her arms cradling her tiny son. She would hold him close, and he would know he was safe, protected and loved.

Lyndsey saw the small lump in her bed. She pulled the object free from the blankets. It was an old teddy bear. It was missing one eye and some of its fur. It looked like it had been in a fight and lost. Most people would throw it away, but she held onto it. It was her father's old teddy bear. A gift from him to her that had managed to follow them over the years. Lyndsey thought about bringing it with her to the hospital and then decided not to. She placed it back on the bed and Teddy sat on her pillow waiting for her to return, its one sad eye seemed to comprehend the enormity of her situation.

With her small suitcase in hand, she left the room. Lyndsey hurried up the stairs trying to beat the next wave of pain. By the time they were in the car, she could no longer speak. Lyndsey was inconsolable. Her mother attempted to help, telling her not to worry, it wasn't that bad, having a baby was uncomfortable and so on.

Lyndsey wished she had the voice to tell her that it was *that bad*, worse even. Instead, she began to disappear, swallowed up by the agony she felt. Lyndsey searched for a place in her mind, far, far away from what was happening to her body. Lyndsey continued to writhe and sweat as she clenched the seat of the car.

It wasn't a smooth delivery. She labored for thirty hours.

Lyndsey's room was scary and cold. The walls were white with strange looking equipment hanging by her bed. There were no pictures or bright colors in the room and everything smelled funny, kind of like the dentist office. There was only one thin sheet on the bed, and she huddled under it.

Other than her mother, no one knew she was here. Her father was at work, but he made it clear he wanted no part in this. She hadn't called anyone and really who would she call anyway. When her mother left the room, she never came back.

Lyndsey lay in her bed alone trying to hang on. She fought the pain, trying to push it back and gain a moment free from it.

Lyndsey's torment escalated. Her labor pains came every few minutes and lasted nearly as long. She no longer feared death. She moved beyond that. Now she prayed for it. Lyndsey wished for a gun. She would have blown her brains out to escape this torture.

The nurse poked and probed her and then she scowled. She was an older woman with a Scottish accent. She declared in her thick brogue that Lyndsey wasn't trying hard enough. Then she strapped a monitor to her stomach. It was attached to the machine next to her and spewed paper in time to her contractions. The nurse ripped the paper graph from the device and waved in her face as if to say, *not good enough.*

The Scottish nurse inserted an IV needle into her hand. The sight of the needle didn't worry her in the least. That little poke was nothing compared to what she was feeling at the moment. Once the needle was in, the nurse taped it to her hand and then attached the IV to a tube. The tube was hooked to a bag with clear fluid in it. There was something in the fluid that would help her have her baby.

The Scottish nurse declared "I'll be back soon," and gave Lyndsey a cold stare before departing. The nurse didn't like her and Lyndsey couldn't think why.

Another pain hit, and it didn't matter anymore. Nothing mattered. Time slowed then stopped. She was in another world now, one of PAIN and everything else ceased to exist.

Lyndsey didn't see the walls or hear the squeak of rubber shoes as they hurried down the hallway. The clear fluid in the bag was Pitocin, and it ran on high through her veins. Lyndsey's stomach, pelvis, and uterus locked in an excruciating spasm.

Pain, more than she could bear, stole her mind and allowed her to escape her body.

Her mind fading to black, her last thought, please, please, let me die.

Then mercifully, she passed out.

# CHAPTER TWENTY-EIGHT

Lyndsey lay in her hospital bed while a team of people, two nurses and her doctor were busy aiding in her delivery. She was in a different room now. This room was white, and there was a large lamp directly over her. In a tray beside her hospital bed were silver tools of all different sizes. Off to the far corner was a bassinette for her baby.

Her doctor picked up a large instrument resembling a pair of pincers and inserted them deep in her vagina. Lyndsey screamed. The doctor pulled hard, and she screamed again. Lyndsey felt out of control like someone else had taken over her body. She wanted to stop the pain but couldn't. Her uterus contracted and pushed the child from her womb. The pain was indescribable. It felt like she was being pulled apart from the inside out. Her innards must be lying on the table out of sight between her widely spread legs.

Above her blue mask the doctored sweated. She gave an enormous pull, and something big slid out of Lyndsey. She pulled the tortuous instrument from Lyndsey and gave it to the nurse. It looked like her mother's tongs. The ones she kept in her kitchen drawer. Except her mother's tongs didn't have blood on them.

A loud cry drew her attention from the bloody tongs, and everything stopped. Lyndsey experienced a profound moment every new mother knows. Her life before the baby was born, and her life after. Once you have a baby, you're not the same person anymore. One minute into her delivery and everything had changed. Her child's cry affected her as nothing else had. Her heart was his forever. Lyndsey laughed and cried as he sobbed.

A stern-faced nurse handed him to her. There were no congratulations or whoops of joy. The medical team was quiet, solemn even. The nurse placed her baby on her chest, and Lyndsey held him close. He skin coated with thick white paste and his head was cone-shaped. He still had blood and bits of her flesh sticking to him. She didn't know that all babies looked this way. Lyndsey wondered if something was wrong with him. Her baby's head was deformed. On the top of his head was a perfectly shaped cone. Like an ice cream cone placed upside down.

Lyndsey touched his head. It was warm and felt okay except the shape of it. She wondered if her son would go through life wearing a hat to cover his oddly shaped head.

"You have a healthy baby boy." The doctor said. "The cone on his head is from being in the birth canal. It isn't permanent. It will disappear within the next few days." She paused, waiting for Lyndsey to respond.

But Lyndsey barely heard her. She was mesmerized with her baby.

"We will take him, weigh him, and then clean him up. You'll have him back soon. In the meantime, we need to stitch you up. I'm sorry about the forceps. You had a difficult birth and will need to rest. Do you have any questions?"

Voiceless, Lyndsey shook her head no.

The stern-faced nurse removed the baby, and she felt the hot, burning sting of the needle being used to freeze her in preparation for stitches. The overhead lamp flicked on and bathed her in heat. She felt the tugging and pulling as she was stitched back together. It occurred to her she lay spread eagle with multiple strangers in the room. Oddly enough she found she didn't care. Life after the baby meant she was more interested in what was happening to him, than what was happening to her.

His little legs kick as the nurse weighed him. He cried as the nurse dipped a white cloth into a washing-up bowl and wiped him down with it. She diapered him and then dressed him in a white undershirt and yellow pajamas with a matching hat. The hat covered his cone entirely. Next, the nurse opened a receiving blanket and placed him on top. Then she rolled him tightly back up. Lyndsey thought he looked like a baby wrap. His adorable little face peeked from the top.

When the nurse brought him to her, Lyndsey opened her arms. Time was precious now, and she had very little of it.

Lyndsey held her precious babe close and thought she had never seen anything as beautiful in her entire life. His skin was smooth and full. His lips were pink and perfectly formed. At the moment his lower lip stuck out as if pouting. Lyndsey kissed his cheek hoping to chase the worry away. Her baby's fingers were tiny replicas of hers. Each was perfect in shape and size. His fingertips ended in beautifully formed little fingernails. Lyndsey opened his blanket and studied his legs and his feet. How could something this perfect and sweet come from her? Lyndsey wrapped him up again. She didn't want her baby to get cold. He flailed his arms, his tiny face scrunched up turning red and he wailed. Had she wrapped him to tight? Was he hungry? Lyndsey's heart plummeted. She would do anything to protect him. She was prepared to give her own life if necessary. She would make the ultimate sacrifice only mother's love could.

Soon.

But not yet.

Her precious baby was soft and snuggly. Lyndsey held in her arms and sang to him. Silly songs. Happy songs. Songs of love. Lyndsey promised when they were both older she would find him. And she would never forget him. Not ever. His soft, shell-shaped ear was smooth under her lips as she whispered into it. She told him his adopted family would love and treasure him. He would have everything he ever needed. He would have clothes and toys, and he'd never be hungry. Most importantly, he would have a mommy *and* a daddy. They would play with him, and their faces would light up when they looked at him. They would love him like crazy, and he would love them back. He would grow up and go to school. He'd be popular and have many friends. She could already see how handsome he was. He may have to fight off the ladies, but she knew he'd figure it out. He would grow into a confident young man and work hard to be successful. He would get good grades and go on to university. He would find a fulfilling career, and he would find love. Real love. The kind that ran deep and survived the ebb and flow of changing seasons. One day, he would have children. He would be a wonderful father. Her son was destined for an incredible life. And he would be so, so happy.

Lyndsey whispered into his ear a final time. She begged him to forgive her and understand she wasn't abandoning him, just the opposite. Lyndsey loved him so much and wanted the best for him. Sadly, she couldn't provide this for him, but she knew one lucky couple would. She placed one last kiss on his head before the nurse took him from her arms. The nurse marched down the hallway, her back stiff, holding her baby. As she walked away Lyndsey's hopes and dreams went with her, each receding footstep was a stab in her heart.

The warm place where her child laid was cool. Her empty arms ached to hold him just one more time. There was nothing left to say or do. She had no tears. She was empty. A hollowed out husk of human flesh.

Lyndsey lay in her bed, staring at the walls and saw nothing. Nothing, at all.

# PART TWO

# CHAPTER TWENTY-NINE

*Ouch! Christ that hurt*! Lyndsey pulled her hand out from under her tray and slammed it down on the bar. She looked at her mangled finger noting the back side of it was split wide open. The cut was deep and to the bone. White spots that looked like grains of rice embedded in her ruined flesh.

Lyndsey felt queasy looking at the blood. She marched over to the dishwasher, it had a rinse sink attached to it. With her uninjured hand, she turned on the cold water and plunged her finger in it. The clear water mixed with her blood and created a rusty trail splattering the bottom of the sink. Her blood dripped on the dirty ashtrays and greasy plates she hadn't had time to rinse.

Lyndsey turned off the cold water and took another look. Dam! She was going to need stitches. Lyndsey walked through the door marked *staff only* and searched for something clean to wrap around her wound. She found a clean-ish cloth on the chair and with her uninjured hand used it to apply pressure and stem the flow of blood. Lyndsey held her finger high in the air and walked back to the bar. Her tray hadn't moved. Dan stood next to it surveying the broken glass. What was once a beer glass was now a deadly weapon, the top half of the glass sheared off and one pointy, jagged edge dipped in blood. *Her blood.*

"What the hell!" Dan barked at her. "Those glasses cost money. I'm taking that one off your paycheck!"

Lyndsey looked at the broken glass. She'd picked it up from a table nearby. Four guys who should have been cut off hours ago sat there. Except in Dan`s bar you couldn't cut your *customers* off. Only Dan could do that, and of course, he never did. Lyndsey needed this job, or she would have told him to fuck off a long time ago. Instead, she pulled the cloth off her finger and showed it to him.

"I think I need stitches. You'll have to manage the bar for a while."

"For that little cut?" Dan snorted, then added, "Go on your own time!"

"Fine, I'll go on my own time. And for the record, I didn't break the glass. Your table of losers over there broke it. I think they need to be cut off." She wiped a strand of hair from her face, wishing she could take the broken glass to him. She wondered how Dan would like that.

Dan couldn't care less. Instead of showing sympathy he just told her to clean herself up and get back to work.

Lyndsey entered the *employee only* washroom. Employee, the word sounded so professional, what a joke! The people working here were anything but professional. Most of the riff raff Dan hired had been fired or quit their previous jobs. Many of them were on social assistance and working under the table. Dan would pay them in cash. Very little cash and they wouldn't have to claim it or pay tax. Kind of like free money, if you didn't mind the cost to your self-worth that is. Lyndsey didn't think anyone working here did.

The staff came and went fast around here. Last night she'd been working with a new girl who hadn't even managed to make it through her whole shift. She walked off halfway through leaving Lyndsey to work the entire floor herself. Lyndsey couldn't keep up with their orders, and the customers weren't happy about it. They bitched and moaned and didn't like waiting for their drinks. Christ, she was tired, and her finger throbbed something fierce. With the little white plastic box opened in front of her, Lyndsey looked through the emergency kit. She removed a roll of gauze and tape from the kit. Lyndsey spied antiseptic spray and gave her finger a good shot. With her injured finger bandaged she opened the medicine cabinet. Dan had a bad back and took pain pills for it.

The cabinet held a dozen bottles. She peered at the labels considering which might be most helpful. Tylenol 3 or Percocet? Lyndsey decided on the Percocet and popped one in her mouth. She looked at the bottle again and took another one. Dan wouldn't miss one little pill. He had plenty and she might need one for later. You never really knew what you might need, and when opportunity knocked, well, there had to be some benefits to working in a dump like this. Lyndsey pocketed the extra pill and headed back to the floor.

Her table of four had made another mess. Two beer glasses lay tipped on their sides, and beer dripped off the table. One of the *gentlemen* had his mouth to the table trying to slurp up the excess beer. The other three hooted with laughter and egged him on. One drunk even went so far as to mash his buddies head into the table giving him a beer facial. Lyndsey hoped he didn't drown in it. On second thought, she didn't care if he did. One less moron to serve wasn't a bad thing, after all.

In one corner of the bar at a table for two, an old couple sat together. They were regulars and came here seven days a week. The old gal drank six glasses of draft beer precisely, and her hubby drank eight. They were sweet really, in a sad, pathetic sort of way. At least they tipped! Lyndsey would get a quarter every time she delivered their beer. They were interested in her too. The old woman asked about her family, and she spoke of theirs. They had a son and a daughter who lived far away. Sadly, they never saw them. The old woman claimed it was too expensive to travel these days. Lyndsey didn't have the heart to tell them if they saved their beer money for a week, they could catch a bus anywhere they wanted. No, she would leave them feeling justified with the lies they told themselves. Besides, they treated her with respect, and she appreciated it. Even if she hadn't earned it respect wasn't something she got a lot of these days, and she was thankful for theirs.

Two years had passed since she first started working here. Lyndsey was surprised the bar was still open. It was old and falling apart. The mahogany bar was the nicest piece of furniture in the whole place. Dan spent hours polishing it every day. Lyndsey liked how she could slide beer to her customers sitting on their stools. It saved her back and her feet.

The pub was like a wax museum. The same people came day

after day. They were the misfits with time on their hands. People who couldn't hold a job or were retired. They spent their welfare checks or pension checks on beer, counting every bit of change they got back from her, making sure she didn't take as much as a dime from them. They needed those dimes. After all, they added up to another beer *don't cha know*. Lyndsey bit back her sarcasm at their greedily hoarded coins and the contempt in their voice when they ordered *just one more*.

Lyndsey looked over at Dan hoping he would do his beer run soon. She wanted a drink and couldn't with him manning the taps. Dan was a strange fellow. He didn't just own the bar he worked there too. Dan liked to keep a close eye on his staff. He was a miserly boss and was kinder to his patrons than his employees. Dan didn't have a life outside the bar. When he wasn't pouring beer, you could find him cooking in the back, with one of his famous grease burgers stuffed in his mouth.

Dan was huge. Lyndsey thought he was three hundred pounds or more. She figured one day soon she'd find him dead from a heart attack behind his well-polished mahogany bar.

Lyndsey's irritation at the world smoothed out. Good. The Percocet was kicking in. It hummed through her body like warm oil, erasing the kinks and lubing her aching muscles. Life was better this way. Stoned, she could glide about the bar for hours. Lyndsey could manage a full house on her own and enjoyed doing it. Stoned, she loved her customers, at least for a little while. Lyndsey spent more time at their table, batting her eyelashes and giving them her full attention. She listened to their woes and made soothing noises. Lyndsey would laugh and tease them. She even remembered their drink orders and had the drinks on the table waiting for them when they came through the door.

Customers love this, and she made them feel special. She didn't know their names, but this she didn't tell. To her, they were Bacardi coke with a twist, or rye, water back, JD on the rocks and a bottle of Bud. She prided herself on remembering their drinks. She would remember even when she hadn't seen them for a long time. When they came back, and they always did, she would have that drink right there waiting for them.

Everyone needed to be good at something, even if it was just to be good at drinking beer, or filling a table, while you drank your fill. When customers ordered beer from her, it was like she worked for them. They were boss, at least temporarily. They were the boss if they had money in their pockets or until the last bit of foam at the bottom of their glass was gone.

Yep, everyone needed a purpose. Hers was serving beer. Lyndsey was good at it. She could run a bar like nobody's business.

Correction, she could run a bar when she was under the influence of drugs.

And that was most of the time anyway.

# CHAPTER THIRTY

*Come on*! Sixty-two dollars and twenty-five cents? The cheap-shits! Lyndsey counted her tip money again remembering to deduct the fifty bucks she spent on coke. Oh, cocaine. It was a necessity that got her through the long hours at work. Lyndsey's table of four left at dinnertime. She carried-walked them to the door. It took her twenty minutes to clean up their mess. God, they were such pigs!

The old and useless departed at five giving her enough time to clean tables and ashtrays, restock the beer coolers and refill the fruit tray with oranges, lemons, and maraschino cherries.

Dan would go home then, for an hour or two and during his absence, Lyndsey would call a secret number, and within minutes her magic white powder would arrive. To reward her delivery friend she bought him a beer. Lyndsey didn't call him her drug dealer all though, in truth, that's what he was. But to call him that would require honesty and a show of good character, traits she lacked.

Her *friend* would cut a line for her right there on the bar if it were empty. If not they'd snort lines in the employee bathroom. Lyndsey took his crisp one hundred dollar bill and rolled it into a straw. She pinched one nostril and inhaled deeply through the other. If it were good shit, a symphony would explode in her head.

Then she would pocket the small flap and hand him the

money. After the ritual was complete, Lyndsey wanted him gone. She couldn't tell him that, she needed him to come back, so she offered to buy him another beer and hoped he would say no. But he never did. So she would get busy with cleaning and stay away from him hoping he'd get the message. Her dealer had a bad reputation. He was well known for selling drugs, and she didn't want anyone to see him with her.

Sometimes he would stick around just to torture her. Of course, if he stuck around long enough, well then, she'd have to be nice to him again, feigning interest where there was none to get more of her magic white powder.

With a twist of the cap, Lyndsey guzzled an entire beer. There were plenty of ways to get free alcohol. Dan's draft beer wasn't metered, allowing Lyndsey to fill her coffee cup multiple times over the day. Her patrons thought she loved her coffee. Lyndsey thought beer helped her pass the day.

The after-dinner crowd was far different than the day crowd. These folks were younger with a lot more money. They spent it fast and carelessly, especially the construction crews. Man, could those boys ever drink! The hard-hat crowd started with doubles and worked their way up from there. Lucky for her, they tipped as heavily as they drank and Lyndsey looked forward to seeing them.

The sixty-two dollars and twenty-five cents in her pocket played on her mind. She should save it for the landlord. Lyndsey was behind on her rent again. With her tip money, she could pay it down fifty bucks.

Lyndsey gave the tables a final wipe shutting the lights off as she went. Dan left her to close up after counting the cash and making his nightly deposits. Lyndsey took a pack of smokes from behind the bar and two bottles of beer from the cooler. She had just snorted her last line so she wouldn't be sleeping anytime soon. The beer would take the edge off when she crashed.

Man, she loved her white powder, but it was a bitch. When it was gone, you better have something else put away because if you didn't, it wouldn't be pleasant. Through trial and error, she founds ways to soften the crash. Gravol or liquor, Valium or weed, either one or all four kept the fiend satisfied. If you couldn't knock yourself out the cravings were intense. To score more, you'd sell your soul, and Lyndsey knew many who did just that.

Lyndsey set the alarm and locked the doors behind her. Hers wasn't the only car in the parking lot. But unlike the others, hers was uninsured, so she would have to drive the back roads home again. Thank God she lived nearby. Lyndsey turned over the ignition and prayed. The car roared to life, and she breathed a sigh of relief. Her rust bucket was twenty years old, and almost everything needed replacing.

Carefully minding her speed, she left the parking lot. Lyndsey noted the big white shiny trucks. The construction company they belonged too would not be impressed they were parked at the bar. Still, she supposed it was better than a DUI or worse, a wreck. Lyndsey hoped the hard-hat crew didn't get caught.

Too bad she couldn't have been more like them. Instead, she chose to drive. Lyndsey never lets a few drinks get in the way of her driving, and one day it caught up to her. It was a little over a year ago. She and her then-boyfriend Johnny were celebrating something. She couldn't remember what, maybe just the fact they hadn't managed to kill each other, *yet.* She had the day off, and they started drinking early.

They were having a great time. Lyndsey made Johnny breakfast, something she didn't usually do, and they'd both enjoyed it. They started with champagne and orange juice and moved on to Vodka. Alcohol increased their potential possibilities, and they talked about all the things they would do that day. First, they would visit friends, then do a little shopping, have a barbeque, and maybe go to the movies later that night. Deciding to do a beer run first, they stocked up in anticipation of their upcoming barbeque. By the time they got home they were both thirsty and had a beer.

Johnny was her newest infatuation. She met him at the bar where she worked. He flirted with her, and she liked that. Before long they saw each other regularly.

Johnny looked at her and said, "You go get the groceries, I think I'll stay here and chill."

Lyndsey wasn't about to do that. If she left Johnny behind, he would drink all the beer, and there would be none left by the time she got back. She shook her head. "Not a chance!"

That's all it took. The fight was on. Lyndsey and Johnny bickered back and forth and drank beer.

Lyndsey and Johnny never did get groceries. They didn't have that barbeque. They never saw their friend's or went to the movie.

When there was no alcohol left in the house, Lyndsey took her car keys from the hook on the wall and left Johnny behind. She drove to the nearest bar with just enough in her pocket to buy her first beer. After that, well, there was always someone to buy her the next one.

A pretty lone woman in a bar didn't need money. As the day became night, Lyndsey drank way more than she usually did. Liquors, hardballs, Jägermeister's, Sangria, apple cider, and beer. It wasn't a combination she would recommend to her patrons. But at the time she never noticed how potentially lethal drinking herself into oblivion could be. Lyndsey was having fun. She sat at many tables that night. Each time someone wanted to buy her a drink, she took it. Around closing time, the room started to spin. Deciding she'd had enough Lyndsey got up from her table and walked out of the bar.

And then nothing.

She came too on a dark road.

Lyndsey was lost.

But not knowing where she was wasn't her biggest problem. She had a much more serious problem than that.

All of the sudden the night wasn't nearly as dark as it had been. The sky lit up with flashing red and blue lights. The alcohol fog lifted. Lyndsey sobered up considerably and became aware of the seriousness of her situation. She was in deep shit and doubted she could convince the cop she drove better with a few drinks in her.

As the officer approached her car, Lyndsey tried to think of a plausible story but drew a blank.

The cop tapped on her window, motioning to roll it down.

Lyndsey rolled the window down and tried not to look guilty.

The cop asked her for her driver's license and registration. Then he turned his flashlight on her, blinding her.

Lyndsey hung her head down hoping he couldn't smell the alcohol fumes. She tried lighting a cigarette, but her hands were shaking too badly.

"Have you had anything to drink tonight?"

Lyndsey spoke to the floor, "just a few and that was a long time ago,"

With an "Hmmf" the cop took her license and insurance papers and walked back to his car.

As Lyndsey waited, she managed to light a cigarette. The nicotine calmed her, and she prayed. *Please God if you make this cop let me go. I promise I'll never drink and drive again.* Fingers crossed Lyndsey waited for the officer to return.

As the cop approached her vehicle, his face looked stern, and her heart sank.

"Please step out of your vehicle," he ordered. His voice was cold, and all business.

Lyndsey stepped out, still hoping it would all work out. But wishful thinking doesn't stand up to reality.

The cop asked Lyndsey to blow into a little machine. She blew a small breath thinking if she didn't blow too hard the device wouldn't register her alcohol intake.

Wrong.

The cop read her rights and circled her wrists in steel.

Lyndsey blew way over the legal limit.

The cop said she had a drinking problem and he hoped she got help for it.

As the prison door clanged shut behind her she shivered. Unable to sleep Lyndsey was awake all night. She wasn't the only drunk here. In cells nearby, drunks cried out and complained. One annoying drunk pounded on the bar slurring, giss me oub here! A splash of water indicated someone was pissing on his wall.

Lyndsey wasn't *anything* like these animals and felt highly offended the cop thought so.

Christ, she was cold. The concrete bed was not inviting. There was no pillow or blanket. There was nothing to give her comfort. Lyndsey curled around herself trying to stay warm. She didn't think things could ever get any worse than this.

Boy, was she ever wrong.

# CHAPTER THIRTY-ONE

Lyndsey set the warm beer on the counter. The fluorescent light above her buzzed with electricity. She popped the top on one can and put the other in the refrigerator. Lyndsey looked at the contents inside, old cheese and a yogurt long past its due date. Oh well, food wasn't her priority anyway. Lyndsey took a long pull from the warm can hoping to calm the edginess she felt.

Cocaine's siren call was irresistible. Lyndsey fought the urge to pick up the phone and spend her tip money. Deep down she knew she was way too dependent on her magic powder. Instead of picking up the phone Lyndsey stood in the bathroom pleading with her image. The mirror was cracked. Lyndsey tilted her head to see properly. She didn't mind though. She stopped looking in the mirror years ago after one particularly bad experience.

She'd been up partying all night and was getting ready for work the next morning. Applying mascara, she locked eyes with the ones in the mirror and was shocked at what she saw there. For looking back at her was someone else's eyes. Her dark, round orbs held no light or warmth. They looked flat and dead. They were the eyes of a stranger.

Lyndsey shrugged off the memory. She was craving, bad. There was no way she could fight them off without help. Thankfully she still had her stash of little blue pills. She swallowed one and put the bottle back in the drawer.

It wouldn't take long for the cravings to recede. Lyndsey

made a mental note to say thank you to Irene who had introduced her to them a month ago. At that time Irene was the new girl. They got along great. And one day Irene showed her the bottle saying the pills helped calm her nerves. She asked Lyndsey if she'd like to try one. Of course, she took it, glad for the opportunity. Irene admitted she had all kinds of pills if Lyndsey was interested. Irene sold them for profit and made good money doing it. When Irene ran out of narcotics and needed more, she made a doctor's appointment and walked out of his office with a prescription in-hand. Irene said it was easy.

But Lyndsey wasn't so sure. She didn't like the blue pill. It slowed her down and made her tongue feel thick and her body heavy. Lyndsey wanted to crawl into bed and go to sleep but six hours remained in her shift. Luckily, she talked Dan into letting her leave early. Lyndsey claimed to be sick and didn't want to give her germs to his customers. If she got them sick, they wouldn't be in his bar spending money.

Lyndsey never took another blue pill while she was working but found they worked great for other things. Other things, like now.

Needing to kill some time Lyndsey washed the few dishes in the sink. The cocaine was wearing off because she was getting hungry. Lyndsey opened the cupboard doors hoping the food fairy had been there in her absence. In the cupboard was four cans of no-name brand soup, one package of Ichiban noodles, a can of beans, and a box of KD.

Opening the beans, she ate them right out of the can. No sense in dirtying another dish and besides she wasn't eating for the enjoyment of it. Lyndsey had stopped enjoying food a long time ago. Actually, she'd pretty much stopped enjoying everything. The sun, the wind, the trees, birds, animals, and people, especially people. Nothing brought her joy anymore. The only time she felt happy was when she had something *more* in her system. More could be anything like a glass of beer, a line of coke, a flirtatious smile. Lyndsey was empty inside. More filled her up. Lately, more came in the form of white powder. Getting high was what her life was about now. She was on a mission for *more*; getting *more*, paying for *more*, keeping *more*. *More, more, more*, it was an obsession that consumed her every waking moment. *More* dictated her words and drove her actions. With *more,* she could conquer the world. Without *more,* she cowered from it.

Lyndsey thought back to the first time she'd tried cocaine. She felt like Super Woman that night. She had no idea the little white lines on the back of the toilet tank could be so powerful and corrupt. Cocaine was like the invasion of the body snatchers, for once you inhaled the seductive powder, it took over your life.

Cocaine took your love and respect, your loyalty and dignity. Cocaine put lies in your mouth and stole your looks, morals, values, and ambitions. Cocaine owned your soul.

You didn't use cocaine. It used you.

Of course, she didn't know that then.

People told her it was addicting, but she didn't believe them. What did they know? Cocaine gave her energy and confidence. She had so much fun that night. It seemed everyone she worked with used the stuff. Lyndsey got hooked immediately. For the longest time, she believed it was her calling the shots. But when she spent money she didn't have, and couldn't pay her bills, when every dime went to feed her habit, Lyndsey knew she was fooling herself.

Just thinking about coke stirred her, awakening hunger, unlike anything she'd ever known before. Cocaine called her name, and she was so damn powerless to resist. Lyndsey hoped the Valium would kick in soon. Without it, she had no chance. Her mind was already plotting ways to could get more money. Her cravings grew stronger blocking out all else. The message was simple; get dope or die.

Lyndsey lay down in bed, closed her eyes and pulled the blankets up to her chin. She pushed back against the fiend. Snuggling deeper into bed Lyndsey hugged her teddy bear, the one she took from her parent's house. As she stroked its soft body, she thought of her son.

Lyndsey whispered into Teddy's ear. "It's okay, baby. You're safe. No one will hurt you. Everything will work out fine."

Her eyes drooped. The noise in her head went away.

The little blue pill worked its sedating magic.

Turning onto her stomach, she drifted off.

Finally, Lyndsey was at peace.

# CHAPTER THIRTY-TWO

Anxiety felt like tiny ants nipping all over her body. Only they don't bite with teeth their nips come through worry, negative thoughts and a sense of detachment. The muted roar inside her head was the worst, though. Lyndsey's hands and feet tingled as she swung her legs out of bed.

She'd lost this battle.

Lyndsey washed her face and brushed her teeth thinking she hadn't slept long but it would have to do. She didn't bother with coffee. She was on a mission now. Lyndsey picked up her purse and took out all the money she had. Not bothering to lock the door she left her apartment.

Three doors down was a door just like hers. For a moment she paused, it was scary to knock on this door. There were dangerous people behind it. As she stood at the door fear battled with need.

Need, won the battle.

Lyndsey banged on the door and waited. Seconds ticked by and she worried he wasn't home. Lyndsey knocked again and nothing.

Just as she was about to turn away, she heard the click of the lock. Thank God someone was there.

Heyman stood in the opening of the doorway. He wore white boxer shorts and nothing else. Nothing else *except* a large white gauze bandage that wrapped around his abdomen. In the middle of the gauze was a big red stain.

"Come in, come in," he commanded. Heyman was small in stature with coal black hair and tiny features. His Asian accent was thick and not always easy to understand. His body language was easy to read, however, and she entered.

Lyndsey followed him into the apartment. It was sparse in furnishings. A single chair and fold up TV tray adorned the kitchen. A chair, ottoman and TV decorated the living room. The apartment was nothing more than a shell anyway, its only purpose a base from which to sell the drugs being warehouse there.

"You're hurt!" Lyndsey exclaimed, stating the obvious.

Heyman only grunted in response as he climbed back into his bed, wincing as he lay down. "What you want?"

"Just a half."

"You got money?" Heyman pointed one long narrow finger in her direction.

"Yes." Lyndsey owed him money already and hoped he wouldn't demand it now. She couldn't imagine leaving here without drugs.

Heyman mulled it over.

Lyndsey looked away from him and stared meekly at the floor.

Heyman reached his decision and opened the bedside drawer. Inside was a Ziploc baggie half full of the white powder she so badly craved. Heyman pulled a small pipe from the drawer. Then he took out a spoon and a lighter, a water bottle and a small bottle of foul-smelling clear liquid. Without a word, he began to cook.

With precise movements, Heyman was a master cook. Lyndsey could tell he had done this many times before and she wondered how he kept his hands so still. They were steady as a surgeon's as he held the spoon to the flame. Lyndsey glanced down at her own hands. They trembled in her lap. She laced her fingers together trying to still her shakes.

Heyman put away his cooking utensils and placed a large rock into his pipe. It was unbelievable how much smoke he could pull into his small body. Heyman seemed able to inhale for hours.

Time slowed as she waited for him to pass her the pipe.

Careful not to appear impatient Lyndsey stared at the floor. She knew her place. If she did the wrong thing right now she wouldn't only lose her opportunity with the pipe; she would also put herself in danger. Heyman was a ticking time bomb, and one wrong word could set him off. Instead of pulling the pipe from him or stealing his dope Lyndsey sat on the carpet beside his bed and waited.

Heyman lit up another big rock.

Lyndsey sat in the cloud of his smoke and covered her mouth. It was getting harder to stay mute and calm. She swallowed her words and tapped on the floor. Lyndsey used every bit of her willpower to control herself. The words rose in her throat leaving a bitter taste.

*Give me the pipe!*

*Give it to me!*

Heyman lit up another big rock and smiled. He was enjoying this.

Lyndsey clamped her lips tightly together. She was on the verge of losing it.

Heyman blew out a large plume of smoke and put the pipe down. All the big rocks were gone. Only crumbs remained.

Lyndsey looked at the crack crumbs and silently begged him not to smoke them all.

Heyman was tripping. His eyes were little pinpoints of madness as he loaded up his pipe with more white crumbs.

Lyndsey waited eyes locked on the pipe.

Heyman held the pipe for a minute toying with her before he passed it over. Lyndsey's fingers brushed his before circling the stem. She brought the pipe to her lips and lit the specks in the bowl. The white blobs melted quickly and for a moment she was content. Lyndsey exhaled, loving the taste of copper and sweet bliss.

It didn't last long though. It never did.

Being a drug fiend was like crossing a line you didn't know was there. If anyone one had told her one day she'd be sitting at the foot of someone's bed, begging for crumbs, she would have laughed in their face, and then probably slapped it.

No, she couldn't pinpoint when it had happened. Maybe bad habits happened over time. Each time she took a drink. Each time she ingested a line. Each time she told a lie.

Drugs erased her.

Not that it mattered really.

Her short buzz wore off leaving her needing more than ever.

Lyndsey put the pipe to her lips again, trying to smoke something that wasn't even there.

# CHAPTER THIRTY-THREE

Time stopped. It lost all meaning. Her skin was getting that greasy, oily film again. Lyndsey sat beside his bed hoping his heart would explode. He'd smoked enough crack that it should have, but unfortunately, Heyman's heart continued to beat, and Lyndsey was forced to beg for crumbs.

Lyndsey ran her fingers over the carpet feeling for little chunks of rock. It wasn't impossible he had dropped some when chopping lines or refilling his pipe.

Yes! Her fingers hit a tiny rock. Lynsey picked it up and popped it into her cigarette package.

Clouds of dark smoke billowed from Heyman's open mouth. He stared at the ceiling touched his bloodied dressing and looked at Lyndsey.

"You creen my bandage." Heyman pointed at his stomach and in his broken English told her what to do and how to do it.

Lyndsey's skin crawled. She didn't want to touch him but would do it anyway. Halfway through his dressing change Lyndsey realized she had not washed her hands. Too late now, she lifted off the rest of his soiled wrapping and studied his wound.

Heyman had a long tear in his flesh. Someone had stabbed him with something sharp and deadly. The wound was infected, and it smelled. The jagged edges circled in yellow-brown discharge.

Keeping her face blank, Lyndsey hid her disgust as she attended his wound. The disinfectant she cleaned him with was pungent. It stung her eyes. She thought it must hurt like hell, but Heyman never flinched. He just lay there on his back staring at her with his black, dead eyes.

With a steely-stare of her own, Lyndsey applied the new bandages. The only sign of life Heyman showed was when a sour-breathed groan escaped his lips and he clenched his fists.

. Lyndsey tossed the dirtied bandages into the trash knowing it was time to leave.

"You go now!" Heyman shouted.

Glad to be leaving, Lyndsey ran out of his apartment. For the moment she had what she needed. It wouldn't last long, but it was enough to get her to where she needed to go next.

Safe inside her apartment Lyndsey lit a cigarette. Her hands shook from suppressed fear. She never knew if Heyman would take a knife or gun to her and she'd seen him do some horrible things. Not able to sit still she paced the room. The urge to move was on, and so Lyndsey paced the carpet stalling the inevitable.

Five minutes later she opened her paper package trying to gauge how long the cocaine might last. Lyndsey would have to ration it, but first, she would do one line.

Just one, nothing more.

From the kitchen drawer, she withdrew an old straw its inside crusted in white from previous use. Lyndsey pulled her razor blade from underneath the cutlery container. With quick chops, she fluffed the rock into powdery lines and then placed the powder on a small square of paper. Satisfied all was ready Lyndsey dipped her long pinky nail in the powder, scooped out a small amount and put it on the kitchen table. She chopped it into fine snow and used her razor blade to form one long thin line. Lyndsey bent her head, inhaled, and the cocaine disappeared. When every last speck was gone, she put it all away, hoping this time she could leave the rest for later.

The shower was warm, but she didn't feel it. Once upon a time, Lyndsey loved baths. She would soak for hours enjoying the caress of warm water on her skin. Now bathing was a chore. It had become another something to get done and out of the way.

Although her skin was pink from scrubbing, she didn't feel clean. Lyndsey felt wretched, defeated, resigned. She was young, yet she was old and broken. Despair didn't wash off. Instead, it got into the pores of your skin, burrowing deep down to fester.

The little cake of soap crumbled in her hand. It held no smell unlike the bars of Irish Spring she used growing up. Lyndsey like the smell of soap. All soaps, even laundry soap. When washing her clothes in the laundromat, she enjoyed the swish and rumble of the machines. Lyndsey liked the warmth of the dryers and the aroma they gave off with their Bounce sheets tumbling inside.

The memory of the little boy surfaced. His mother carried overflowing baskets of dirty laundry, and the child toddling behind her trailed a well-loved blanket along the floor. He clutched a torn and soiled blanket tightly in his chubby little fist while sucking his thumb. In his other hand, he held a stuffed toy rabbit. The child was young, and he needed a bath. His clothes were dirty as if he had colored on them with felt pens, leaving

bright streaks of yellow and red on his T-shirt and jeans. He had
a full head of sandy-colored hair and the biggest blue eyes she
had ever seen.

Lyndsey thought he was adorable!

The little boy turned to her and Lyndsey thought she might
melt. This child was about the same age her son would be.
Lyndsey wondered if her son was as cute as this little guy. Her
heart ached.

The little boy's mother busied herself with sorting laundry,
quickly filling two washing machines. The little boy left his
mother's side and walked over to her.

"Timmy, don't you bother that lady," his mother called.

"It's okay. I have a son his age. He's not bothering me."
Lyndsey responded.

The child's mom nodded, and Lyndsey scooped him off the
ground. She plopped him on her lap and told him silly stories
while playing puppet with his leaky rabbit. Timmy snuggled into
her and pulled his *banky* tight. A few minutes later he was asleep
in her arms. Timmy had long eyelashes and his face smooth. His
breath was sweet, his body soft and warm.

Timmy was the picture of innocence. Lyndsey wished she
could stop time for him. She didn't want him to lose his
sweetness.

The laundry mat was warm, Lyndsey began to drift. It was a
pleasant feeling. She wasn't all the way under but she wasn't
fully awake, either. The drift was a special place where your
troubles disappeared, and your body was weightless.

From a distance, Lyndsey heard Timmy's mother. "I told

you no more sucking your thumb!"

Timmy's mom ripped him from her lap ending their short nap with a startling abruptness.

Timmy whimpered when his mother yanked his arm high in the air. Pulling on his thumb to make her point she scolded. "Only babies suck their thumbs, and you're a big boy!"

Lyndsey didn't think Timmy looked very old. Her eyes widened with concern as Timmy's mother pulled a bottle of hot sauce from her purse and generously doused his small thumb with it.

Timmy's eyes bulged, and his face scrunched up. He wailed, long shrill cries of protest.

Timmy's mother's face scrunched up, too. Not in fear but in anger, as she force-fed Timmy his spicy thumb. She pushed the offending digit in Timmy's mouth and held it there for what seemed like an eternity. Finally satisfied, she removed it. Timmy's mom put her face close to his. "Bad boy. Bad, bad, boy. You had better smarten up and don't you *ever* do that again!"

But Timmy's mom wasn't finished yet. She poked him sharply in his tummy saying she'd cut off his thumb next time she caught him sucking on it.

Lyndsey couldn't stand to hear any more. What could she do? If Timmy weren't here, Lyndsey would pound his abusive mother into the ground. The urge to beat on her was strong. But Lyndsey didn't want Timmy to see his mom getting hit.

In the end, Lyndsey turned her head away. She couldn't watch anymore, or she would lose her shit, and ultimately, it would be Timmy who paid

When Timmy left with his mom, he glanced at Lyndsey. His cheeks were wet with tears. He looked scared and confused. Lyndsey thought Timmy had aged since first stepping into the laundry mat. He wasn't as innocent as he had been only a few moments ago.

Lyndsey's heart hurt at the unfairness of it all.

Timmy held his thumb stiffly out in front of him as he marched out the door trailing his blanket.

One last look over his little shoulder and Timmy was gone.

# CHAPTER THIRTY-FOUR

The towel circled her head like a turban. Lyndsey smelled of soap and lotion. Naked she stared into the closet. There wasn't much there. Lyndsey had moved many times in the past. With each new move, she left personal belongings behind. Sometimes she did and grab-and-run. When you're getting evicted you don't always have a lot of time to pack. So now she only kept the necessities.

There would be an eviction notice on this door soon. The landlord had given Lyndsey three warnings. Each time he asked for the rent money, she promised to have it for him the next day. Lyndsey had a million excuses; *my boss is sick, my paycheck is late, my purse got stolen, your check is in the mail, the bank held my funds.* She had a million excuses alright. The only problem was she'd already used most of them.

Her current boyfriend, Drake, gave her enough money to pay utilities and rent before he left. Drake was the first boyfriend to quit her. Before him, she used replacement therapy.

Replacement therapy was something she made up to prevent heartache. Why mourn a lost relationship when you could replace it? Lyndsey met hundreds of men in the bar, and so when one left, it was easy to replace them.

But Drake was different.

Drake never belittled her or called her names. Since moving in he never once touched her in anger. And Lyndsey had tried her best to make him angry. Calm relationships were boring. She thrived on chaos. In her experience, if you weren't angry with someone you didn't love them very much. When Drake refused to get angry, Lyndsey got mean. She would pick fights and complain about stupid things. If Lyndsey could push his buttons and get him to react, then she was justified in taking advantage of him. That way she had an excuse for spending their money on drugs instead of rent, food, and bills.

For a long time, Drake put up with her crazy behavior. That is until recently when he told her that she needed help. Lyndsey couldn't believe it, him telling her! As if he didn't have problems too, Drake was no angel that was for sure. But she had to admit he wasn't nearly as unhinged as her.

For the first time, Lyndsey didn't have anyone waiting in the wings. There was no replacement therapy. Although there were still plenty of guys she could have picked from, they weren't her kind. These men were bottom-of-the-barrel kind of guys. The ones who didn't work, or if they did, got fired frequently. They were the ones with kids but never paid their child support. They were the ones on welfare and scamming governmental aide support programs. They were the ones who would leach off her, and let her do all the work while they sat in the bar drinking away her tips.

Now that Drake was gone, Lyndsey missed him. She didn't believe him when he threatened to leave her unless she got her shit together. Christ, as if she could! If it were that easy, she would have done it a long time ago.

Why would anyone choose to live like she was? Of course, it

didn't happen overnight. She thought back to her first bar manager. Chuck was Italian, a good-looking ladies' man, with a big cocaine habit. Chuck was also generous, at least with his cocaine. It had been a slow night in the bar and she and her co-worker Diane had taken turns snorting rails in the back room. Lyndsey hadn't thought much of it. Unlike weed she didn't feel wasted, she just felt happier, more social, and she couldn't stop smoking. Lyndsey chain-smoked a package of cigarettes in no time at all.

Cocaine gave her incredible energy and stamina. It was easy to get. Chuck sold it, and she bought him from him on every shift. At first, she and Diane would split it. The little flap of cocaine would last them all night long, and they even had a little left over. For a while, they pooled their tips and bought cocaine with it, but then something changed between them. Their easy friendship became fraught with suspicion. Now when they split the small white flap, they would both need to be there. They didn't trust the other to be fair, so they both watched eagle-eyed, making sure the division was even fifty-fifty.

One night it occurred to Lyndsey if she sold drugs not only could she do them for free but she wouldn't have to worry about running out. There were plenty of opportunities to sell in the bar. It wouldn't be a problem getting rid of her product.

At first, Lyndsey was nervous. She kept expecting to be busted or found out.

The addicts she sold too were pathetic. The depth of their sickness was unbelievable. She felt superior to the crack heads and junkies.

If only Lyndsey had known, this was a preview of her life.

Drug dealing started small. It was risky, and Lyndsey was cautious. But word got out and her number of customers increased. So far she'd managed to keep herself in free product and even made a little money at it. Each time she made a deal her confidence grew. Before long she felt invincible and decided it was time to play in the big leagues. Lyndsey fronted half an ounce. She had big plans, promising her dealer to pay off her debt in two days.

The thought of all the money she would make excited her. With the half ounce she bought, Lyndsey added another two grams of filler. It stretched her profits, and her customers never noticed. But it was the weigh-in ritual she liked best. It took the better part of the afternoon, cutting little envelope flaps and weighing them. Lyndsey sampled every package.

Lyndsey was in fine form when she met Diane at a local, watering hole. They both had so much to drink that night. Cocaine made you thirsty and allowed you to consume large quantities of alcohol without feeling drunk.

With so many paper flaps in her purse, Lyndsey felt generous. She gave Diane one calling it a freebie. When Diane left, saying it was late, Lyndsey was still raring to go. She hailed a cab headed for downtown and went to an after-hours bar.

There she met a new crowd of people and when the bar closed she followed them to a house party. It didn't bother her that she didn't know anyone there. It was easy to make friends when you had cocaine.

As if she was the God Father, Lyndsey cut massive lines on

the living room coffee table. At once her new friends were at her side, fetching her beer, and laughing at her jokes. She was famous, adored and she loved the attention.

Euphoria ruled the night. Lyndsey was having the time of her life. Her new friends were cool. They liked drugs as much as she did and bought up most of her stock. They didn't have any money on them but promised to stop by her workplace and pay her the next day.

As if they'd know each other for years, this new crowd and she were connected. Time flew, and Lyndsey never noticed that people were leaving.

As dawn was cresting the horizon, only Lyndsey and two guys remained. The newly lit room brought the first hint of reality. Shame crept across her body bringing a new awareness with it. The two guys that only moments before had been her best friends were now strangers. Bottom-of-the-barrel, kind of strangers. One of them was missing his front teeth. A sure sign of meth mouth and both were skinny, with greasy hair and sores on their face.

Oh God, she knew what they were thinking.

*Want more, want more, want more!*

*Gimme, gimme, gimme!*

The dreaded hour had come, it was go-home time. Thinking she'd have one more for the road Lyndsey reached into her pocket and pulled out the baggie.

It was empty.

How had that happened?

Panicked, she scanned the table-top looking for the missing

flaps. When she didn't see them there, Lyndsey got on her hands and knees and crawled under the table.

Nothing!

She looked at the coffee table again and started counting. The empty flaps littered the table, all except six. One she'd given away and five she sold. Sold to people, she'd never seen before and didn't even know their names.

Lyndsey stumbled out to her car. The sun was shining. The birds were singing. It was a beautiful day. She looked at Mother Nature's artwork and wished for black. At least she could hide in the dark but out here in the light of day; the truth was glaring.

Awash in shame and misery, Lyndsey wanted to crawl under a rock and die. She owed a lot of money and had nothing to show for it.

A heavy weight settled on her chest. Lyndsey struggled to stay calm.

As she drove off into the bright day sun, dread pierced the gloom of her vehicle, reaching its tentacles into her brain. With a pounding head and squinting against the sun, Lyndsey racked her mind looking for ways to get her out of this predicament.

Nothing came to her. There was no get-out-of-jail, free card.

Only one word whispered in the seclusion of her car.

It repeated itself over and over again.

*Loser.*

*Loser.*

*Loser.*

# CHAPTER THIRTY-FIVE

The fiend was powerful. Lyndsey was on the hunt again. Just as she was leaving her apartment, Tracy yelled down.

Tracy was a long-term tenant. Her housing checks were deposited straight to their landlord. Tracy was pleasant enough, but Lyndsey avoided her because she was always broke and looking for a handout. Tracy would knock on Lyndsey's door asking to *borrow* a cigarette, or a cup of sugar, sometimes a beer.

But mainly Tracy wanted her time. She was lonely and liked to talk.

Lyndsey didn't like idle chit-chat. She'd never seen the point of it.

"Hey Lyndsey, I got paid, and it's party time up here!" Tracey yelled her voice high with excitement. "Come on up!"

*Paid* meant her welfare check had come in. Tracy was a generous woman on welfare Wednesday. She would splurge on anyone who happened to walk by. Only she spent her month's money in one day and then lived like a bum the rest of the month, begging and borrowing until the next check came in.

Not that it was any of her business. This was one day of the month Lyndsey *was* glad to see her. She knew what party time meant and called out, "I`ll be right there!"

Tracey was waiting for her at the door, dressed for business in a clean pair of jeans and a form-fitting blouse. Tracey wore large silver hoops in her ears and thick make-up on her face.

Tracey's hair was freshly shampooed and hung in a long shiny curtain down her back.

"You look nice," Lyndsey offered. She was quite surprised really. Tracey usually wore old sweats and a large grey hoodie. With her hair in a ponytail or clipped up on top of her head.

"You're pretty hot yourself." Tracey offered back.

Lyndsey had lost weight and thought she did look hot. One of her customers recently commented she looked like a scarecrow. But Lyndsey didn't believe him, and Tracey's comment confirmed it.

Tracey's three children didn't live with her. She had them every other weekend. The Ministry of Families and Children removed them from Tracey's home one day after an unscheduled visit. Tracey's youngest daughter answered the door, still dressed in her pajamas although noon. None of Tracey's children were in school that day, and her small apartment was a disaster.

The social worker wasn't able to rouse Tracey. She called for an ambulance and a foster family. Tracey was diagnosed with alcohol poisoning and declared unfit for parenting. A family member came forward to take her children. Tracey had to undergo psychiatric evaluation and detox.

Tracey tried to stay away from drugs and alcohol. She really did, but when she couldn't get her children back as quickly as she hoped, she went back to it.

Today Lyndsey would have to hear about it all over again. It was the price of admission, one she was willing to pay.

Lyndsey sat down on Tracey's leather couch. It was a cast-off from her parents. Brown in color, it was creased and worn but very comfortable. Lyndsey sank into its soft cushions and waited for the rant.

Tracey cut a big line for Lyndsey and put her share in a spoon.

Lyndsey cut her line in two and inhaled the first one. She helped herself to Tracey's cigarettes offering one to Tracey. Tracey shook her head no, busy with her spoon.

It was strange what you can get used too. Lyndsey was more comfortable with it now, watching Tracey cook her next hit. She used a small torch and before long the powder and water in the spoon merged as one.

"You won't believe what those assholes have done now." It started. Tracey blew on her spoon. "They want me to take a drug test before I can see my kids. Can you fucking believe that? I mean whose kids are they anyway?" Tracey never looked up as she pushed the syringe through the cotton and sucked up the liquid in the spoon.

Thank Christ, Lyndsey thought.

Tracey stopped talking for a moment, held the syringe up and pushed on the plunger. A small droplet of clear liquid escaped the sharp point and Tracey continued. "I mean how the fuck do those assholes sleep at night?"

Saving the ash from her cigarette, Lyndsey reached for her next line.

Tracey held out her arm and pushed on a vein. "Can you imagine what kind of a monster you must be to take kids away from their mothers?"

Lyndsey ground her cigarette out, eyeing the white powder

left in the paper flap.

"Ouch! Ow!" Tracey cried, plunging the needle deep.

Lyndsey pondered doing another line or cooking some to smoke.

"Shit I missed. I'm terrible at this." Tracey cried, pulling the needle out.

Yep. It was time to smoke. Lyndsey wondered if Tracey had ammonia in her kitchen.

Tracey pushed on the crook inside her elbow. "I mean, Christ, a single mother, doing her best to raise three children on her own…" she trailed off spying a raised vein.

Lyndsey might not have to cook. She still had Heyman's rock.

Tracey emptied the syringe. "Awe, that's better," she murmured orgasmically.

Lyndsey pulled the pipe out of her purse and filled it with ashes.

"Raising kids on your own isn't easy to do." Tracey swiped at the blood oozing from her puncture. "I'd like to see them try it."

Lyndsey placed a small crack rock on top of the ash and opened her purse looking for her lighter. She'd just had it, now where did it go?

"Here use this." Tracey handed her the propane torch and restocked her spoon.

Lyndsey lit the little rock in her pipe. All she got was a small lungful of smoke.

Tracey took the torch back and applied the flame to the back of her spoon. "My kids are lucky. I worked my ass off for them and look where it got me."

The dragon awoke, and it was starving! It only took one rock to awaken this beast.

Lyndsey wasn't herself anymore. A greater need consumed her, and it shouted *more!*

Tracey waved her full syringe in Lyndsey's face. Her pupils had disappeared. "I should blow the fucking place up."

Lyndsey looked at the pile of powder on the table. She reached into her purse and pulled out her razor blade.

Tracey pulled the needle away from Lyndsey's face and punched it in her arm. She pulled on the plunger drawing blood into the syringe. "I should you know, those bastards deserve to die!" Tracey pushed the plunger all the way down, emptying the needle.

Lyndsey helped herself to Tracey's cocaine.

Tracey dropped the needle, her body becoming stiff. Her eyes rolled, and she fell to the ground. White foam came from her mouth as she started to shake.

Tracey's body bounced up and down on the ground convulsing.

Lyndsey moved her onto her side in the recovery position.

Tracey's bladder let go. A wet stain appeared on the crotch of her jeans.

The air reeked of urine.

Tracey was doing the chicken. It was the first time Lyndsey had seen it in person.

Lyndsey shook her head in disgust and refilled her spoon.

# CHAPTER THIRTY-SIX

Lyndsey covered Tracey up and left her on the floor. Then she helped herself to a large spoonful of Tracey`s dope. By the looks of her, she was doing Tracey a favor. Tracey didn't need to get high again. She needed help.

Lyndsey felt justified for stealing Tracey's drugs. She honestly didn't think she was doing anything wrong. She'd become so good at making excuses she was blind to her actions. Lyndsey was the victim, the underdog. And when opportunity knocked, she answered.

As Lyndsey cooked up her dope, Tracey became more alert. Her eyes were less glassy, and she was moving around. The last time Lyndsey and Tracey went on a binge was in this apartment. It was one day after Welfare Wednesday. Tracey picked up an eight-ball and was in high spirits. She was so proud of herself that day. For a change, she wasn't talking about MFC but her daughter's birthday. Between puffs, on her crack pipe, Tracey told Lyndsey about her plans. It was her daughters sixth birthday, and Tracey was throwing a party. She'd gone shopping at the Dollar store buying party hats and balloons. Tracey had put money away for the ice cream cake her daughter requested.

Tracey's little girl had begged her mom for a bike. Tracey took another hit off the pipe, and she passed it to Lyndsey. Grinning wide, Tracey got up saying she'd be right back. When Tracey returned, she was pushing a small pink bicycle in front of her. The look on Tracey's face said it all. *I love you, my precious daughter. You're my world.*

Life had been so sweet at that moment. They were happy, both of them getting into the swing of things as they planned the birthday. There would be balloons and cake. Should they have hot dogs or hamburgers? Lyndsey thought it should be hot dogs. The kids were young and probably couldn't eat a whole burger. Tracey wasn't sure but thought hot dogs would probably be cheaper. They discussed what the kids would drink, Kool-Aid, pop, or juice? Lyndsey declared juice a healthier choice and passed the crack pipe back to Tracey, who continued with the birthday plans.

Tracey pulled out a carton of smokes and tossed Lyndsey a pack. Lyndsey told Tracey she was proud of her, to shop ahead was a great idea. Tracey's smile slipped from her lips, when admitted she purchased the birthday supplies early because she was worried she would spend all her money before the birthday leaving her daughter without a present.

Once the truth was out, it couldn't be unsaid.

Tracey and Lyndsey grew quiet. It was awkward as they passed the pipe back and forth, avoiding each other's eyes.

Tracey broke the silence first, stating what Lyndsey had also noticed.

*We're almost out of dope.*

Euphoria died, and doom descended.

They smoked their last pipe full and sat, staring at the table, at the walls, at the carpet. Before long they were crawling on the ground searching for the elusive crumble. Any white speck on the carpet would do. They picked lint off the carpet, put it in their pipe and lit up in a desperate attempt to smoke *more*.

Tracey opened her purse and pulled out the cake money. She would find a way to repay it by the weekend. It wasn't a big deal. Lyndsey agreed to pay Tracey back.

Together they went down the hall and knocked on Heyman's door. The cake money only bought half a gram, and they went through it quickly. There was an urgency present, and they both felt it. The less dope you had, the bigger it got. Lyndsey and Tracey swallowed lungfuls of smoke hoping that somehow, magically it would be enough.

It wasn't.

This time Tracey took the carton of cigarettes, minus four packs. When she returned from Heyman's, she was holding two rocks.

Two.

Teeny.

Weeny.

Rocks.

They were gone in five minutes.

Lyndsey wished she had weed or Gravol or something that would knock them both out. But she had nothing, so instead, she smoked another cigarette. Her throat was raw from smoking, and the carpet lint hadn't helped either.

Tracey didn't say a word, her face sagged with that hopelessly lost look only a dope addict knows. She sat cross-legged on the carpet and eyed the bike. Coming to a decision, Tracey stood up. Her body moved as if it belonged to somebody else. Tracey walked in stiff, jerky steps, coming to a complete stop every few feet and then walking again. Tracey was just a puppet, something more potent than she pulled her strings.

Lyndsey shivered, catching a glimpse of this powerful enemy. It was massive, this giant puppeteer. It held *all* the strings, and they weren't just attached to Tracey's body. They were attached to her too.

Addiction was callous, cruel and uncaring.

Tracey lost the battle, pushing the bike in front of her she left the apartment. As she crossed the kitchen, Lyndsey looked at the bike one last time. On it was the ghost of Tracey's daughter. Her little girl laughed and squealed with delight. As Tracey opened the door, her child's smile disappeared as understanding dawned. Lyndsey heard her cries echo in the apartment.

*No Mommy! Please don't do it! Mommy! No!*

The door opened. Tracey and the bike disappeared.

Five minutes later Tracey returned, in her hand she held *more*.

# CHAPTER THIRTY-SEVEN

Tracey got up slowly. She looked as if she'd aged twenty years. Carefully she stood and fought for balance. She teetered on her feet, swaying just a little. Her eyes were dull and her words slurred. "Whaa happed to me?"

"You had a seizure."

"I fee funnee." Tracey rocked on her feet and grabbed the arm of the couch. Carefully she lowered herself down and sat next to Lyndsey.

Lyndsey tried not to flinch and slid over putting distance between them. Tracey smelled awful, and Lyndsey didn't want her wet clothing to touch her. "Why don't you have a shower and clean yourself up?"

"In a while," Tracey replied, her words clearer. "You used all my coke!"

"No there's some left." Lyndsey pointed to the small mound.

Tracey picked up her bloodied syringe and held it out to Lyndsey. "You do it for me."

Lyndsey didn't want to argue, so she scraped the last bit of coke into the spoon. She went through the motions mechanically, not wanting to think. It didn't work though. As Lyndsey held the spoon to the flame, she wondered how this was happening. When had it become normal to sit beside a urine soaked friend holding their bloodied syringe to the fire? When did seeing someone seizure on the floor stop mattering? Why am I helping her die?

Lyndsey felt dead inside, and her hands never shook once. She couldn't stay and watch. The coke was gone, and so was she. It wasn't kind. It wasn't nice. Lyndsey hated using her friend and felt awful about it.

Back at her apartment, she glanced at the clock. Jesus! She was supposed to be at work soon. There was no way she could go in like this. Lyndsey was way too fucked up, and not even her superior acting skills could get her out of this one.

Her body buzzed. Her brain was on fire, probably from dopamine overload, and her nerves jumped around like sand fleas. Lyndsey hoped she didn't get fired, but at the moment couldn't rouse any great concern over the idea. It wouldn't be the first time that was for sure. She had a history of being fired. Not that it was entirely her fault, her habit had made her undependable. She didn't want to be a shitty employee, but the trouble arose from not being able to predict what would happen when she used. It was a crapshoot. She might come home; she might not. She might spend all her money; she might not. She might show up for work; she might not.

No, she couldn't predict what would happen because she didn't know herself. Lyndsey wasn't lying when she said she'd be right back. She meant to keep her word, but hadn't figured out how to do that yet. For once there was *more* in her system she wasn't in charge.

The paper stapled to her door read *EVICTION NOTICE* in big bold letters. Shit! Now, what was she supposed to do? Lynsey put her key in the door, but it wouldn't budge. The landlord had installed new locks while she was away.

*Fuck.*

All she had with her were her purse and its contents. Damn, she wished she could get in and at least get some of her belongings.

Christ, she was screwed! First, her boyfriend had left her, now she was probably fired and to top it all off she was homeless. Thank God she still had her car. But it had no insurance on it and was almost out of gas.

Lyndsey needed a cigarette bad. But she was out of those too.

Not sure where to go, she went to her car. She could probably beg Tracey for a night on her couch, but she couldn't bring herself to do it.

When she got outside, it was dark. Lyndsey didn't know what day it was anymore. She found her car. It was lopsided, one tire needing air. On her way to work one day, she'd run over a nail. It wasn't a problem as long as she'd remembered to fill it up every day.

Of course, she didn't remember, and Drake teased her about it. "What would you do without me?" He grinned over at her as he filled her tire.

Drake had bought the car for her. It wasn't much as far as cars go. It was an older model, Chevy Impala. It was white, and he was always washing it. Drake used to tell her "You may not find me handsome but you'll always find me handy."

She could see him now. His lips turned up as he sluiced soapy water over her 'new' car. She looked at the car now. It wasn't just lopsided. It was dirty. The car wasn't washed since

Drake left. Before that really, because he'd been mad at her for a long time and had barely spoken to her, let alone washed the car. At the time, Lyndsey thought he was acting like a big baby, all overprotective and jealous.

Lyndsey had met Drake at work. He wasn't like the other guys who were always hitting on her. Drake was quiet. He wasn't loud or grandiose like her other customers. What she liked best about him then was he tipped well. Drake would come in the bar dressed in his work clothes. He worked in construction and Lyndsey thought he looked pretty damn sexy in those steel toed work boots and snug-fitting jeans.

Lyndsey flirted with him as she did with all her customers, but Drake wasn't buying it. He was polite, but that was all. That was the moment Lyndsey become interested in him. She'd always liked a challenge and added Drake to her list.

Her mind snapped back to the present moment. The parking lot was cold. Lyndsey missed Drake more than she could have imagined, and thinking about him brought tears to her eyes.

If only Drake were here, he'd make everything better. But he wasn't here, and Lyndsey was just now feeling it.

Christ, she needed a cigarette! Pulling open the ashtray Lyndsey spotted the longest butt and pulled it free. The half-smoked ciggy was bent and the filter covered in ash.

Lyndsey placed it between her lips and lit up.

It tasted old and bitter.

Like ash and death.

# CHAPTER THIRTY-EIGHT

With no place to go Lyndsey drove around aimlessly. The enormous weight of her situation was heavy. She was lonely, depressed and hopeless. Lyndsey missed Drake like crazy and berated herself for ruining everything.

That's all she ever seemed to do.

Ruin things.

And it wouldn't stop.

Not unless she made it stop.

A few miles down the road Lyndsey pulled into her favorite park. It was a place she and Drake had walked hand-in-hand, many times. The park was a reminder of better times, and brought back good memories. The parking lot was vacant. Lyndsey parked under a big tree hoping no one would notice her there.

Lyndsey crawled into the back seat, covering herself with an old blanket that she and Drake used the first time they were here. It was soon after they'd met. Lyndsey flirted shamelessly with Drake, but still no date. Lyndsey thought Drake wasn't interested in her and this only made her more determined to get his attention. He had come into the bar as she'd been getting off work. Lyndsey had too many 'coffees' that shift and was feeling particularly brave.

With a bottle of cold Bud in her hand, Lyndsey sauntered over to his table. "Mind if I join you, boys?" Not waiting for an answer, she sat down.

Drake sat with a customer she knew well. Bob worked in construction too and was a frequent patron of the bar. A regular, as Dan would call him. Bob was a regular all right, a regular pain in the ass. Lyndsey had tried to get him cut off but failed to do so. Bob was a sloppy drunk, and in comparison, he made Drake look even more attractive. Lyndsey didn't stay at their table long. Just long enough to finish her beer.

Before leaving Lyndsey tore her match cover in half, wrote her phone number down and placed it in front of Drake. "Call me sometime."

Her bravado faded, her cheeks burned, and Lyndsey hurried out the door. All the way home she cursed her ridiculous impulse.

When Lyndsey pulled into her driveway, she could hear the phone ringing. Not wanting to miss the call she ran to unlock the door. Lyndsey thought it would be her girlfriend on the other end. They'd made plans to hit the clubs that night, and she couldn't wait to go. Out of breath, Lyndsey picked up the receiver. "Hello," she puffed.

It wasn't her girlfriend on the other end. It was Drake. After that they were inseparable. For a time they were happy. Except for when she tried to ditch him for *more*.

That night Lyndsey was surprised to hear his voice on the other end of the phone. Lyndsey canceled her plans with her girlfriend. Romance won over more, for once.

Drake showed up at her door with flowers and a bottle of wine. He wore clean jeans and a button-up shirt. The baseball hat was gone, and she could see the top of his head for the first time. His hair was still wet from his shower. Instead of steel-toed boots, he wore black leather boots on his feet.

They each had a glass of wine before going out to dinner. With an unexpected wit and charm Drake entertained her for hours. The smile never left her face as she sat listening to his hilarious stories. Drake ordered another bottle of wine with their meal followed by two snifters of cognac. Lyndsey was by no means a cognac connoisseur, but she followed his lead and swirled the liquid in her glass.

Drake offered her bites of his steak. Lyndsey was full, and it wasn't sitting well. Her stomach had shrunk, and all the liquor she drank wasn't agreeing with the rich food she'd consumed.

The ride back to her place was a blur. Lyndsey used every ounce of willpower not to vomit in his car. The hot sourness rode high in her throat making her stomach roll. Lyndsey opened her door just in time. Her dinner came up on the side of her driveway.

Embarrassed, Lyndsey wanted to disappear. Lyndsey did what she always did when things got rough. She ran. Lyndsey bolted for the door not wanting to see the look of disgust on Drake's face.

But Drake was faster than her. He grabbed her arm as she opened the door. Startled she yelled. "Don't look at me!"

Drake just put his arm around her and walked through the door. Lyndsey shrugged off his arm and bolted for the bathroom. She hoped Drake would have left by the time she got out.

But no such luck.

Lyndsey saw Drake outside. He was in her driveway with a hose in his hand. Drake twisted the water tap getting the water pressure just right. Then he sprayed down the spot where her regurgitated dinner had been. But he didn't stop there. Drake cleaned the entire driveway before he was satisfied. When he finished, Drake coiled the hose around his arm and placed it on the ground beside the water tap.

As he came through the doorway, he commented. "I need to buy you a hose hanger." Drake stomped his wet boots on the carpet and winked. They sat on the couch together, and Lyndsey relaxed. She'd found the one man who wouldn't humiliate her.

They slept together on the couch that night. Each at separate ends, with only their legs and feet, touching. Lyndsey fell asleep and when she woke the room was ripe with the aroma of freshly brewed coffee.

A loud noise scratched at her window breaking her train of thought. Lyndsey peered out the glass.

The eerie darkness of the night played tricks on her mind.

Lyndsey double-checked the car doors making sure they were securely locked.

Her mind ran wild, imagining someone hiding in the dark, waiting to pounce on her.

Cold air blew through her vent, and she hunkered down in her blanket.

The wind picked up, and something tapped at her window.

# CHAPTER THIRTY-NINE

Lyndsey had once heard that it's darkest before the dawn, but she didn't think she could wait any longer. Dawn was a long way off, and she had given up. Lyndsey had never seen the point of her life. She was a walking disaster.

She wished she could go back in time. If she could, she would go to her field. The one with the tall grass where she played for hours her only company, her imagination. As a child, she would imagine herself a bird soaring through the sky or a lion prowling through the grass as she stalked nearby insects.

She was innocent and sweet, her heart pure. But time had not been her friend. Her heart was black, decaying and shriveled. Her imagination was not her friend, either. It fed her fear and paranoia. Lyndsey knew her thinking was irrational and yet it made perfect sense to her. She was always two things. Good and bad. Pretty and ugly. Fat and thin. Nice and mean. Honest and a liar. Caring and could care less. Hopeful and hopeless, and lately, just hopeless.

Lyndsey was so tired and wanted her life to be over. In a way, she'd been trying to end it for some time now. She risked heart attack and overdose every time she took a hit off the crack pipe. But she didn't care, and if she did feel concerned, her two things would kick in. I can die, I won't die. It could happen, it won't happen.

Lyndsey first thought about suicide after a three-day binge.

Her binge started as it always did, with a few drinks. After her shift was over Drake stopped by wanting to give her a ride home. He'd just gotten paid and had been out grocery shopping. Drake said their cupboards were full. Drake liked supporting their little family.

"Just one beer," she'd begged him.

Drake waved his arm at the door. "We've got ribs at home, and I just put the potatoes in the oven. We can make a salad when we get back. And there's beer."

"Please, just one." Lyndsey pleaded. "I need to unwind. I'm not ready to go home yet."

Drake scowled, his happiness fading. He had experience with her *just one* and looked at her now, clearly torn. "Just one," Drake agreed.

Drake and Lyndsey found a table and soon others joined them. Customers and friends alike, wanting to buy them a beer. Before long, drinks were lined up in front of them. Lyndsey was having a great time when Drake reached over and whispered in her ear, "I'm hungry, let's go."

For a moment everything stopped as she looked into his eyes.

Drakes' eyes hardened in preparation for what was coming.

Lyndsey was pissed off. She was having fun, and the last thing she wanted to do was to go home. What she really wanted was to purchase more and had been about to suggest it to Drake.

Before she could say a word Drake shook his head. "The potatoes will burn."

"I don't give a shit. Quit being such a party pooper!"

Drake's jaw thrust out. "You said just one, and you've had four!"

"Quit trying to control me, you freak! Christ, what are you, my mother?" Lyndsey's raised voice got the attention of the rest of her table.

She lowered her voice. Something ugly had taken over. It was far stronger than her love for Drake. She would stop at nothing now. She must have more.

Hoping to appease Drake she told him to go home. She'd be along soon. Why she'd be home before he knew it. She even asked him for money saying she needed gas and cigarettes.

Drake reached in his pocket and put a fifty in front of her. Then he kissed her cheek and said goodbye. He was far too nice. At the time she hadn't appreciated him. The nicer he was to her, the more she took advantage of him.

Before long the people at Lyndsey's table changed. Some left and others joined them. Her dealer had come and gone long ago. Since his departure, Lyndsey hadn't been at her table much. She spent more time in the bathroom snorting lines than anywhere else. Lyndsey thought she fooled them, with her drug paraphernalia tucked into her bra. But in the end, it was she who was the fool.

By then she was soaring, and it didn't matter. Everything was bright. She laughed more. She talked more. She loved more. One of Drake's friends asked her to dance, and as he brought her back to her table, she saw that the people sitting around it were strangers. The ones she started out with had gone home.

Lyndsey didn't care though and sat down at the table as if

they were her new best friends. It never occurred to her at these times she was putting herself in danger. Lyndsey never acknowledged fear. With more, she didn't have any. She was ten feet tall and bulletproof. It was only when more ran out that fear began.

Lyndsey played the chameleon adjusting her words and attitude to fit the present company. She matched them word for word, drink for drink, and shooter for shooter.

One of the big burly guys winked at her passing a tinfoil package under the table. Lyndsey grasped it touching his roughened fingertips at the same time. "Thanks!" The folded square was big. Lyndsey pulled the folded edges apart and looked at the fluffy pile. "Wow! Thanks!"

Lyndsey and her burly friend were the last ones to leave. They closed down the bar, but they were just getting started. Lyndsey walked out of the bar not knowing where she was going. Not that it mattered, she had what she needed for now. Lyndsey placed the tinfoil package in her purse and snapped it close. She wasn't going home, not for a long time. That would be such a drag.

Lyndsey got on her new friend's bike. With the borrowed helmet strapped securely to her head, she held hugged his back. The motorcycle was loud. As they roared out of the parking lot, she scooted closer to him.

For a moment she thought about Drake. As if she were looking through a window she saw him pacing with the remains of his dinner growing cold on the plate. His face lined in worry and anger, the burnt potatoes resting on top of the stove.

For a split second, guilt prickled her conscious and then it was gone.

The night disappeared in a cloud of gasoline fumes as the Harley's engine revved *more*.

# CHAPTER FORTY

Between the painful memories of the past and the even more painful reality of the present, Lyndsey started to shiver. Death whispered in her ear. It would be so nice to go to sleep and never wake up. She was tired of hurting and even more than that, she was tired of inflicting pain on the people who meant the most to her. Her gone would be doing them all a favor.

Lyndsey could still see Drake's face as she'd walked through the door that final morning. She hadn't slept in three days, she hadn't eaten either. Lyndsey looked like someone you saw on the streets. Her clothes were dirty, her hair greasy, and her face smeared in three-day-old makeup.

Baffled, Lyndsey lost count of the days, trying to calculate by the light outside the grimy window. She'd watched it fade to black twice and thought she'd been away from home two days. She was in a crack-shack. At least she was pretty sure that's what it was. People came and went at all hours. They'd scared her at first, dressed in their rags and muttering to themselves, their fingers blackened and calloused from continually flicking their lighters.

Lyndsey's hands looked like that too in the end. Her finger-pads thickened with the beginnings of the chronic crack user paw-like fingertips. Crack hadn't been the only thing being consumed in that shack either. Lyndsey sat on the floor next to a girl younger than herself. The girl told her she was a runaway.

Sally shot the drug in her arm with a nurse's ease and then went nuts. Sally ranted gibberish and picked at her face. She insisted cops and FBI agents were after her. Sally's frantic gaze searched the building returning over and over to Lyndsey. Her eyes tilted back and forth as Lyndsey reassured her she was safe.

Sally had moved closer to Lyndsey, and it was horrible. The odor of her unwashed body reached her nostrils and made her want to vomit. Sally smelled rotten, like meat that had gone bad and her face wore open scratch marks. They were raw, bloodied and wept reddish tears down her cheeks. Some of Sally wounds were deep and healed over. Others were fresh. Sally picked at them all opening new craters on her face.

Lyndsey's heart broke for her.

The burly guy on the motorcycle left shortly after arriving. Lyndsey had managed to ditch him, and he wasn't very happy with her. He called her every name in the book before stomping off. Lyndsey thought he was going to hit her, he raised his arm to do so, but at that precise moment, something changed. The noisy crack-shack became still. They had eyes on them, so instead of hitting her, he shoved her, sending her crashing into the wall. As he turned away from her, he tossed out, "bitch" and left.

Lyndsey ran out of cocaine sometime the next day. She would have left then if it weren't for the generosity of Sally. Sally didn't want her to leave and offered to share her meth. Lyndsey had never used crystal meth before and told Sally she didn't do needles. As if by not shooting it into your vein, somehow meant you didn't have a problem. Lyndsey felt superior. But Sally never noticed. She just showed Lyndsey how to use the new drug.

Lyndsey caught on quick. Before long she had the straw in her mouth chasing the little wisps of smoke coming from the broken piece of glass Sally held the lighter too.

That was when she'd lost all track of time.

Lyndsey became engrossed in a small pile of pebbles she found on the floor near her. She played with them for hours, lining them up and making designs. Lyndsey was sure there was a message or spiritual meaning in the shapes and repeatedly moved them around trying to figure it out. From time to time, Sally would put the broken glass under her face, and Lyndsey would breathe in through her straw chasing little black wisps of smoke.

The pebbles were driving her mad. Lyndsey was losing her mind. They consumed her from the inside out, and her hands flew around arranging them this way and that. She didn't feel hungry or thirsty or tired. She was obsessed with her pebbles.

The drugs ran out. Sally left. Lyndsey hadn't even noticed her departure and then sometime after, she'd gotten up, too. It happened fast. She'd been playing with the pebbles which were lined up neatly in the shape of an L. They'd been magical, and then they weren't. Suddenly they were just rocks. The spell broke, and she made her way out.

Lyndsey could barely remember getting home. She walked a long way and lost track of time. Finally, arriving home, Lyndsey barely made it through the door. Drake was waiting for her, and she was vaguely aware of him as he ran her a bath. He washed her, saying little. He cleaned away three days' worth of filth and depravity. He lathered her hair with shampoo and scrubbed her until her skin turned pink.

The water felt nice, but she didn't. He could clean her all he wanted, but she knew she would never be clean again. She was too broken, and that was something the bath water could never touch.

Drake fed her soup and gave her a bottle of Gatorade. She'd cried with the hopelessness of it all. He'd put her to bed, and when she awoke, she was alone.

All alone.

Lyndsey almost did it then. She looked for her blue pills hoping to swallow enough that everything would go away.

On her way to the bathroom, she'd passed the kitchen and saw the envelope. Lyndsey knew he was gone from the first second her eyes opened. The apartment felt different without him. Curiosity and dread coursed through her as she'd torn open the envelope. Inside was a note. Lyndsey glanced at it briefly before stuffing it into her purse. It was the wad of bills attached to the note she was after. Lyndsey read enough to know he was gone and the money was for their rent and the bills. Drake was going away, and he left her enough money to cover the remaining time on their lease. Of course, she hadn't paid the rent. She meant to, she really did. But it never happened.

In the end *more* had gotten it all. It took her home and her job. It took Drake and all his hopes and dreams. It took everything she had, and now she was going to give it one last thing.

Lyndsey reached into her purse knowing exactly how she

could make that happen.

# CHAPTER FORTY-ONE

Lyndsey couldn't see a damn thing. The starless night was black. She felt around in her purse searching for the pill bottle when she heard it again. *Tap, tap, tap.* The sound resembled fingernails scratching the glass. Her heart accelerated with a fresh wave of panic, and she dropped her purse. Adrenaline heightened her senses, and every nerve tingled. Lyndsey was sure the very devil himself was out there, awaiting her arrival as he ran his fingers over the glass.

Well, he wouldn't have to wait much longer. Lyndsey bent down to retrieve her purse. The cars floorboards were cold. She felt an empty crumpled up pack of cigarettes she had tossed there weeks ago. Her fingers touched a cardboard coffee cup, a plastic water bottle, and unidentified paper debris. Then her fingers touched her purse. A sharp object poked her when she wrapped her hand around the strap.

Ouch, that hurt!

The obsidian-black night was endless. Blindly, Lyndsey lay her purse on her lap and opened the clasp. As she felt inside, she recognized the shape of her pill bottle. She felt around for the matches and lit one. The small flame gave off enough light to see inside her purse. Lyndsey reached in to take out her pill bottle when she spotted Drake's note. She pulled it out. *Shit.* The match fizzled out burning the end of her finger. She lit another one and opened the folded piece of paper. Trembling, she began to read.

*Dear Lyndsey,*

*I love you. I have from the first moment I saw you. I gave you my heart, and you crushed it. As you fell further and further under the spell of drugs, I too, have fallen hard, under the spell of you. It scares me this spell. For I feel lost. I don't know who I am anymore. I do things I would never have imagined doing. The love I feel for you is making me ill. I don't like what I've become. I've given you my life, and we have both lived a tragedy. Together we are toxic. It sickens me, our fighting, arguing, your lying and stealing from me, and me making excuses for you. If we kept this up, we would become even more pathetic than we already are. I can see it now, me nursing you back to health so that you're strong enough to leave me and get high again. It's such a crazy game, and I'm losing my mind. That's why I must leave. I'm going away to get help. It's not only you that likes a few too many beers. I'm scared to death at what you're becoming and I pray one day you'll stand up and fight for your life as I'm now fighting for mine. I've left you enough money to cover the expenses we committed to. I hope you spend it wisely. But that's your problem now. Please don't contact me. I wish you well.*

*Drake*

The match burned down, and there was only blackness.

*Oh, my God.*

What had she done?

If only she'd said no to *more* her life would look very different right now. Lyndsey imagined what things might look like if she wasn't so messed up. She could be married by now, with two children and a dog. She would have other animals as well. Maybe a rabbit and a hamster, a cat and if she had enough land a horse. She'd always wanted a horse. Lyndsey would be happy, content even. It would be enough for her, and she would be good for her family. Her love wouldn't hurt them the way it did now. Lyndsey would be a loyal wife, a good mother, and a nice person. She would love her family unconditionally and feel immense satisfaction seeing their smiles. Lyndsey would get great joy in pleasing them. With such a beautiful family she would find her son and get him back.

Her son... Lyndsey's imaginary world broke apart.

Tears spilled down her face at the thought of her son and what could have been. Hope was painful. Lyndsey knew she would never have those things. That life was for somebody else. Someone who didn't come with a self-destruct button. No, this was her best option. Killing herself was the kindest thing she could do for everyone involved. Lyndsey didn't know what happened to you after you died, but just in case she whispered a small prayer.

*Please God, if I get the chance to come back, please make me a better person. Please make me kinder, and less selfish. Please make me pure and please don't let me use drugs. And God, if you can't do that, please allow my sleep to be eternal and never awake to cause harm again. Amen. Oh and another thing God, please let Drake find what he is looking for and most importantly please take care of my son. I give him to you to love and cherish, to be both mother and father too. Thank you and Amen.*

More at peace than she would have believed possible Lyndsey was ready to meet her maker. She lit another match and inventoried the contents of her pill bottle. Two Percocet, three yellow Valium, five sleeping pills, six Tylenol three and eight Advil. She wasn't sure if it would be enough. Just in case it wasn't, she put the pills back into the bottle and searched for the one more thing she would need. Lyndsey was almost never without it. Her fingers touched every square inch of her purse but couldn't find it. Frantic, she felt inside her purse again, but it wasn't there. The razor blade was missing. There was no way she could do the job right without it.

*Now what?*

Lyndsey remembered the sharp object on the car floor. It might work. She leaned over the seat and ran her fingers along the ground. Rocks and pebbles scattered at her touch bouncing off the car matt. So much dirt had accumulated since its last wash. Lyndsey felt the hard, sharp object and carefully picked it up mindful of its pointy edges.

Lyndsey lit another match and looked at the object in her hand. It was a beer bottle, her favorite brand. Dear God, she wished she had a beer right now. Lyndsey couldn't remember tossing the bottle, but then she couldn't remember much. The glass she held was the pointy sheared-off stump of the beer bottle.

The jagged *little edges* beckoned.

Her heart raced wildly.

Lyndsey opened the bottle of pills.

# CHAPTER FORTY-TWO

*Almost over, almost over, almost over, the mantra ran through her head.* Lyndsey choked down the pills. She chewed each one, knowing they would work quicker that way. The pills were bitter and hard to swallow. She remembered the plastic water bottle and reached down to grab it. The water was old and likely infused with bacteria, but it didn't matter. Lyndsey didn't have to worry about germs anymore.

Hysterical laughter broke from her lips. Lyndsey felt strangely giddy, relieved and scared all at the same time. She twisted the cap off the bottle and placed it to her lips. Watermelon wafted in the air. Only it was sour watermelon now. The fruit-flavored water had turned to vinegar. Lyndsey took a small sip anyway.

Bad idea. She gagged on the sour water. Saliva flooded her mouth. When her nausea passed, Lyndsey popped another pill in her mouth and chewed until there was nothing left but paste.

Each time she swallowed, she was closer to death. Lyndsey felt strangely indifferent at the thought. It was like she was removed from herself and reading a book. She had more empathy for the fictional character than she did herself.

Lyndsey wondered if she should write a note and felt another surge of panic. Why hadn't she thought of that before? What would she write and who would she write it to? Lyndsey started to compose one in her head. *Dear Blank*, she pictured her mom, her dad, and her sister, and what about Drake?

*Dear Mom and Dad,*

*By the time you get this note, I'll be dead. I'm not sure why I'm writing to you. I guess it's what one does in a situation like this. I wish I could think of something to say and the fact that I can't, really says it all.......* trailing off Lyndsey drew a blank.

Lyndsey had no words, and they had never heard her anyway. She decided to skip the note altogether. They would figure it out soon enough, and it wasn't like she had anything worthwhile to leave. She hoped her sister would take her car. Other than that she had nothing, nothing but a pile of bills and maxed out credit cards. Lyndsey hoped Drake didn't get stuck with those. Her debt wasn't his fault.

It was a sad way to end her life, but it would have been even sadder not to. Lyndsey hadn't wanted to live for a long time, trapped in a body where she was too sick to live, and too afraid to die.

With a sigh of relief, Lyndsey placed the last pill between her lips and held it there, trying to work up enough spit. She bit down, and bitterness coated her tongue. This time it didn't bother her at all. Lyndsey thought her mouth must be going numb and knew her body would soon follow.

A sudden craving for a cigarette had her pulling the ashtray open. Lyndsey fished around the ashes and grasped at the last remaining butt. She needed the kick of nicotine to help her with what came next. Lighting one of her last matches, Lyndsey took a long pull and blew out smoke. Then she picked up the piece of beer glass next to her. Slowly she sawed at her wrist. It didn't hurt that much. Feeling encouraged she cut deeper, slicing open flesh.

*Oh, that hurt!*

It was too soon. Lyndsey must wait longer, and let the pills do their job. She pulled the blanket tight around her.

*Are you there, God? Are you real? Please be real.*

Pictures of her life played behind closed eyes. They ran back and stopped when she was a child. Tears fell as she looked at the lonely little girl she'd been. This sweet baby never had a chance. She'd been born an anchor, to parents who didn't want her, and she spent her life searching for love. Lyndsey saw her little dog, Suzy. Her tail wagged back and forth as she spotted Lyndsey. For a moment Lyndsey thought Suzy was in the car with her. She felt Suzy's wet kisses and tongue on her hand. Or was it her tears? It didn't matter. Lyndsey pulled Suzy closer snuggling her warmth. Or was it the blanket? Lyndsey was getting confused. Her head rested on her hands, and she felt Suzy nestle in beside her. The little pup had come when she needed her most.

Drifting again, she knew it was time.

Lyndsey could barely keep her eyes open. With rubbery fingers, she picked up the glass and began to cut.

*Jagged little edges* sliced through her wrist. Warm blood ran down her hand. It was surprisingly comforting.

Her last conscious thought was of her son. He would be seven today. Lyndsey wrapped up all the love she had left in her dying body and sent it his way.

*I love you.*

*I love you.*

*I'm sorry.*

Her pulse weakened, and her breathing slowed.

As her hand opened the jagged piece of glass fell to the floor, and Lyndsey thought no more.

# Part Three

## Home Sweet Home

# CHAPTER FORTY-THREE

The little boy couldn't sleep, spying the kite in the corner of his room he giggled. He was supposed to wait for Mommy, but she was taking sooo long. His bedroom was growing lighter. The boy thought morning was close. Mommy had promised to take him to the park today, so that he could fly his new kite. It would fly high in the sky. The child giggled again imagining it. *Zoom, zoom, zoom.* It would go fast! He might even fly it to the moon!

The boy looked at his kite as he bounced on the bed. It was a big, red and yellow dragon. The first time he saw it in the store, he cried. But he had been a baby then, only six. Today he was seven, and he wasn't afraid of dragons anymore. He pestered Mommy until she gave in. And last night she let him open it early before his special day.

Thinking of his special day brought on another round of giggles. The boy bounced even higher. Oh sure, he wasn't supposed to bounce on his bed, but he thought it would probably be okay because this wasn't *his* bed. It was Aunt Sally's. They were staying with Aunt Sally for a few days while Daddy was away on business. But Daddy was coming back today, and Mommy was making him a Spiderman Cake. The little boy wasn't sure who he liked more, Spiderman or dragons. Maybe he could have both?

The boy jumped from his bed and ran into the kitchen. "Mommy, can we go to the park now?"

"Breakfast first, my little man, then the park," Mommy said with a smile and began to sing. "Happy birthday to you. Happy birthday to you. Happy birthday my sweet little prince. Happy birthday to you."

"Mommy, you're silly. I'm not a prince!"

He liked it when Mommy sang. Mommy made his favorite breakfast, French toast with whipped cream and strawberries and when he finished eating, they left for the park. The child hoped it would be the right kind of park. It couldn't have too many trees or he wouldn't be able to fly his kite.

Mommy held his hand as they walked. She said the park wasn't far from Aunt Sally's house. He wasn't sure if big boys still held their Mommy's hand, but he let it go for the time being. Besides, he liked holding Mommy's hand, as long as no one was looking of course.

Luckily, it was still windy. The little boy worried that the wind would stop. It was windy last night, and the tree branches scratching on Aunt Sally's window scared him. The child feared it was a scary monster scratching on the window, but Mommy said it was just tree branches. So he stopped being scared and went to sleep. The wind sure didn't scare him now. The little boy leaned into it; he liked the way it felt on his skin.

When he saw the park, he stopped mid-skip. It was just right! It didn't have a lot of trees, and there was a playground with swings and a slide. It even had monkey bars. He loved monkey bars! Mommy said it was cuz he was such a little monkey. But he wasn't a monkey. Mommy was just silly. Next to the playground was a big open field. And it was just perfect for flying kites! The child opened his arms wide. It was going to be a great day!

Mommy helped him set up the kite for its first flight. She showed him how to check that the strings were on good and how to run with the kite so the wind could catch it and fly it off the ground. He watched as his Mommy made it fly high, high up in the sky. The dragon looked down at him and he giggled again.

"My turn, Mommy! My turn!"

Mommy handed him the strings. He held them just like she did. The boy ran as fast as he could. The kite begins to lift off and then it was up, up, and away! The child laughed and shouted with excitement as he flew his kite.

A big gust of wind came out of nowhere and tugged so hard he lost his grip on the string. His kite sailed through the air and landed in a tree with a car parked under it. Tears welled in his eyes, and he rubbed them away. He didn't think big boys should cry, but one got loose anyway.

Mommy hugged him. "Sweetie, don't worry we'll get it back for you."

They walked over to the tree, and Mommy pulled on the tail of the kite, trying to loosen it. The little boy stood near the car hoping his Mommy could get the kite down. He looked over at the car wondering if he could climb up on it and help Mommy reach his kite. The car looked empty. The boy moved closer and looked inside. It wasn't empty. Something was in the back seat. It was a big lump with hair the same color as his. The little boy thought the bump was a lady. He wondered why she was sleeping in the car and who had colored her red.

"Mommy, Mommy, look at the lady!"

"Just a minute love, I've almost got it," Mommy said, giving the kite tail a ferocious pull.

"Mommy, look! Somebody colored the lady all red! Isn't that silly?"

Mommy came over to the car and looked inside. Her face went white and her eyes looked funny. "Oh my God!"

Mommy pounded on the window, but the lady didn't wake up. Mommy picked him up and began to run.

"Mommy? My kite! Mommy! Where are we going?"

The child bounced up and down in his mother's arms as she ran. Mommy ran fast! "We're going to get help." She said in a huffy voice.

The little boy thought Mommy was funny and he giggled again.

# CHAPTER FORTY-FOUR

Lyndsey came too in a cacophony of strange noises. More like screeches really, followed by moans and wailing. Everything was black. So she was in hell then. Her throat was sore. But that wasn't the worst of it. Her stomach felt bruised like someone had used it for a punching bag. Her severed wrist hurt. Lyndsey tried to move it but couldn't. She couldn't move at all.

"Wake up sleeping beauty."

"Hmm."

"Wake up!"

Someone pushed on her arm. Lyndsey retreated into darkness. A sharp sting brought her back. Lyndsey opened sand-encrusted eyes to see a nurse drawing blood from her arm. "Where am I?" She croaked.

"You're in the hospital. The doctor will be by shortly to speak with you."

"What happened? Why am I here?"

"The doctor will be here soon." Without any other explanation, the nurse gathered her vials and left.

Lyndsey wore a dark blue hospital gown. Her wrist wrapped in a thick gauze bandage and there was an IV inserted in her uninjured hand. Lyndsey's teeth felt furry, and her mouth was dry.

The room she was in was small. The walls were curtains, and they were pulled tightly closed. Through the crack in the curtain,

Lyndsey saw a chair. A man sat in it. His scrubs were lighter in color than the ones she wore. The man stared at her curtain and Lyndsey looked away.

"Ahh!" Someone moaned from nearby.

Where in the hell am I? Lyndsey inched off the bed and felt a stabbing pain in her bladder. She pulled the sheet back she looked down. A clear tube inserted in her vagina ran down her leg and over the side of the bed. The tube was attached to a plastic bag with urine in it.

Was this really a hospital? "Excuse me," she called to the man outside her curtain.

The man just sat there as if made from stone. He never bothered to look up.

"Excuse me!" Lyndsey tried again.

Nothing, he didn't move a muscle. Maybe he was deaf.

The moaning stopped, and someone shrieked. "Please help me!" More voices joined in. One woman made bird noises. "Tweet, tweet!" A man with a low voice called for his Mom. Someone grunted as if they were sitting on the toilet. Lyndsey chewed her knuckle. The background noise was pure crazy. Like a lunatic lullaby from the soundtrack of insanity. Lyndsey was in the land of the shattered and broken.

She needed to get out of here. Lyndsey pulled her gown up and tugged on the tube. Ouch! She quickly abandoned the idea of pulling it out. Maybe she could take the bag with her, but what about the IV in her arm? And what was in the IV? Was she on drugs? Was she hallucinating?

"Hey!" She tried again, yelling at the statue sitting on the chair. Still nothing, but she had seen him move. Just briefly, but at least she knew he could hear her.

*Was she in prison? Why did she have a guard? Where am I!?*

The curtains closed in on her. Lyndsey pulled her hair and screamed. "Someone please help me! Please, I need help! Someone help me! Someone! Help! Me!"

In a full-blown panic, she wreathed on the bed. A nurse opened the curtains and stepped into her room.

Without a word, the nurse inserted a needle into the IV at her bedside.

Lyndsey's hand burned, and coldness ran up her arm.

Then everything went black.

# CHAPTER FORTY-FIVE

Her eyes were heavy. Lyndsey was having troubles opening them. She felt sluggish and lethargic. Lyndsey rubbed her eyes and wondered where she was. Her mouth tasted awful. Like someone had used it for their toilet.

Lyndsey was in a different room. This room was white, and so was everything in it. She lay on a white, plastic covered lumpy mattress on the floor. The walls were padded with thick foam. The blanket covering her was the only thing that wasn't white. It was off-white and the small, hard pillow her head rested on was white with a rust colored stain. The only thing of any real color was the funny looking toilet standing alone in the corner of the room. It was silver stainless steel, and it looked like it was molded, with no corner edges, just rounds. And it didn't have a toilet seat.

Lyndsey still wore her dark blue gown, but this time she had no tubes attached to her. Someone must have taken them out while she slept. The thought of being violated sent fear racing through her.

Lyndsey got up off the mattress and wobbled. She was shaky and weak as a newborn kitten. The only door held a small window, and she peered out of it. There was a hallway outside her door. It was wide and shiny and looked very clean.

"Hello?" She called out to the empty hallway. Her guard was nowhere around. "Hello?" Had she been abducted? Why? Who would want her?

Her stomach rumbled, and she pressed her legs tightly together. Her bladder was ready to burst. Lyndsey eyed the strange looking toilet. Urgency outweighed modesty as she squatted above it, not wanting it to touch her bare skin. When she finished, Lyndsey couldn't find the flush handle. What kind of toilet was this? Who made toilets you couldn't flush? Christ almighty, where in the hell was she?

There was nothing in the room to wash her hands with so she rubbed them on her scrubs. Lyndsey paced back and forth as she tried to figure out what to do. The thought of the un-flushed toilet bothered her. She didn't like the idea of her bodily waste on exhibit for all to see.

Her stomach rumbled again. Lyndsey couldn't remember the last time she had anything to eat. All she remembered was sitting in the back seat of her car. She remembered swallowing the pills and cutting her wrist. And then warmth. After the initial cut, she stopped experiencing pain, and a floaty-feeling came over her as if she was drifting on a tranquil sea.

Well, she was back from her sea voyage. This crazy-house was as far from tranquility as you could get. Determined to get some answers, Lyndsey strode over to the door.

Lyndsey pounded on the thick steel door. "Hey! Hello! Is anybody home?"

Where was everyone? Lyndsey banged on the door with her good hand. The hard steel bruised her knuckles.

Lyndsey looked through the little window again. Could she break it? Even if she could would she fit through it? Lyndsey pictured herself stuck, hanging half in and half out of the window.

Maybe she could jimmy the door? Lyndsey looked at the doorknob. It was steel, and when she pulled on it there was no give. Where in the hell was her purse? Christ, she needed a cigarette!

Too tired to stand she sat on her mattress. Shivering with anxiety Lyndsey chewed her cuticle. The scream built inside, gaining power. It crawled up her throat, and she couldn't keep it in.

Lyndsey opened her mouth. "Please Help Me. I don't know where I am!"

She screamed until her throat was raw. She screamed until she cried.

Lyndsey lay huddled and broken on her lumpy plastic mattress. Her chest heaved, and her throat labored to swallow. Her body hitched with intense emotion. Her sobs slowed, and her anger returned.

This time her scream was raw and gritty.

Lyndsey screamed until she was mute.

# CHAPTER FORTY-SIX

All the ruckus hurt her ears. The people's whines and wails were annoying, and the only relief she got from the noise was when a nurse walked by and closed the door.

Soft footsteps approached Lyndsey's bed, and she wiped her face hoping to hide the tears.

"Lyndsey, I'm Dr. Murphy."

She couldn't look. Lyndsey stared at the wall as tension coiled inside her body. Bracing for what she might see, she forced herself to turn around. He was standing next to her mattress on the floor, and to her surprise, he asked: "mind if I join you?"

Before she could answer, he plopped himself down beside her. He didn't look old enough to be a doctor. His hair was long, and he wore jeans below his white lab coat. He didn't seem nearly as threatening sitting, as he had standing.

"You're not a doctor."

"I assure you I am. At least that's what the physician's board of medicine says. I'll be your doctor during your stay with us."

Lyndsey eyed him suspiciously. *What did he want? Was this a trick?* "I don't need a doctor. My arm is healing nicely."

"Well, that's good because I don't fix arms. Lyndsey, I'm not *that* kind of doctor." He said with a small, sad smile.

"Well, what kind of doctor are you? Where am I?" Lyndsey's voice quaked and to her horror tears began to fall. She swiped furiously at her eyes.

"I'm a psychiatrist, and you're in the hospital." Dr. Murphy answered, with the same sad smile.

Maybe he didn't like his job? Lyndsey wondered what had made the doctor so sad. But she didn't wonder long. As his words sank in, she bristled.

"I don't need a shrink! I'm not crazy! I want to go home!" The last word *home* caused her eyes to well up again. Shit, home? She didn't have one anymore. Where would she go?

"No one said you're crazy, Lyndsey. But healthy, well-adjusted people do not try and end their lives by swallowing a lethal dose of pills and cutting their wrist." Dr. Murphy's tone was gentle.

Lyndsey blinked back tears and remained silent.

Dr. Murphy shook his head. "Do you remember arriving at the hospital?"

"No."

"You were very close to death. We pumped your stomach, and you received two units of blood." Dr. Murphy shook his head again. "You got here in the nick of time."

"How did I get here?"

"You were brought in by ambulance. Someone saw you, a little boy actually, who told his mother."

"Yeah? Well, maybe I didn't want to be lucky." Lyndsey glared at the doctor angry to be woken from eternal sleep.

Dr. Murphy squared his shoulder. "Yeah? And that's why I'm here."

"What?" Dr. Murphy wasn't making sense.

"Lyndsey, do you know how many people get a second chance in life, like the one you've just gotten?" The sad smile was gone. Dr. Murphey's face wore an inquisitive look.

"What are you talking about?" Dr. Murphy made her head hurt. He was the crazy one not her.

"Think about it. You've just done your best to kill yourself, and by all means, that should have happened. Another thirty minutes and it would have. The question you should be asking yourself is why you're still alive."

Wow! And this guy claims to be a doctor? It didn't take a rocket scientist to figure it out. "I'm alive because some busybody wanted to play hero and called 911. Hello! Are you sure you're a doctor?"

"I'm sure, bear with me. Do you know the ambulance received the call for you at six thirty a.m.?"

"So what does that have to do with it?" She looked at him her brow wrinkled in frustration.

"Why would a mother and her son be in the park that early in the morning?"

"Who cares?"

He took a breath and continued. "Not only that, these two were from out of town. Had they been at home they wouldn't have found you, and we wouldn't be having this conversation."

"I still don't get it?"

"Well, maybe you were *supposed* to be found. Did you ever think there's something planned for you, something greater than you ever imagined?"

"Yeah and maybe pigs fly, too?" Lyndsey snorted.

"Well maybe they do, and we just can't see them." He was smiling now as if he had said something funny.

But Lyndsey wasn't laughing. "Wow, you're about the craziest person I've ever met. I can see why you're a psychiatrist. You must be your best patient."

"Okay, I'll try and simplify this for you. You tried to kill yourself and -"

Lyndsey broke in. "I didn't try and kill myself. I just wanted to go to sleep and not wake up."

He took another breath and began again. "Okay, you wanted to go to sleep and not wake up, which, in clinical terms, we call committing suicide or trying to take one's own life." He poked his tongue in his cheek making a bulge on one side of his face, deep in thought. After a moment he continued. "And because of divine intervention you didn't die, now I'm going to ask you to try and open your mind, just a little." Dr. Murphey's eyebrows drew together over his soft brown eyes.

Lyndsey stared at him wondering what he meant.

"Think about it, a family from out of town who just happens to be at the park in the dawn hours of early morning. That's by no means usual. In fact, I would say it's very unusual indeed. It gets even stranger because it was a very special day for the little boy who first saw you. They wouldn't even have been at the park unless it had been that particular day."

Sensing something strange beginning in her body, she almost whispered her next words. "What was so special about the little boy's day?"

Dr. Murphy replied. "It was his seventh birthday."

# CHAPTER FORTY-SEVEN

"You couldn't know that!" Lyndsey shouted. What the hell was this guy doing, messing with her head this way?

"I only know because I just got off the phone with the mother of the little boy."

"You're so full of shit! Why would she be calling you?"

"Because, believe it or not, Lyndsey, she cares."

Wow, this guy was off his rocker. Thinking a complete stranger could care about her. What world did he come from? "Listen, I don't know who you think you are, but why don't you crawl back under the rock you just came out from and leave me the fuck alone!" Lyndsey's face was red with anger.

Dr. Murphy just looked at her. The small, sad smile was back. "She called because she was concerned and wanted to know if you were okay."

"Yeah right, as if she cares about me after I ruined her kid's birthday with my bloodbath!"

"He didn't know it was blood. He thought you were sleeping and someone had colored you red. His mother says he's fine. In fact, he wants to draw you a picture."

"Well, I don't want it. I don't even have a fucking wall to hang it on. Now please leave me alone." She turned her back on him, wanting nothing more than to go to sleep. Her body curled into a tight little ball.

Dr. Murphey stared at her and scratched his head.

Lyndsey pleaded. "I don't want you here. Would you *please* go away."

Dr. Murphy nodded. "I'm going to prescribe something to help you sleep. The nurse will be by with it shortly. The orderly should be bringing your dinner soon. After dinner, I want you to rest. I'll be back tomorrow. We can talk more then."

She listened to his footsteps as they faded away. Oh, my God. It couldn't be, but still, oh my God, even if it wasn't. It was still a little boy on his seventh birthday. Dr. Murphy had been right about one thing. What were the odds of that ever happening and why had it?

So he was a psychiatrist. And she was in the looney-bin. Why was she here? She wasn't crazy! What was she going to do? She had no home, no job, no money, no family, no Drake, no hope, no *more*. No *more*!

A sudden craving hit. Lyndsey's mouth watered and her heartbeat accelerated. Oh, what she wouldn't give to have some right now! She didn't have any money, but maybe someone here did? She could always check a few pockets and see what she could find. Well, that was if she ever got out this locked room.

Right then keys rattle outside her door. Lyndsey turned and watched it open. An old orderly carried a tray carefully into her room. He placed it on the ground next to the mattress she sat on. He wore grey scrubs with white runners. The white of the runners matched the white of his hair. Lyndsey thought the man was too old to be working. The orderly's shoulder stooped from age or life, and his face was wrinkled. He flashed a crinkly smile at Lyndsey, and his whole face moved.

The old orderly left his keys hanging in the door. Lyndsey thought about pushing him out of the way and locking him in her room. Lyndsey wondered if the keys would get her out of the building. She looked at him again. He grinned at her and turned back to the door.

The orderly retraced his steps and pulled the keys free from the lock. Maybe he had read her mind? He clipped the keys on his belt and sat cross-legged on the floor next to her. His knees creaked as he lowered himself to the ground. The orderly pulled the cover off her food. It looked pretty tasty. The dinner tray held the chicken, mashed potatoes, carrots, and peas. There was a paper napkin on the plate and a cardboard cup of milk. Lyndsey took a sip. It was a little warm. Not a fan of warm milk, she put it down.

The orderly took a final look at her. He appeared satisfied with what he saw. He stood up and said he would be back later for her plate. She watched him retreat, taking the precious keys with him. If he hadn't smiled at her just then, she thought she could have done it. She would have pushed him hard and ran past him before he could get up. By the time he was on his feet, Lyndsey figured she'd have the door locked and the keys in her possession.

But even if she got free, where would she go? And what would she wear? She didn't think the blue hospital gown was appropriate. The gown clearly stated she was from the land of no return. If anyone saw her fleeing the building wearing it, they would stop her.

Her dinner smelled good. Lyndsey was hungry. She wanted

to dig in, but something was missing. She couldn't see a fork or knife. What the hell was she supposed to eat with? It took her a moment to figure it out, and she hadn't done it consciously. Lyndsey picked up a piece of chicken and nibbled on it still wondering where the utensils were when it occurred to her she'd found the answer.

Lyndsey ate every crumb. She thought about licking the plate but decided against it. The milk was tepid, but she finished that off too. Besides, she wasn't sure where her next meal would come from. Wasting anything would be foolish.

With a full stomach, her cravings eased. Lyndsey pushed the tray aside using the napkin to clean her fingers. She ran her hands through her hair. It was stringy and greasy and lay in a tangled mass down her back. With her fingers as her comb, Lyndsey pulled through the snarls freeing up the worst of the knots.

The door opened, and this time two people entered her room. Jesus, she was having a regular party. The old orderly was back. He bent down scooped up her tray and said, "Good job!"

Lyndsey felt like she was in third grade again. It was the same feeling. Like you did something right, and you were important. Only now she knew better. Lyndsey frowned at the old guy not fooled by his sweet nature.

The orderly took her tray and left leaving her alone with the nurse. The nurse placed a cuff around Lyndsey's bicep and squeezed. Lyndsey never bothered to ask the nurse her name and the nurse didn't mention it either. The nurse murmured "good" and wrote something down on the sheet of paper attached to her clipboard. Then she changed Lyndsey's bandaged wrist.

With the wrapping off Lyndsey got her first look at the damage she'd inflicted upon herself. She counted the stitches running up her arm.

The nurse looked at her. "You're lucky. They're healing nicely." The nurse looked tired. She had dark pouches under her eyes, and she spoke in clipped sentences.

Lyndsey felt exposed. Like everyone knew her ugly little secret. She was sure the nurse was angry. Was it because she tried to take her own life? Why did people care? Lyndsey stared at the floor with hair hanging in her eyes wishing she could disappear.

"Here are the sleeping pills the doctor ordered for you." The nurse pushed a Dixie cup in Lyndsey's direction. Inside were two little tablets.

Lyndsey swallowed the tablets gladly, wanting nothing more than sleep.

The nurse paused at the door. "The doctor will be back in the morning. He'll decide what's to be done with you then. Have a good rest. Good night."

When Lyndsey was certain the door was closed, and she was alone, she used the weird looking toilet. Somehow it had flushed itself. There was nothing but clear water in the bowl. Lyndsey crawled into bed pondering the strange phenomenon. The plastic crinkled under her body and she wondered how many other crazy people had slept here.

Crazy people like she, tortured demonized human lumps of flesh. It wasn't a very comforting thought. She didn't have to worry though, the sleeping pills kicked in and slowed her thoughts. Lyndsey struggled against it. She felt overly sedated but was no match for the pharmaceutical knock-outs.

Lyndsey was out.

# CHAPTER FORTY-EIGHT

The squeak of a shoe hitting the floor woke her. The cuff circled her arm again. "Go away." Lyndsey rasped, her throat sore.

It was dark, and she was angry at being woken up.

The nurse deflated the cuff and removed it from Lyndsey's arm. Lyndsey's had a headache, her head was thick, and she felt woozy. Her tongue felt like sandpaper.

The nurse moved away from her bed and left the room. Lyndsey could just make out her back as she retreated.

Feeling tired and groggy it wasn't long until she was fast asleep once more.

The next time Lyndsey woke up it was daylight. Her hospital room was bright with light, and she was miserable. Thick headed, dry-mouthed, sore-eyed, achy, and pissed. Lyndsey was itching for a fight.

With no watch and no clock on the wall, Lyndsey had no way of knowing what time it was. She stared at the white walls hoping this was her last day here.

Keys turned in the lock, and the door creaked open. The old orderly stood in the entrance. He pulled the keys free before stepping into the room. In his hands was her breakfast.

He walked over to her and carefully lowered the tray.

Lyndsey's stomach rumbled betraying her indifference. With knobby fingers, the orderly lifted the lid on the tray exposing a hardboiled egg, toast, banana, and a paper cup of orange juice.

The orderly's wrinkled face beamed and he offered up a cheery, "Good morning to you."

Lyndsey rubbed the sleep from her face, looked up at him and asked. "What's so good about it?"

The old man looked surprised by her question. "Why it's a new day. A new start! It doesn't get any better than that."

Lyndsey picked up her toast and chewed. It was warm and buttery. The toast was delicious! Funny, she couldn't remember toast tasting quite this good before. Lyndsey looked at the orderly ready to give him hell, but the sight of his kind face changed her mind. Instead, she asked. "Aren't you a little old to work here?"

The orderly through back his head and laughed. His laughter was loud, youthful and infectious. Before long, Lyndsey was smiling too. At what, she couldn't say.

The orderly wiped tears from his eyes and slapped his knee. Then he looked her square in the eye. "You couldn't keep me from this. It's what gets me out of bed in the morning. I would do it for free, but my boss insists on paying me."

"Why do you want to work here?" Lyndsey waved at the white walls. "Doesn't your work with crazies put you in danger?"

"These crazies, as you call them, were me. I was in and out of here more times than I can count." The orderly shrugged. "This was my second home, my first being on the streets."

"What?" Lyndsey hadn't expected that! She was shocked this kind old man had once been insane and lived on the streets.

"It was pretty bad." The old man rubbed his stomach. "My body was failing, my liver shutting down and the docs didn't think I'd make it. One doctor even sent a priest in to see me. The priest read me my last rites."

"Wow!" Lyndsey couldn't believe it. "So you almost died?"

"Yep. I was pickled. I drank anything I could get, cooking sherry, cheap wine, hand sanitizer, rubbing alcohol. It didn't matter what it was. If there was alcohol in it, I drank it. I don't think I had a sober minute in over ten years." The orderly shook his head at his tragic tale.

"Ewe! Hand sanitizer and rubbing alcohol? Why did you drink that? I mean that's pretty gross!"

"Why do any of us do what we do?" The orderly shrugged. "Something is missing in us. A hole, I guess you could say, and we fill our bodies with whatever takes the pain away. The trouble is, it only lasts for a little while then we have to go and do it all over again."

Lynsey shook her head. "I just can't see you living on the streets or drinking those things."

The orderly chuckled. "Whether you can see it or not, that's what I did, and it should have killed me. I might not have cut my wrist but make no mistake, me drinking poison was the same thing. When the priest came to see me, I was glad. I was happy to be going home at long last. I was tired of living, and I wanted nothing more than to go to sleep. I wasn't afraid to die. I welcomed it."

"Me too!" Lyndsey exclaimed. "That's how I felt."

The orderly looked at her and nodded. "I know the feeling.

When the priest told me all my sins would be forgiven if I asked God for forgiveness, I thought, okay I have nothing to lose here. I prayed for forgiveness and got ready to die. But it didn't play out that way. Instead, to my surprise, I woke up the next morning. It was me, but it wasn't. I felt different somehow. Like something had changed in me that was beyond my comprehension, but none the less it *had* changed. I knew it. I could feel it."

Lyndsey propped an elbow on her knee and asked. "What do think happened to you?"

"I don't think I'm meant to figure it out." One shaggy grey eyebrow arched high. "The best I can come up with is what the priest told me."

The orderly's story piqued her interest. She'd never met anyone like him before, and Lyndsey felt a bond with the old guy. It was something she hadn't felt in a long while. "What did the priest say to you?"

"Well. The priest said the likelihood of me living were very slim. My liver was end-stage cirrhosis, and the doctors figured I only had days left. But, if by chance I was one of the slim few who pulled through, then my life would be governed by a different purpose."

"What does that mean?"

"I believe what the priest meant was instead of serving the bottle; I'd serve humanity.

"You mean you'd be a slave? Why would you want to do that?"

"No, not like a slave at all. That's what I'd been." The

orderly cleared his throat. "I was indentured to my thirst. It controlled my life, took everything I loved and tried to kill me. I befriended the devil and prayed to die. The only way you win against the devil is through God and service work. I help others such as yourself. Helping you helps me. That's where I find freedom and peace of mind."

Lyndsey shook her head. "That doesn't make any sense."

"It doesn't have too." The orderly argued. "It just works. I can't explain this to you. It's something you'll have to feel for yourself. I only know when I talk with you and the others who are here, it fills me up in a way the bottle never could. I'm at peace, I'm content, and I'm happy. So you see, it's never too late." The old guy smiled a big smile, and it shone right through his eyes.

Something shifted in Lyndsey. Like a gust of strong wind blew all the ugliness from her heart and new possibilities appeared. Lyndsey's eyes welled up. There were a million questions she wanted to ask the orderly, yet she was still cynical. Torn, Lyndsey thought the orderly was full of shit, yet she also believed him. Her head and heart warred, and she felt unsettled.

The orderly bent to pick up her tray. He looked at her sincerely. "Good luck. I believe in you. I know you can are destined for great things. And one day you'll know it, too."

It was weird watching him leave. The orderly was dignified. Lyndsey almost asked him to stay. She enjoyed talking with him. However, asking him to stay behind and keep her company would imply she needed him. So instead of asking him to stay, Lyndsey watched him go. The orderly turned in the doorway, a grin lighting up his face. The old guy was sure sweet. And he had something elusive, Lyndsey couldn't quite put her finger on it. It was warm, and happy and alive. The word came to her then, and it was a perfect fit.

Hope.

The old guy had hope, and somehow a little of it had rubbed off on her.

His smile brightened the room long after his departure.

Thoughts flew through her mind, and Lyndsey was overwhelmed. She'd never heard a story like his before. Lyndsey wondered how the orderly had found the courage to face his demons.

Hers were strong. Lyndsey had never believed she stood a chance against them. She viewed herself as weak, not good enough and not worthy.

The old guy was a lot stronger than she was, that's for sure. Lyndsey couldn't see herself serving humanity like he had chosen to do. It was just the opposite. She didn't like people. Or at least, she didn't feel comfortable around them.

The only time Lyndsey enjoyed socializing was when she was high. High, she loved everyone. High, she felt connected to people. High, she was on top of the world.

And yet she wasn't high now.

The orderly had awakened something in her.

Lyndsey felt confused. The sweet glow of moments before shifted and grew dark.

Why would a complete stranger bare his soul to her? What did he want from her? Was he laughing at her behind her back?

Was he messing with her head?

Lyndsey eyed the closed door suspiciously. She wanted answers. *Now.*

Anger brought her to her feet. She's been a fool to listen to him. Not able to sit still Lyndsey paced. Eight steps one way, then ten the next.

Someone was at the door.

Lyndsey tensed, ready for whoever was on the other side.

# CHAPTER FORTY-NINE

Lyndsey's fists clenched as Dr. Murphy stepped over the doorway and nodded.

Not bothering with niceties she blurted. "I want out of here right now!" Lyndsey stood inches from the doctor's face. She refused to be held hostage one more minute. Her temperament was ugly.

"You are free to go." Dr. Murphy side-stepped her gaining a foot of personal space. "I can't keep you here any longer than today. But before you go, I'd like to discuss your plans." Dr. Murphy's tone was gentle. Perhaps he was unaware Lyndsey was ready to explode.

"Seriously?" Lyndsey's voice rose. "My plans are none of your business!" Her eyebrows drew down, and her lips narrowed. Lyndsey stepped into Dr. Murphy's personal space again, giving him a hard stare.

"That's where you're wrong, Lyndsey." Dr. Murphy took two steps back. "You *are* my business. You made me your business when you decided to take your life. Now it's my responsibility to know your plans, and help you improve on them if possible."

"I don't want you to know my plans!" Lyndsey didn't even know here plans! She stalled for time. "What if you don't like them? Will I still be able to leave?"

"First, I must be certain you won't harm yourself, or anyone else for that matter, before we talk farther."

"What do you mean?"

"Well," Dr. Murphy looked up at the ceiling and gathered his thoughts. "Lyndsey, are you open to the idea of getting help for yourself?" He gave her a piercing look as if his stare could unfold the great mysteries of her mind.

"You didn't answer my question." Lyndsey returned the stare.

"What question?"

"If you don't like my answer will I still be able to leave?"

"Let me ask you again. Are you planning on harming yourself? Do you feel suicidal now or are you planning suicide?"

Lyndsey took a risk. "I never really wanted to die. It's just that…" She stammered. "It's just I don't know how to live." *Oh man, she wasn't getting this right at all.* "I mean, of course, I know how to breathe and eat and all the basic things but I don't know how to *live*. It's difficult to make you understand when it feels so confusing to me."

Dr. Murphy harrumphed, scratched his head, and looked at her blankly.

Lyndsey looked at him hard trying to judge the harrumph, and then decided he was clearing his throat. She began again. "It's like when I want something badly, and then I get it, for a little while life is good and then it's not anymore. I do something to ruin it. Then I wish I never ruined it and I can't understand why I did. It's like there are two of me. One is kind and loving and the other, well, she's an evil bitch."

"That's good, Lyndsey, keep going." Dr. Murphy

encouraged, his lips lifting in an inviting smile.

Lyndsey paused for a moment then began again. "I can feel it you know. The loving, caring person feels calm, and her heart is full. She wants to be around people she loves, and spend time with them, talking or going for walks. Maybe even watching movies and cuddling. Then it's like pressure builds and instead of loving, I get critical. I start finding faults with everyone. Like the way they talk or how they eat or what they wear. It's stupid. But at the time it takes over, and before you know it, I'm trying to get away from them."

"And then what happens?" Dr. Murphy queried.

"Well, it starts getting pretty bad then." Lyndsey shrugged. "It's like the affection I feel turns into something else, and once that happens, the only thing I want to do is to get high. I usually go to the bar where I run into someone I know, and I end up partying for days."

"For days?" Dr. Murphy clarified.

"Yep." Lyndsey nodded.

"Okay. And how do you feel then?"

"A little crazy because here's the bizarre thing, whenever I go to the bar I tell myself I'm just going out for a little while. I mean it. I really do. You could strap me to lie detector when I say it, and you would see I'm telling the truth. Then somehow, days go by, and it's like I haven't noticed. I'm high, and I can't leave. Sometimes my head will say *go,* but my body refuses to obey."

"Does that worry you?" Dr. Murphy asked.

"Yes, a little." Lyndsey replied honestly, "but then my mind tells me not to worry and that it won't happen again."

"Hmm." Dr. Murphy murmured and scratched at his chin.

"You're not going to keep me here are you?"

"You still haven't answered my question. What are your plans?"

"I'm not planning on hurting myself again if that's what you mean. I don't have anything in concrete. I was going to swing by the bar where I work and see if I still had my job and then, I guess I'll go from there."

"What do you think might happen if you *swing by the bar* as you put it?"

"I haven't gotten that far. I don't know, but I hope I still have a job and that I can come up with enough money to get a cheap room tonight."

"And what if you can't?" Dr. Murphy countered.

"I don't have a plan B," Lyndsey admitted.

"Well here's an idea for you, how about if we skip the bar for the moment and I offer you a better plan." Dr. Murphey's brown eyes went wide.

Lyndsey figured she didn't have much to lose by listening. The doctor might let her leave if she appeared willing to go along with his plan, whatever that was. Then again, maybe he was pretending to care so he could set her up? But why would he do that? Lyndsey couldn't figure out which way to go so she went with her gut. "What's your plan?"

Dr. Murphey's eyes lit up. "My plan is for you to enter a dual-diagnosis residential
inpatient treatment program. The length of stay is open-ended

and individual, meaning you'll be there until you're well enough to live successfully off campus. You will learn a lot about yourself. Lyndsey, you deserve to be well. Group therapy will help you develop a healthy relationship with your feelings and function more successfully in life."

Lyndsey shook her head. "I don't have the money for that."

"Don't worry about that." Dr. Murphey placed his hand on Lyndsey's shoulder. "I know the CEO of this program and believe you'll qualify for the grant. They have scholarship monies to fund cases just like yours. Think about it. You'll have a roof over your head, three meals a day, and a warm bed. And most importantly, you'll be surrounded by people who understand you."

Lyndsey smiled, hiding her true feelings. "I think I'll check out the bar first thanks. If I can't get my job back, I'll get back to you."

"I don't think that will work. You've passed the point where you can predict what might happen. If you leave today and do things your way, your future might be nonexistent. I don't want to see that happen for you."

Shit, she could see where this was heading. Lyndsey was pretty sure if she said no then he wouldn't let her leave. So she studied him for a time, trying to figure out what she should do.

"Can you give me a few minutes to think about it?" Lyndsey asked.

"What's to figure out, Lyndsey? On the one hand, you have life, on the other, death. Which hand do you choose?"

Oh God, he was all serious now. It had been a trap. Lyndsey thought Dr. Murphy looked mad. She didn't want him to be mad. If he was angry, he might keep her here. Lyndsey wanted out. And maybe a cigarette, and if she was honest, what she wanted most of all, was *more* and she knew exactly where to get it.

So instead of arguing with the doctor Lyndsey opened her mouth and surprised him. "Yes, I'll go," Lyndsey answered in a quiet voice, hanging her head low so he couldn't see her eyes.

"Great!" Dr. Murphy smiled wide. "I'll go make the arrangements and be back with your belongings!" Dr. Murphy bounced out of the room, his shoulders high.

Lyndsey lifted her head and watched him go.

A smile lifted her lips, and she grinned.

It was too easy; manipulating people was a skill every addict was good at.

Dr. Murphy may have thought she held her head lowered in shame. But that wasn't it at all. Lyndsey hid her head because she didn't want the keen doctor to see her truth.

And the truth was no way was she going to treatment!

But she would take the ride. Then she'd ditch the driver and be high before nightfall.

Going to treatment was most definitely *not* on her list of things to do today.

No way was she was going.

No chance in hell.

# CHAPTER FIFTY

A new orderly brought in Lyndsey's lunch. This one was young and silent. He dropped the tray beside her and left without a word. As she ate lunch and waited for the doctor's return, Lyndsey was relieved. She didn't want to lie to the old guy. Telling him she was off to treatment didn't feel right and she suspected he would know she was lying. Lyndsey felt protective of her new friend and didn't want to hurt him.

Sitting still was hard. Lyndsey wished she could run off the nervous energy she felt. Lyndsey hoped Dan wouldn't be mad at her. He had a hard time keeping employees and she was a hard worker. Hopefully, that would work in her favor.

Once she was in the bar, Lyndsey figured she could call her dealer and front a half gram until later that night.

Where was doctor Murphy? He was taking forever! Lyndsey looked at the remains of her lunch. She'd eaten most of her chicken noodle soup, only the crusts remained of the tuna fish sandwich, and there was a wrapped package of oatmeal cookies. Lyndsey put the cookies under her sheet. She was full but might want them later.

Finally! The jingle of keys alerted her to a new arrival. The smile slid from Lyndsey's face as she noted it wasn't Dr. Murphy but two male nurses who stood in the doorway. The oldest nurse carried a clipboard and the younger one a white plastic bag.

The older one introduced himself as George. He handed Lyndsey the clipboard and explained the paperwork she was reading. George said she was being discharged into the care of the treatment facility and the paper she signed, gave Dr. Murphy permission to share information regarding her case.

Lyndsey read the rest and looked at George. "What information is being shared with the treatment facility?"

"Medical information." George rumbled. He was a big man with a deep voice. "Like the medications you got when you arrived, that sort of thing."

"Oh, okay then." Lyndsey took the pen and scratched her name across the bottom of the document. It didn't matter what she signed because she would never arrive at the facility anyway.

George took the clipboard back from her and put the pen in his pocket. "Gerry there," George jerked a thumb at the young man holding a plastic bag marked Personal Belongings "has your clothes. We washed them, and they're ready to wear."

Lyndsey took the bag from Gerry and looked inside. Her clothes were clean. No evidence of blood told the gruesome tale of her suicide attempt. The clothes might be clean but looking at them sent a quiver through her. If circumstance were different, she would be lying on a morgue table in these clothes. Lyndsey took a deep breath and pushed the horrible image away. Her purse poked out from beneath a pair of jeans. Lyndsey pulled it free and opened the clasp, looking for her car keys. She searched every pocket inside the purse, but her keys were not there.

"George. My car keys are missing. Where's my car?"

George reached into the plastic bag and withdrew a sheet of

paper.

Lyndsey eyed the form. "What's that?"

George nodded at the sheet of paper. "That's where your car is."

Lyndsey took the paper and quickly scanned it. On the letterhead was the name of a towing company that had her car. Lyndsey read through the text feeling alarmed. The towing company charged an impound fee as well as a daily fee, meaning every day that her car was there, she owed them more money.

Lyndsey set the papers in her lap and looked at George. "I can't afford this. How am I supposed to get my car back?"

George just smiled at her. "Good thing you won't be needing it. I'm sure the treatment center will help you figure it out."

Fuck. Lyndsey needed her car. Now, what was she going to do? Shit, shit, shit. George signed his signature on the paper with a flourish and then stood up.

"Why don't you get dressed? I'll be right out the door, and when you're ready, we can leave."

"But what about Dr. Murphy? He wanted to see me before I left."

"We can stop at his office on the way out if he isn't here first." George turned to Gerry. "Right?"

Gerry nodded in agreement. He paled in comparison to George. Lyndsey wondered if Gerry was mute because he never said a word during their exchange. Maybe he was afraid of her? She would have been if she was in his shoes. Most people never got the chance to work with crazy people. Maybe Gerry was in training.

Alone again Lyndsey put her clothes on underneath the hospital gown. It was an awkward way to get dressed, and she had to struggle with the clothing. Her toe caught in the hem of her jeans, and Lyndsey landed on the mattress face first. It was the first time she felt grateful for the plastic-covered lump of foam. Lyndsey dressed quickly. She didn't want anyone walking in on her while she changed.

Out of her hospital garb and back in street clothes once again, Lyndsey folded the dark blue hospital gown and placed it on her mattress. She put the little cloth slippers she'd been wearing in her purse along with the cookies she'd stashed earlier. Lyndsey brushed her hair and wished for a bath. How could she go to the bar looking like this?

A knock sounded on her door, and George and Gerry walked in.

Lyndsey put down the brush. "George, where can I can grab a shower?"

George looked at his watch and shrugged. "The treatment center is expecting you. Don't worry about showering. You can have one after they've checked you in."

"Oh, okay." Maybe it was better this way. Lyndsey would go to the treatment center, grab a shower and find someone to help her get her car back. Then she would be out of there. If she got her car, she could swing by her place and try to pick the lock. That way she could get some of her belongings back.

Lyndsey wished for Drake. There wasn't anything he couldn't do. He even knew how to pick locks. Lyndsey thought about the time she had locked herself out of her apartment. She was doing laundry two floors down and left her keys inside on the kitchen counter. She was standing outside her apartment door wondering what to do when he snuck up behind her.

"Boo!" Drake growled in her ear as he swept her into a great big bear hug.

"Drake! Oh, thank God you're here! Do you have your keys?"

"I do," Drake grinned, "but we won't need them. Watch this!" He winked happy to show off and flashed her a devilish smile. Then he turned to the door and inserted his credit card into the locking mechanism. In not time Drake had the door unlocked and opened.

Sorrow filled her heart. Why hadn't she appreciated him then? Lyndsey was sick at the thought of how careless she'd been. Drake and been able to pull off a locked door but she doubted she could. Drake made it look easy. But then he did that with everything he touched.

"You ready?" George asked, interrupting her thoughts.

"I guess so?" Lyndsey was terrified, but wouldn't let George see that.

The three of them walked the wide shiny hallways she'd looked at through the window of her door. The floors were spotless and buffed to a high gloss. The air smelled of wax, and cleaning solutions. As Lyndsey walked, she had mixed feelings about leaving the hospital, and it surprised her.

Lyndsey wanted to thank the old orderly for his kindness. "George, can you tell that old orderly thanks for all his talks. And that I appreciate them."

"Will do," George replied as they walked.

Lyndsey passed the front desk where two nurses sat. She recognized the older one and gave her a shy little wave. The nurse watched her passing and gave her a curt nod in return. Next to the front desk were office doors with three different names on them. George led her to the correct door and knocked.

"Come in."

George opened the door for her, and she got her first look at Dr. Murphy's office. It wasn't what she'd been expecting. Lyndsey imagined a psychiatrist's office with dark paneling, leather couches, and a big wooden desk.

But Dr. Murphy's office was sparse. There were no rugs and no leather couch. He had a wooden desk, but it was beaten up and scarred. Dr. Murphy sat in a high backed chair padded with faux leather. Two chairs faced his desk. The chairs looked like cast-offs from a thrift store. Dr. Murphy's desk was messy with files and paperwork. Other than his framed university degrees, the walls were bare.

As Lyndsey stepped into Dr. Murphy's office, he looked at her and grinned. "Good luck, Lyndsey! I'm so proud of you for making the right choice. The treatment facility is excited you'll be joining them, and they put together a care package of sorts. You'll find extra clothing and toiletries. Anything else you might need you can purchase at their store on campus. Please don't worry about money or anything else for that matter. Your scholarship covers everything you need. The only thing you have to focus on is getting well."

"I don't know what to say, um thank you?" Lyndsey felt

guilty.

"No thanks necessary. Just get well. That will be all the thanks I need. Oh, and before I forget, here." Dr. Murphy passed her a large brown envelope.

Lyndsey took it wondering what it might be. Carefully she opened the flap not wanting to tear it. Inside was one sheet of paper. She pulled it out to get a better look. It was a drawing done in crayon of a little boy holding a kite. The child had drawn himself beside her car with a big smile on his face. Above her car was a bright rainbow. He must have used every crayon he had to color it. In one corner of his picture, he had drawn a smiling sun. At the bottom of the page, the little boy wrote Git wel son.

Lyndsey felt overcome with emotions.

Dazed and heartbroken, George led her to the car.

# CHAPTER FIFTY-ONE

In the back seat of the car, Lyndsey stared unseeingly out of the window. The trees many shades merged into a giant green smear. The telephone poles were blurry matchsticks. Passing cars raced by as hurtling blobs of colors heading to destinations unknown. Lyndsey didn't notice the tall buildings they drove by, only glimpses of great grey shadows, caught in her peripheral vision.

Lyndsey saw only one thing. A little boy's drawing. She looked at the little boy in the picture again. His artwork was really quite good. The child had colored his hair the same as hers and drawn a big smile on his face. His grin spread from ear to ear. Everything about the picture yelled *happy*. Even the colors looked cheerful. The rainbow screamed hope. The sun's smiling face and the boy's smile all but shouted love. But it was the three little words written at the bottom of the page that caused her heart to hurt. GIT WEL SON. *Get Well Soon, get well soon, get well soon.* Over and over his message rang vibrating in her head. *Get, pound. Well, pound. Soon, pound.*

Lyndsey felt like vomiting. Not able to dislodge the image of the picture it stuck there like a barb, taunting, hurting and annoying. She felt trapped, sitting here on her way to treatment, a little boy's words ringing in her heart. Lyndsey was exhausted, sleep beckoned. She leaned against the window, cushioned by the soft padding underneath her. The car's tires met the pavement with rolling smoothness. The engine hummed a comforting white noised lullaby.

The car was warm, and her stomach was full. Lyndsey began to drift, not quite sleeping but not awake either. It was a place she loved, and if her brain had been alert, she would have stopped to ponder that for a while. But it wasn't. It was in sleep mode, and she hung there in that space, without body or thought, in a place where she just *was*.

Unfortunately, she wasn't there long. Lyndsey became aware as the car slowed, then turned onto a bumpy road. She looked out the window and noticed the forest. Trees lined both sides of the pavement and met far overhead. Lyndsey thought it was like driving through a tunnel. Only this tunnel was alive and pretty.

The car slowed and came to a gate. There was no sign, just a big, black wrought iron gate. Through the bars, Lyndsey could see the gravel driveway curving to the left. To the right of it was a well-manicured green lawn. George pressed the button on the intercom attached to the gate and announced their arrival. Before he was finished speaking the black gate opened, allowing them access.

George drove through the opening and Lyndsey turned her head and watched the gate swing closed behind them. It was a little like going to her execution. Panic swelled. She was trapped!

Lyndsey's palms became sweaty, and she tapped George on the shoulder. "George, please turn around. I can't do this! I've changed my mind. George, do you hear me?"

George drove on not giving any indication that he heard Lyndsey.

Fear rocked her. Lyndsey tapped his shoulder again. "George, please, I've changed my mind, and I want to turn around right now!"

Not stopping George answered. "Where would you go, Lyndsey?"

"Anywhere but here. Oh my God, George. Please turn around!"

George sighed and then growled. "Not good enough, Lyndsey, the truth is you've got nowhere to go and *here* is where you need to be. You'll see. Believe it or not, there will come a day when you're thankful for this ride."

"I'm not a prisoner! I order you to turn around!"

"Lyndsey I'll have no part in your self-destruction. I will not drive you back. If you want to leave, you're on your own. We're here now so at least give it a chance. If you still want to leave tomorrow, fair enough. But don't leave before you even get there. Isn't that what you've been doing your whole life? You keep quitting on yourself girl and look where it's gotten you."

The car rounded a curve, and George pulled up in front of an enormous cedar sided building. It was a beautiful structure with a green metal roof and big wood trims. Lyndsey expected something more institutional looking, like a hospital. This structure looked like a large chateau for a vacation rental in the mountains or something out of a Home and Gardens magazine. It was quite lovely. A little piece of heaven and it was the last place on earth she wanted to be.

Trapped by her seat belt, Lyndsey flung it off, wondering if she should bolt from the car and how she would get over that gate. But before she could open the door gravel crunched underfoot with the sound of footsteps approaching.

Lyndsey froze with indecision. Two people stood next to the car. By the size of their smile, they thought this was a joyous occasion. Lyndsey despised them immediately.

Her hand reached for the handle, ready to run. But it was too late.

The man with the biggest smile opened her door and leaned in his head. He put his face close to hers. Lyndsey noted his shiny hair and peppermint breath. He flashed a big bright grin at her. This dude would be a shoe-in for a commercial selling toothpaste with his large white teeth.

Beaming at her as if she'd just won the lottery he said, "Welcome home."

# CHAPTER FIFTY-TWO

*Jesus! Where was she? What the hell was this?* Lyndsey looked up into his smiling face. The man reached a hand out to her. She ignored his hand and stared at him. He smiled so big he was in danger of cracking his face. The only thing missing from his appearance was the white robe and shaved head. Was this a cult? Lyndsey wondered who else would employee serene, smiling zombies as their greeters. The second man, not to be outdone by his buddy, joined in on the act with a heartfelt, "Welcome."

*Unbelievable!* Was that the only word they knew around here? With a frown on her face, Lyndsey got out of the car and brushed past the outstretched hand. George exited the driver's seat at the same time, bringing her meager belongings with him. It wasn't a heavy load. The hospital had given her a clean gown, a pair of slippers and a housecoat.

George placed the bag in her hand and gave her a gentle push in the direction of the front door.

Lyndsey turned on him and snarled, "Don't you touch me!"

When she turned to face the building, the serene zombies smiled as if nothing unusual was taking place. Her nasty mood and apparent dislike didn't seem to bother them in the least. Lyndsey wondered if they were medicated. Maybe they put lithium in the cornflakes. Or maybe it was in the drinking water, or juice? Happy juice! Isn't that what she'd been serving all along?

One of the zombies linked arms with her. Lyndsey pulled her arm free and followed beside this strange group of people. This crew was touchy-feely. Not her kind of people at all.

George waited for her at the front door. He pressed a button. The door chirped, and then it opened. Lyndsey was confused. She'd expected to see patients shuffling around in white housecoats and slippers, maybe muttering *you're going the wrong way,* but that's not what she saw.

Instead, she looked at big open rooms. The floors were a light glossy hardwood. The walls painted in soothing earth tones. The four entered a smaller reception room with double glass doors. It was just as nice as the rest of the building.

Behind a large oak desk was another serene, smiling zombie. She looked up as they approached and smiled at Lyndsey. "You must be our new admission. We've been expecting you. Welcome."

*Holy Shit!* What had she gotten herself into? There were swarms of people on the other side of the glass door. They moved fast and with purpose. Most of the people she saw dressed casually. But Lyndsey did notice a few suits and women in dresses with high heels. They all carried clipboards and books. Lyndsey noticed most people carried a coffee cup with them. They looked well-kept and freshly bathed. Three people locked eyes with her as they passed, and smiled.

One body broke free of the swarm, heading in her direction. A woman crossed the threshold and used the fob hanging from her neck to gain access to the room where Lyndsey waited.

Lyndsey noticed the small red light beside the door turn from red to green as the women entered. When she stepped through the doors, they automatically swept shut and the light returned to red.

Awareness dawned on Lyndsey. "Jesus Christ, George! This is a locked facility! Take me back this instant or I'll call the cops and tell them you're holding me against my will."

Clipboard lady spoke before George could. "It's only locked to keep from people coming in. That's for your protection. Not everyone here wants to be identified. The doors to leave are unlocked. You can go anytime you want. See?" To prove her point, she walked over to the door they'd just entered, and pushed down on the bar.

The door swung wide. Lyndsey didn't trust the woman and decided to try it for herself. She pushed down on the bar expecting it to stay locked but it opened easily under her touch. Lyndsey stood half in and half out of the building. Sweat beaded her upper lip. Her body tensed with adrenaline, ready to run.

Lyndsey was good at running. Whenever life got tough, she ran.

Only if she ran right now, she didn't have enough money to make a call. Lyndsey smelled, and she looked terrible. No, she couldn't go anywhere looking like this. The time wasn't right. Not quite, not yet.

Lyndsey turned her back on freedom and entered the reception area for the second time. Her face blank, she asked, "Now what?"

Those two little words created a roomful of energy. George

enveloped her in a big bear hug and patted enthusiastically on her back. "Way to go, Lyndsey. Good choice! Way to go, kid!"

The zombies bounced with enthusiasm as if Lyndsey won a gold medal in the Olympics and repeated George's words. "Way to go! Good choice!"

Lyndsey had never met such strange people in her life. They scared her with their smiling faces and positive words.

The woman with the clipboard squeezed Lyndsey's arm and answered. "Now we get started."

# CHAPTER FIFTY-THREE

Lyndsey didn't know it at the time, but she witnessed something most people never got to see; her birth announcement *now we get started*. The words had held no meaning then. She didn't know she stood at the fork in the road of her life. To her, they were just words. How could she know four little words would change her life forever?

Lyndsey said a tearful goodbye to George, amazed at how close she suddenly felt to him. She clung to him for a brief minute and then forced herself to let go. The last small hope of escape was leaving, at least for now.

The lady with the clipboard smiled. "I'm Kathy. I'll be doing your admission. Please come with me." She flashed her fob at the red light, and the glass doors swung open.

Lyndsey followed her through the opening trying not to flinch as the doors hissed closed behind them. She'd never been in a building this beautiful. At one end she could see multiple leather couches looking out over a cobblestone patio. The patio was large and three-tiered, offering a waterfall with picnic tables and comfortable looking patio furniture. The third tier held a gazebo where people gathered to smoke.

Kathy, aka clipboard lady, noticed her interest. "After we finish your admission, you'll get a tour of the building, and I'll show you to your room."

Kathy grabbed Lyndsey by the elbow, and led her down a short hallway with a door labeled *Admissions* above it. Kathy offered her a glass of water from the pitcher standing on the desk. Lyndsey drained the glass in one swallow. It was ice-cold and tasted delicious. She poured another glass of water and leaned back in the chair.

Kathy asked questions Lyndsey didn't have answers for. "What is your address? Place of employment? Spouse? Family contact numbers, telephone number…"

On and on it went and Lyndsey fumbled to come up with answers.

Kathy looked at Lyndsey. "When was the last time you used? How much do you use and how often?"

Lyndsey hid her smile. That one was easy, as much as she could, as often as she could, would have been the correct answer. But no way would Lyndsey tell this straight looking lady that. Instead, Lyndsey said, "I don't use drugs much. The last time was a few months ago. And I don't use them to get high. Sometimes I work double shifts at the bar, and I need the energy, it's like drinking a double espresso." Lyndsey shrugged. "It's no big deal."

Kathy looked at her and murmured, "Hmmm."

After a few more questions Kathy wrapped up the interview. Lyndsey was feeling smug. She had snowed this naive lady who would tell her boss they'd made a big mistake. Lyndsey didn't belong here, she wasn't an addict and then they would let her go. Lyndsey better hurry. She needed a shower and money. Otherwise, there was no hope of getting her car back.

Kathy held the clipboard tightly to her chest and led Lyndsey down the hallway. At first, the hall was empty. Lyndsey wondered where all the people were. It didn't take long to find out One by one the doors along the hallway opened, and bodies rushed past her.

One young man banged into her and ran off. Hey!" Lyndsey cried at his departing back. Lyndsey turned to Kathy. "That staff member is rude! And where are the patients?"

"Those *are* the patients, Lyndsey."

"What! You're kidding!" Lyndsey stopped mid-stride and stared at the people walking by.

They didn't look sick. This crowd was loud and goofing off. The hallways were more like a high school than a hospital. Confused Lyndsey looked at Kathy. "I thought hospitals were supposed to have sick people in them?"

"Oh make no mistake, these people are sick. It's a devious sickness because you can't always see it. Addiction is like cancer, by the time you figure out you have it, the damage has already occurred. And just like cancer the sooner you find it, the better your chances are of recovering from it."

What the hell was this lady talking about? Partying was

nothing like cancer! It was fun, not lethal. "Whatever," Lyndsey replied as they continued walking.

Lyndsey checked out the *patients*. They were of different ages. Some were her age, some younger. There were people her parents' age, and a few looked like grandparents! Wow, guess it took all kinds.

Kathy veered off down a smaller hallway leading to a flight of stairs. Her steps were sharp and precise. Lyndsey got the message, *hurry up*. Kathy glanced over her shoulder likely to reassure herself Lyndsey was still following as she led her down the stairs. Kathy's fingers rat-tat-tatted on the back of the clipboard, and she smiled seeing Lyndsey fast on her heels.

The lower level of the building was painted the same soothing earth tones as the main floor. Too bad Lyndsey wouldn't be staying long enough to enjoy it.

Kathy stopped in front of an opened door. She tapped briskly on the door before entering. There were four beds in the room. In one of the beds was an elderly woman sitting up with a mound of pillows behind her back. The bed sheets covered her legs.

The room reeked of alcohol fumes and something worse. The old woman moaned and clutched her stomach. "I'm going to throw up."

Kathy handed Lyndsey the plastic bag holding her belongings and turned to leave.

Before exiting, Kathy smiled at Lyndsey. "Make yourself at home."

Kathy left the room leaving Lyndsey alone with the old lady.

The old lady looked at Lyndsey and cried. "Help me!"

# CHAPTER FIFTY-FOUR

Lyndsey was frozen, rooted to the plush carpet she stood on.

The old lady made gagging sounds and swung the top half of her body over the bed. Her head hung upside down, and her lips peeled back exposing false teeth. The woman's mouth went wide, and she vomited.

The old women spewed into a black plastic garbage can. The vomit smelled sour, and Lyndsey gagged.

The old lady thrashed on the bed. Lyndsey feared she might fall off. After several long agonizing minutes, the old woman stopped heaving and took a deep breath.

Lyndsey looked around the room wondering how she could help. She spied fresh linen hanging from a towel rack in their adjoining bathroom. Lyndsey removed the facecloth and twisted the faucet marked cold. When the facecloth was saturated, she wrung it out and turned off the tap.

Worried the old woman might be dead, Lyndsey hurried back.

The woman was slumped in bed, her body sprawled at an upward angle. Her mouth remained open showing dentures that looked too big for her face. She wheezed, her breath rattled in and out. Lyndsey was sure each new breath would be her last.

Lyndsey pushed the vile trash can to the side and placed the cool cloth on the woman's brow. She was tiny and shrunken, her body nothing but bones. The old woman reached out a frail arm, and her eyes blinked open. Baby-blue eyes met hers.

The old woman grasped her arm and began to shake. Lyndsey's arm went up and down in time with the old woman. Before she could free her arm, Lyndsey heard voices in the hallway. Someone yelled and stomped nearby.

The door opened with a loud bang hitting the wall beside it. Lyndsey jumped. A woman her age glared. "Who the fuck are you?"

The angry woman wore short black spiky hair and lots of tattoos. She flung herself at the bed closest to the window and tossed the white binder she carried, in the trash.

Lyndsey wondered if she should introduce herself or slap the nasty bitch. She decided to be firm but friendly. "I'm Lyndsey and who are you?"

Before they could get converse further, the old woman yanked on her arm, this time with surprising force. Her bony fingers pinched as Lyndsey helped her sit up. The old lady peered at Lyndsey. "That's a nice name, I'm..." she trailed off a blank look coming over her face. She started shaking again and closed her eyes.

"Oh shit! I'll get the nurse!" The angry lady ran from the room.

Lyndsey used her body to keep the woman from toppling off the bed. The old woman bounced up and down unaware of her bizarre dance.

Lyndsey held onto her until the nurse got there. It wasn't a long wait, but it seemed like hours. In reality, only a few minutes passed before the angry woman was back with the nurse at her side.

The nurse seemed unfazed by it all and calmly began to wrap the blood pressure cuff around the old woman's arm. As she inflated the cuff, still she looked over at Lyndsey. "Meet your new roommates. This is Ruth," the nurse nodded at the old woman attached to the cuff, "and that's Becky."

The nurse removed the blood pressure cuff and looked at them. "I'll be back shortly. Ruth needs her medication. Why don't you two girls get to know one another?"

The nurse seemed unaware of the tension between Lyndsey and Becky. As she left the room, they stared at one another.

They weren't making friends.

They were ready to fight.

# CHAPTER FIFTY-FIVE

"Ahh," Ruth gurgled, and the tension broke. Lyndsey and Becky rushed to her side.

Ruth's eyes were open. Lyndsey looked at Becky. "What is wrong with her?"

"They think she might have wet brain."

"What's wet brain?"

Becky twisted a short lock of hair and then said. "I think it's like when you drink way too much and the alcohol kind of pickles your brain."

"Oh? Poor Ruth!" Lyndsey wondered if an open mouth was a symptom of wet brain. Ruth's mouth resembled an open garage door with all the messy contents in full view. Ruth licked her teeth and wheezed.

Dear God Lyndsey hoped to never look like that!

Ruth raised her arms like a baby would to their mother. She hooked a gnarled hand on Becky's arm.

Startled, Becky screamed.

"She did that to me too!" Lyndsey admitted.

Becky's animosity disappeared. "This place is beyond weird!"

"No shit!" Lyndsey nodded in agreement. "Why are you here?"

Becky stared at her as if to size her up. Then she answered, "My parents wouldn't get off my ass. The band wouldn't get off my ass. The whole fucking world was on my case. So to shut them up, I came here." Becky studied a tattoo on her forearm and shrugged. "It's no big deal, I sing in a band. Three other guys and me. We're on the road a lot. We play most of our gigs in the bar. They tell me I drink too much, and well, other things. But what do you expect? That's life on the road, right?" Becky looked at Lyndsey. "Why are you here?"

"Um, same, sorta. Well not really. I mean my parents aren't involved in my life. They couldn't wait for me to leave home. There is this guy though, well, I mean there *was*. It's complicated…" Lyndsey trailed off at a loss for words.

Before either of them could say anything else, a petite brunette strode into the room. Her smile said she ate from the same bowl of cornflakes as the serene zombies did. The brunette carried a small suitcase which she plopped down on the bed assigned to Lyndsey.

"Welcome, Lyndsey." The brunette nodded in her direction. "My name is Linda, and I work as support staff here." Linda opened the suitcase. "Here are some items you'll need during your stay with us. These are just a start, but it will get you through the first little while. If you need anything else, please speak with your counselor."

Linda stacked the clothing up in a neat pile on her bed. Lyndsey looked at it and felt a rush of emotion. Why were complete strangers so nice to her? What did they want? She was feeling suspicious but covered it by saying "thanks."

Linda opened the closet nearest to Lyndsey's bed. "You can put your clothes in here."

Damn it. Lyndsey didn't want to put the clothes away, seeing the suitcase gave her a better idea. Not wanting to reveal her idea she responded, "I will later."

Linda met her eyes and said, "How about now? I can help you if you like."

Shit, Linda wasn't going to leave until Lyndsey put the clothes away. Frustrated and feeling like a small child, Lindsey obeyed. There were new underwear and a sports bra, which she wouldn't be caught dead in, three pairs of socks, cotton pajamas, one zipped hoodie, and a pair of sweatpants. There was also three T-shirts, one white, one grey, and one pink. And a pair of white Converse runners.

Lyndsey shoved the clothing in the closet refusing Linda's help. With the clothes put away, Lyndsey reached for the suitcase.

Linda's fingers met hers, and she took the suitcase. "Lyndsey you won't need this. I'll take it with me."

As Linda walked out of the door, another woman walked in. This one had a stethoscope dangling from her neck and a glass of water in one hand. Where Linda was petite, this one was big. Lyndsey thought the woman was at least six feet and built like a Mac Truck.

The nurse approached Ruth's bed and reached into her pockets.

Lyndsey watched her closely. The nurse pulled out a vial of pills. Were they pain pills? Narcotics?

Lyndsey hoped the nurse would leave the bottle behind.

The nurse placed two tablets in Ruth's mouth and glanced

over her shoulder at Lyndsey. "Don't you have something better to do?"

Lyndsey's face reddened, and she turned her head away.

Becky stood behind the nurse making funny faces. She raised her middle finger and grinned.

Lyndsey stifled a grin.

It was surreal, watching Becky make fun of the nurse. Lyndsey turned away from Becky trying to think of a way to exit this funny farm. She could always put her clothes in a plastic bag. Or maybe the old lady had a suitcase that she could borrow. It didn't look like Ruth would be going anywhere any time soon. Lyndsey would ask Becky if she could borrow a few bucks. Then she could hitch a ride to the bar, but first, she needed a shower.

Lyndsey looked at Becky. "Can I borrow your shampoo?"

Becky's eyes widened, and she put a finger to her lips.

The nurse swung in Lyndsey's direction. Hand on hip and finger-pointing, she said. "No borrowing and no shower until after dinner."

Oh for fuck sake! Lyndsey was fed up with all the crap. What bull shit, she thought, and craved a cigarette.

Lyndsey reached into her purse feeling for the pack George gave her. Who did they think they were talking too? She wasn't a moron or a fucking two-year-old. Anger turned her vision red.

Lyndsey snatched up her cigarettes. The pack caught on a piece of paper which fluttered from her purse. Lyndsey watched it hit the ground landing face up.

It was the picture the little boy had drawn. His message was loud and clear.

*Git wel son* looked her squarely in the face.

# CHAPTER FIFTY-SIX

The dining hall buzzed with noise. Lyndsey thought it sounded a little like the bar where she worked. As they drew close, the buzz became voices. There were a lot of people there! Lyndsey hurried to follow Becky's disappearing back. She didn't want to go in alone.

The treatment center was enormous. Lyndsey felt small and lost as she stuck close to her roommate. Instead of drywall, the dining hall walls were glass. Through them, Lyndsey saw dozens of long tables. Seated at the tables were the people she glimpsed earlier. Becky stopped at a long line forming outside the doors.

Lyndsey was hungry and wondered why they had stopped.

Before she could ask Becky turned to her and explained, "It's not our turn yet. We have another ten minutes to wait, but if we don't get in line early all the good food is gone." She pointed through the glass. "There are some real pigs here. They eat everything in sight." Becky's foot tapped. She never stayed still.

Sandwiched up against Becky's back Becky looked at Lyndsey over her shoulder and asked. "Are you hungry?"

"A little," Lyndsey admitted, not wanting to say she was starving.

"I'm not. But I'll force myself to take a few bites." Becky scrunched up her face as if eating was something disgusting.

Ten minutes went fast. Lyndsey people-watched checking out her new peers. It was easy to spot who the popular were, the princesses and the jocks, the bad boys, and the nasty girls. It was a lot like high school. The only difference was most of the people standing in this line were way older.

Lyndsey saw a blond woman with pouty lips tease the four men standing nearby. Wow! The woman had breasts big enough for three. She rubbed them on a middle-aged man standing next to her. "Oops!" She giggled. "Sorry about that! The girls are always getting in my way!"

The older folks stood in little groups together wagging their eyebrows and rolling their eyes at the ridiculous shenanigans of youth. The oldest people had walkers with seats built in them and sat dozing in their chairs. Others waited patiently, their eyes averted staring at the floor. The youngest crowd was the loudest. They joked around and ridiculed the rest of the people in line.

Lyndsey pried herself from Becky's back and thought about the picture. It had gotten to her, and she'd been tempted to tear it into little pieces so she wouldn't have to look at it anymore. But she hadn't been able to bring herself to do so. The image of the little boy's smiling face had stopped her cold. So instead of tearing it up, she taped it to the bulletin board above the desk in her room.

The doors opened expelling the five pm dinner crew. Bodies swarmed past Lyndsey as she moved along, automatically following Becky.

Becky looked back at her. "You need to grab a tray then just do what I do."

"Okay," Lyndsey said, imagining cattle at the feeding trough.

Seeing Becky pick up a tray, Lyndsey picked one up too. They walked at a snail's pace. The food smelled delicious and Lyndsey's mouth watered in anticipation. The menu board announced tonight's meal. Roast chicken, rice pilaf, asparagus with a side salad, and vegetable soup. The dessert was strawberry ice cream.

Lyndsey placed her tray next to Becky's on the ledge set up for this purpose. Lyndsey counted five chefs standing over hot stoves stirring pots of food. The server looked at her with a blank expression. Not sure what to do Lyndsey pointed at the food she liked.

The server ignored her request and heaped her plate with food, balancing a multi-grain dinner bun on top.

"This is too much." Lyndsey began but stopped short when Becky jabbed her in the ribs. Lyndsey followed Becky to a table. "What the hell was that for?"

"Never give your food back. Trust me. Someone will want it. If you give it to them, then they owe you a favor." Becky bent her head and devoured the food on her plate.

Lyndsey eyed Becky thinking she was an odd duck. Why did she say she wasn't hungry and then eat like she was starving? Lyndsey picked up her fork feeling unnerved. She didn't like eating with these many people around her and preferred dining alone. Lyndsey thought this was a throwback to her childhood days. She was not good at table talk.

Forks clattered on plates as her dining companions rose, heading for seconds. Lyndsey wasn't surprised they could eat so fast. Food was not a priority when you were high and when you weren't, your body was starving and made up for it.

Lyndsey picked at her food and ate a few bites. Her eyes landed on a young man sitting apart from everyone else at the table. This badass leaned so far back in his chair Lyndsey thought he was in danger of falling on his ass. He turned his head her way and caught her stare. Lyndsey blushed, looking away. That's all she needed, another asshole in her life. Lyndsey thought about Drake then and felt the familiar twinge.

Badass corrected his chair and banged on the table, interrupting her thoughts. "If you're not gonna eat that give it to me."

It wasn't a question. As Lyndsey was getting ready to tell him where he could stick it, Becky jabbed her again. Lyndsey closed her mouth while Becky pushed her plate down the table. Becky grabbed her arm saying "they were going to the little girl's room."

Lyndsey pulled her arm from Becky's and followed her to the bathroom.

Becky pushed open the bathroom stall door. "For Christ's sake, Lyndsey, don't piss him off!"

Lyndsey opened the door next to Becky's and sat down. She didn't need to pee but craved privacy and didn't know where else to find it. She loathed treatment, and with every passing minute, the urge to bolt was growing stronger.

Lyndey ran through her plan looking for flaws. She figured as soon as dinner was over she would shower. Then, when everyone was asleep, she'd check pockets looking for money. When she had enough coin, she'd take off. Before dinner,

Lyndsey had checked the bedroom window. She was pretty sure it wasn't alarmed. Lyndsey had been a pro at sneaking out windows when she was younger and thought she could still pull it off.

Becky flushed the toilet next to hers. Lyndsey felt better with a plan and the tension she'd been carrying earlier, released. Automatically she flushed the toilet and then wondered why she had. Her mood was much improved, leaving the bathroom. Lyndsey would do her best to avoid everyone, and when she got her first chance, she would be gone.

Deep in thought, Lyndsey followed Becky back to the table. If she were lucky, she would find enough money to rent a hotel room for the next week. Who knew? Maybe she could even ask Becky for help.

As they neared the table, Lyndsey stopped dead in her tracks. Her chair was no longer vacant. In it sat badass. He leaned way back and grinned. The chair wobbled as it fought for balance.

Lyndsey's good mood deflated like a pricked balloon.

# CHAPTER FIFTY-SEVEN

The fire alarm blasted a high-pitched warning, stopping Lyndsey in mid-step. She pushed Becky out of the way and reached for her chair. She had intended to knock the chair out from the unwanted occupant landing badass on his best feature. Lyndsey hoped the fall would deflate his arrogance and take him down a notch or two. Lyndsey had been ready to shove the chair from under him when the fire alarm went off.

Too late now, badass was already up and looking around. The fire alarm was loud. The whoop, whoop, drowned out any chance of conversation. People covered their ears and rose to their feet. The loud noise was chaotic and exciting. It was the same feeling Lyndsey got when she was at a club or party. When drugs and alcohol weren't available to get you high, chaos, drama, anger, food, caffeine, nicotine, flirting, exercise, and fire alarms would do. Her peers lit with excitement.

Once again Lyndsey stayed close to Becky as she followed her out of the dining hall. The large crowd was like a well-orchestrated mass moving as one towards the closest exit door. Once outside they grouped-together in the lower parking lot as the alarm continued shrieking its maniac whistle.

Two of the serene, smiling zombies holding their precious clipboards stood in the group with Lyndsey. As she looked around, she noted the chaotic scene. There were different responses to the chaos unfolding. Some people covered their ears, others laughed, and some were crying.

Lyndsey saw many groups like hers around the perimeter of the building. Once again she wondered how many people were here. One of the serene, smiling zombies separated herself from the group and in a loud voice began to take roll call. She shouted each of their names loudly making eye contact to be sure the correct person was answering.

Becky leaned close and whispered in her ear. "They have to make sure we're all out. Don't want any of druggies burning up in the building, probably bad for business."

Lyndsey giggled. "Yeah, it brings the meaning of cooking your dope to a whole new level." Lyndsey and Becky squealed with laughter.

Lyndsey couldn't smell smoke but reverently prayed the building was on fire. At least she wouldn't have to go back in, and that part of her problem would be solved. Hell, maybe the place would even spring for a few nights in a hotel. She could probably run off in this chaos, no one except Becky would know she was gone. But then again she still needed a shower.

It was better to wait. Bored, Lyndsey people watched. It kept her amused, and she'd been doing it her whole life. Lyndsey remembered when she was little, and her family would be traveling together in the car. She watched people passing on the street or in their vehicles. When they stopped at a traffic light, Lyndsey would study the families waiting next to them. She noticed parents and children who looked happy and talked to each other. The parents' faces were soft, not hard and etched with anger.

Lyndsey would look at her parent's and wonder what it was like to have that kind of family. Even as a little girl she had felt an intense longing for nurturing, love and connection. Loneliness was a powerful feeling, and it brought tears to her eyes. But tears weren't okay in her family. Letting them fall meant she risked getting hit or yelled at. To survive, Lyndsey shut her feelings down. Now she viewed tears as a sign of weakness and to be avoided at all cost.

Lyndsey pushed the memory away and looked at the ground. She kicked at pebbles and one skittled over the top of Becky's shoe.

"You okay?"

"Yeah. I guess."

Of course, she wasn't okay. None of them were okay, or they wouldn't be here. That itchy, nasty, ugly feeling gnawed in her belly. She knew it well. Lyndsey wanted to strike out at the people standing closet to her, for no other reason than she didn't want to be alone in her misery.

Lyndsey had to get something in her and soon. The need for something, anything, *more* was building. With nothing to distract Lyndsey for the moment, reality snuck in and punched her in the face.

Reality was the one thing she couldn't do.

At least, not stone cold sober. The obstacles and problems Lyndsey faced were daunting. For some reason, Lyndsey always ended up in places she didn't want to be. Other people didn't seem to struggle at life the way she did. Lyndsey didn't understand why she felt overwhelmed or why her life had to be so hard.

There was only one thing that could help her now.

Lyndsey went over her plan. It was only a matter of a few hours, and she would be out of here. Just minutes really, if you added them all up. It wasn't the smartest thing she was about to do. But desperate times called for desperate measures.

The fire alarm stopped bleating, and silence ensued. The all-clear came down for everyone to return to the building. The serene, smiling zombies assured their patients all was well. There was no fire. It was a false alarm. To most that would be good news. But addicts weren't most people. People like her got a rush from chaos. Normalcy bored them. Instead of comments like, yeah we're safe! Lyndsey heard grumblings and people saying bummer. Now we have to go back in.

Lyndsey stayed silent as she followed the retreating mass of bodies moving through the front door. She walked behind Becky and counted.

Two hundred was the total.

Only two hundred more minutes.

Lyndsey had a lot to do in that short period and hurried through the doorway heading for the shower.

As she stepped over the threshold, there were only one hundred and ninety-nine minutes to go.

# CHAPTER FIFTY-EIGHT

The doorway jammed. There were too many people trying to get through it. Lyndsey got squished in the crowd and felt panicky. She flashed back to a time when she was at a rock concert. There were thousands of people attending. Many were already drunk, as they waited in line for the doors to open. Lyndsey was one of the first to arrive and stood at the front of the line next to a wall of glass and steel. The sun was hot and the drinks potent. As the concert opening drew near, and the doors remained closed, the mellow mood shifted to one of hostility.

The chant started far down the line and gained in strength as it caught on. "Let us in, let us in, *let us in!*"

The chant grew in force as thousands chimed in fueling it with anger and energy. The people in line pushed as if to bulldoze their way through the front doors. Lyndsey and the other people at the front smashed against the glass doors. She'd known true terror then and felt it now. Lyndsey stumbled, but the bodies jammed in the doorway held her up. A minute later her peers broke through and the doorway cleared.

People scattered into various parts of the building still unknown to her. Lyndsey found herself standing in the hallway not knowing which way to turn. She was lost, in more ways than one.

Tears welled, and she swallowed fighting to subdue her emotions. She loathed this weak feeling! *Stop your crying, or I'll give you something to cry about.* Her Dad's voice never far away reminded. Her tears were pathetic and embarrassing. Once upon a time, she had no control over them, but now she did. Lyndsey took a deep breath and drew on her anger. It was never far from the surface, and she'd learned anger was far better than tears. She would find her room if it took all night then she would have her shower. If anyone tried to stop her this time, well, it wouldn't be pretty.

Lyndsey followed the unfamiliar hallways. It seemed like she'd been walking forever and she was getting frustrated. If she could find the stairs that led to the lower level, she would find her room.

Open doors lined the hallway. The rooms all looked similar. Each had a bed, a dresser, an armoire, a desk and a chair. The furnishings were new, and the beds all wore the same quilts. The rooms were spotless. The treatment center must hire a large cleaning crew to keep it this nice.

Lyndsey turned right and found herself in a long hallway. She passed a laundry room where a young man stood behind an ironing board. He glanced up as she came into view looking surprised to see her. His surprise faded, and he said. "You're not supposed to be here!" Then, "Do you know how to iron?"

What the hell? Lost in a treatment center, with fire alarms beeping, a roommate almost dying and a young man ironing, what was this? Lyndsey felt like Alice. She'd fallen through the rabbit hole and was on a bad acid trip. Rehab was weird, and she wanted out!

The young man waved his hand. "You're in the men's wing

you know. If they catch you here, you'll be kicked out."

The man ironing was a kid. He should be in high school hanging out with his buddies, not in a place like this. He had a stocky build and would look perfect on a football field. The kid was the picture of health, with big blue eyes and black wavy hair.

The iron puffed grey smoke. "Careful. You're burning your shirt" Lyndsey said, smelling the scorched, burnt fabric as he lifted the iron off to view the damage underneath.

"Oh shit!" He wailed. "That was my favorite shirt."

His shirt had a large brown spot. All it was good for now was the rag pile.

Lyndsey walked over to the wall and unplugged the iron. "You have to put water in it, or your clothes will burn. Look this is how you do it." She turned the tap on in the laundry room sink and showed him how to fill the steam portion of the iron. Once it was full Lyndsey returned it to the ironing board and plugged it in. She moved the iron over the sleeve demonstrating how steam erased wrinkles. "It won't burn if you put water in it."

"Wow! I've never ironed a shirt in my life. My mom always did it for me." The kid looked sad as if someone had run over his favorite pet. His big blue eyes filled with tears.

The sense of strangeness returned. Lyndsey was having a hard time believing she was having a conversation about laundry with someone she'd never met before and yet as she looked at him he felt familiar. Like she knew him even though she didn't.

The kid reached out a hand. His lip trembled, and he said, "I'm Tommy."

Tommy's eyes were big and wide open. A tear trailed down

his cheek and disappeared beneath his jaw. Tommy's eyes were like a mirror to his soul, reflecting hurt, fear and confusion.

Oh God, she knew those eyes. She'd seen them many times before.

Now Lyndsey knew why Tommy seemed so familiar.

It was the eyes. Lyndsey was seeing in Tommy what she'd been trying to hide from for years. Lyndsey hadn't expected this. Although Tommy might only be a kid, his eyes told a different story. He had the eyes of a soldier or someone who had seen far too much ugliness in his young life. His eyes looked haunted by the ghosts from his past.

Yes, she would know these eyes anywhere. For her eyes were identical. Lyndsey felt sorry for Tommy and stepped close enveloping him in her arms. She hugged him hard hoping to share his pain so he wouldn't have to carry the weight of it all alone.

When Lyndsey hugged Tommy something ugly released within her and warmth filled its place, Lyndsey felt safe. Her eyes watered and this time she didn't fight it. Tears fell landing on Tommy's shoulder.

Lyndsey and Tommy hugged tightly, two broken ends coming together for a brief period. No words were necessary. Lyndsey had never felt this comfortable with another human.

When she stopped shaking, she looked at Tommy, grinned and said, "I'm Lyndsey."

# CHAPTER FIFTY-NINE

The hot pulsing water was delicious. Lyndsey couldn't remember a shower feeling this good. She lathered herself with a rose scented bar and the small shower stall filled with steamy floral aroma. Becky gave her a brand new disposable razor. Lyndsey bent to shave her stubbly legs. She ran the blade over her legs until all the hair was gone and only smooth, soft skin remained. Lyndsey squirted shampoo into her palm and lathered her hair. The fragrance of coconut and pineapple mixed with floral, creating a heady scent.

Lyndsey's eyes brimmed with tears. Something was wrong with her. She felt happy, and little things like a shower and shampoo brought her joy. Lyndsey was appreciative that she was warm and clean. She'd never really thought about it before. Bathing was just another thing to get out of the way. Why had she never even noticed how good a shower felt?

Lyndsey toweled off with a thick fluffy towel. It was rough and smelled of fresh air as if hung outside to dry. Was there something wrong with her nose? Scents were exaggerated and more powerful. Lyndsey thought the shower had done more than wash away her dirt. She imagined the lather circling the drain had removed something dark, sinister and ugly.

Lyndsey hung up her towel feeling lighter, and less burdened. There was something alive and energetic moving in her. Maybe it was the after-effects of the drugs she'd consumed in the loony bin, but whatever it was, she felt happy and yet fearful at the same time. These positive new feelings scared her. Lyndsey wondered if she was hallucinating, it might explain all the strange new sensations she was experiencing.

Lyndsey brushed her hair amazed at how soft it felt. Her long locks cascaded down her back tangle free. Lyndsey saw a jar of body butter on the shelf and helped herself to it. The moisturizer was slick on her newly shaven legs, leaving them soft and glossy.

As Lyndsey returned the jar, a twinge of unease pierced her blissful fog. She dressed hurriedly in her new clothes throwing her old ones into a plastic bag. Lyndsey needed a suitcase and thought about looking in Ruth's closet. If there were a suitcase, she would borrow it and leave Ruth a note saying she would pay her back.

Lyndsey opened Ruth's closet and was surprised. Her clothes hung with precision, and the closet was neat and tidy. Lyndsey didn't see a suitcase but noticed a large black beach bag that she thought would do nicely. Lyndsey reached in to pull it out for a better look when someone spoke behind her.

"What are you doing in my closet?"

Lyndsey jumped, caught red-handed. Her cheeks burned as she turned away from the closet and looked over at Ruth. Only minutes before Ruth was lying on her bed, with her eyes closed. Lyndsey assumed she'd been asleep or in a stupor.

But Ruth was neither. She looked at Lyndsey with eyes clear. Her tone accusing she repeated her question. "What are you doing in my closet?"

Lyndsey's face grew hot with embarrassment, and she stammered the first thing that came to mind. "I...I thought it was my closet." Her cheeks flamed bright red. Lyndsey looked away from Ruth and stared at the floor.

"Come here....please." Ruth patted the bed beside her.

Lyndsey shuffled over sitting as far from Ruth as possible without toppling from the bed.

Ruth looked at her once more. Gone were any signs of confusion or the violently ill old lady. Ruth appeared to have lost a decade or two in her sleep. She looked at Lyndsey with a knowing look and repeated her question. This time in a softer tone. "What were you doing in my closet?"

Lyndsey looked at Ruth and her mouth filled with the lies. She was a good liar. As she opened her mouth to make up a bullshit story nothing came out but a squawk. Lyndsey cleared her throat and tried again. "I – she broke off. Lyndsey was horrified. In the past, she'd gotten away with things she shouldn't be doing because of her quick thinking and ability to make shit up. But now, sitting on Ruth's bed, she'd gone mute. Even worse, her body was betraying her! Lyndsey's mouth trembled and her eyes filled with tears.

With a deep breath, Lyndsey tried to compose herself. She looked at Ruth and opened her mouth. "I was just..." Lyndsey trailed off.

Ruth sat up in her bed, resting against two plump pillows and locked eyes with Lyndsey.

The gig was up.

No words were needed. Somehow Ruth knew exactly what

Lyndsey was doing in her closet. Now she was waiting for Lyndsey to tell the truth.

Lyndsey shrugged, her cheeks burned, and she looked at Ruth. "I was trying to find a suitcase."

Lyndsey told Ruth everything then, holding nothing back.

Becky entered the room and sat on the bed with them. Lyndsey filled her in on what had happened and finished with a short version of what had been going on in her life recently. At times Lyndsey stopped talking and gulped back tears. In these moments Ruth would give her hand a reassuring squeeze, and Becky gave her a brief, awkward hug.

The woman tried to help her. All three of them were so new at this. When they got too close to one another, or their feelings became too intense, they would withdraw into their familiar shells. Intimacy was a new experience. None of them could cope with it for long without their shield of intoxication.

After Lyndsey finished telling her story, Becky shared hers and then Ruth opened up. Lyndsey was amazed at how much they had in common and yet how different they were from each other.

Ruth said she had tried many, many times to quit drinking. She had been hospitalized more times than she could count. Ruth lost her husband and children, and she wasn't allowed to spend time with her two grandchildren. In a moment of closeness, Ruth pushed the covers aside and exposed her abdomen. "They say my liver is shot, if I drink again I'm going to die."

Lyndsey looked at Ruth's shrunken body and wondered what the large lump protruding from Ruth's stomach was, but before she could ask, Ruth pointed to the bump. "That mound is my liver sticking out. The doctor says I'm in the final stages of cirrhosis. I pickled my poor liver it with all the booze I drank." Ruth laughed as if her death was a funny thought.

Lyndsey couldn't believe what Ruth was saying. She seemed indifferent and spoke as if talking about someone else. Ruth didn't appear to comprehend how close to death she was.

Lyndsey looked at her with concern. "You won't drink again will you?"

"Probably." Ruth chuckled, with a sly grin on her face. "After all, you can't teach an old dog new tricks. Besides, I like it too much. I couldn't imagine my life without a nice drink."

"But Ruth, you can't drink!" You're going to die." Lyndsey said, hoping to make Ruth understand the seriousness of her situation.

"Oh be careful, dearie, you're beginning to sound just like *them*." Ruth wagged a finger at Lyndsey. "Don't worry. I won't die. They only say that to scare you, and you know if I do, well, that would be okay too. But I won't die. I've been to rehab many times and believe me the counselors all say the same the same thing *if you use one more time you're gonna die*. Well, I say screw you to their scare tactics. Now go ahead and take that bag so you can get out of here."

Becky had grown quiet and sat huddled in a ball on the bed beside her.

Lyndsey felt tense and wasn't sure how to handle it.

Ruth was clearly insane. Lyndsey thought it was probably a waste of time trying to talk sense into her. Lyndsey wanted to shout at her, at Becky, too.

Becky looked like she was six again. She had grown smaller as she pulled into herself on the bed.

Lyndsey jumped up needing to get away from them.

How was this possible? Only moments before the three of them had been so close, connected even. What was she thinking opening up to these idiots? Impatience and anger swelled in Lyndsey. She needed something to alter her mood quick, or she would start screaming and throwing things.

Sick and miserable Lyndsey returned to Ruth's closet and tugged the black bag out of the corner. She filled it with her newly gifted purchases. Lyndsey balled up her clothes and threw them in the bag hoping to vent her frustration. But it only seemed to make things worse.

The alarm clock ticked loudly on Ruth's desk.

Lyndsey recalculated, one more hour, maybe two at the most.

Lyndsey hoped she could make it.

# CHAPTER SIXTY

Twelve chairs faced each other in a large circle. All the seats were full. Lyndsey looked around in disbelief. She had no clue why she was here. She'd been tossing clothes into the black bag when footsteps approached their room. Lyndsey managed to stuff the black bag back in the closet and out of sight when one on the serene zombies entered their room. With her smile firmly in place, the staff member informed Lyndsey it was time for reading group. Lyndsey argued she was too tired, but the woman just smiled at her and led Lyndsey through the hallways to the group room.

The serene zombie said all patients must attend reading group. But this was like no hospital she'd ever seen before. It pissed her off. Lyndsey sure as shit wasn't a *patient.* Hello? Did she look like she was wearing hospital clothing? What was wrong with the people here? Lyndsey's misery grew, feeding on her dark thoughts.

When the staff member-zombie opened the door to the group room the first thing Lyndsey noticed was the circle, and then the books. The people in this group read from a blue book, Lyndsey had received upon admission. The chairs held many who wore the same calm expression, as the serene, smiling zombies. Were they all staff members? How many people worked here?

The lady in charge introduced Lyndsey to the group. Once more she heard the dreaded *welcome* and found herself shuddering. Lyndsey knew of many cults, but she'd never seen anything like this.

A man read from the blue book and talked about God. Lyndsey almost shit herself. She was right! This was a cult.

At least now she had proof. Rehab was a God camp for the hopeless and broken and if she weren't careful she would turn into one of the serene zombies.

Lyndsey noted the people in the chairs took turns reading a passage from the blue book and then sharing their thoughts on what they had read.

The only one Lyndsey knew in the group was Tommy. He sat across from her, his eyes wide and bulging. As Lyndsey looked at him, she felt like laughing. Tommy wore his feelings on his sleeve. By the look on his face, she knew what he was thinking. Run!

Lyndsey thought Tommy looked hilarious. She fought to keep her laughter inside. But a snort escaped through her nostril making a strange noise.

Lyndsey's face grew warm as heads turned her way. Her laughter died as embarrassment and anger took its place. Lyndsey sat up and glared at the people sitting in the chairs. "What the hell are you looking at?"

There was no response. And after an awkward pause, the man next to her resumed reading.

Then it was Lyndsey's turn to read. The man to her left thrust a blue book at her. With a calloused finger, its nail-bitten to the quick, he pointed to the passage she was to read. Lyndsey looked at the words printed on the page. *We admitted that we*

*were powerless over alcohol – that our lives had become*
*unmanageable.*

Powerless? What did that mean? Lyndsey was confused and fumbled the book in her haste to have it out of her hands.

The people in the group stared at her, waiting for her to read. Lyndsey passed the book back to the man who had given it to her. It was like a game of hot potato. She didn't want to be the one who got stuck reading from the blue book.

In her haste to give it back, Lyndsey dropped the book. It landed on the floor with a loud bang. Half the people jumped in their chairs, and the other half pulled their knees tightly to their chests and curled up in a ball.

Lyndsey picked up the book and offered it to the man next to her. As she did, she got her first good look at him. She noticed his hands lay loosely in his lap. They were bruises and dark brown and red spots on the back of his hands. His arms were toothpick thin with track marks running up his forearms. On one arm was an abscess that looked nasty!

The book weighed heavy in her hands. Lyndsey tried again to pass it to the man only he never acknowledged her. He appeared unresponsive, sitting in his chair with his hands open. The man's eyes were vacant. Poor bugger. The lights were on, but he was gone.

Not sure what else to do Lyndsey said, "Um, I'll pass."

A lady sitting across from her shrieked like a parrot. "You can't pass! You can't pass! Someone tell her! She can't pass!"

One of the serene zombies spoke calmly. "It's okay Jean. This is Lyndsey's first day here. We can let her pass for now."

*Holy shit!*

Lyndsey needed to get out of here and *fast*! The woman who sat next to the vacant man reached for the book. She was about the same age as Lyndsey and dressed in a skirt and blouse with low slung heels and a big flashy wedding ring on her left hand. Her nails painted in glossy pink nail polish and her hair cut in a sharp-looking bob. Lyndsey thought she might be the CEO of a successful company and wondered what she was doing sitting here with the riff-raff.

"Hi, my name is Jan, and I'm an alcoholic."

Lyndsey almost fell off her chair.

Jan spoke sincerely. "I can relate to this." Jan read the paragraph which had baffled and offended Lyndsey. *Step One. We admitted that we were powerless over alcohol – that our lives had become unmanageable.* Jan seemed confident as she explained her thoughts to the group. "The first time I read this it didn't make any sense to me. Powerless means you're weak, and I've never seen myself that way."

"That's what it means! You're weak! You're weak!" The woman resembling a parrot shrieked.

"I used to think so, too," Jan admitted. "But I've changed my mind. Let me explain why." Jan tapped the blue book and looked at Jean. "Just before I got here I went on a bad bender. I mean *bad*. I was away for three days. As I was getting ready to go out, I had a glass of wine with me in the bathroom. I was applying my makeup when my daughter came in. She begged me not to leave. My child doesn't like me to drink, and I was feeling angry with her. I was impatient with her whining. I just wanted her to stop and leave me alone with my glass of wine. But she kept begging me not to go, so I got down on my knees and looked her square in the eyes. I pinky swore I wouldn't be long. I was only going out for a few hours, and then I would be back. I hugged my little girl and told her not to worry. I'll never forget the look on her face. You see she wanted so badly to believe me. She looked at me, her big eyes full of hurt and hope that maybe, *please god maybe*, this time it might be different."

The honesty in Jan's story and the image of her little girl broke Lyndsey's heart. Her eyes filled with tears and she wiped them away. Lyndsey squirmed in her seat feeling uncomfortable. Her emotions were all over the place! Lyndsey hoped no one noticed her reaction. She stared at the floor wishing she were invisible.

Jan paused, and Lyndsey snuck a glance at her. Her eyes were red, and she was breathing hard.

"I really meant it you know." Jan's voice got quiet. "Every single word. It was the truth. I wasn't lying."

"Then why were you gone for three days! Huh? You're lying! *Liar.*" Jean hissed.

"No Jean, I wasn't lying, and that's how I know what powerless means. You see when I told my daughter I'd be back in a few hours I was telling the truth. If I hadn't been drinking, I never would have broken that promise. I would move heaven and earth to make sure I never hurt my little girl. But when I took that first drink, she became somehow *less* important to me. It's like the alcohol took away everything that mattered in my life. It was selfish and wanted me all to itself. Alcohol never shared me with anyone." Jan stopped.

Lyndsey saw the raw emotion on her face, and the depth of it made her look away.

The group room was quiet. You could have heard a pin drop.

After a moment Jan said. "I thought about killing myself you know. At the end of it, when I'd sobered up long enough to realize I'd been away for three days. Facing my little girl was more than I could bear. I couldn't even bring myself to see her. When I came home that morning, my husband drove me straight here."

A woman sitting next to Jan passed her a Kleenex. Lyndsey used the back of her hand to swipe at her nose and noticed most everyone had tears in their eyes.

Jan dabbed her eyes and tucked the Kleenex up her sleeve. "So, *powerless over alcohol,* means that when I take that first drink I no longer have the power to predict when I might come home, or what I might do, or how much I might spend, or who I hang out with and most importantly, it means that it becomes more *powerful* than the love I have for my child. I'm truly *powerless* when I take that first drink. Sometimes I come home, but mostly I don't. And if I do manage to make it home, I'm not nice to be around. I punish my family for ruining my fun. I make them pay for it. If my husband wants me to leave a party early, I'm a nasty bitch to him for the rest of the night. I pick fights with him letting him know I'm not happy. Then the next morning I feel horrible for acting that way. I can't tell you how many times I've tried to have one or two drinks, hoping this time it would be different and I could drink like everyone else. But no matter how I change it up, it beats me every time."

Jean piped in. "Every time! Every time! It beats me every time." Jean might sound like a parrot, but she was nodding her head to what Jan had just shared.

Lyndsey's leg vibrated on the floor.

Up, down.

Up, down.

Up, down.

Lyndsey glanced at the wall where an industrial looking clock hung.

Thirty more minutes.

Lyndsey put a hand on her leg.

It still shook.

# CHAPTER SIXTY-ONE

Lyndsey left the group room shaking. Tommy took her by the arm and steered her down the hallway. After a few steps, she asked. "Where are we going?"

"We need a cigarette," Tommy replied as they rounded a corner and headed for the doors to the courtyard.

The outside area looked tastefully designed. Lyndsey stopped for a moment taking in the scenery. She saw a stone and brick patio and bright flower gardens. Mature trees lined the property, and lush green grass carpeted her feet.

Tommy tugged on Lyndsey's arm and led her up the stairs to the smoking area. The garden area below was beautiful but vacant. The small patch of land above them was where most of the patients hung out. As Lyndsey stepped up to the third tier, she got a closer look at the gazebo. The scent of freshly cut cedar wafted from the lumber. Smoke poured from the Gazebo. It wasn't on fire. The smoke came from the dozens of smokers jammed inside. Lyndsey entered the pool of smoke, took a cigarette from Tommy and lit up.

An elderly man gripped a walker. His skin was grey. He put the cigarette to his blue lips and inhaled. Half the cigarette disappeared. Through a plume of smoke, he looked at Lyndsey and said. "Hey miss, there's no borrowing allowed here."

Tommy retorted. "Piss off, Frank! Cut her some slack. She just got here."

Frank seemed to consider Tommy's statement and shuffled over to them. Squinting at Lyndsey, he asked. "And what brings you to this fine establishment, miss?"

Lyndsey sucked on her cigarette as a baby sucked its pacifier. She needed this hit of nicotine and hoped it would soothe her frayed nerves. Her entire life was upside down. Lyndsey was off kilter and feeling unhinged. She'd lost Drake, and was homeless, she had tried to kill herself and ended up in a loony bin and now this! Could she do anything right? Of all the places she'd been this was by far the strangest.

And Lyndsey knew strange!

Strange had been her childhood. Strange had been her family. Strange was her life.

Lyndsey looked at the group of misfits around her and blurted. "You know its four days today. At least I think it is. Four days! I can't remember the last time I was clean and sober for that long."

It was weird vocalizing her thoughts. Lyndsey took a long drag hoping to feel better. But the cigarette didn't help. Her nerves were on fire. Lyndsey felt like she may snap soon. Why had she said that? She hadn't meant too. What was happening to her? Her mask was slipping. It was exhausting trying to hold herself together.

Lyndsey took a deep drag, inhaling as much as she could suck into her lungs. She blew out smoke, feeling slightly better, eyed the filter and took another drag. This time the smoke was bitter and tasted like cotton. Lyndsey coughed and ground out the cigarette below her heel.

Frank cleared his throat. "Ahem." Frank's puny chest swelled. "Been here twenty-eight days myself."

"Of course it doesn't really count," Lyndsey admitted, ignoring Frank. "I don't know what drugs they gave me at the crazy farm and I would never have been sober this long if I hadn't been locked up. But still, four days! I couldn't get four minutes before let alone four days. I couldn't get out of bed without something to snort or smoke or drink. I didn't have the energy. I was too sick, and the only thing that got me going was *more*." Lyndsey clapped her hands over her mouth horrified at what she'd just said.

"More of what?" Frank asked and gasped. His grey wrinkled face scrunched up as he fought for breath. Frank made choking sounds that rumbled deep in his lungs. Frank's coughs turned wet. It was pretty disgusting. Lyndsey thought Frank had been smoking for a very long time.

Tommy cut in trying to explain. "More of everything! More of anything, just *More*."

Lyndsey nodded at Tommy relieved he understood. Just talking about it brought on an intense craving, like the drugs were right next to here. She tasted bitterness in the back of her throat. Her pulse quickened, and her nostrils flared. Lyndsey smelled the slight acidic chemical aroma. Her body thirsted for more, the way one would thirst for water if caught in the desert for days without a single drop. Lyndsey was *so* thirsty. She was parched.

"Lyndsey, *stop!*" Tommy yelled in her face.

Lyndsey felt the pinch of Tommy's fingers digging into her

arms.

"Stop," Tommy said again. His voice trembled and he was shaking too.

Lyndsey blinked, back on solid ground. The last traces of cravings dissipated as she returned to the present moment.

Frank looked at Lyndsey with concern. His fingers were white as they gripped the walker and his grey face beaded with sweat. Frank pulled a hanky from his front pocket and dabbed his face. For the moment he was speechless.

Tommy drew in a ragged breath and said. "Please be careful Lyndsey. Drugs are powerful." Tommy looked at her. "Even talking about them can be dangerous."

Lyndsey felt the stares and turned to look at the rest of the group huddled in the smoke pit. They were a twitchy lot, with legs bouncing and cigarettes inhaled at warp speed. Lyndsey knew the feeling, one of needing something, anything really, to be comfortable in your skin. When *more* wasn't available, you turned to what was. In rehab, the filler was gossip, flirting, cigarettes, and food.

As Lyndsey observed the crowd of strangers around her, she felt angry. Why was she here with these sick people? She didn't like the way they looked at her. She didn't like the way they looked, period! Frustrated, she turned on the crowd and snapped. "What the hell are you all looking at? Why don't you mind your own damned business?"

One woman came forward. She smiled at Lyndsey and said. "It gets better you know. Every day you'll find it gets just a little bit better. Hang in there hun; you're worth the wait."

*Are you kidding me?* Lyndsey wondered who in the hell this woman thought she was. Under normal circumstances, she wouldn't be seen with this woman. It was hard to tell her age. She could have been twenty or forty or anywhere in between. You could tell by looking at her she had lived a rough life. The woman's voice was raspy, and her front teeth were missing. But it was her eyes that caught your attention. They didn't fit with her appearance at all. Her looks said homeless and drug addict and beware. Her eyes should have been dead, vacant, without a spark of life left in them. But that's not what Lyndsey saw there.

The woman offered her hand to Lyndsey. "I'm Teeny," she said. "I know my name is a little weird, but I got it while living on the streets and it kinda stuck." Teeny grinned utterly unaffected by her missing front teeth.

Lyndsey wondered how Teeny could be so confinement without her teeth.

Teeny's eyes locked on Lyndsey's. It was unsettling. Teeny grinned again, and her eyes lit up with love. Her eyes were not the eyes of a corpse but of someone who was happy to be alive.

Teeny's hand remained outstretched, cautiously, Lyndsey shook it. "Nice to meet you Teeny. I'm Lyndsey, and I have to go. I have, um, something I must do right now." Lyndsey pulled her hand free fighting the urge to clean it on the side of her leg.

Teeny nodded, smiled and said. "Nice to meet you. Maybe we can spend some time together later on?"

"Um, maybe." Lyndsey fought the urge to run from the group and tried to appear calm.

Tommy looked at her with his big eyes. Lyndsey managed,

"I'll see ya later."

Frank reached out and gave Lyndsey a feeble hug. He was all bones and sagging skin. Frank smelled like an ashtray and medicated topical ointment. Lyndsey knew the smell from her grandfather, who used the cream to ease his aching muscles. Frank looked up at her from his shrunken perch. He had one hand on the walker, the other on her shoulder. Frank leaned on her heavily and said. "See ya soon, kid."

"See you, Frank." Lyndsey wished she could smile at Frank, but she was fighting tears. Lyndsey moved out from Franks hold and walked down the stairs.

This time Lyndsey knew where her room was. As she passed through the glass doors, Lyndsey couldn't wait to be gone. She found the staircase and ran down the steps. Lyndsey skipped the last few stairs and jumped to the landing below.

Lyndsey ran through the hallway eager to reach her room. Excitement built as she thought about freedom, just moments away.

Lyndsey opened the door to her room with anticipation.

It was time.

# CHAPTER SIXTY-TWO

On tip-toe, Lyndsey walked past her roommate's bed. Ruth huddled under her sheets. Lyndsey hoped Ruth was sleeping soundly. She didn't want a big scene when she left.

Lyndsey opened the cupboard drawers and pulled out the black bag. She looked inside wondering if she'd forgotten anything. Yes! Her purse! She reached into the back of the closet and found it. Lyndsey opened the clasp and looked inside. Her wallet and cigarettes were there. Her makeup, *shit.* There was no way she was leaving without that.

The bathroom was dark. Lyndsey closed the door and hesitated. She couldn't see anything and would have to risk turning on the light. As she flicked on the switch, Lyndsey tensed hoping it wouldn't wake up Ruth. When nothing happened Lyndsey packed her makeup into an old makeup bag that barely zipped closed. She worried a staff member would come barging through the door demanding to know what she was doing.

She finished in the bathroom and tiptoed into their bedroom.

With a quick glance around the room, Lyndsey had an idea. She would put her pillow under the blankets on her bed. It was a trick from years ago, and it would buy her some time. Lyndsey plumped up her bed to look as if she were still sleeping, should anyone check. The moon outside her window was full and gave off enough light to see. Lyndsey placed her black bag on her bed and snapped it closed. She had packed enough clothes to get her through the first few days.

Once she got to the bar, everything would fall into place. Someone would buy her a drink, lend her money, and let her use their couch for a night or two. And if that didn't work out, there were other options. Ones she didn't want to think about right now. Lyndsey hoped she didn't have to go that route.

With one last look at the room, Lyndsey was ready to go. She wondered if she should say goodbye to Ruth but decided not to wake her up. Lyndsey thought her bed looked good. A quick glance in the room and it would fool whoever was checking. Her desk was empty and her eyes lifted to the corkboard above. Damn! She forgot about that. The picture from the little boy hung there, looking at her with its smiling faces and *Git wel son*.

The picture represented something Lyndsey didn't want to think about, and she felt torn. She wished she could take it with her but didn't feel it was the right thing to do. Lyndsey wouldn't be getting well anytime soon where she was going, and as much as she hated to do it, she decided to leave the drawing taped on the board. Lyndsey hoped the next person to fill her bed would fulfill the little boy's wishes. Innocent little boy's artwork did not belong where she was going.

Ruth stirred in bed, and Lyndsey froze, waiting to see if she would wake. Ruth mumbled as she tossed and turned.

Was Ruth dreaming? Lyndsey stood still and listened.

"Don't! Don't go. Wait." Ruth's voice was thick with sleep.

Lyndsey's pulse kicked up a notch when Ruth kicked her legs out and sat straight up. Ruth's eyes opened.

Ruth reached out a hand and said. "Don't." And then, "just wait."

Shit! Was Ruth awake?

Ruth rubbed her eyes and made clearing sounds in her throat. "Get my purse," Ruth said, her voice low from sleep.

"Ruth?" Lyndsey wondered if Ruth was talking in her sleep.

"I'm awake." Ruth nodded and leaned back against the headboard. "Go get my purse. You need money. Now hurry! They'll be doing bed checks soon."

Money? Was Ruth giving her money? Feeling more hopeful about leaving Lyndsey opened Ruth's closet and pulled out Ruth's purse. It dangled heavily from her arm.

Lyndsey walked to Ruth's bed and passed her the purse.

Ruth took the purse from Lyndsey and sat it on her lap. She opened the clasp and asked. "How much money do you need?"

"Um, I don't know, maybe fifty dollars?" Lyndsey hated this. She felt like a bum waiting for a handout.

"Nonsense, dear." Ruth shook her head. "Fifty won't be enough. Here, take this."

Lyndsey held out her hand to take the money Ruth thrust at her. Her eyes widened at the thick wad she held in her palm. "Ruth, this is too much, I can't take it."

Ruth closed Lyndsey's fingers around the bills. "Don't worry. I have more money than I can spend. Please, you would be doing me a favor, besides you will need it."

"I'll pay it back, Ruth. I will. I promise. Thank you." Lyndsey knew she shouldn't be taking this money. It wasn't hers, and Ruth wasn't well enough to make this decision.

Lyndsey felt guilty and ashamed as she stuffed the bills into her pants pocket.

Ruth tugged on her shirt. "Will you visit me, Lyndsey? I'm lonely you know, and my family doesn't want anything to do with me. Maybe you could be my family. I'd like that."

"Uh, sure Ruth, I'll try, I mean. I'm not sure how happy the staff will be to see me around here after tonight though."

"I'm sure it will be fine. Don't even give it a thought. I would like you to bring me a wee little gift if you will."

*Oh, oh, here it comes.*

"I'd like you to *please* bring me a wee nip of Gin. For medicinal purposes only, of course."

Lyndsey backed away from Ruth and shook her head. "I...I don't think I can."

"Of course you can! Now get going!"

*Oh my God, what have I done?*

There was no way she was coming back here.

As Lyndsey turned her back on the room and Ruth, she was disgusted with herself. She needed to leave right now!

Lyndsey walked to the window and dropped her black bag on the floor. She pushed the window up and picked up her bag.

A cool fresh breeze brushed her face.

Then all hell broke loose.

# CHAPTER SIXTY-THREE

Lyndsey screamed with the alarm. "Damn, shit, *Christ*! How do you turn this thing off?" The alarm shriek was deafening and to make matters worse the window wouldn't open far enough for her to climb out.

Oh my God! The noise was going to wake the entire building! Lyndsey pounded on the window hoping to make the alarm stop.

*Beep, beep, beep*!

There were no wires visible, no off button, and no alarm that she could see. Maybe it was motion censored?

With no way to turn the alarm off, the best she could do was damage control. Lyndsey ran to the bedroom door and closed it hoping to minimize the noise. She flipped on the light switch knowing she only had minutes before a staff member arrived at her room.

Lyndsey propped a chair under the doorknob, to buy more time. The loud shrieks made her knees shake. She crossed the room and ran her hands over the window glass feeling every inch. The window was stuck halfway up. Lyndsey couldn't move it. Nor could she see anything resembling an alarm. No electrical wires ran inside the glass or to any outlets in her room.

Lyndsey was about to bolt from the room when she noticed Ruth.

Poor Ruth was sitting up in bed, crying. Her eyes rolled as

she covered her ears to protect them from the piercing shrieks. Lyndsey thought Ruth looked like a spooked horse. Lyndsey crossed the room to Ruth's side. She didn't look good. Lyndsey hoped Ruth wasn't going to seizure again.

The noisy alarm and Ruth's poor health weren't Lyndsey's only problems now. She heard voices coming from the hallway.

Someone pounded loudly on their bedroom door.

A female voice yelled. "Open the door!"

Lyndsey looked at the window again. Maybe she should try and break it? The door would hold for a little longer but what about Ruth? She couldn't just leave her like that.

Damn, she had been so close.

Lyndsey patted her pocket and felt the bulge of bills. If she was going to stay longer, she better hide the money. But where?

Lyndsey mind raced to come up with another plan.

Then she had an idea. In the wee hours of the morning, when she knew everyone would be sound asleep, she would simply walk out the front doors. It should be easy. The front doors might be the only opening in the building that wasn't alarmed.

Until then where could she hide the money?

Ruth bounced up and down on her bed. Lyndsey had another idea.

She put a hand on Ruth. "Hang on. You're okay."

Lyndsey reached into her pocket, pulled out the wad of money and stuffed it far under Ruth's mattress. Hopefully, it would be safe there until Lyndsey could come back and get it.

"No!" Ruth garbled, clawing at her arm.

Lyndsey squeezed Ruth's arm and walked over to their door.

She had no idea how to explain all this.

Lyndsey removed the chair from underneath the doorknob. What had she done?

Worried about Ruth, she only just managed to get out of the way before the door flew open. Six frowning people stood in the doorway.

Uh, oh. It was going to be a long night.

Lyndsey faced the crowd ready to be lynched when her night went from bad to worse.

Ruth's headboard banged against the wall. Lyndsey watched distraught as Ruth bounced up and down on her mattress. The covers had come off exposing Ruth's thin legs. The air was suddenly pungent with a sharp odor, and the sheets under Ruth turned yellow.

Holy shit! Ruth had just pissed the bed!

A staff member took Lyndsey by the arm. No serene, smiling zombies this time. These ladies were mad! The other staff turned to help Ruth as the one holding Lyndsey's arm marched her from the room.

Lyndsey dug her heels into the carpet. "Wait! I want to make sure Ruth's okay."

The ex-serene zombie snorted. "Haven't you done enough for one night? The doctor will be here shortly. Ruth will be well-looked after." The woman's harsh expression softened a little when she saw Lyndsey was worried.

Lyndsey noticed Becky standing in the opening of the door. Becky watched her with a strange look on her face. Lyndsey looked at her. "Becky, can you make sure she's okay?"

Becky didn't respond. She just looked on with closed lips.

As Lyndsey left her bedroom, she glanced back at Ruth. Ruth was lying in bed with her eyes closed. Thankfully, the shaking had stopped. As Lyndsey turned to leave the room, she stopped short.

Was she seeing things?

Lyndsey looked at Ruth again. Ruth opened one eye and looked straight at her. Ruth closed her eye and opened it again. Lyndsey couldn't believe it. Ruth had just winked at her!

Ruth's lips curled upwards.

Lyndsey grinned in response.

The female staff member went through the door with Lyndsey at her side. They walked through the hallway and up the flight of stairs. Lyndsey didn't fight the woman leading her. She barely paid any attention to her at all.

Ruth's wink flashed like a neon sign. Lyndsey couldn't get the image out of her head. Had she really seen Ruth wink? Maybe her eyes were playing tricks on her? Was it even possible? Over and over she replayed it. Ruth's lip curling ever so slightly as she winked at Lyndsey.

Wow! That Ruth was quite a gal. Lyndsey's admiration for her raised a thousand fold.

The female staff member stopped outside an office door and taking the fob from her neck, ran it over the keypad and the door buzzed open.

Lyndsey thought the office too pretentious. Whoever had decorated it like big formal pieces in bold colors that didn't look very comfortable to lounge on.

When the door closed the female staff member let go of Lyndsey's arm and said. "We need to call your family and let them what you've been up to."

Lyndsey shook her head. "Yeah? Good luck with that. You'll have to fill them in on the last six or seven years too. They don't even know I'm here."

The woman raised an eyebrow and looked at Lyndsey like she might be lying. "Okay, then. We won't call anyone tonight. Your counselor will be here in the morning. We can talk more about it then. Maybe you'll feel better with some sleep." The woman paused and then added, "by the way, my name is Mary. I'm one of the support staff here."

"Well Mary, my name is Lyndsey, and I'm one of the *patients* who will be *leaving* here!"

Mary's face remained blank. "Lyndsey, you can talk to your counselor about this in the morning. In the meantime, we are going to put you in a different room so we can be nearby. In case you uh, need us."

Lyndsey needed to get back to the room she'd been sharing with Ruth and Becky. She wanted to see if Ruth was okay and also to get the money. Lyndsey decided to play along. She knew if she appeared docile the staff wouldn't watch her as closely. So she looked at Mary and nodded.

Mary lit up. "Way to go, Lyndsey, each time you make the right decision, you take another step towards getting better." Mary grinned, resembling her former serene self.

Lyndsey mimicked Mary's smile and thought to herself, the only right decision I'll be making is to get the hell out of here.

Mary continued talking, but Lyndsey tuned her out. She looked at Mary and watched her mouth move. *Blah, blah, blah.* It was all foreign to her and Mary may as well have been speaking in another language for all Lyndsey understood.

Mary was animated, and her eyes sparkled. "You'll know a new freedom and a new life." Lyndsey thought if Mary's smile got any bigger her jaw would break.

Maybe Mary was on drugs? She sure the hell was on *something.* You didn't get like that all by yourself.

"Just for today, that's it, Lyndsey, and sometimes if you can't do that, it's just for this minute."

Lyndsey yawned, the last traces of adrenaline leaving her body. "Can I go to bed now?" she asked, interrupting Mary's lecture.

"Of course you can. Come on. I'll take you there right now."

Lyndsey followed Mary, walking fast to keep up with her quick, energetic steps. *What the hell was Mary on? Speed?* Whatever it was Lyndsey wished she had some. Her eyelids felt thick and her legs heavy, each step harder to take than the one before it. Mary turned and noticed she had fallen behind.

"Almost there," Mary sang.

They hadn't gone far when Mary stopped in front of a door. They were in a short hallway with four doors. Lyndsey read the names on the three closed doors. The first door said *Dr. Green, Physician*, the second door, *Dr. Marvin, Psychiatrist.* The third said *Examination Room* in big bold letters. It was the fourth door that Mary opened. This one just said *Chapel.*

Lyndsey crossed the threshold as cautiously as if she were

descending into the bowels of hell.

Mary struggled to open the couch which she assured Lyndsey was a bed. Other than the couch, there was little else in the room. A small night table stood beside the couch. On top of the night table was a lamp that gave off a soft, welcoming glow and cast a shadow over the small crucifix that lay next to it.

The crucifix was interesting. Lyndsey wondered if someone had forgotten it here. She picked it up and looked it over. It was surprisingly heavy. Lyndsey studied the tiny figure engraved on the cross. It was a beautiful piece and spoke to her in a language needing no words.

Mary finally got the bed free. It was already made up and looked inviting. Lyndsey crawled into it fully clothed. It was heavenly.

Mary dimmed the lights and said she would be right back with Lyndsey's PJ's and toiletries.

Lyndsey never even heard her leave. She wasn't aware of Mary's departure or that she'd returned with a few of her belongings.

Lyndsey was unaware that Mary looked upon her and didn't have the heart to wake her to get into her pajamas.

Lyndsey was unaware of the smile that lit Mary's face as she watched Lyndsey sleep. Mary pulled the soft comforter up tightly around Lyndsey, leaving only her face and hand exposed.

Lyndsey was unaware her face was smooth and peaceful in her sleep and that she clutched tightly to the crucifix in her hand.

# CHAPTER SIXTY-FOUR

She woke briefly in the early morning rolled over and drifted off again. Asleep, she floated like a balloon, weightless. She was free and content, in a space where there was no time.

Lyndsey's eyes snapped open. Something hard and pokey embedded in her cheek. Lyndsey lifted her head and spotted the crucifix lying below. Her cheek burned, and she touched it. Great! Lyndsey felt the indentation and hoped it wouldn't last long. She sat up in bed, rubbed the sleep from her eyes and finger-combed her hair. Her mind was already racing.

First Lyndsey needed to get the money from under Ruth's mattress. Then she'd go. Before she could think anymore, there was a soft tap at the door.

Lyndsey looked up to see Mary. "Don't you ever sleep?"

"I will soon, I'm going off shift and just wanted to say goodbye." Mary gave her a funny look.

Lyndsey felt awkward and wasn't sure what to say. "Um, that was nice of you."

Still looking at her strangely Mary said, "There's a cross on your cheek."

"Yeah, I must have fallen asleep on it. I sure went out fast."

"Well, I'm glad you had a good sleep. Things always seem better in the light of day. Will you be here when I get back for my shift tonight?"

Mary's tone implied caring and Lyndsey couldn't figure her

out. Why should Mary care if she was there or not? If she was gone wouldn't Mary's job be easier? One less patient she would have to look after. Lyndsey picked up the crucifix and held it in her hand. It was still warm from her body's heat. She'd seen pictures of them before but had never actually seen one up close. The pictures didn't do it justice at all, and Lyndsey wondered how someone could sculpt something so small with such precise details.

"Earth to Lyndsey." Mary smiled. Her eyes kind.

Lyndsey hated it when people were nice to here. It was so much easier to be a bitch when nobody cared. But looking at Mary, Lyndsey knew she cared. Not only that, Mary had hope. Lyndsey couldn't tell her to go to hell. Or to mind her own business. She didn't want to be responsible for diminishing the light shining from Mary's eyes. But she didn't want to lie to her, either.

Torn, Lyndsey opted for the truth. "I don't know Mary. If I can, I'll go."

Mary's shoulders sagged. "Well until you do know, can you do me a favor?"

Lyndsey felt guilty for upsetting Mary and asked. "What's the favor?"

Mary's eyes sparkled as she grinned. Mary had nice white teeth. Lyndsey wished hers were as white. "Would you hold onto the cross until you decide, for me?"

"I don't believe in God. Mary. I stopped believing a long time ago. I'm not sure I ever did."

Mary reached out and touched the crucifix. "You don't have

to use the word God."

Lyndsey shrugged. "Even if there ever were a God, I wouldn't want anything to do with him. I mean what kind of God lets the horrible things that happen in our world, continue to go on?"

"That's humans doing those horrible things Lyndsey. Not God. Besides, you're getting hung up on the word God, and that's not what I'm talking about."

Lyndsey bristled. "Well then what are you talking about Mary? When I was a little girl and scared to death, I used to pray to God. I prayed that he would give me a family that loved me. I prayed that he would make Daddy stop hitting me. I prayed that my parents would stop fighting. I prayed I would stop having nightmares so terrifying I was afraid to fall asleep. I prayed my mother would leave my father and find us a happier home. I prayed my parents would get divorced. I prayed someone would save us. Then I prayed for my Father to die."

Mary's eyes were wet with unshed tears. "Oh, Lyndsey. I'm sorry."

Lyndsey continued, it felt good to get it out. "Praying to God didn't change anything, Mary. Things only got worse, and something festered in me. It was ugly, dark and hateful. I stopped praying to God and started taking care of myself. I learned to control my fear. I stopped trusting people. I discovered the world we live in is brutal and unfair. I grew up fast. While my friends played with dolls, I was learning survival tactics. Do you know what those are Mary?

Mary shook her head no,

So Lyndsey told her. "Survival is getting them before they get you. Tears are for the weak and the helpless, Mary. And I learned *never* to be helpless again."

Mary wiped her eyes. Her voice thick with emotion. "You never deserved that Lyndsey. I'm so sorry that was your experience. Every child deserves so much more."

Lyndsey tossed her head. "Well, I must have deserved it because it's what I got and *nobody* stepped in to change it."

Mary touched Lyndsey's hand. "No, Lyndsey, you didn't deserve that. What you deserved was unconditional love. You deserved the truth, which was you were precious and priceless and beautiful. You deserved to feel safe. You deserved to be held and cuddled. You deserved healthy parents. You deserved-"

Lyndsey was getting pissed listening to Mary and cut her off. "Holy Christ, Mary! What world are you from? No one ever told me I was loved or any of those things. What I was told was that I was *bad* and stupid and to smarten up. I was told I was never good enough and that everyone else's children were much better than me. And then, when I needed them most, I was told I was a slut and shameful. Then I wasn't told anything at all. Just silence. That was the worst."

Tears rolled down Mary's face. Lyndsey saw compassion for the little girl she'd been.

Lyndsey remembered her. She'd been skinny. All knees and elbows with bangs that hung crookedly over her forehead. She hadn't started to go bad yet. She was still innocent. The little she had been curious with a million questions and no one to ask. So the child made up her own answers. She had a great imagination and kept herself amused. Back then the world was an amazing place, and she could study a bug for hours. The child loved all the little creature she met each day. They became like family to her. The little Lyndsey was so sweet and pure. Lyndsey wished she could reach back in time and hold her.

Mary's arm circled Lyndsey in a hug, and she stiffened. Lyndsey was uncomfortable with the embrace.

Lyndsey looked over Mary's shoulder at the child. Little Lyndsey was lying stiffly on the floor in her parents' bedroom. She had just started having the horrible nightmares. She was experiencing a terror that only someone living in a war zone could know. She was small and helpless, and it felt big. Her terror was a living thing. It breathed in the darkness and held her frozen in its grip. Terror entered her mind destroying sanity and force-fed paranoia. Lyndsey was only a child, and there was nowhere she could turn for comfort.

Tears fell from her eyes and dripped on Mary's shoulder. Mary's arms were warm and safe. Lyndsey sobbed. Oh, that poor wee girl. She lay curled stiffly on the floor praying the nightmares would stop as she lay next to the only hope she had left. Her mother.

The black, ugly hard thing inside Lyndsey crawled up her throat exploding in ugly cries.

Mary rocked her as her mother couldn't. Mary whispered in Lyndsey's ear. "Ssshhh, there now. You are safe. You are loved."

For a moment, Lyndsey *did* feel loved.

She and Mary rocked together, taking comfort from the

other. They shared a special connection now.

After the tears stopped, Lyndsey felt awkward again and pulled free of Mary's arms. This was all very new and very strange. She was overwhelmed and raw with everything that had taken place.

Mary released Lyndsey and said, "Thank you for sharing that with me. It was such a privilege to hear your story. I hope you tell me more."

Lyndsey shrugged. "I'm still not sure I'll be here when you get back." Lyndsey added. "But thank you, I appreciate your support."

Mary opened the door and looked at Lyndsey. "Don't forget. Hold onto that cross."

Lyndsey looked at the cross in her hand. "I don't believe in God, Mary."

Mary smiled. "I know you don't. But maybe you will learn to believe in love."

With that, Mary left the room.

# CHAPTER SIXTY-FIVE

The little woman was an Amazon. She stood *maybe* five feet tall. Lyndsey thought she probably didn't weigh more than a hundred pounds. If that, but her bearing was gigantic. The little woman looked to be in her late forties. Kinda old, but she still looked good. The woman's hair was blond, and her eyes sky blue. At the moment they locked on Lyndsey.

Lyndsey's head spun. She'd met her counselor shortly after Mary left. Lyndsey expected a matronly woman not this little pit bull of a thing before her. Lyndsey was eating breakfast when Barb marched up to her chair, tapped her on the shoulder and said, "Come with me." It hadn't been a question.

Lyndsey followed her to the office. She hoped this meant she was one step closer to leaving.

Unfortunately, she wasn't.

Instead, Barb introduced herself, saying she was Lyndsey's counselor. Not wasting a moment Barb got right to business. She waved a piece of paper in Lyndsey's face and then pushed it across the desk.

Neither Barb nor Lyndsey moved, locked in a silent battle of wills.

Barb nudged the sheet of paper closer to Lyndsey. "I can sit here all day if you like. There's nothing I have to do right now that's more important than this." Barb leaned back in her chair and crossed her arms.

Power struggles were not her thing. Lyndsey pushed the sheet of paper away.

Barb said it was a contract saying she wouldn't leave before talking to staff and they would hold her personal belongings for the next twenty-four hours.

Lyndsey didn't want to sign the contract. She wanted to leave. If only she could get to Ruth's room, then she had an idea.

Lyndsey looked at Barb. "If you let me visit with Ruth I might sign the contract."

Barb stood, pushing back her chair. "Let's go."

"Wait! I was hoping for a *private* visit." Lyndsey glared at her.

Barb looked up at her. Her body language screamed *powerhouse*. Barb's brows raised. "I think there has been enough private visiting for now. I go with you, or you don't go."

"Fine!" Lyndsey reverted to the age of two as she stamped her foot and pouted. Lyndsey took her anger out on the chair she sat on, shoving it out of the way. The chair scraped across the floor and bumped into the desk with a loud bang.

Barb looked at her and Lyndsey was embarrassed. What was wrong with her? She was crying one minute and having temper tantrums the next. She was on an emotional roller-coaster, and she didn't like it.

As if speaking to a not very bright child Barb said, "I'm going to put your poor behavior down to PAWS and excuse it for the time being."

Lyndsey gaped at her. "I'm not a dog. What the hell are you talking about? I don't have paws."

"I don't mean the kind you find on a dog. PAWS stands for post-acute withdrawal syndrome. I think you're experiencing it, which would explain why you're oversensitive and acting irrationally."

Barb was an iceberg. Just looking at her made Lyndsey cold and she fought the urge to shiver. Barb opened the door and walked down the hallway. Lyndsey followed Barb, walking fast to keep up.

Lyndsey's leg muscles screamed in protest. She didn't feel good. Her bones ached, her stomach was woozy, and she thought she might be getting the flu. Lyndsey lagged behind Barb wondering how she could ditch her.

She spied an open door and thought about hiding in the room.

As if able to read her mind Barb turned in her direction. "Come on."

"You're going too fast." Lyndsey huffed. Barb had one speed. FAST.

Barb laughed. "Lyndsey, if you were going any slower you would be in reverse. Now come on. I don't want to lose you."

"I can't walk that fast," Lyndsey whined and then felt mortified.

Barb scowled. "Lyndsey if you want your life to improve, you need to learn how to push yourself harder."

The hallway crowded with people. All the noise hurt Lyndsey's head. She felt dizzy, and she was hot. She caught up to Barb and blurted, "I don't feel good. I think I'm getting the flu. Can I get a Tylenol?"

Barb shook her head. "Of course you don't feel good. You've been poisoning yourself for years. How did you expect to feel?"

*Jesus Christ*! This woman had the nerve to call herself a counselor? More like a prison guard or a prosecutor. There didn't seem to be an ounce of warmth or sympathy in her body. Opening her mouth to blast Barb, the words died on her lips.

Barb was as big as any gigantic dwarf Lyndsey had ever seen. She held herself ramrod straight. Her shoulders were back, and her cold blue eyes drilled little holes into Lyndsey. Lyndsey wanted to tell Barb to fuck off. But instead, she said, "I didn't use very much, and it wasn't for years."

Barb laughed as if someone had told her a joke. Then she marched off down the hallway.

Lyndsey stayed with her this time. Damned if she was going to let this little woman think she was in control. Lyndsey intensely disliked Barb. She tried not to think about how sick she was feeling and quickened her steps to match Barbs.

Two steps later she was miserable. Her bones ached and throbbed. There must be a Tylenol around this place somewhere. Maybe Ruth would have one. She would check the medicine cabinet when she got to their room.

A tall skinny woman stopped to speak with Barb. Her name was Gloria. Barb made introductions, and Gloria gushed, "Ooh, you're *so* lucky to have Barb for your counselor. She's great, and you should hear her in lecture."

Barb, not fazed by the compliment at all said, "thank you. I'll see you in group later."

Gloria moved off looking star-struck as if Barb had been an

actual celebrity, not the annoying little pit bull Lyndsey had briefly known.

Lucky my ass! If it weren't for bad luck, Lyndsey wouldn't have any luck at all. It was just her luck she had to get the worst counselor in rehab.

Her luck was about to change though, and quick. All she needed was the money hidden in Ruth' mattress and *see ya later Barb*!

Pain stabbed at Lyndsey's knees as she went down the stairs. It was as if the fluid lubricating her joints had dried up. A Tylenol 3 would fix her aches quickly. Maybe she could get one before leaving? She'd spotted the doctor's office last night. Maybe she could get one there?

The lower level was quiet. The silence was soothing to Lyndsey's sore ears. The woman's wing smelled nice, like laundry soap, baby powder, and shampoo.

That was weird, too. Lyndsey's senses, especially smell, worked better than it had in a long time. She was picking up scents she hadn't noticed in a while.

Barb opened the door wide. "After you."

Lyndsey passed in front of Barb trying not to touch her as she entered the room.

A few steps in she stopped.

The room was vacant, neither Ruth nor Becky was here. Ruth's bed was immaculate. Made with military precision. A tossed quarter would have bounced off the blankets.

Anger spiked her tone, and Lyndsey snapped at Barb. "Where's Ruth?"

Barb looked like the cat who had swallowed the canary. She grinned at Lyndsey and said. "The gigs up."

# CHAPTER SIXTY-SIX

The circle sat twelve. The people in eleven of the chairs all stared at her. Lyndsey had been *grouped*. She was in the hot seat. At least, that's what Lyndsey called it. Barb called it CBT or cognitive behavioral therapy.

The purpose of this group was to help Lyndsey modify her thoughts, beliefs, and perceptions, and to change her usual pattern of behaving. Apparently, this was done through feedback which Lyndsey was getting now.

One group member said she had an indifferent attitude. Lyndsey zoned him out and thought about Becky. She would like to get her hands on her, her fingernails and teeth, too. Becky had ratted her out, and Lyndsey thought about ways she could get back at her.

"You appear hostile." A little pimple faced boy spoke up, as other members of the group nodded their heads in agreement.

Of course, she was hostile! She wanted to wrap her hands around Becky's neck! Lyndsey wished Tommy was in the group with her. At least there would be one person on her side.

Lyndsey still couldn't believe it. The empty room. No Ruth, no Becky and then Barb marching her back up the stairs. They hadn't said a word. The only noise came from Barb's shoes as they clicked on the tile floors.

When they entered Barb's office, Becky was waiting for them. With Becky was another woman who was there to *support*

Becky!

Becky looked at Lyndsey and blurted. "Ruth told me what happened. I can't believe you took advantage of her that way, Lyndsey. I had to tell. I was worried about you and Ruth."

"You were worried about me?" Lyndsey gave Becky a hard look. "Yeah right! Sure you were!"

Becky's eyes narrowed. "It was all an act you know. Ruth just pretended to have a seizure to try and distract the staff from the fact you had been trying to sneak out, and you had hidden the money."

Lyndsey wanted to jump across the desk and wipe the smug look right off Becky's face.

"Anyway," Becky continued. "It backfired on both of you because when you left the nurses came in and got Ruth. They also changed her bed, and that was when they found the money hidden there. I don't know why she put herself out like that for *you*. She was *my* roommate first, and she never did anything like that for me. And frankly Lyndsey you're just not worth it!" Becky tossed her head flipping a thin strand of hair in her face.

Barb interjected. "You're coming off pretty high and mighty here, Becky. And you sound judgmental. Giving feedback isn't about judging someone's character. It's saying what you see, stating the facts, without judging."

"Oh, okay." Becky sneered. "Well, I *see* Lyndsey stealing from an old lady!"

"Have you ever stolen from anyone before?" Barb inquired.

"What! This isn't about me?" Becky pouted.

"Just answer the question."

"I don't see the point." Becky looked like she was about to cry. "I never really stole before, I just sorta borrowed things. I always meant to pay them back. I'm not a thief, unlike someone else in the room!" Becky's eyes darted at Lyndsey.

"Becky! That's enough." Barb bared her teeth.

Becky whimpered. "It's not fair. Why does everyone like Lyndsey so much? I've been here longer, and no one even notices me." With a shaky finger, Becky pointed at Barb and mewled, "You're playing favorites."

Barb looked at Lyndsey and Becky and said, "You two have a lot in common. Becky, I want you to tell your group about our meeting today. Lyndsey, come with me."

Lyndsey shot Becky a look that said *you're dead* and left the room with Barb. Back at her office Barb pushed the contract at Lyndsey and said. "Sign it or leave. If you leave, you'll be going back to the psychiatric unit where they will hold you for further observation."

"I'm not going back to the hospital. I keep telling everyone that I'm not sick. What is wrong with you people? Why can't you hear me?"

Barb tapped her ear. "I hear just fine. It's you who seems to have that difficulty."

Lyndsey rolled her eyes in frustration. Communication with this woman was like talking to a brick wall. "What part of *I am not sick* don't you understand?" Lyndsey questioned through clenched teeth.

For the first time sadness flickered in Barb's eyes. "Not only are you sick, but you're also terminally ill. Lyndsey, you're dying, and you don't even know it. That's how sick you are."

Lyndsey wanted to shake this woman. "I don't have cancer. My heart is fine. My lungs are good. My liver is working. I'm not dying. I am *not* sick!"

"How do you know?"

"What?" Lyndsey asked feeling thrown off track.

"How do you know you're heart's fine, you're lungs are good, and your liver is working?"

"Duh! Well, obviously they are. I'm still standing here."

"Yes, and you shouldn't be." Barb met her eyes. "Didn't you just try to kill yourself? What would you call that? Would you call that *well,* Lyndsey?"

Wow! Barb certainly didn't beat about the bush. "You need blood work done. You've done damage to yourself. Besides the obvious, I mean."

"I'm *not* sick! I was just…" Lyndsey trailed off at a loss for words.

"You were just what?"

"I was just trying to…" Lyndsey couldn't come up with anything.

Barb twitched and huffed. "Are you going to sign this or not. I have other things to do, and if you're going to sign this contract, I don't want to waste any more of my time. The choice is yours. I would recommend that you stay. At least long enough to understand how sick you are."

God, she was tired. Sick and tired. Lyndsey just wanted to go to bed. Her body was sore, and she couldn't think straight. And trying to get this crazy woman to see the truth was wearing her out. Maybe she would stay. Just for one more day. Lyndsey would get some sleep and then she could find Ruth, and they would work something out.

Lyndsey reached for the contract and signed her name. She looked at Barb wanting the last word. "Okay. I'll stay, but only one more day."

Barb nodded as if it expecting nothing less and announced. "Group in ten minutes, head to the kitchen and grab a quick bite first."

So much for sleep, Lyndsey thought. A sharp jab to her side brought her back to the room. Pimple boy glared at her. "Not listening!"

Lyndsey sat up straighter in her chair and glared back.

# CHAPTER SIXTY-SEVEN

Lyndsey was snoozing in the stuffy lecture hall when the woman's voice roused her. The lecture title on the whiteboard read *Seven Stages of the Family Disease*. Lyndsey wondered what kind of sick trick they were playing on her now. Her ears perked up as she listened to the lecturer talk about her family.

Who told this woman lecturer about her family? Lyndsey hadn't mentioned a word about them other than to say she hadn't seen them in years. The woman with the microphone talked about walking on eggshells. She said in alcoholic or unhealthy homes, just saying the wrong thing could set off an explosion. The woman described the family as hypervigilant, meaning to be on guard, or an increased state of alertness leaving family members feeling sick and exhausted. She said the family walked a tightrope and communication was closed, questions strongly discouraged. The lecturer said the family system was one of dictatorship and rigid rules. And the enabler protected the alcoholic and made excuses for them.

Oh my God! This woman knew her family!

The lecturer went on to give examples of some things an enabler might say; "Your dad had a rough day, that's why he yells at you, or he drinks because it eases his stress." The lecturer said addiction is a family disease because *everyone* gets sick. The whole family makes excuses for the alcoholic and tolerates neglectful and abusive behavior.

The lecturer described another scenario where it was the son who was the alcoholic. He was sleeping in his room, and it was late afternoon. His parents were arguing. The father wanted to wake up his son and kick him out of the house. The mother didn't agree, saying her son needed his sleep. Had the son been awake he would have told them both to go to hell. His head was pounding from drinking the night before. But the son didn't have to deal with any of it. He slept blissfully unaware as his parents fought with each other.

Lyndsey fidgeted in her seat wondering when she could sneak out. She saw Becky watching her and turned away.

The woman with the mike continued. "The father was angry with his wife for protecting their son and babying him. The mother was angry with her husband for being such a lousy father. The boy's younger sister sat on a couch nearby not noticed as her parents tore verbal strips off one another. The sister was used to this. She was the *invisible* one. No one ever noticed her. Her parent's attention was *always* on her older brother."

Lyndsey knew exactly how the girl on the couch felt and her heart went out to her.

The women with the microphone paused for a moment to take a drink of water before continuing. "The family car sat in the driveway no longer usable. Billy, their son, had crashed it. The mother was feeling frustrated. She turned on her daughter and said if she were a better sister and more understanding of Billy, maybe this wouldn't have happened."

Lyndsey fidgeted. Her seat was too hard. She scribbled furiously on her paper.

The lecturer said. "By now Billy's family is sicker than him.

They blame each other for Billy's actions. The family is not rational. They communicate by hurling insults and swearing. They point the finger at one another.

Lyndsey thought of her family. She felt a stab of remorse for fighting with her sister. They'd turned on each other, like a pack of starving hyenas.

The lecturer continued. "We know the son was intoxicated. Billy was high as usual. But that only explains his actions. His family was sober, and yet they were acting crazier than Billy. Billy's mother stayed up all night waiting for her son to come home. His father hadn't gotten much sleep, either. He lay awake stewing about his wife and how their son seemed to be getting all her attention. The father felt angry and resented being neglected."

Lyndsey remembered her parents' fighting. She'd been so worried her mom was going to be hurt. Her mom was so much smaller than her dad. Lyndsey feared she would find one of her parents dead and she didn't think it would be her dad.

The lecturer cleared her throat and resumed. "By this time the mother has a closer relationship with her son than her husband. She feels he needs her and she wants to protect him. The couple argues openly as their daughter sits nearby going unnoticed."

Lyndsey remembered all the times she'd spent in her room, alone.

"They belittle one another and call each other awful names. They point fingers and yell. They call up every hate-filled instance from their past. Sometimes their arguments will escalate to the point of violence."

Lyndsey remembers the thrown dishes and breaking glass.

"Sometimes the police are called but usually not. Dad just leaves. He storms out. He might go to work and stay there for twelve to fifteen hours a day. Or maybe he goes out and has a few drinks, too. Mom just cries. She cries and cries and tells their younger daughter what a jerk her father is. Maybe they divorce, but usually, they don't. They just stay together growing more miserable over the years."

Lyndsey remembered the tears. She cried buckets of them.

"Billy, he sleeps. He feels pretty good when he wakes up. He's the only one who got a good night's rest. When he leaves his bedroom, he finds his mom and hits her up for another fifty. His mom doesn't tell his dad. It's their little secret. Mom doesn't feel bad about giving her son money. If her husband weren't such an asshole, she wouldn't have to keep so many secrets."

Lyndsey remembered all the secrets her mother kept from her dad, the calls that came from school to inform her mom of her absences. The sneaking out at night.

"The daughter, she does what she can to make her mother happy. She gets good grades in school. She is a high achiever. She only wants to be noticed. She *craves* attention and will grow up and marry someone just like Billy because emotionally unavailable men are all she knows.

Lyndsey thought about *him*.

"Billy, he goes out and gets drunk again. Why wouldn't he? He doesn't have any of the mess of his drinking. His family takes care of him. Billy gets all the fun, and they keep paying for it by cleaning up his mess. Billy knows his family is screwed up and thinks to himself *if you had such a messed up family, you'd be drinking, too!"*

Lyndsey thought about the booze she'd stolen over the years from her father's liquor cabinet.

"Mom ends up on Ativan or sleeping pills. She never tells anyone what's going on. The only person she confides in is her daughter. She tells her daughter *everything.* By now mom sleeps a lot, and her eating habits have changed."

Lyndsey pictured her mother in her room, the door shut.

"You never see Dad anymore. The house is quiet."

Lyndsey remembered the long silences. Miles and miles of it, only to be filled with outbursts of rage.

"Billy meets someone like Mom and moves out. He's got a new champion now, someone who will love him and look after him."

Lyndsey thought about *him* again.

"Mom takes antidepressants. Sometimes she doesn't get dressed. Mom is heading for a nervous breakdown. She might even think about suicide."

Lyndsey blinked back tears and wondered how her mom was doing.

"Out of the entire family, Billy is the only one having any fun. He never gives his family a second thought. He has found his one true love, and it's not in the *human* form."

Lyndsey saw her dad's glass of rye on the kitchen table.

"Dad seldom thinks of his family, either. He has moved on. He may have remarried, probably to a younger wife, one that will pay attention to him. Or maybe his life is simply consumed with work and he doesn't have to think at all."

Lyndsey remembered the little white pills.

"The family is sick, and they don't know it. They still think Billy is the sick one. Mom continues to blame Dad and believes she's a victim. She's done nothing wrong. If only everyone else would get their act together, then she would be all right."

Lyndsey thought of her mom and all the wasted years.

"Without treatment for the *whole family*, they'll continue spiraling downwards. Their bodies will breathe, but their spirits will die."

Lyndsey thought of her mother's blank face.

"The days will get longer and harder to get through. Life will become a task, something to be done and gotten out of the way. They will lose their joy. Some will contemplate suicide, and others will commit it. But most will continue living in their misery, wondering where it all went so wrong. They will wait for the *sick person* to change. Year after year, they just wait."

Lyndsey wept, her heart was breaking.

"Without enablers, Billy has nowhere to go. He would be forced to grow up and take responsibility for his actions. Billy can't stay sick by himself. He doesn't have to worry though. His people would rather die than make him take responsibility."

Lyndsey thought of the belt and her mother's excuses.

"And that's what they're doing. When you live your life taking care of someone else, you stop living. If the disease of addiction doesn't kill you; the disease of enabling will. There are worse things than death and living in misery *forever* is one.

Make no mistake, folks. The family disease is a *deadly* one. Each person in the family is affected. Without treatment, this illness continues from one generation to the next."

Lyndsey wondered about her grandparents. She never knew them, and maybe this was why.

"So thank your lucky stars you're here and pray to God you don't pass this on to anyone else. Thank you for listening."

There was a small smattering of applause. Lyndsey was stunned with disbelief. The lecturer had described her family to a tee.

Bodies pushed past her chair, and the lecture hall emptied out.

The whiteboard blurred.

Lyndsey sat frozen to her seat.

The lectures words rang in her ears.

# CHAPTER SIXTY-EIGHT

A paper plane landed on her clipboard. Lyndsey put down her pen and looked up.

Tommy grinned over at her. "Whatcha doing?"

Lyndsey said "I" and dissolved into tears. The lecture weighed heavily on her mind, and she hadn't been feeling right since.

Tommy's mouth formed an O, and he sat down beside her. "What's wrong Linds?"

Lyndsey sniffed, she felt all quivery inside. "I don't know, um, *everything*? That lecture got to me. At first, I thought the woman was talking about my family, and I wondered how she could have known. Then I felt sad for the family she was talking about, and I couldn't get my family out of my head. Then I just felt awful for my family. I miss them. I've never missed them before, and it feels weird. It's hard to believe my family is sick. I always thought my dad was mean and my mom naive. I've never looked at them, or me, as *sick*."

Tommy nodded in agreement. "My mom's like that too, you know. She hardly says a word anymore. She stares at me with her big, sad eyes, and oozes depression. Dad cheated on her with his secretary, and it doesn't help that I'm here."

"Seriously? Your family's like that, too?"

"Yeah." Tommy snorted. "And I took advantage of it. Mom would tell me her long, sad tale and then I would ask her for money. Like payment for listening. She told me things that were pretty gross, too. She talked about Dad and his new girlfriend. Mom was always complaining Dad didn't give her enough money."

Lyndsey twirled a lock of hair around her finger. "Sometimes when my dad was drunk he would tell me stuff, too. It's sad you know. I liked him better when he was drunk even though he was pathetic. When he was sober, I didn't like him at all. I don't think he liked himself, either. I wish I would have known he was sick and not just an asshole."

Tommy shrugged. "What difference would it have made, Linds?"

"A lot, I think. Maybe I would have been nicer, more understanding. Being sick isn't your fault, is it?"

Tommy picked up the paper plane and smoothed the creases. "I'm not sure. But being sick still doesn't give you or me, or him, the right to treat people the way we have."

"I wonder why mom didn't know."

"Your mom probably did." Tommy put the plane down on Lyndsey's clipboard and looked at her. "Sometimes it's easier to stay stuck than to move on to something new."

Lyndsey thought about what Tommy said. It sounded right.

Tommy tapped the sheet of paper in front of Lyndsey. "What's that?"

"Barb gave me this assignment. It's probably a waste of time. I don't think I'll be here long, but she seemed to think it was important. The assignment is to help me see what drugs and alcohol did to my relationships."

"Who did you put down?"

"I was only going to write about Drake, but Barb said I had to add my family, too. So I put down Drake, my sister, my mom, and my dad. It should be the other way around. I wish my Dad would look at the damage he did to us. I'm stuck though. I can easily see the damage I did to Drake but its way harder with my family. I keep coming back to the damage they did to me."

"It's not that hard, Linds. Did you ever steal from them? Lie to them? Hurt them? Put them in danger?"

"Um, yeah, but I thought they deserved it."

"Yeah, but that's not the question, right? Just focus on your part. Not theirs and it will be easier for you to answer."

"You know what's really weird?"

"What?"

"Barb says I forgot to put the most important person in my life on this piece of paper. I didn't even give them a thought. It was like that person didn't exist to me. Oh, shit!" Lyndsey wiped the tears running down her cheeks.

Tommy leaned in closer, looking concerned. "Who did you forget, Lyndsey?"

"Oh, Tommy, Meeeee! I forgot about *me!*" Lyndsey wailed.

# CHAPTER SIXTY-NINE

Lyndsey sharpened her pencil and scratched her head. She looked down at the paper and chewed her lip. *Describe a time in your life when you felt a power greater than yourself guiding you.* Shit, she didn't know how to answer that. *What do the words Higher Power mean to you?*

She thought back to group earlier that day. The word God had kept coming up. God this, God that and Lyndsey piped in with "God damn it, I'm sick of the word *God*." She'd blurted it out, and was surprised at her outburst. Feeling embarrassed. Lyndsey waited in silence for Barb's ax to fall on her head. But it never did. Instead, Barb threw her head back and laughed. Then she asked. "Can anyone else relate to Lyndsey?"

Some of the people in group twittered nervously, and others visibly relaxed.

Lyndsey breathed a sigh of relief and got honest. "When I hear the word God I think of the guy nailed to the cross. It pisses me off because it's like if you don't believe in God, you're going to hell. And if you do believe in God, you must obey a strict set of rules. Then, if you make one mistake, you're going to hell. It seems pretty rigid to me."

Tommy nodded. "Yeah, and the guy on the cross didn't do anything wrong and look how he ended up!"

"Besides. " Lyndsey admitted. "I don't want to believe in anything that punitive. I lived that way my entire life. And I was never good enough."

"Okay." Barb nodded. "Then what do you believe in, Lyndsey?"

"I don't know," Lyndsey faltered.

Barb's eyebrows raised. "Come on, take a risk. God can be anything you want. What, where, when, or who, have you have felt most comforted?"

Lyndsey thought about the field of tall grass and all the little creatures she met there. She thought about her little dog, Suzy. Lyndsey thought about Drake. She took a giant step out of her comfort zone, eyed the group and decided to go for it. "When I was little, I loved playing outdoors. I would play for hours. I was curious about all the little creatures. I felt safe and nurtured and... Full. Not like eating full, but like a full heart. I know that sounds corny, but it's true. And I guess the other thing…is *love*. I want to be loved so badly. I feel like I've been searching for it my whole life…" Lyndsey trailed off afraid she had said too much.

The group room was quiet. Lyndsey's cheeks burned, and she expected people to laugh at her. But no one was laughing. Instead, heads bobbed up and down around the room. The people in this room could relate to her. She blinked back tears grateful to be understood.

Barb smiled and looked at every person in the group. "What Lyndsey is describing is spirituality. Religion is for people afraid of going to hell. Spirituality is for people who have already been there. Lyndsey, it looks like you've found your God after all."

"What? I don't understand."

Barb sat forward in her chair and looked at Lyndsey. "You

said nature made your heart full. Maybe your God can be the *Great Out Doors*."

"What? You can't change it like that can you?"

"Why not?" Barb replied. "The idea of God is to comfort. It can be anything you want it to be. The God of your understanding should love you unconditionally and have your best interest at heart."

"Well, what if you don't like the outdoors?" Tommy asked.

"What makes you feel better, Tommy?" Barb questioned.

"I don't know. I guess talking in these groups have helped."

"Okay then," Barb smiled. Why don't you make your God these groups? A *Group Of Drunks* is your higher power."

Tommy's eyes grew wide. "Isn't that blasphemous or something?"

"Not at all," Barb replied. "The God of my understanding isn't rigid. He works with the belief system that works for me."

Tommy scratched his head, and he looked dubiously at Barb. "Well, I guess…" He trailed off, not convinced.

"It's all right, Tommy. We don't have to figure it out today. Just try and stay open to the idea. Okay? Or if you find your existing belief system is more comforting than the one I described, stick with that." Barb announced group was over and walked out of the room.

Lyndsey doodled on her paper. Her mind was full and her body tired. She decided to put the assignment away for the night and work on it tomorrow. Lyndsey couldn't believe it. She was five days sober!

She crawled into her new bed. Barb had asked her to move

rooms. The bedroom she was in now had two beds. Lyndsey's roommate slept next to her while she stared at the ceiling. Her contract was up tomorrow, and she could get her purse and ID back. Lyndsey reached for the clipboard on the night table next to her. The little boy's drawing taped there. Lyndsey studied the picture through a thin sliver of moonlight. *Git Wel Son* and smiling faces.

If only it were that easy. Was it even possible? Lyndsey wondered if she'd ever drawn smiling faces when she was little. Lyndsey pressed the clipboard to her chest, drifting off.

"Lyndsey! Wake up!" Jan stood over her.

Lyndsey's eyes blinked open. "What?" She croaked.

"You were yelling. You woke me up." Jan looked alarmed.

Then it came back to her. She'd been in a dark alley arguing with a toothless man. His face was sunken, and he had a weak chin. The back of his head disappeared into the grey hood attached to his sweatshirt. Lyndsey didn't know him. The man's face was shrouded in the dark. Lyndsey played tug of war with the crack pipe in his hand. Although the man's face was a blur, she could see the big rock sitting on ash in the bowl of his pipe. Lyndsey's mouth watered as she fought the man for it. She sank her teeth into his hand and gagged. The man's flesh was rotten. The stench filled her nostrils as she spat out a chunk of his hand. The pipe flew through the air and landed on the ground. Lyndsey watched it all in slow motion, seeing the pipe shatter as it hit the ground. The crack-rock rolled next to it. Lyndsey bent to pick up the crack, but before she could grasp it, ghostlike forms surrounded her. "Nooooo," they moaned. Lyndsey felt their icy fingers on her. The ghost figures danced around Lyndsey preventing her from picking up the crack.

"Lyndsey," Jan touched her shoulder. "Are you okay?"

Lyndsey was cold. Her heart raced with fear. Sweat beaded her brow, and she felt clammy. Her breath came in ragged gasps, and she glanced nervously around the room expecting to see the hideous little man lurking somewhere in a corner.

"Lyndsey?"

"I'm okay," Lyndsey rubbed her eyes. "I had a nightmare."

"Well, you sure were yelling."

"What was I yelling?"

"You were yelling *no,* but it was more like you wailed it. And you didn't sound like you. It was creepy!"

"I'm sorry for waking you up."

Jan squeezed Lyndsey's arm. "Don't worry about it. Did you have a using dream?"

"A using dream? What's that?"

Jan replied. "When I first got here I had using dreams all the time. For me, my dreams were about bottles of wine. I used to hide wine in the closet at home. I would pretend I was cleaning, but really, I'd be drinking wine in the closet."

"What?" Lyndsey was irritated, and Jan wasn't making sense.

"Anyway," Jan continued not noticing Lyndsey's bad mood. "The dreams started a week after I got here. They were vivid! I could smell the wine. I was so close to tasting it. Something would always happen before I could drink it and I woke up wanting it so bad." Jan sighed.

"I guess mine was sort of like that," Lyndsey grumbled. Christ, Jan was a chatterbox. It's way too early for this. She looked at the clock on the bedside table. Three forty a.m. If she had gotten through the window the night before, what would she be doing right now?

"My counselor calls them using dreams." Jan prattled on.

"I almost had it," Lyndsey said to the ceiling. "I was fighting with this creepy little guy, trying to get the crack pipe from him and I bit him. It was disgusting."

"So it was a using dream, then. Don't they seem so real?"

"All I could think about was getting the crack from him. I didn't care about anything else. I would have had it too, but these weird shadows kept saying no, no, then I woke up. It was real though. Like if I could have smoked it, I would have gotten high."

Lyndsey was heavy with dread. The dream left her feeling antsy and skittish.

Jan straightened Lyndsey's covers and returned to her bed. "I hardly have them anymore. Thank God. It'll get better. My counselor says it's the way your addiction works. If it can't get you while you're awake, it will get you in your sleep."

Oh, that was a comforting thought! Lyndsey tossed and turned long after Jan had gone to sleep. Her mood was dark and ugly. She felt like something powerful was squeezing her.

Lyndsey stared at the clock focusing on the bright red numbers. The clock hissed softly, and the numbers moved.

Four eleven.

Lyndsey watched the clock and saw the piece of flesh lying

next to the chunk of crack.

Click.

Four twelve.

*Fuck it.*

Lyndsey got out of bed.

# CHAPTER SEVENTY

Lyndsey never meant to stay. She'd just been too tired to leave. She thought she'd go when she had the energy to work up another plan. Lyndsey couldn't remember the last time she had been so exhausted. Just breathing wore her out. It was like she was dragging a heavy anchor. Walking anywhere was difficult. Lyndsey felt like an old woman, with aches and pains in every muscle and joint.

All she wanted to do was sleep. But they wouldn't let her. The staff was always getting her out of bed. Lyndsey was miserable. To make matters worse, she couldn't get any pain medication. Before rehab and at the slightest sign of an ache or a sore throat she popped and pill and voila! The pain disappeared. The odd time she couldn't get her hands on codeine, or narcotic medication, she would stay in bed and sleep.

There were times she would spend three, four, even five days in bed, only getting up to eat and use the washroom. When she did finally leave her bed, Lyndsey was weak and sore, but she had never suffered as she did now. What she wouldn't give for a Tylenol!

"Lyndsey," Barb's eye blue eyes pierced her misery. "Would you like to share with the group?"

"Ah, no thanks. I'll pass." Lyndsey was deep in thought and wanted to get back there. Plus she found this particular group a waste of time. She was tired of listening to people whine about their lives. Lyndsey didn't have much in common with them, either. The people in this group were *really* sick. Lyndsey wasn't even close to their level.

Barb clapped her hands once and sat up leaning into the group. "Lyndsey you don't get to pass. Rehab isn't a game you're playing. You're fighting for your life, and you've already used up all your passes. Get off your high horse and join the rest of us."

Barb is such a bitch! Lyndsey thought. Lyndsey glared at her counselor. "Well, if you really want to know what I'm thinking, here it is; I wish I didn't feel so sick because then I'd have the energy to get the *fuck out of here!*"

Barb shrugged. "Okay, you're dope sick. Can anyone else relate?"

Heads nodded. Lyndsey looked around the room taking in the end-stage addicts. She looked at Barb and shook her head. "Of course they can relate to dope sickness. They're sick. Look at them!" Lyndsey pointed a shaking finger around the room before continuing. "And I'm not dope sick."

A skinny female sat to Lyndsey's right. She was covered in sores and scratched at one when she spoke to Lyndsey. "I never thought I was dope sick either. I always put it down to being tired, or I had the flu."

Lyndsey looked at her surprised. "Ah, no offense but it's pretty clear you're messed up."

The skinny woman stopped scratching and pointed one long bony finger at the bandage on Lyndsey's wrist. Then she mimicked, "Ah, no offense but it's pretty clear you are too."

"That was a mistake! It's not the same thing at all." Lyndsey couldn't believe this skinny woman thought they were alike.

"Yeah, well so were these!" The skinny woman snorted and pointed to the scars on her cheeks and arms.

Lyndsey thought the people in the group were too far gone to understand, but she tried to help them. "I was going through a bad time. I admit I messed up, but I would never have gotten as bad as you guys are. I never used a needle, and I had plenty of opportunities to try one. I'm not dope sick. I'm not a junkie, and I'm not an alcoholic!"

Barb looked around the room. "Addiction is a disease. It's not about whether you use needles or glue or drink or snort or huff or any other way people get high. Don't minimize by comparing needles to alcohol. They're both deadly. The only difference is IV drugs will get you to bottom a lot quicker than alcohol."

"That's not true! Needles are disgusting, and they're much worse," Lyndsey argued.

"No," Barb shook her head. "It's all the same. A person can drink for years before they hit their bottom. In that time they torment their families, friends, and workplace before dying or going to treatment. Because it's legal, it only appears to be the lesser of the two evils. But make no mistake. Alcoholism is a progressive and deadly disease. It's the same as any other addiction. And families suffer a lot longer with it than they do with any other drug."

No one spoke. All eyes were on Barb.

"Being an addict isn't as much about what you use as it is

about the way you manage your life. With addiction, your family, work, finances, physical health and mental well-being unravels. It's not about what you use, or don't use, or even how much of it you're using. It's about how you *live*. Addiction lives in hiding, dishonesty, isolation, lying, shame, guilt, chaos, blame, secrecy, resentment, and feeling different from other people. Addicted persons become self-absorbed and struggle with self-pity. They live in denial and delusion. They're impulsive and irrational. Addiction has less to do with what you use and more to do with *why*.

"Then why do I use?" Lyndsey challenged Barb.

Barbs clear blue eyes met Lyndsey's. "You use for the same reason everyone else does, to feel better. A person using needles gets the same relief as a person drinking. It's just faster. All of you in this room got the same results. No matter what you use, you are powerless over your addition, and your life is unmanageable."

Lyndsey bristled. "My life isn't unmanageable." She argued.

Barb's eyes narrowed. "That's right, Lyndsey, your life is doing incredibly well, and that's just a cute little bracelet you're wearing on your left wrist."

Lyndsey glanced at the not so white bandage circling her wrist. It had started to itch. She rubbed it on her pants and looked incredulously at Barb. The woman was mean! Lyndsey wasn't sure she was sane. Lyndsey fought to remain calm and wondered how she could get through to her counselor and peers. As if talking to a group of dim-wits Lyndsey spoke slowly. "I already explained. It…was…a…mistake."

Barb waved at the group. "How many of you thought you didn't need to be here?"

Every hand in the group raised. Lyndsey scrambled to say something, anything, to convince the group of misfits she didn't belong here.

The skinny female sitting next to her joined in. "I lived in my car for a while. I didn't think much of it. I knew lots of people living on the streets, and I thought I was much better off than they were. In a way, I kinda looked down on them. I still had my car. They had nothing. I didn't think I was screwed up. I thought everyone else was."

Barb smiled encouragingly at the skinny woman and said. "What changed your mind, Lorna?"

"Well, I ended up losing my car. I pawned it to buy dope. When the dope was gone, and I was crashing, I had no place to go. It was awful. I was hungry and cold, and I saw things that weren't there. I thought the devil was after me and a young boy took me by the hand. He helped me find a shelter and stayed with me until my paranoia had passed. The kid and I got to talking, and I told him my story. He told me his story too. The kid was two years sober. He worked on the streets helping people like me. Anyway, we were talking, and I said my life was so messed up because of what everyone had done to me."

Lyndsey stifled a yawn. She hated these groups! The people never seemed to shut up. Lyndsey needed a cigarette and thought about sneaking one in the bathroom. Before she could get up, Barb jumped down her throat. "Lyndsey, are we keeping you awake?"

Lorna never missed a beat. "This young guy says to me, well who are all the people you think have messed you up. So I give him this great big list of people, and he says, who do you think is the common denominator? I was never any good at math. I don't know what he means, and he says real simple-like. The common denominator is *you*. And just like that, I know it's true. *Me,* I'm the common denominator."

"Jesus, speak English for Christ's sake!" It was all she could do to stay in her seat. Lyndsey was on the verge of screaming.

"What Lorna means is your biggest problem is you." Barb folded her fingers and then continued. "Think about it. Your best thinking got you here. If you continue to trust your thinking, you'll get the same results you've always gotten. The definition of insanity is doing the same thing over and over again, expecting a different result."

Lorna nodded. "And it gets worse, each time. You try and do it differently, but it doesn't work. It's easier to blame everyone else for the way your life has turned out. I lost my car, and I blamed the drug dealer. I got scabs on my face, and I blamed the people who made the meth. I spent all my money, and I blamed the government for being a tight-ass with my welfare checks. I got kicked out of my place, and I blamed the landlord. My life was a disaster, but it wasn't my fault. Eventually, I was high all the time. Then I *had* to use because I was dope-sick. The things I did to get my drugs weren't my fault. I needed dope." Lorna shuddered, visibly impacted by her words.

Lyndsey nodded. Her head moved on its own, and she was shocked. She had more in common with Lorna than she'd thought. Lyndsey knew the blame game well.

The group was quiet.

Honesty shone its bright lights into the small room, and the stark reality was blinding.

With nothing to distract her and no one to blame, Lyndsey sat with the truth of her making.

The weight was stunning.

# CHAPTER SEVENTY-ONE

She was enveloped in darkness, climbing a long staircase. Lyndsey could barely make out the step in front of her. The climb was steep, more like climbing a mountain than a staircase. Above Lyndsey, the stairs disappeared into a pocket of light. Her feet lifted to the stair above knowing she needed to reach it. She huffed from exertion and quickened her steps. Lyndsey climbed and climbed. At times a wispy tendril of white light would touch her, giving her a brief glimpse of the paradise ahead. The white light ignited energy, and she basked in the feeling. Her body now strong she climbed the stairs tirelessly. A great gust of wind came from behind her, almost knocking her off the stairs. It was a cold wind, howling in compliance and procrastination. She slowed her steps and trod cautiously. Something ugly wanted her off this staircase. She must be careful. The woman felt the angry presences in the dark surrounding her. Guided by the white light above, she took the next step and then the next. The white light held her steady, guiding her forward. She knew she was in danger. The darkness wanted her back. But she held steady to the white light, and it stayed with her. Now she could feel it on her face. The white light held back the darkness. She was getting closer.

\*\*\*

Lyndsey awoke to feel refreshed. She slept well, and her aches and pains were gone. The dream stayed with her, and

Lyndsey thought about the white light. She imagined it enveloping her with its bright aura and healing her broken soul. Lyndsey experienced a jolt of energy. She felt something she hadn't felt in a very long time.

Hope.

She jumped out of bed and stopped short. It was time to do things differently. Lyndsey knelt beside her bed. She wanted to say thank you, but she wasn't sure who to say it to. After a brief hesitation, she decided it didn't matter and began. *Thank you for my life, thank you for my hope, thank you for Drake and all the kind people I've met here. Thank you for everything.*

Lyndsey was embarrassed, being on her knees was a humbling experience. What if someone saw her? Lyndsey rose, feeling disappointed. She never said the one thing that mattered. It was a miracle she never thought possible. To hell with my pride! Lyndsey got down on her knees. She closed her eyes and in a soft whisper said what was on her mind from the moment she woke. *Thank you for my sobriety.*

Lyndsey was two weeks clean and sober today.

She made her bed and took a long hot shower. As she toweled off, she looked in the mirror. Her cheeks were rosy, and she had a sparkle in her eye. Lyndsey was surprised at how *alive* she felt. And she wasn't high!

A belly-laugh burst from her lips as she left her bedroom. It was a great day, and she was hungry. Lyndsey wondered what was for breakfast and went to the kitchen to find out.

The dining hall was loud, alive with energy. It was Sunday, visiting day, and the patients were in high spirits. Lyndsey poured some cereal and then sat down beside Jan. She wanted to tell someone she was two weeks clean and sober but felt embarrassed about it at the same time. Not knowing if she should say anything, Lyndsey picked up her spoon and shoveled cereal into her mouth.

Jan's hand was shaking. The cereal on her spoon wobbled its way to her mouth. Lyndsey looked at Jan questioningly.

Jan put the spoon down and turned to Lyndsey. "I'm a mess," she said, bursting into tears.

Lyndsey stopped eating and patted Jan's shoulder. "What's wrong?"

"My husband is bringing my daughter to visit me today. I don't know what to tell her. I don't want her to know what a screw-up Mommy is. She thinks the sun rises and sets on me and now…and now; she will know the truth. Lyndsey, it will crush her! No child should ever know how screwed up their parent is."

Lyndsey thought back. "I think children know. In my family, I knew something was wrong. Nobody talked about it, but it was there. And it got bigger. Because we didn't talk about our problems, they kept growing. You know, I was always wondered if I'd done something wrong. If only we had known the truth. The elephant in our house was my dad. He was sick and had a drinking problem. It's scary when you're a child, and you know something is wrong, but nobody is talking about it. As a kid, I asked questions. My parents told me I wasn't seeing or hearing the things I saw and heard. You start to feel like you're crazy and your family's problems are your fault. You know where that leads you."

Jan's lips turned down. "My daughter is young. I wish I weren't sick. I hate being an alcoholic! It's not fair to her," Jan wailed.

Lyndsey reached for Jan's hand. "Her mother *is* sick, and she's working on getting better. Your daughter is a lucky little girl. You have to believe that. Every time you talk about her, your face lights up. Not every child has that, you know. I didn't. I was a nuisance, not a gift. I was an albatross hanging from my parent's neck. Jan when you speak of your daughter I can feel your love. If I can feel it, she can too. With love, anything is possible. Don't you think?"

Jan squeezed Lyndsey's hand. "I sure hope so. Do you think I've screwed her up permanently? She must think I've abandoned her."

"I don't think you've screwed her up permanently, Jan. I don't think you've abandoned her either. Remember what we learned in our group? When we get high, we abandon everything that matters to us. Like when you were at home sneaking drinks in the closet. All you thought about was getting your next drink. That's a form of abandonment. When you were with your daughter, you wished she wasn't there so you could drink. The bottle was more important than she was. Now that you're here, you're doing the work, so from now on she will always be number one."

Jan didn't look convinced. "But my child is young, and she won't understand any of this."

"Maybe it's not that complicated." Lyndsey shrugged. "Tell her that you love her. Play with her, color with her, do the things that she likes to do. Actions speak louder than words. Make the day about her. That's all she needs. That's all any little girl needs. Your daughter needs to know she is loved and she matters. When parents put their needs first, over their children's, the child feels neglected and hungry for attention." Lyndsey flashed on him.

"Thanks, that's what I'll do then." Jan picked up her spoon, this time without shaking. "I'll tell her mommy is sick, and it's not her fault. I'll tell her how much I love her and I'll make this day about her. Lyndsey, I would love you to meet her."

Lyndsey felt torn. Today was the day she had chosen to leave. Only, something had changed in her, and she didn't feel as sure now. For once Lyndsey felt hopeful, and she wondered if it would last.

Not sure what to do Lyndsey pondered her decision when someone tapped her on the shoulder.

Lyndsey looked up to see Mary's smiling face. A rush of affection for Mary came over Lyndsey. But before she could tell Mary how happy she was to see her, Mary said. "Come with me."

A frown crossed Lyndsey's face as she looked at Jan and then at Mary. "Where are we going?"

Mary grinned widely and reached down for Lyndsey's arm. "Hurry, you have a visitor!"

# CHAPTER SEVENTY-TWO

Her eyes devoured every inch of him. Lyndsey stroked his callused hand, and then his arm. She leaned against his shoulder liking the way his body warmed hers. Drake smelled yummy. He looked good, too. He'd filled out and wore a goatee.

Lyndsey still couldn't believe it.

Drake put his arms around her, grinned and said. "We need to talk."

Lyndsey thought, oh, no!

Drake's lips smiled, but his eyes were serious.

Lyndsey's stomach sank. Why couldn't he wait? Just a little longer, that's all she wanted. Lyndsey feared what Drake was about to say. As long as they stayed here like this, on the couch, connected, everything was fine. She didn't want Drake to talk. She just wanted to touch him.

Drake pulled away from her. "I'm glad you're getting help, Lyndsey. You need it."

Lyndsey tensed. She wasn't the only one who needed help! She almost flung the thought in his face, but she didn't want to scare him off. Lyndsey bit her lip and tried to calm herself. She was angry at Drake for saying that to her. She didn't want him to go, but man, she was pissed!

Not knowing how to react, Lyndsey remained mute.

Drake looked at her, sensing her turmoil. "You know I've

been getting help myself. After I left you, I started seeing a counselor. He suggested I attend a program for codependency. It was the best thing I ever did. I'd spent so much of my life blaming everyone else for the problems in my life. I felt so helpless. Only when I was looking after someone else did I feel needed and in control. I'm not proud of it, but the only way I felt good was when you did." Drake ran a hand through his hair and sighed.

Lyndsey wanted to say something to make him feel better, but when she opened her mouth, nothing came out. She was tongue-tied.

Drake picked at his goatee. "The counselor said I was sick because I'd made my well-being dependent on another. When you felt down, so did I. It was my *job* to make you happy. I thought it was because I loved you and I was a caring guy. But I've since then I've learned I was actually trying to make myself feel better."

"But you are a caring guy!" Lyndsey objected.

In spite of Lyndsey's objection, Drake continued. "Of course the people I chose to look after were pretty sick. Like you, Linds. You never appreciated my efforts. So I felt sorry for myself, and I was miserable. Misery consumed me. It was all I thought about. My counselor said I was behaving like a victim. I gave you way too much power. I blamed you for making me miserable, but I ignored the fact I continued to stay. The longer I stayed with you, the more I blamed you, and the worse I behaved. I even blamed you for the way I was acting, as if my quality of life was your responsibility! God. It was so much easier to blame you than to look at myself."

Lyndsey scooted close. "Don't say that, Drake. I *was* the problem. I could be such a bitch sometimes. I can't believe I picked partying over you, but drugs had such a hold over me. I don't know if I can ever explain it to you. It was like I lost my mind. I was crazy to put anything before you. It's so hard to put into words how horrible it was. I was consumed too but in a different way. All I could think about was *more*. If I didn't have dope, I panicked. I didn't know I was addicted and sick. I thought I was having fun and that I was a selfish, horrible person."

"Yeah. That was the confusing part." Drake tipped her chin up and looked into her eyes. "We had some beautiful moments together. There was something deep in you that spoke to me. Lyndsey, I gave you my heart. I really did you know. Only you stomped on it, and I got sick. Every time you were out of my sight I wondered who you were with and what you were doing. I'd show up for work, but I was never really there. All I thought about was you. You were my obsession. I became a shell of a man and despised myself for it. I was your revolving door. You could come and go as you pleased and I was there to pick up the pieces. I'd make threats to leave, but never follow through. I felt weak, and then I started hating you."

Pain filled her chest. She'd hurt this man deeply. "I'm sorry." She whispered.

"It feels crazy you know." Drake drew a ragged breath. "Loving and hating the same person."

Lyndsey nodded, she did know. She'd felt that way about her

family.

"I even hated that I loved you. When I left you, I could barely work up enough energy to get out of bed in the morning. I had to force myself to eat. I quit drinking and tried to bury myself in work. I couldn't sleep, and that's when I went for help. My mom suggested it. I think it was hard on her seeing me like that."

"Oh God! Your mom must hate me!"

Drake snorted. "I don't think she's your biggest fan, but what do you expect?"

Shame clawed her. The day darkened. Lyndsey grabbed at Drake's arm, wanting to tell him how badly she felt but her vocal cords seized. All that came out of her mouth was a high squeak.

Drake never noticed Lyndsey's distress. "You know I thought if I could just love you enough, more than anyone else ever had, I could fix you. That somehow, my love was going to be the magic key, and we would live happily ever after. You know what I found out, Lyndsey?"

Her throat unlocked, and she whispered. "What did you find out?"

"I found out that I'm more in love with the idea of *love* than, I am truly *in* love with you."

OH. MY. GOD. Here it comes.

Lyndsey's pulse sped up, and she asked. "What do you mean?"

"What I mean is what we had together was sick. I thought it was love. But real love doesn't look like that. You know, it's not your fault. There was something in me that needed someone like you. Like you needed drugs, I needed you. If I hadn't found you, I would have found someone like you. A messed up chick who needed fixing or rescuing, and was emotionally unavailable."

The thought of Drake with someone else punched her right in the stomach.

"What I'd always thought was love, wasn't. Real love isn't needy, and it wants the best for the other person. It isn't clingy or possessive. It isn't jealous. It doesn't have ulterior motives. It doesn't want anything in return. It just *is*. And you can't give love if you're sick. You can't receive it, either. The stuff we thought was love was endorphins. You get the same high from endorphins as the cocaine you snort. It's heady stuff, but it's not love."

"What do you, you, mean?" Lyndsey stuttered.

"I mean, we were pretty sick together. I used you because of the way you made me feel. Lyndsey, I loved the way I felt around you, at first, anyway. And you loved the way you felt with coke. We were both doing the same thing, just in different ways. I blamed you for my fucked up life, and you blamed your family. It's all the same thing."

"So you never really loved me?" Lyndsey tried not to whine and sound pathetic.

"Not in a healthy way, but I think we can change that." Drake nuzzled her hair and whispered in her ear. "What do you say?"

Lyndsey swallowed the lump in her throat and blinked.

Her mouth trembled, and she smiled a wobbly grin.

"I say yes.

Drake smiled at her.

It was a start.

# CHAPTER SEVENTY-THREE

Lyndsey was high as a kite. Her pupils weren't pinned. She wasn't crawling on the carpet looking for more. There were no pipes, syringes, or pill bottles. She had not consumed alcohol. Lyndsey wasn't high on dope. She was high on hope. There was a spring in her step, a song in her heart, and a smile on her face. Her life had taken a giant U-turn. Just weeks before she tried to kill herself and now she had hope. Lyndsey was shocked at how drastically her life had changed in such a short period.

Hope was the little flame that whispered to the soul, yes you can!

Lyndsey was alive. SHE WAS ALIVE! God, she was giddy. When you had one foot in the grave and lived to tell about it, life was sweet indeed.

Hope brought color back into her world. Lyndsey's senses were in overdrive. One afternoon while on a walk with Jan and Ruth, Lyndsey stopped suddenly. "Look!" She stared in awe at a Fir tree. Isn't it beautiful?"

"It's just a tree," Ruth replied.

"No, it's more than that. Come here." Lyndsey touched the tree bark. Its texture was rough, patchy, furrowed, and scaly. The bark was dark and thick with swirls of silver running through it. The earth smelled of leaves and moss. It was a woodsy-pine smell that brought Christmas to mind.

"It is pretty." Jan looked at Ruth. "If you cut it down you

would see circles inside, like a bullseye. If you count the rings, you'll know how old the tree is."

Lyndsey jumped in front of the tree arms spread wide. "Don't you dare cut down this tree!" She cried pretending horror. Then she grinned. "I've never seen a tree as pretty as this."

Jan ran a hand over the bark and turned to Lyndsey. "Maybe you never looked."

"How so?" Lyndsey asked.

"Sometimes we don't see what's right in front of us. At first, all these trees look the same, but when you look closely, you can see the differences. If you're not paying attention, they're just blobs." Jan shrugged. "Maybe you never looked. Or maybe your thoughts were on something else so when you looked; you didn't see."

"How could I miss something as large as a tree?"

"It's easy. Our thoughts are powerful. They override sight. I used to like gardening. I loved smelling my flowers and feeling the wet earth in my hands. The more I drank, the more time I spent in my head. I was constantly worrying or fixing on something. I stopped seeing the flowers. I still worked in the garden, but it had become a chore."

"Do you miss your garden?" Ruth asked, patting Jan's arm.

Jan touched Ruth's gnarled fingers and nodded. "I do. You'll probably think I'm off my rocker, but I think that tree is our answer."

Ruth reached a hand to Jan's head. Jan smiled and stepped closer to the tree.

Lyndsey asked. "What do you mean?"

"Well, look at the tree. I mean *really* look at it. To see it properly you must be with it. You can't be thinking about yesterday or tomorrow or next week. You must be in the present moment. When you concentrate on the tree, you clear your mind. You're not worrying, obsessing, or stressing. This tree represents sound mental health. If we can find a way to stay out of our heads, maybe we'll become as healthy as this tree."

Weirdly, it did make sense. In rehab, Lyndsey learned negative thinking was toxic. It affects the way you think about yourself and the world and interferes with work/study and everyday functioning. Negative thinking made her sick and sarcastic, and she wanted to get high all the time. Lyndsey was starting to realize becoming well was more than just quitting drugs and alcohol. It was changing *everything*, her thoughts, actions, the places she went, the people she hung out with, her job. Oh, no! Her job! How could she stay sober working in the bar?

Lyndsey was overwhelmed just thinking about all the changes she would need to make. Instead of running with it she eyed the tree. She noticed the swirly patterns in the bark. Lyndsey ran her fingers over the crevices. Anxiety faded and she turned to Jan. "You know, this works!"

The three woman giggled like school children. They linked arms and continued walking. Lyndsey looked at her two friends. "You know what else is strange?"

"What?" Jan and Ruth answered in unison.

"That we're laughing so much. Think about it. We're in rehab fighting for our lives. And here we are laughing."

"All three women laughed at the absurdity.

Lyndsey wiped her eyes. "It feels so good to laugh again."

Jan's forehead wrinkled. "I think laughter must be good medicine, but you're right, we are fighting for our lives. Addiction is such a confusing disease to have. I know I'm sick when I'm detoxing, shaking and throwing up. It's when I don't feel sick, and I feel good, that I get in trouble. My head tells me I'm okay. One little sip won't hurt me. Then it builds, the thought becomes louder, it crowds out everything else and bam! I take that drink. It's scary how quickly I'm back to where I started, and it gets worse from there. I'm serious. I can't trust my thinking."

Ruth cocked her head. "They stopped doing frontal lobotomies years ago. Shock therapy is out, so you're stuck with it. You can't turn off your thinking now, can you?"

"I think we can," Jan insisted. "Isn't that what steps two and three are all about?"

Ruth dropped Jan's arm and looked at her. "I'm not sure. I may have missed that class. Be careful Jan. You don't want to get brainwashed."

"You're wrong, Ruth. I do want to get brainwashed."

"Why would you want that?" Lyndsey asked.

"Because brainwashing is the only hope I have. If something drastic doesn't happen to change my thinking, I'm doomed to a life of misery. The worst part is I don't go there alone. I have a choice. I can buy into what we're learning in treatment, or I can keep doing things my way. I know where *my* road leads. I've never been willing to take direction before. This time I decided to do it differently. I have to give it a try. It's the only hope I have. And hey," Jan shrugged. "If it doesn't work, my misery awaits."

Lyndsey shuddered. "I don't like the word brainwashed. It makes me think of zombies."

Jan pointed at finger at Lyndsey. "Isn't that what we were? Stoned out, zombies? We were dead to ourselves and our family. Besides," Jan's lips turned up in a grin. "My brain is filthy! It needs a good washing."

The three woman rounded the corner taking them to the main doors, howling with laughter. The mood shifted as they got closer to the building. Their laughter faded and the three woman grew quiet.

Lyndsey pushed through the front doors and stopped short seeing Barb.

Barb cocked a finger at Lyndsey and said. "Come with me."

Lyndsey's muscles tensed. "Why? What's wrong? Where are we going?"

Barb looked at her. "Lyndsey breathe."

Lyndsey sucked in air.

Barb's face softened. "We're going to a family conference. Yours."

Alarm slammed through her. "But who's here?"

Barb locked eyes with Lyndsey and spoke two words that filled her with dread.

"Your family."

# CHAPTER SEVENTY-FOUR

They sat in a circle frozen in their old tableau of angst and hostility. Nothing had changed. It was still as awkward being with her parents as it had always been. Lyndsey, once again feeling like a huge disappointment, had gone mute. She stared at the ground refusing to look at her parents.

The room was tense, and Lyndsey wanted to run.

Barb introduced herself and then went over the goals of the family conference. Barb wanted her parents to talk about their feelings as Lyndsey progressed in her disease.

But Lyndsey's parents hadn't been able to do that. Instead of expressing their feelings, her dad blamed Lyndsey. She was a big disappointment. She failed at everything. She never tried hard enough. She was lazy. It went on and on. Lyndsey had heard it all before.

Barb held up a hand and looked at Lyndsey with concern. Then she spoke to Lyndsey's parents. "I want you to think about a time you felt closest to your daughter. Now I want you to tell Lyndsey about it."

Lyndsey's mom spoke for the first time. "Lyndsey was a cute little girl. She had a ton of energy and asked a lot of questions."

Her father added. "Too many questions. She never stopped talking."

Barb glanced at her dad. "Was that a problem? "Did her

questions bother you?"

Lyndsey's mom spoke first. "We were young and not prepared for a child. Our life together was chaotic, and then I had another child. I was sick with worry and too exhausted to keep up with two little girls."

"What was that like for you?" Barb asked.

"It's such a blur. I did the best I could. I made sure my children had clothes and food but as far as what was on my mind, I never knew if there would be enough money to pay the rent or buy groceries." Her mother's chin quivered.

Lyndsey stopped looking at the floor and stared at her parents in astonishment.

Lyndsey's mother spoke again. "If I didn't hide our money he spent it on alcohol. I hid bottles and poured them out. My thoughts were on my husband and how I could keep him from drinking again."

As Lyndsey listened to her mom, she was able to see it from her side. She knew the addict's family was sick too.

"And what about you?" Barb asked, staring directly at her father.

"What do you mean, what about me?"

"What was that time like for you? You had two young daughters. That must have been a big responsibility."

"What do you think it was like? It was hell. That's what it was. The only time I had any fun was when I was drinking."

"So you liked drinking?"

"Of course I liked drinking!" Her dad stared at Barb incredulously. "I loved it. That was the only time I got any relief from my life. I was working full time, going to school, and I had two little girls. I didn't know anything about little girls but I was responsible for them, and it scared the hell out of me."

Her dad's nostrils twitched. Lyndsey thought he might yell, or cry. He did neither.

Her dad blew out a breath. "I was barely old enough to be responsible for me. We didn't plan on having kids, they just happened, and we weren't ready."

"Did you ever think what it must be like for them?" Barb asked.

"For them?" Her father snorted. "What about me? Did you ever think what it was like for me? I'd gone from having all the freedom and fun a guy could want to live in a worn down dump, and working my ass off, only to come home to two whiny kids, and a nagging wife."

Barb folded her hands together and looked at Lyndsey's dad. "So it didn't bother you, drinking, instead of spending time with your children?"

"Are you kidding? It bothered me all the time. I'd look at Lyndsey, and she would be watching me. She used to think the world of me, you know. Lyndsey would run to the door when I came home from work. She was so happy to see me. She liked sitting on my lap, and when I left the house, she would cry. It got so I couldn't look at her anymore."

A lump grew in Lyndsey's throat. She remembered when she had worshipped her dad.

Barb asked. "Why did things change?"

"Lyndsey was a little brat so I would have to spank her. She never seemed to learn her lesson though, no matter how hard I spanked."

Her mother jumped in. "You spanked her too hard."

Her father shot back. "And you were too soft."

Barb interjected. "How hard did you spank Lyndsey?"

Her dad looked at Barb. "As hard as I could. Lyndsey was a tough little bugger. I thought if I hit her hard enough, she'd learn her lesson. She never did though."

"What lesson were you trying to teach her?" Barb questioned.

Her father's eyes widened, and he huffed. "To listen to me and do as told."

Barb shook her head. "But weren't you drunk most of the time?"

"No, not most of the time, just sometimes."

"But she was a child." Barb pointed at Lyndsey. "How was she supposed to know the difference?"

Lyndsey's dad threw up his hands. "Look, I wanted her to learn from me. Do as I do. Isn't that a father's job, to lead by example?"

"But you did teach her," Barb argued. "You taught her well."

Surprised at the compliment her dad asked. "How so?"

"You wanted Lyndsey to be like you. You tried to beat it into her and guess what. It worked! She *is* just like you. She likes to be the boss, she likes to argue, *and* she's a drunk."

For once her dad was speechless.

Lyndsey squirmed in her seat and stared at the carpet.

# CHAPTER SEVENTY-FIVE

Her mother cried first, then Barb. Lyndsey was surprised at Barb's tears. Lyndsey viewed Barb as an ice-sculpture, not human. But she was wrong. Through Barb's tears, Lyndsey felt the first ounce of compassion for herself and her family. They were in trouble from the very beginning. Her parents were young, emotionally immature and not equipped to deal with the challenging reality of their life. They really shouldn't have had kids. Children had no business in their unhealthy relationship, but then they hadn't planned on children. It just happened. Lyndsey knew first-hand about that.

Barb said her family did the best they could with their limited set of skills. It was time to put the past behind them and create a new future.

Lyndsey wondered if they could.

Barb looked at her dad. "It's never too late. Even when Lyndsey has grey hair, you'll still be her father."

"Yeah, well, I hope she's smartened up by then…" Her dad trailed off, his voice cracking.

Lyndsey couldn't believe it! Her dad cared about her.

Her mother sniffled next to her. Lyndsey looked at her and saw pain. Her mom was like the tree. Lyndsey realized she'd never really seen her mom before. She'd been a blob, a blur. Her mom was there, in their house, like the Chesterfield was there. Lyndsey was sad she didn't know her mom. She'd been so caught up in her pain; she hadn't noticed the rest of her family was hurting too.

Lyndsey's lips clamped closed, trying to stop the sob from exploding. Her chest heaved. Her eyes watered and she breathed through her nose. Grief washed over her, and shuddering sobs ripped through her body. Years of ugliness and pent-up pain gushed out. They all hurt. Why hadn't she noticed? Lyndsey sobbed, hiccupped and choked on snot.

Barb nodded. "You're okay, Lyndsey. Don't fight it. Let it come out."

Barb's words brought on another round of grief and Lyndsey wailed. Her body shook from the force of it.

Lyndsey's mom's cried silent tears as she looked at her daughter.

Lyndsey's father was white as a ghost, knuckling the chair handles. His lips turned down when he looked at Barb. "Jesus Christ! Did I cause this?"

Barb spoke softly. "Part of it, yes. But what you're experiencing are pent-up emotions. Your family has stuffed their feelings for a long time, and now they're coming out."

"Well can't you fix them?"

"There's nothing to fix," Barb answered.

Her father looked sheepishly at the group. Not being in charge was a new experience for him. "Well, what do we do now?" He asked Barb.

"Now I ask how you're feeling," Barb answered.

Lyndsey's dad squared his shoulders, looked at the three women, and barked. "My ears hurt!"

Barb's eyes lit up, and she smiled. She rolled her shoulders and said. "Your family has begun the healing process. You can be proud of yourselves. For the first time, in a long time, you sat down together and listened. That's what healthy families do. They talk to each other, and they listen. In alcoholic families, only the addicted person gets their needs met. But in healthy families, everyone has a voice."

"Hmm." Her dad sat up and stared at Barb. "Are you saying we're all fixed?"

"Not even close!" Barb answered, with a smile. "What I'm saying is if you *all* work hard, *maybe* we can get this family back on track."

Lyndsey's father corrected Barb. "You mean if Lyndsey works hard we can get this family back on track."

Barb shook her head. "Nice try. Addiction is a family disease. Lyndsey didn't get her by herself. Now *dad*, what are you prepared to do about it?"

"Wait! How did this become about me?"

Barb said. "We have a program for family members. I think you should go."

Lyndsey's dad's eyes widened. "But I don't have a problem! I quit drinking two years ago."

Barb wheedled. "You going would help your daughter."

"Well, I...um..." Her dad looked around the room. His eyes fell on Lyndsey, and he frowned.

"Why don't you think about it?" Barb encouraged. "You don't have to decide right now."

Baffled by the sudden turn of events Lyndsey's dad sat back

in his chair and gave her a mean look.

Lyndsey had never seen anyone stand up to her dad before and for a moment she felt badly for him. The feeling passed when she heard Barb's next words. "Lyndsey, can you tell your parents what you need from them?"

"I...I...don't need anything." She stuttered.

"Of course you do," Barb argued.

"I can't think of anything." Lyndsey wished Barb would shut up and she could disappear under her chair.

"We all need something from the people we love." Barb eyed the three strained faces. "You need support, respect, honesty, trust, loyalty and to know your family has your back. When division happens you build a defense system to protect yourself from hurt. These walls keep others from getting close to you. Instead of interacting with your friends and family in a healthy, loving way you, you interrogate in a demanding, selfish way. If you don't have the basics of a healthy relationship, it's better to not be in one at all."

Lyndsey's cheeks burned. She felt like she was five years old again.

"Of course it will take a while. But today is a great start." Barb stood and shook hands with her parents. She walked them to the door and said. "I'll keep you updated on Lyndsey's progress. I hope you'll think about our Family Program."

Lyndsey watched them cross the threshold. Her parents were smaller than she remembered. He mother's eyes were red and puffy. Her father's face was grey. Lyndsey stammered. "Ah... thanks for coming." Her cheeks burned. Lyndsey wished she could talk to her parents without feeling so uncomfortable.

Her parents looked older than she remembered. Lyndsey felt defeated and responsible for their heartache. They rounded the corner and disappeared from her view.

They never even said goodbye.

# CHAPTER SEVENTY-SIX

"Stay right here," Barb ordered and left the office. Lyndsey didn't think she could move anyway. She was shell-shocked. She hadn't seen her parents in so long. Her dad didn't look like a monster. He was older and more human. Lyndsey wondered why they'd come. The image of her mother silently crying would haunt her forever. Lyndsey picked at a cuticle and wondered now what?

She thought her parents were probably arguing by now. Alone in their car, were they hurling insults at one another and building walls?

Lyndsey hated feeling this way. Guilt was such a son-of-a-bitch, heavy feeling. She'd always felt responsible for her parent's happiness. Once again, she had failed them miserably.

The door opened breaking her train of thought.

Barb entered the room with Tommy and Jan in tow. "Look what the cat dragged in!" She exclaimed.

Lyndsey wondered if drama turned Barb's crank. But she didn't wonder long. Her eyes filled with tears and she blurted. "Jesus, I'm a Goddamn water tap! I've never cried so much in my life! What the hell is happening to me?"

Barb threw open her arms. "You're healing, Lyndsey. To get better everything needs to come out. Right now, it's coming out."

"Well sorry, I'm not usually such a baby. I'll try and get myself together."

Barb closed her arms and looked at Lyndsey solemnly. "Please don't. If you stuff your emotions, you'll get sick. When you try to control your feelings, they end up controlling you."

Tommy looked at Lyndsey as if to say *what's she been smoking?*

Barb caught their look and laughed. "It doesn't sound right, does it? But it's true. Have you ever watched little children? They haven't learned how to control their feelings yet. If they're mad, they let you know immediately, and then in the next second, they're laughing again. They get it out, and they're over it, just like that." Barb snapped her fingers.

Jan looked at Barb. "It's not always wise to say how you're feeling. I mean what happens if the person you tell uses it against you?"

"Then they're not safe people. Your job is to find people who are safe. I brought you and Tommy here so that you could be Lyndsey's safe people. Lyndsey has something she needs to tell you."

"I do?" Lyndsey questioned.

"You most definitely do," Barb assured her.

"I ah," oh man! She was such a baby! Did everybody go through this? Lyndsey didn't want friends right now. She couldn't stop thinking about her parents. *Please, please, please, let them not be fighting!*

"What is it, Lyndsey?" Tommy questioned.

"I just had my family conference."

"Oh, wow! Are you alright?"

"I think so. But I feel like a big loser. I'm such a

disappointment. I've always felt this way. Like there's something wrong with me. I've never been good enough. I never measured up. And I feel awful right now. I'm so worried my parents are arguing because of me."

Barb interjected. "Lyndsey, if your parents are arguing, it's not your fault. They were arguing long before you were born and they will be arguing long after you leave. It's learned behavior. They don't know any other way to communicate with each other."

"Barb, did you see my mom's face? My mom was in pain."

"I did see her face. Pain is an appropriate emotion given the situation. It's only pain, Lyndsey. Pain is an uncomfortable feeling. She won't die from it."

"It sure looked like she was dying from it."

"Lyndsey, she'll die sooner from *not* expressing her emotions. When you keep your feelings buried, your blood pressure rises. You can get headaches, stomach aches, ulcers, migraines, heart disease, and other chronic health issues. If you're an alcoholic, you'll drink over hidden pain. Those of us coming from alcoholic families never grow up emotionally. We don't know how to deal with our feelings and are overwhelmed by them. So we avoid them. Then we wonder why we never feel close to other people."

"So why don't we? Feel close to people, I mean," Jan asked Barb.

"To be close with someone, you must be intimate with them."

Tommy snorted. "Yeah, like I'm just going to have sex with

everyone I meet."

"Don't you already?" Lyndsey teased.

"Intimacy isn't about sex, Tommy. Although that can be part of it." Barb smiled.

"If intimacy isn't about sex, then what's it about?" Lyndsey asked.

"Intimacy means you open up. You share what's going on with you. Think about it this way, *Into Me You See*. You don't hide your thoughts and feelings. You share them. You take down your walls and allow yourself to be vulnerable with the people you love. Of course, to do that, you need someone safe. Someone who will be truthful with you, and not tell you what they think you want to hear."

"What happens when people aren't safe?" Tommy asked.

"Then you build walls, spiked with thorns and topped with barbed wire. Should someone get close enough to you and try and climb those walls, they'll get hurt. The purpose of your wall is to keep others out, even when you might want them in. It's something you have learned to do. Just like your parents fighting, Lyndsey. It's all learned behavior," Barb explained.

"But how do we unlearn it?" Jan asked.

Barb thought for a moment. "To start, try being honest, open and willing. Practice being truthful with each other. Work on staying open, even when you hear things you don't like. Put aside your defenses and take risks. Let yourselves feel uncomfortable and talk about it. Get more experience with your feelings, instead of trying to micro-manage them. You'll be amazed at how quickly you become emotionally comfortable.

Your emotional age will catch up to your physical age and pretty soon you'll stop feeling like a scared child. Fear is just fear. It won't paralyze you. Pain is something you share. Embarrassment will always be uncomfortable, but it passes quickly. Instead of being emotionally crippled, you'll be emotionally fluent. Then you're on the way to having the life you've always deserved."

"Are you saying all we have to do is talk about our feelings and we'll get better?" Tommy's eyebrow raised as he looked at Barb.

Barb nodded. "I'm saying that's a big part of it, but not *all* of it. When someone breaks, it's usually more than one thing wrong. We have physical needs, emotional needs and spiritual needs. When these needs aren't met, we wither and die. Like a plant without water.

"Wow! Why don't we learn this stuff in school?"

"I wish we did, Tommy." Barb sighed. We'd all be better off. Sadly, it seems the human condition ignores our emotional health. When this happens, we get mentally sick, and our physical bodies start breaking down. We die spiritually when loneliness sets in. But there is good news. This is all reversible. Try it out for yourself and find out. You'll notice the difference immediately. Sharing your thoughts and feelings with someone you trust is the best narcotic on the market. You feel better instantly and no hang-over."

"Maybe addiction should be called a *feelings disease*, or more accurately, a not wanting to feel disease," Lyndsey added.

Barb nodded her head. "Maybe it should."

# CHAPTER SEVENTY-SEVEN

A blur of thoughts and feelings raced through Lyndsey's head. She was so grateful to be sitting next to Drake. Her pulse kicked up a notch as she eyed him. Drake's face was tanned and peaceful, his eyes closed. Lyndsey thought he had the longest black eyelashes she'd ever seen. With their hands joined, Lyndsey loved the way her smaller, smooth hand, fit in his larger, calloused one. She closed her eyes and leaned her head back against the chair. The sun was warm and felt gentle on her face. Voices murmured, and a bee buzzed nearby.

Lyndsey's eyes blinked open. She was way too excited to keep them closed for long. She studied the dark stubble on Drake's cheeks and the swoop of his eyebrows. And the slow, steady movements of his chest, rising and falling with each breath.

"I can feel that you know."

"Feel what?" Lyndsey asked.

Drake opened one eye. "You're staring at me."

"I can't help it," Lyndsey giggled. "You look good!" And he did, too. Without his usual look of worry, Drake looked healthy. "You know, I've been thinking about us a lot lately, and I think I need to thank you."

"What for?"

"Well," Lyndsey drew in a deep breath. "This might sound strange, but I want to thank you for leaving me."

"You want to thank me for *leaving you*?"

"I do." Lyndsey nodded. "If you hadn't left. I wouldn't be here. I would have kept using and hurting us both. Drake, I thought everyone in the world was against me. I was toxic. That's the best way I can describe it."

"I know you were." Drake squeezed her shoulder. "Believe me, I felt it."

"I still can't believe it. I pinch myself every morning just to be sure this is real. There's a warm, quiet in me and it brings happiness to my heart."

"That emotion is joy, Lyndsey." Drake's tone was soft and tender.

Lyndsey traced Drakes hand with her fingers. "I feel so grateful and so...*changed*. I almost died. Many don't get a second chance. It's like a collision, my old life before and my new one after. I feel like I've lived two lives in one body. It's crazy, but I think I needed every minute of my past, to get me where I am today." Lyndsey stopped and wiped away a tear.

Drake pulled her close.

Lyndsey spoke into Drake's shoulder. "It's humbling you know when you understand how sick you are. At first, I thought this place was a cult. I fought everything geared to make me healthy. Those first few days were tough. I embraced the disease and didn't even know it!"

Drake stroked Lyndsey's hair. "I know what you mean. I think everything happens for a reason. Especially the shit you don't like or understand. Pain is our teacher. The hard part is learning not to take it personally. I guess that's what it's all about… Drake trailed off. His fingers moved down her body.

Lyndsey heard the smile in his voice.

"And I'm *learning* I have a hard time keeping my hands off you." Drake teased.

"Hah! I think that's a lesson you already knew," Lyndsey teased in return.

When had mere words become so intoxicating? Lyndsey enjoyed talking to Drake and looked forward to getting to know him better, without being high.

"When do you think you'll graduate rehab?"

"I don't know. A few weeks ago I was counting the days. I couldn't wait to get out of here. Then I passed thirty days and stopped counting. Now, well, it doesn't seem as urgent."

"It's a good thing they have their windows alarmed." Drake nuzzled her ear.

"I know! Can you imagine if I left then?"

They locked hands and grew quiet.

When Lyndsey spoke, it was in a whisper. "I would have died."

"I know."

"I'm so lucky."

"I know."

"Thanks for leaving me."

"You're welcome."

"You know what?"

"What?"

"I think the best is yet to come."

"I know it is."

"And you know what else?"

"What?"

"I love you."

"I love you, too." Drake smiled and looked into Lyndsey's eyes.

Lyndsey allowed herself to look. To really *look*. It was awkward. She wanted to pull away from this intimate moment, but she held on.

They grinned at each other like a couple of fools.

Mary walked by and said. "Sorry guys, five more minutes."

As Mary walked passed them, Drake said. "I hate this part."

Lyndsey kissed Drake's finger-tips and nodded. "Me too."

They stood up both reluctant to be saying goodbye. Lyndsey walked Drake to the end of the driveway. She watched him as he got into his truck. She blew him a kiss, and he caught it through the window.

Lyndsey waved until Drake was long gone.

At the end of the driveway, she stood alone, but Lyndsey wasn't lonely.

A smile of satisfaction tugged at her lips as she returned to the rehab center. A car drove slowly passed her. Lyndsey moved to the side of the driveway letting them pass. Another new arrival, by the looks of the people inside. The car crawled by her and Lyndsey glimpsed the man and woman in the front seat. They looked pale and stressed out. Lyndsey saw the patient, sitting in the back seat. The woman screamed and beat her fists on the rear window.

She felt sad for the passing family.

The car came to a stop at the entrance doors, lurching up on the curb before settling back on the pavement. Mom and Dad got out of the car on unsteady feet.

Lyndsey watched the parents open the rear door.

Then all hell broke loose.

The woman inside screamed as if someone was murdering her.

As Lyndsey walked by the car, she glanced into the back seat. Woah! The alcohol fumes were strong!

The woman's Dad tried to pry her fingers free of the seat. The woman was drunk, disheveled and slurring as she hurled profanities at her aging parents.

The front entrance doors swung open. Two support staff came to the aid of the distraught parents. They managed to get the drunk woman out of the car.

As the group passed her, a support member nodded and said to the woman. "This is Lyndsey. She's a patient here, too."

The staff smiled at the drunk woman as if this were an everyday occurrence. Which for them, it was.

Lyndsey smiled and looked at the woman. She slouched upright between the support staff, barely able to stand.

Lyndsey spoke the first words that came to mind. "Welcome home."

The drunk woman looked at her with hate-filled eyes. Her face twisted in a snarl and she spat. "Fuck off and leave me alone!"

Lyndsey smiled at her and walked into the building.

# Two Years Later...

Lyndsey lay on the lounger and stretched. A fat bee hovered near the rhododendron tree. The savory aroma of roast beef scented the air. Lyndsey's mouth watered and her stomach rumbled.

Last night she laid awake next to Drake listening to him breathe. She was too excited to sleep, and the coffee hadn't helped either. She'd gone to her home group and met up with Ruth, Tommy, Jan, and Mary. At the AA meeting, a young man shared his story. He was new to sobriety and wanted support. Lyndsey and her friends stayed after the meeting to talk with him. It was nearing midnight when she drove home. When Lyndsey pulled into her driveway, the light above the back door was on. It was a welcoming beacon that cast a soft glow over the handcrafted plaque Drake made for her. *HOME SWEET HOME.* Lyndsey stopped in front of the plaque running her finger over the words. There was no place on earth she would rather be.

"Go! Go!" Drake said from the kitchen. He shooed their little dog out from under him. The sliding door swooshed open, expelling an excited little bundle of fur.

A wet tongue licked her hand and Melee's ball dropped in her lap.

"Arff! Arff!" Melee barked. *Throw the ball. Throw the ball!* Melee's tongue poked out the side of her mouth, and she bounced up and down.

Lyndsey laughed and picked up the ball, throwing it as far as she could. It sailed across the deck and onto the lawn. Melee flew after it. She lunged through the air landing on the grass and ran after the ball. An interesting smell distracted Melee, and she stooped suddenly. Her head cocked as she eyed the grass.

Pots and pans rattled in the kitchen. Drakes was ramping up.

Lyndsey supposed she should get up. Her family was coming for dinner tonight, and she wanted to change her clothes.

So much had happened. Lyndsey went back to school and completed her diploma in social work. Her bartending days were over. Now she was looking for a job working with troubled kids or supporting people in early recovery.

Drake started his construction business and had two commercial projects on the go. He stood by his motto, *if you can't find me handsome, you can always find me handy*. Lucky for her, she found him both.

Drake and Lyndsey shared a deep love. They had seen each other at their worst and worked hard to become better people. Their relationship today was solid. They were friends, lovers, and partners in life. They didn't always see eye to eye, but they didn't have to. Lyndsey appreciated their differences, and when an argument arose, they had the tools to work through it. Every day her love for Drake grew stronger. They had a beautiful, sober life, together.

Lyndsey's relationship with her family had improved. She regularly spoke to her sister. They shared childhood memories and tears. They laughed together, poking fun at their parents, and each other.

With her parents, it was baby steps. But they were learning how to fit together in peace, love, and harmony. They'd come a long way, and Lyndsey was proud of them.

Drake hummed *Happy Birthday,* and Lyndsey grinned.

The sliding glass doors swooshed open, and footsteps drew near. "Lyndsey, I have a surprise for you," Drake said. "Close your eyes."

Lyndsey closed her eyes.

*"Happy Birthday to you. Happy Birthday to you. Happy Birthday, Dear Lyndsey. Happy Birthday to you!"* Drake sang.

Lyndsey opened her eyes and saw a cupcake with candles on it. Drake held it close to her so she could read the message printed in icing.

*Git wel son.*

The flames danced in the wind. Drake cupped them with his hand and said. "Make a wish, Lyndsey!"

Lyndsey closed her eyes and drew a blank. Her eyes popped open. "I can't, Drake. I already have everything I want. I'm happy, I have you and my family back. Every morning I wake up and wonder how I got so lucky. .. Lyndsey trailed off overcome by gratitude.

Drake thumbed a tear from her cheek and whispered. "Come on, Linds, there must be something you want."

Lyndsey had climbed out of hell. She learned she wasn't a loser. Or a junkie, or weak-willed. Addiction is a brain disease that rewires the cerebral cortex resulting in poor impulse control and impaired judgment. Lyndsey was never bad. She was sick.

Today she was thriving, healthy and free. As long as she

stayed connected to people in recovery and didn't use drugs or alcohol, she would remain that way.

Lyndsey kissed Drakes cheek. "I have everything I want, but there is one thing I need."

She remembered something Barb had told her.

*If you want to hear about miracles, go to church.*

*If you want to walk among them, go to a meeting.*

Lyndsey closed her eyes and made her wish.

*Dear God. Please guide me in my decisions and direct me through this day. Amen.*

Lyndsey took a deep breath and blew out the candles.

She was two years clean and sober today.

# About the Author

Internationally recognized author, Lorelie Rozzano, is a writer, blogger and recovery advocate who works in the field of mental health and addiction helping individuals and their families recover from substance use disorder. As a daughter, mother, wife, and survivor, she offers insight into the world of chemical dependency. Lorelie has given thousands the glasses they need to see addiction from every angle. She has written several books on the topic, including **Gracie's Secret**, **Jagged Little Edges, Jagged Little Lies**, and **Jagged No More**.

42933896R00267

Made in the USA
Lexington, KY
21 June 2019